**W9-CAM-529**

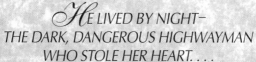

"*CAPITAINE*, PLEASE," RENÉE WHISPERED.
"YOU MUST NOT DO THIS."

"By *this*," he inquired with a frown, "do you mean this—" He kissed her shoulder and retraced the path he had taken from the tender crook of her neck. "Or do you mean this?" He threaded his hands into her golden hair and held her while his mouth moved boldly up to claim hers.

She made a small sound in her throat, but he only pushed his fingers deeper into her hair and held her closer. His tongue coaxed her lips apart and traced their sleek, soft contours, but he ventured no farther than her guarded gasps allowed.

"As I said," he murmured, "life is full of dangers. It should be lived to the fullest while we have the chance because it could all be taken away from us tomorrow."

"Do you say this because you truly believe it, m'sieur," she asked breathlessly, "or because you wish to take me to bed?"

"I am saying it because it is the rule I live by . . . and because I want very much to take you to bed. . . ."

*Dell Books by Marsha Canham*

Pale Moon Rider
The Blood of Roses
The Pride of Lions
Across a Moonlit Sea
In the Shadow of Midnight
Straight for the Heart
Through a Dark Mist
Under a Desert Moon
The Last Arrow

# PALE MOON RIDER

*

# MARSHA CANHAM

A Dell Book

*Published by*
*Dell Publishing*
*a division of*
*Bantam Doubleday Dell Publishing Group, Inc.*
*1540 Broadway*
*New York, New York 10036*

*This novel is a work of fiction. Names, characters, places, and incidents either are the product of the author's imagination or are used fictitiously. Any resemblance to actual persons, living or dead, events, or locales is entirely coincidental.*

*ISBN: 0-440-22259-1*

*Printed in the United States of America*

*Published simultaneously in Canada*

*January 1999*

*10  9  8  7  6  5  4  3  2  1*

*OPM*

*To my beautiful new grandson,*
*Austin Mitchell Edward Canham*
*I can feel the Chief smiling*
*over my shoulder every time I hold you.*

*

*Behold the wandering moon*
*Riding near her highest noon,*
*Like one that had been led astray*
*Through the heaven's wide pathless way.*

—John Milton

* ☽

# Prologue

It was a fine night for treachery—dark with a pale moon rising. The silence was profound enough for the shadowy figure seated on horseback to hear the soft slither of the mist curling around the trunks of the trees and the moisture dripping off the sleek surfaces of the leaves overhead. He felt the chill of the night air through the heavy wool of his greatcoat and kept the uppermost of two collars standing high, almost touching the brim of his tricorn. A glitter of wary eyes showed through the narrow gap between the collar and hat; they were the only feature that would have been visible even if the light of a dozen lanterns surrounded him.

"Horses," came a whisper from the shadows to his right.

Tyrone Hart nodded by way of acknowledgment even though the gesture went unseen. He had already heard the pounding of hooves on the road, the churning of wheels, and the rattle of traces.

The whisper came again, sparked by a hint of excitement. "Double-braced. Big bastard by the sound of it."

The highwayman's long, thick lashes momentarily descended as he transferred the reins into one gloved hand. After running the other briefly along his stallion's neck, he reached beneath the flap of his greatcoat and withdrew a long-snouted pistol. One of a fine pair of flintlock snaphaunces he wore belted to his waist, the weapon was as exquisite as it was deadly. Silver-mounted, with gold inlaid barrels, the walnut stock was carved with grotesques and floral patterns, the designs highlighted by rich foliate work. Similar snarling monsters shaped the locks—one for each of the over-and-under barrels, making each pistol capable of firing two shots before it needed reloading.

Tyrone curled his long, gloved fingers around the curved stock and, through force of habit, raised the gun to his nose; a gentle flaring of the chiseled nostrils verified that both pans were primed with gunpowder. In the past eight months there had been only one instance when either he or Robert Dudley had been caught off guard during the course of a robbery, and even then, it had been more of an annoyance than a threat. A fat, oafish lord, returning from a night of gambling and drinking, had tried to impress his beautiful young companion with his bluster and had made a clumsy attempt to retrieve and discharge his own gun when Tyrone's back was turned. A calm, accurate shot from one of the snaphaunces had raised a ribbon of blood on the nobleman's hand and sent him into a dead faint, face-down in a puddle of mud.

Hart spared a glance into the shadows where Dudley's horse was nickering with impatience. His own black brute, Ares, named after the god of war, stood like a block of granite beneath him, motionless, soundless, unseen in the gloom save for the wary puffs of steamy breath blown into the surrounding mist.

Hart concentrated on the moon-washed ribbon of road again. The coach was intermittently visible through the trees as it approached along the winding track. A single brass riding lamp was mounted on the roof, its glow not only making it easy to track the vehicle's progress along the road, but also defining the silhouette of the driver seated in the front box.

"A fancy rig, all right," Dudley whispered. "Two matched geldings, marquetry on the doors . . . can you see if it has a crest?"

"Not yet."

"No outriders. No escort. What do you make of it?"

"I make it a curious enough sight to warrant a closer look."

"Talk at the White Swan tonight was that the governor is getting quite apoplectic at the number of good citizens being waylaid on his roads. I heard he dressed your friend Colonel Roth down in front of the entire regiment and by the time the governor was finished frothing at the mouth, the colonel was so livid, he slashed his fencing partner half to death during a practice session. And that was with dulled blades."

Tyrone's dark eyes narrowed. Colonel Bertrand Roth was neither his friend nor a very inventive adversary. He was a pompous braggart who had specifically requested a transfer to Coventry four months ago in order to oversee the capture and hanging of the elusive highwayman known to the local citizenry as Captain Starlight. Since issuing his vow to see Starlight hanging from a gibbet before Christmas, there had been a marked increase in patrols and coaches sent out as decoys full of soldiers. And while Hart did not take the threat lightly, he did not think this particular conveyance was part of any such scheme. For one thing, it was far too grand to be trusted into the hands of Roth's oafish dragoons. For another, Tyrone possessed an uncanny, and usually reliable, instinct for danger, and the only thing he sensed about the polished, well-appointed coach approaching them now was that the occupant was inviting trouble by being out so late at night on such a deserted stretch of road.

Caution, nevertheless, was the name of the game, and caution had kept him playing—and alive—for the past six years.

"If Roth is behind this, we will know it soon enough."

He gave the reins a gentle tug, wheeling Ares around. The coach was just drawing abreast of them now, and it would take at least six minutes for such a cumbersome vehicle to navigate the upcoming section of the road where it snaked between two forested hills. A man on horseback could cover the distance in half the time by cutting over the crest and be waiting in position with a pretty ambush on the other side when the big spoked wheels crossed the midpoint. He and Dudley had ridden the route, paced it, timed it half a dozen times by daylight, and he was confident enough to keep Ares to an easy lope. Thin filaments of displaced fog curled in their wake, closing like a curtain behind them. The horses' hooves made almost no sound as they passed over the spongy earth, and as Tyrone rode, he looked up and noted the moon where it flickered through the tops of the trees. It was full and blue-white, ringed with a gauze-like aura of menace. A good moon for the business they were about.

They reached the ambuscade with plenty of time to spare, and Tyrone, dismounting briefly, dragged a rotted branch out of the shadows. It was no thicker than a man's wrist and would be nearly invisible from the tall perch of the driver's box, yet it would feel as if the coach had struck something large enough to have caused potential damage to the wheels or axles. The driver would naturally be obliged to stop and inspect, and when he did, Dudley would be there to assure him there was nothing to keep him from continuing on his journey . . . once the passengers had been relieved of the burden of any valuables they might be carrying, of course.

It had been Dudley's idea to switch roles tonight. If it was a trap, he would feel much better having Tyrone's guns behind him in the shadows. Hart was not completely comfortable with the arrangement. Dudley had suffered a badly broken leg several years back and walked with a heavy limp. On horseback, he was as light and swift as any man, but if there was trouble and he was unhorsed for any reason . . .

Tyrone pushed the thought aside before it was finished. Dudley was well aware of the risks: They both were.

As the sound of harnesses and rolling wheels approached, he swung easily into Ares' saddle again. He shrugged the collar of his coat higher and adjusted the brim of his tricorn lower and, after looping the reins over the front of his saddle, drew the second snaphaunce from beneath his greatcoat and thumbed both forward hammers into half-cock. Ares responded to the pressure of his master's knees and stood still as stone, man and beast becoming one with the mist-drenched shadows.

# *✲ ☽ Chapter 1*

*T*he horses were maintaining a comfortable canter when they passed over the log. Being unsprung, the body of the coach jumped as high as the wheels when they struck, rocking back and up then lurching violently forward, twice in rapid succession. As expected, the tremendous cracking sound of the rotted wood breaking made the driver draw back on the reins and put his foot to the brake handle. The matched pair pranced to a stop and Dudley waited until the coachman had climbed down from the box—not a quick job, as it turned out, for he took his sweet time and seemed much put out by the inconvenience. He had one gloved hand braced on the front wheel for support and was bent over, squinting at the undercarriage of the coach, when Dudley emerged from the shadows by the side of the road.

"I bid ye good evenin', sar. 'Ad a wee mishap, 'ave ye?"

His greeting, delivered with his best cockney accent, had no effect. The horses were stamping and snorting, and the driver was half covered by the body of the coach, poking at the axle to check for damage.

Dudley leaned forward and lifted the bottom edge of the curtain-mask that now covered most of his face. *"Evenin', sar! 'Avin' a bit o' trouble are ye?"*

This time the driver's head came up sharply enough to make contact with the edge of the wood frame.

"Mary and Joseph—" He backed away from the coach,

his hands rubbing the top of his head. "There is no need to shout, my good man. I may be old, but I am not deaf!"

Dudley straightened in his saddle and raised his pistol so the driver had no trouble seeing it in the yellow spill of light from the coach lamp. "Not blind either, I trust?"

With fastidious care, the driver tugged the front of his livery to smooth the wrinkles. Tall and thin, he had a face as lined as a prune, bearing an expression that bespoke too many years of serving the nobility to tolerate impudence from a mere brigand.

"I assure you my eyesight is more than adequate." He glared at the gun, then glared at the masked highwayman with equal disdain. "So this is what you are about, is it? Robbing honest travelers in the dead of night?"

"Aye, that it is," Dudley admitted candidly, and raised his voice again for the benefit of those inside the coach. "An' such a fine night, too, I'd like t' invite all the 'onest folk t' step down an' get a ripe lungful o' fresh, 'eathen air. Lively now, one at a time."

The pale blur of a face appeared at the window. A moment passed while Dudley's figure came under harsh scrutiny, then the unmistakable sound of a softly muttered curse.

"*Mon Dieu*, this cannot be him."

The strongly accented pronouncement took Dudley briefly by surprise, delivered as it was by a distinctly feminine voice.

" 'Appens I might be," he answered, increasing the gruffness in his voice. " 'Appens I might not, dependin' on 'oo ye were expectin'. Either way, I've a gun in my 'and an' a finger willin' t' pull the trigger, so when I say 'stand an' deliver' I'd be quick as spit t' do as yer told!"

The blur remained at the window a few seconds longer than Dudley found comfortable before a second whisper prompted the driver to turn the latch and open the door. He held out a gloved hand to assist a cloaked and hooded figure disembark one wary step at a time, dragging a handful of carefully gathered skirts in her wake. She had her back to the light so that Dudley could see nothing other than the bell shape of her hood and cloak, but there was no mistaking the richness of the silk garment.

"Frenchie, eh? 'Eard tell' that them o' ye what escaped sneezin' in th' basket brought away 'arf th' crown jewels stitched in yer 'ems."

"Sneezing in the basket? *Qu'est-ce qu'il dit?*"

The question was directed in a low whisper at the driver, but Dudley answered. " 'Ad yer 'ead lopped off. Like this—" He held up his left hand to display the stub of a pinky finger. "Felt the kiss o' ma-dam gill-o-teen. Aye, an' I truly 'ope you an' yer friends brung a fine selection with ye tonight." He chuckled and steadied his aim on the coach door. "Rest o' ye now: Out ye come, one at a time, 'ands where I can see 'em."

"There is no one else," the woman said with an exasperated sigh. "I assure you I am quite alone."

"Alone? Ye're travelin' the Chester 'pike in th' middle o' th' night . . . *alone?*"

"I was told . . . that is, I was led to believe . . ." She stopped and seemed to reconsider what she had been about to say, and ended up expelling a huff of misted breath instead. "But I can see I was sadly misled. You cannot possibly be the one they call *'Capitaine Clair d'Etoile.'* "

"Eh? Cap'n 'oo?"

"Captain Starlight. I was led to believe he might be out on a night such as this." She paused and glanced up at the smeared disc of the moon. "I paid an outrageous sum for this information, but I can see now I was merely being played for the fool."

"I did warn you it would be a waste of time, mad'moiselle," the driver said, his hands clasped primly behind his back. "But as usual . . ."

"Yes, yes." Another puff of breath marked the

woman's disappointment. "You warned me, and I did not listen."

Dudley raised his gun and scratched his jaw with the snout. " 'Old up a minute 'ere. Are ye sayin' ye *paid* someone t' tell ye where t' go so's ye could get robbed?"

The driver provided the answer with a righteous sniff. "I advised mad'moiselle most emphatically against it, warning her she was just throwing good coin after bad, for what manner of highwayman advertises where and when he will be stalking a particular road? Indeed, this so-called Captain Starlight certainly would not have been able to elude capture for as long as he has if every unwashed jackanapes raising a tankard knew his business."

"And so he would not," came an amused voice from the shadows behind them. "Nonetheless he *would* be extremely interested to know where this information was purchased and from whom."

The driver and the woman both whirled around to stare at the shifting layers of mist. Even Dudley was somewhat startled, for he had not expected Tyrone to reveal himself without due provocation. Now he seemed to materialize like a ghostly specter out of the blackness at the rear of the coach, with nothing to lend horse or rider substance save for glints of light reflected off the stallion's bridle and the gold foliate work on the brace of leveled snaphaunces.

"*Capitaine Clair d'Etoile,*" the woman whispered.

*

There was a lengthy pause, time enough for the mist to settle around the stallion's legs again, before Tyrone offered a slight bow. "At your service, mam'selle. Did *I* hear correctly: You have been looking for me?"

She continued to stare, for so long he was forced to gently prompt her again.

"Oh. Yes, m'sieur. Yes—" She took a halting step forward, her hand pressed over her breast as if to keep her heart in place. "I must speak with you, m'sieur. On a matter of some importance."

Dudley glanced nervously over both shoulders. "I don't like it, Cap'n. Don't like it a-tall."

His features masked behind the raised collar of his coat, Tyrone surveyed the shadows on either side of the road, searching for any sign of movement. He tuned his hearing to the forest and the hills, trying to catch the accidental nicker of a horse or the snap of a twig beneath a boot, but if it was some ingenious new trap set by the persistent Colonel Roth, his instincts were not detecting it.

His gaze settled on the woman again. *Foolish* and *naïve* were two words that came instantly to his mind, for she obviously had not considered the personal risk involved in her quest. There were few, if any, grown men who would venture out on their own along this deserted stretch of road, and he was curious in spite of the glared warnings Dudley was attempting to convey across the pale circle of lantern light.

Ignoring his partner as well as his own common sense, he uncocked the snaphaunces and tucked them into his belt. One long leg swung over the back of the saddle and he dismounted, the coarse earth of the road crunching loudly under his boots as he came forward.

"What the bloody hell are you doing?" Dudley asked urgently, his accent lapsing in surprise.

"The lady has gone to a good deal of trouble to find me. It would be most ungallant of me to send her away disappointed."

Dudley lifted the bottom edge of the curtain-mask to hiss, "Are you insane? The woods could be crawling with dragoons!"

"If you see any, shoot the driver first, then come and fetch me." Tyrone held out a black-gloved hand, inviting the woman to accompany him to the far side of the road. "Mam'selle—?"

When she hesitated, clearly not expecting to have to leave the comparative safety of the coach, he moved his head the slightest degree to let her see the glitter of his eyes. He had not chosen the fanciful name of Captain Starlight. It had been bestowed upon him by a near hysterical female victim who had sworn there had been nothing mortal between the rim of his tricorn and the top edge of his collar—nothing but a phantom space and a clear view of the starlight beyond. The story, much embellished from one telling to the next, had spread like wildfire, reinforced by the inability of anyone to get close enough to disprove the assumption that they were dealing with an otherworldly being.

"I can promise you, mam'selle, despite what you may have heard, I am quite earthbound. You did say you wanted to talk, did you not?"

The hood moved fractionally to indicate a nod, and she gathered up the voluminous folds of her cloak, following in the direction of his invitation. He did not stop by the roadside, and when she would have balked again, he cradled a hand beneath her elbow and led her up the grassy side of the slope. The mist and shadows thinned measurably as they reached the top of the low knoll; conversely, the moon was brighter and bathed the surrounding countryside in a pale wash of luminous light.

Tyrone released her elbow and walked slowly around the crest of the knoll, scanning the forest, the hills that rolled out on either side, the scant patches of road visible through the mist. He paid particular attention to the eerie pools of fog that had collected in the hollows; the moon gave them the look of puddled cream, the surfaces smooth and motionless enough to betray any disturbance, stealthy or otherwise.

"I assure you, m'sieur, there are no soldiers lying in wait. I have come on my own."

He stopped and turned his head to glance in her direction. He was just a black silhouette against the midnight sky now. His clothing was wool and did nothing to attract any light, whereas the woman's cloak was brocaded silk and shimmered blue-white against the darkness. Her hood was still in place, shielding her face from the moonlight and he moved deliberately around behind her, forcing her to turn with him as he spoke.

"You said you had a matter of some importance you wanted to discuss?"

"Indeed, m'sieur. But first I must know if I can trust you to keep what we say here tonight between your lips and mine."

His slow prowl ended and he arched an eyebrow, for he could see her mouth clearly now. It was a perfect bow shape with a full lower lip, lush and soft, and the image her words conjured started a smile spreading across his own lips. "You would accept the word of a common *voleur* to guarantee a confidence?"

"You speak French, m'sieur?"

*"Un peu.* A little."

*"Bon,* for although I have studied English for many years, there are still words and phrases I do not understand and cannot properly express."

"You seem to be doing just fine," he said, looking around again. "But my time is limited, and my friend is not known for his patience."

"Then I have your word, m'sieur?"

Amused at the irony of her insisting on the word of a thief, Tyrone affected a deep and solemn bow. "You have it indeed, mam'selle. Anything we say . . . or do . . . here tonight will go with me to the grave."

"In that case"—she drew a deep breath and braced herself—"I wish to hire you."

The request startled him and he peered intently at her through the darkness. "Hire me?"

She nodded and the silk threads in her hood sparkled like stardust. "I require the help of someone with your

. . . special talents . . . to assist me in an endeavor of *great* importance."

Two, three long puffs of steamy breath came through the edges of the standing collar before Hart asked, "Exactly what special talents might those be?"

"I wish you to commit a robbery, to stop a coach on the road and relieve the passengers of their valuables."

He leaned forward, almost certain he had not heard correctly. "You want to hire me to rob a coach?"

"This is what you do, is it not?"

"Well, yes, but—"

"The occupants of this particular coach will have with them valuables of a particular interest to me."

"What kind of valuables?" he asked bluntly.

"Jewels."

"Jewels?"

"*Oui*, m'sieur. A necklace, a bracelet, earrings . . . all of a matching suite, all of the finest, most exquisite rubies and diamonds. For your help in assisting me to obtain them, I would be willing to pay you a handsome fee."

He studied her in thoughtful silence for a long moment. The forward rim of her hood still cast a shadow over her face, but his night vision was excellent and her complexion fair enough to reveal a very delicate Parisian nose that complimented the luscious ripeness of her mouth.

"Rubies and diamonds," he murmured. "The suite must be worth a small fortune."

"Several tens of thousands of your English pounds," she agreed without demur.

"Then, if it would not seem too presumptuous of me to ask, what would stop me from simply stealing the pieces and keeping them for myself?"

She was ready for the question and he saw a tight smile flatten her lips. "In the first place, m'sieur, you do not know upon which road, in which coach, on what night the jewels might be found—nor will you discover this without my aid. *Deuxièmement*, you are, as you say, a common thief. You would find it difficult, if not impossible, to receive a fair price, or indeed, to sell them at all without drawing the attention of the authorities. I, on the other hand, will simply appear to be another displaced aristocrat forced to sell off precious heirlooms to survive."

"You don't think the owner might raise an objection or two?"

"I *am* the owner, m'sieur. The jewels were given to me as a betrothal gift."

He was taken by surprise a second time, but said nothing as she continued to elaborate.

"On the fourteenth of this month, I am to marry, m'sieur. During the week prior to the happy event, there are bound to be several dinner parties and soirées where I will be expected to wear the jewels. On the way to one of these entertainments, it is my wish that you waylay the coach and rob me of my valuables. If you are successful, we can then meet the next day—at a place of your choosing, if you wish—where you will give me the jewels and I will pay you your fee."

Hart approached the woman's glimmering silhouette one measured step at a time, forcing her to tilt her face higher and higher the closer he came. Her hood slipped back, but at the same instant a filmy veil of wind-driven clouds drifted over the moon, and he gained nothing more than a dawning suspicion that she was neither as naïve nor as foolish as he had initially supposed.

"If the jewels were given to you as a betrothal gift, why do you have to steal them?"

"Because I have no wish to marry the man who gave them to me." She said it in a way that made it sound as if it were the most logical presumption in the world and he was a dullard to ask. He was so intrigued by the crushed-silk sound of her voice that he barely noticed the insult.

"It was not my choice to marry him," she was saying. "Nor was I even consulted when the decision was made.

I have been . . . how do you say . . . *bartered*. Like an object. Sold by my uncle who wants only to be rid of me, rid of the burden and expense of feeding and clothing and keeping me. He arranged this marriage to relieve himself of an embarrassment, nothing more. And because I came to this country with nothing, I am expected to be grateful for his charity and meekly accept whatever fate that he, in his wisdom, sees fit to arrange."

Tyrone's brows lifted again. "Most women in your position would not consider it such a terrible fate, mam'selle. Most women take it as a matter of course that they are expected to marry for money, position, influence. If you are looking for love—?"

"Love?" The word was expelled on a puff of impatience. "Do not mock me for being an ignorant little French peasant, m'sieur. For centuries, my family has married to make alliances and gain power. I know full well the value placed on a woman's womb—we are simply here to be used for breeding more men."

Tyrone's momentary surprise at her candor changed to amusement. "Be that as it may, mam'selle, few women would find it tiresome to marry a rich man rather than a poor one."

"Indeed, the man to whom I am betrothed has money and he has jewels to lavish on his wife," she said with quiet vehemence, "but he is also a brute. He is coarse and vulgar and looks at me always as if I have no clothes on. He—he makes my skin crawl, m'sieur," she added with a convincing shiver, "and if I had some other way of escaping him, be assured I would take it."

Tyrone looked around at the utter stillness of the countryside. "You were obviously able to escape his clutches tonight. With a coach and two fast horses at your disposal."

"He is in London. So are the rubies," she said by way of saving him another question. "Both he and my uncle are due to arrive in Coventry at the end of the week."

"May I assume your uncle is unapproachable in the matter?"

"You may assume, m'sieur, that you are my last resort."

"And a rather desperate one at that," he pointed out, "although I credit your nerve and imagination for originality."

She looked steadfastly up into the dark slash of shadow between his collar and tricorn. "I am French. I am an *émigré*. Your country is at war with mine and I am allowed to claim refuge here only through the grudging patronage of those who fear that the revolution might reach across the Channel and arouse England's common masses. I have no friends, no other family, nowhere else to turn. My uncle makes no effort to conceal the fact that I live on his charity, but he has threatened to withdraw even that much if I refuse to comply with the arrangements he has made. The jewels will provide me with the means necessary to get away."

"And to live comfortably for quite some time," he added dryly.

Although he could not see her entire face beneath the shadow of her hood, he sensed a burning resentment toward his sarcasm.

"I am not afraid of doing without, m'sieur. I have done without a great many things for the past seven years, since the night the good citizens of Paris marched on the Bastille. More recently, I have done without my parents, my grandparents, my aunts and uncles and cousins—all of whom died on the guillotine. I have hidden in barns and ridden in dung carts while soldiers hunted and searched the countryside for escaping *aristos*"—she spat out the derogatory term with icy disdain—"and I have lain cold and hungry for days on end praying that just once more before I die, I would feel warm again." She stopped and had to visibly gather herself before adding, "But I am not here to solicit either your pity or your help if you do not wish to give it. I have come fully expecting you to demand payment for your services."

Now, that was a nice touch, he mused. It added the right amount of sincerity to an all-around commendable performance. A shimmering waif comes to him in the moonlight, appealing first to his sense of chivalry and if that fails, strike at basic greed.

"You are right in that much, mam'selle," he agreed without the slightest hint of modesty. "I would expect to be paid a good deal more than any one of a dozen other road hawks you might have approached with your proposition. Thus I am prompted to ask again: why bring this to me?"

"You have a reputation for daring, m'sieur, and for success—a thief *sans égal*, without equal. In six years you have never once been caught, your face has never been seen, your actions never betrayed though the reward for your capture is two thousand pounds—more money than most *citizens ordinaire* will earn in a lifetime."

Another nice touch, he thought: flattery. And if that failed . . . ?

"It is also whispered that you have no love for those who would rob and cheat and steal from the poor. That you have often left gifts of coin for those who might have starved or gone without shelter otherwise—"

"Mam'selle—" Unable to hold his humor in check any longer, Tyrone laughed. "You have me confused with another legend, I'm afraid. It was Robin Hood who robbed from the rich to give to the poor. If I choose my victims from among tax collectors and fat landowners, it is because they carry more coins in their pockets than farmers and clerks do. As for giving away my ill-gotten gains, I assure you the rumors are just that: rumors. I would consider such generosity to be a rather glaring flaw in the character of a true thief, not to mention the logic of someone who is engaged in my profession strictly for profit—which I am."

"Then . . . you will not help me?"

There was still a lingering threat of laughter in his voice as he answered, "I am not in the habit of hiring myself out."

She seemed genuinely taken aback by the rejection. It struck him as the ingrained reaction of someone born to the nobility who could not fathom a peasant's reluctance to slash open his own flesh in order for some curious, bewigged aristocrat to debate a point of anatomy. It was not a response someone could fabricate, regardless of how good an actress one might be, which convinced Tyrone that at least part of her story rang true. There were parts that did not, however, and he was mildly curious to know what she was hiding . . . and what she would do next.

One of his questions was answered when she raised her skirts as if she were about to depart. *"C'est dommage,"* she whispered. "I am sorry to have wasted your time."

She started back to the road, but had taken no more than a few steps when his voice stopped her. "I said I was not in the *habit* of hiring myself out, mam'selle. I did not say I would not do it."

She glanced over her shoulder and for one long suspended moment, the moonlight shone full on her face. Tyrone had amassed enough impressions to suspect there was a very lovely woman hiding beneath the hood, but not even his finely tuned perceptions had prepared him for the full extent of her loveliness. His breath, in fact, stopped somewhere in his throat. The combined effect of a lushly pouting mouth, a nose as slim and delicately refined as on a porcelain figurine, and eyes large and luminous had an immediate and startling impact on the way the blood flowed through his veins.

"You could try seducing me, mam'selle," he murmured.

*"Pardon?"*

"Tempt me. You said you would be willing to pay me

handsomely for my services. What do you consider 'handsome'?"

She let the hem of her skirts settle onto the dew again and turned fully around to face him. "Would a thousand pounds pique your interest, m'sieur?"

"Not as much as two," he countered bluntly.

"Two!"

"It will be no easy ride in the moonlight, mam'selle. There is, as you aptly pointed out, a considerable reward on my head and no lack of men out there who are not above shooting first and asking questions later if they think they have me in their gun sights. Furthermore, if the jewels are worth as much as you say they are, you will be well able to afford it."

"On the other hand," he shrugged and adjusted the rim of his collar higher, prepared to lead the way back to the coach, "if the price of freedom is too steep—"

She straightened her arm and extended a slender, gloved hand toward him.

"Two thousand," she agreed. "And no price is too steep to pay for freedom."

Tyrone pondered the businesslike gesture a moment before taking the delicate hand in his and grasping it firmly to seal the pact.

"I will need more details, of course. But not tonight. My comrade should be about ready to burst his seams by now, and besides . . . I would say we both need time to think things through very carefully, for—like the act of losing one's virginity—once the deed is done, it cannot be undone. Shall we say three days? If, in that time, you are still determined—"

"I am not a virgin, *Capitaine*, nor will I change my mind." Her hesitation had been barely perceptible and she hid it well by using the time to extricate her hand from his. "Only say where and when you wish me to meet you and I will be there."

Tyrone almost smiled, and certainly would have if the

hairs on the nape of his neck were not prickling upright like the spiny quills on a hedgehog. He relished the secure feeling of knowing his instincts had not been corrupted by the shine in her eyes or the faint tremors he had felt in her hand. She was obviously not telling him the whole truth, but at the same time, she looked so eager, and so desperate, he played the charade to the end.

"I will expect you to come prepared to tell me everything you know about the events planned for the week of your wedding. If I think it can be done, I will do it. If I think there isn't a hope in hell of succeeding, I will tell you that too. But I will also warn you, mam'selle, that if I think you are lying at any point," he added softly, "I will not hesitate to wring your lovely neck."

*  ☽

# Chapter 2

Renée Marie Emanuelle d'Anton stared out the window of the coach, her heart pounding as if she had run all the way down the hill. She had not, of course. She had forced herself to walk as calmly as she could beside the tall, black silhouette, taking fastidious care where she placed her feet on the slippery grass, wary not to brush too close or appear to cringe too far from his side. Arriving back at the coach, he had handed her inside with a cavalier bow, and Finn had climbed into the box, snapping the horses to attention, driving away as if nothing out of the ordinary had occurred—as if she had not just met and invited the most elusive, most hunted criminal in five parishes to rob her at gunpoint and steal a fortune in jewels.

She sank back against the seat and closed her eyes.

After four failed attempts to lure the elusive Captain Starlight into the open, she had begun to think he truly was a phantom, a figment of someone's obsessed imagination. On each occasion, Finn had visited the surrounding inns and taverns ahead of time and left discreet hints that someone rich and important would be travelling the Chester turnpike that night. Each time they had set out, Renée's nerves had been stretched taut with fear and apprehension, not knowing what to expect. After all, there were no guarantees that the brigand who stopped them would be the *right* brigand. Or even if he was, that she would be able to go through with her plan.

It had only been Finn's staunch presence by her side that had kept her from fainting dead away when she had seen the first rogue. He had sounded like a thief should sound, with an accent as impossibly coarse as English wool. Renée's mother had been English by birth and had insisted her daughter become proficient in the language of her homeland, but the tutors in Paris had enunciated every word clearly and meticulously, using only proper, upper-crust inflections Renée could expect to hear in the finest parlors and ballrooms of English society.

She imagined that the only time such a vulgar brigand could have spent in any parlor or ballroom was if he had robbed the inhabitants. She had all but resigned herself to yet another failure when the figure of the second highwayman had emerged from the darkness and mist. Her heart had vaulted clear up into her throat, and the sight of him—all black shadows, black clothing, black beast—had very nearly caused her knees to buckle with fright. She had known who he was without having to ask for confirmation of his identity as the phantom Captain Starlight.

Yet it was no phantom who had led her to a canny vantage point above the mist, and no phantom who had listened with amused curiosity to her proposal. He had been careful to keep his back against the moonlight so that what little of his face was exposed was kept constantly in shadow. Only once had she caught the faintest impression of a bold, straight nose and dark eyebrows, an impression that could fit a thousand men without betraying a clue to their identities.

He had kept his voice deliberately low as well, revealing nothing beyond its deep and mellow resonance. His words bore no distinctive accent—though she would hardly be the one to admit to any expertise in that regard—nor had he identified himself in any other way. He *seemed* taller than the average man, but that could have been credited to the combined effect of the standing collar and tricorn. Even the greatcoat he wore had disguised his frame insofar as she could not say if he was broad or lean, muscled or soft.

Muscled, she decided. And lean, like the body of a jungle cat she had seen once in the zoo at Versailles. Everything about him, in fact, reminded her of some sleek, dangerous beast who kept to the shadows and struck without warning. Finn had related some of the stories he had overheard the servants telling, and it was said *le capitaine* could shoot the button off a coat at a hundred paces. Once, when he had been challenged by a master swordsman, he had left the hapless duelist gasping on his knees for mercy. He was cautious, deliberate, vigilant, and perceptive. He appeared and disappeared without so much as a swirl of mist to mark his presence, and sometimes—if the stories were to be believed—on nights when the moon was very high and bright, he could be seen galloping along the crest of a distant hill, laughing at the ineptitude of the soldiers he had left far behind.

A shiver sent her nestling deeper into the corner of the coach, and she realized she had not paid heed to any passing landmarks. Careful not to lose hold of the lap robe, she reached up and tapped on the roof, and almost at once, a panel in the rear of the driver's box slid open.

"Mad'moiselle?"

"Are we nearly at the crossroads, Finn?"

"It should be just over the next rise."

"*Vraiment*," she said softly, "I am so cold, my toes are like blocks of ice."

"Harwood House is but another half hour away. If you would prefer to go directly home—"

"No, Finn. No, in even such a short time, I fear my toes and fingers might snap off and my courage desert me altogether. A few moments by a warm fire, and I shall be fine."

He snorted, muttering something about headstrong foolishness, and before the panel slid shut, she could hear the cracking of the whip overhead to spur the horses to greater speed.

The posting house that sat at the crossroads was an old timber and plaster building, with gabled overhangs defining the upper storeys and a steeply sloped thatch roof mounting clusters of brick chimneys. Slits of light glowed through the front window shutters, but it still required the impatient stamping of Finn's boots on the wooden floor to bring a round-faced woman bustling out of a back room to greet them. The inn catered primarily to travelers who sought relief from the bone-rattling roughness of the turnpikes. There was also a scattering of locals who chose the Fox and Hound both for its isolation and for the discretion of the innkeeper, and it was apparent, by the way the woman cast a sly glance along Renée's cloaked and hooded figure, she expected her to fit the latter category.

"M' lady is chilled," Finn said in his most imperious manner, attempting to discourage the impression at once. "She requires something restorative to drink, preferably warm, as well as a few moments' respite by the fire, if it can be arranged."

The woman raised the three pronged candelabra she was holding and inspected Finn's face as well as his livery. When the smoky light flickered over Renée's features, the woman clucked her tongue. "Lud," she muttered. "You do look blue as a bruise, child. Come on through then, and I'll put you as near the fire as you can get without charring. As for you," she noted Finn's red nose and purpling ears, "you can go through to the kitchen and our Violet will fix you up with a bowl of hot broth."

Finn looked guardedly at Renée. "I would prefer not to leave you on your own, mad'moiselle."

"It is all right, Finn," Renée said wearily. "I will call if I need you."

"Are you quite certain?" He had lowered his voice and

deepened his frown. "I am not the least comfortable with the surroundings."

Renée managed a weak smile. "I will be fine, Finn. Go and warm yourself. We will not be here any longer than necessary."

Grudgingly, he relinquished her into the proprietress's care, and Renée was led through a stout oak archway into the parlor, a large room paneled with oak sheets and dominated by a huge wooden fireplace along one wall. Half of the room obviously served as a taproom, the other had groupings of small tables and chairs where customers could dine or simply converse in private. Apart from a solitary gentleman who sat in a corner reading a copy of the *Coventry Mercury*, the room was empty. Renée might not have noticed him at all had the light beside him not reflected off his shock of red hair, making it seem to burn as brightly as the candle flame.

The innkeeper identified herself as Mrs. Ogilvie and pointed to a wooden settle positioned directly in front of the hearth. "Can't get you any closer, m'lady, unless you'd care to sit inside the chimney corner."

"This is fine," Renée replied as she sat.

"I'll return in a moment, m'lady. We takes proper care of our guests, as you'll see."

Staring at the flames in the hearth and stretching her toes as close to the heat as she dared, Renée tried to control the fresh onslaught of butterflies that were rolling around in her belly. But there were just too many, and then Mrs. Ogilvie was bustling beside her, placing a cup of wine and a plate of cheese and bread on a small table. Nodding her thanks, Renée cradled the pewter goblet in both hands and took slow, measured sips hoping the spicy drink would kindle some warmth in the rest of her body. She had not removed either her cloak or her hood, and in short order, her face was rosy from the heat, and the dew-soaked toes of her shoes were beginning to steam faintly.

A shadow approached the side of the settle and startled Renée into looking up.

"Might I be permitted to refill your cup, my dear?"

The red-haired gentleman was holding out his hand and, without waiting for her answer, took her goblet and filled it from the tankard of wine that had been hooked over the grate to keep warm.

He cut an elegantly lean silhouette as he bent over the fire. His breeches were skin tight, while his jacket was tailored high in front to show the rich brocading of his waistcoat beneath. The collar was fashionably high, with deep lapels folded down in front to accentuate the multiple layers of a pleated white cravat that had been arranged to flatter the sharp, angular lines of his face. His hair, more orange than red this close to the brighter firelight, was plaited into a neat tail in back with two precisely rolled curls left to sit over each ear.

He topped up his own glass and, careful to lift the long swallow tails of his jacket aside, joined her in the high-backed wooden cocoon of the settle.

He saw where her gaze was fixed and smiled. "Ah, yes. I had forgotten . . . you have never had occasion to meet me out of uniform before, have you? And in truth, I find the regimental wigs rather more of an affectation than a statement of fashion."

Amber-colored eyes more suited to a bird of prey than an officer in King George's Royal Horse glittered with reflections of the firelight as he studied her profile. "Your driver had no difficulty finding the inn?"

"No," she said quietly. "None."

"I know it is a little farther out of the way than the last one, but I prefer to err on the side of caution."

Renée took a sip of wine and the hawk-like eyes slid down to the small bead of wetness that lingered on her lower lip.

"To be seen meeting too many times in the same place

would surely give rise to gossip and speculation," he added. "Neither of which would suit our purposes."

Watching her face, he leaned back against the settle and steepled his fingers together under his chin. "Am I left to conclude by your apparent lack of enthusiasm that our little . . . venture . . . was once again unsuccessful?"

Renée tried to keep the loathing out of her eyes as she turned, finally, to face him.

"As it happens," she said softly, "we were stopped not five miles from here."

For an entire minute he did not move, did not betray a reaction. Someone more intimately acquainted with the facial nuances of Colonel Bertrand Roth might have noticed the thin rim of white that began to glow around his nostrils, or the tiny blue vein that rose and began to throb in his temple. To Renée, it seemed as though he hardly troubled himself to blink.

After a moment, he slowly leaned forward, forcing the words out through his teeth. "Are you certain it was him? Are you certain it was Starlight?"

Renée's focus shifted from his face to his hands where they had dropped to grip the caps of his knees like claws. She concluded he must have passed several nerve-wracking hours waiting here at the inn, for his nails had all been chewed down past the quick; the left thumb was savaged so badly, a drop of fresh blood was being squeezed from the torn flesh.

"It was Captain Starlight," she said. "I am quite certain."

"*Quite* certain? I remind you, there have been more than a few enterprising fellows taking to the roads these days thinking a gun and a black horse will cause their victims to throw money at them in terror."

"It was *le capitaine*. And I am *absolutely* certain because I spoke to him."

"You *spoke* to the bastard!"

"Was that not what I was *supposed* to do, m'sieur?" she asked angrily. "Was that not the purpose for this entire masquerade?"

Roth settled himself back against the riser of the bench and clasped his hands beneath his chin again, ignoring her question for a more pressing one of his own. "Did you see his face?"

"No. He had his collar well up and his hat well down. He was all in black and . . ."

"Yes . . . and?"

"And—" she hesitated, thinking Roth would not want to hear that the highwayman was bold and dashing. "He was extremely careful, m'sieur, that I should not see more than what he wanted me to see."

"Not very enterprising of you, my dear. I had hoped for a little more ingenuity on your part."

"What would you have me do, Colonel? Reach up and remove his hat, turn his face to the light, and demand his name?"

Roth pursed his lips. "So. You spoke to him. And you told him . . . what?"

"Exactly what I was supposed to tell him: that I wanted to hire him."

"And?" The glowing whiteness where he pressed the pads of his fingertips together belied the almost nonchalant tone of his voice. "He didn't think it an odd request?"

"He thought it very odd indeed. He wanted to know why I should want to do such a thing."

"Were you *convincing*? Did he believe your explanation?"

A flush crept into her cheeks. "Why should he not have believed me? It was the truth, for the most part. I am being forced into a marriage not of my choosing; I am being used like a pawn in a game of terrible consequences and if I refuse to do either of these things—"

"If you refuse, Mademoiselle d'Anton," he interjected,

"your brother will be taken before the King's Bench and put on trial for attempted murder."

Renée's anger, her rage, her hatred for Roth at that moment rose like a lump in her throat and threatened to choke her.

"Antoine did not attempt to murder Lord Paxton."

"He was found kneeling over your uncle's body. The gun was in his hand, the barrel was still hot and smoking. My God, woman, you were there, you saw it."

"I heard the shot and I ran to see what had happened, but whoever shot Lord Paxton had already fled through the back door. Antoine was—"

"Holding the gun above the earl's head, likely preparing to make amends for his poor aim."

"He was moving the gun out of the way, trying to see if Lord Paxton was still alive."

"Indeed, head wounds do tend to bleed like the devil. Which is why they can be so deceiving . . . and undoubtedly disappointing to someone who would have only had a chance to make one clean shot."

"Antoine did not shoot him," she said, closing her eyes against the weight of her frustration. "There was someone else in the room."

"Is that what he told you in his inimitably quaint way?"

She opened her eyes again and reacted with unblinking disbelief to Roth's casually vicious remark. No, Antoine had not told her anything, not in the conventional sense of the word. Antoine had not been able to speak a single word or make the smallest sound since the day they had fled Paris. Roth knew this. He knew it and his eyes glittered with pleasure at the pain his cruel words caused.

"He is only a boy," she said softly. "He is not yet fourteen years old."

"English law is quite strict in its penalties for attempted murder, regardless of the accused's age. He could be imprisoned for the rest of his natural life or transported to penal labor colonies in Australia. Or he could be hung. He could also be set free, Mademoiselle d'Anton, dependent entirely upon Lord Paxton's generous nature."

"Which will improve considerably if I agree to help you capture Captain Starlight?" she asked in a whisper.

"A small enough price to pay, I should think."

"If you have never been betrayed, I suppose it would be considered a small thing."

"Oh, come now. You cannot compare the illustrious Captain Starlight's position to that of the political eradications in France. He is a *thief* and a *cold-blooded murderer*, with no uncertainties whatsoever regarding either charge. He is destined to swing from a gibbet, regardless of whether you assist in his arrest or not. For him, there is no choice, no possible salvation. On the other hand, your brother . . ." He shrugged meaningfully. "As you say, he is only a boy. He has his entire life ahead of him. A life you can make easy for him . . . or very, very difficult."

Renée regarded him the way she might look at something repugnant on the bottom of her shoe. He quite literally made her skin crawl, which it did now as he leaned forward and blinked once, very deliberately, like a reptile.

"You might also want to take into consideration the part I have played in all this," he recommended softly, running the tip of one spidery finger along the sleeve of her cloak. "Why, if I hadn't been in London the evening of the . . . incident . . . there might not have been a calmer head present to prevail over Paxton's anger. Your brother might have been hauled away upon the instant to a rat-infested cell in Newgate instead of the comparative luxury of your uncle's estate here in Coventry."

"He is still watched, day and night, by your men, by the servants. He cannot set foot outside the door without someone questioning his intentions. Or following him."

"For his own protection, I assure you."

"For your convenience, you mean. What good is a hostage if he cannot be taken upon the instant?"

The bony finger finished its lazy meandering along her arm and curled upward again to rest under his own chin. His face was only inches from hers, close enough for her to smell the pomade he used on his hair, and close enough for her to see the top layer of dried skin on his lips crack as he smiled. The smile itself was an artificial and postured display of too many teeth crammed into too small a mouth; it made her think of a picket fence with all the stakes toppled together.

Roth noted where her gaze lingered and he leaned even closer, emboldened by her apparent interest. "With the weather so unpredictable these days, I took the liberty of arranging a room for myself overnight. We . . . could have a private supper sent up and . . . discuss how we might be of further help to one another in the future."

It was not the first time he had made an overture, nor was he the first man coarse enough to suggest she use her body to win favors. Renée had come to realize, in fact, that being French, she was commonly expected to be a harlot, or at the very least, a woman not fettered by any moral inhibitions. She was not unaware of her own beauty, but had come to regard it as more of a curse than a blessing, especially when men three times older than herself pushed her into corners and offered her trinkets for a lusty fumble under the stairs. Or when clearly repugnant reptiles thought there might be a feather's chance in a windstorm that she would willingly accompany him to a private supper in a cheap tavern.

"Colonel," she murmured in her very best harlot's voice, "if I thought for one second I could keep the contents of my stomach intact while I played whore for an Englishman, I would just as easily have sold myself for the glorious procreation of Robespierre's bastards."

Roth stared. The laugh started low in his throat, and because it was so seldom the product of genuine mirth, it sounded more like a harsh, grating bark when it left his lips.

"You have wit, my dear, and the true pride of the *ancien régime*. I imagine some men admire those qualities in a woman, although I would have thought someone in your position would be inclined to show a tad more humility—unless, of course, you have grown fond of the sound of whispers behind your back and the sight of villagers who spit in the streets as you pass."

Renée felt a surge of warmth in her cheeks that had nothing to do with her proximity to the fire. The inhabitants of Coventry held no love for French émigrés. Most of the villagers had sent a husband or a brother across the Channel to fight in a war that had too many uncomfortable similarities to the embarrassing loss they had suffered at the hands of the American colonists. If the French wanted to abolish the monarchy, if they wanted to do away with the greed and corruption of the aristocracy and put the government into the hands of the people, who were they to interfere? Why should English commonfolk have to send their men to fight and die in a foreign land when their own nation was ruled by a king who was given to fits of madness and the major portion of the wealth was in the hands of the ruling nobility, as it always had been. The villagers did not understand why, if their country was at war with France, there were so many French nobles seeking asylum, and more important, why these émigrés had full bellies and warm beds while they still went barefoot and ate crusts.

Renée was seldom inspired to venture too far from Harwood House. She was regarded with suspicion and open disdain, for although she had been a victim of Robespierre's madness and the Terror had taken every last member of her father's family to the guillotine, there was no sympathy to be found in the villagers' company.

Only persecution and contempt. The sooner she was away from here, the sooner she could break free . . .

Aware of Roth's eyes watching for any flicker in her expression, she moistened her lips and said quietly, "The captain has agreed to think about my request."

A coppery eyebrow quirked upward. "Only *think* about it?"

"I imagine he wants some time to decide if it is a trap or not. He . . . has agreed to meet with me again."

Roth drew a deep, thoughtful breath and leaned back against the settle. "When? Where?"

"In three days' time. I am to be at Stonebow Bridge at precisely midnight. From there, I am to travel north on the Birmingham turnpike until he intercepts me—which he will only do if he is certain no one has followed me and there are no soldiers lying in wait."

"The Birmingham turnpike?" Roth's eyes narrowed. "There are twenty miles of flat fields and moorland flanking either side of the road."

"Perhaps that is why he chose it."

Roth seemed not to have heard her. "Only one other rogue, Dick Turpin, was able to evade capture so long and that was because he knew every bush and bramble, every foxhole and cave within ten miles of his lair. The villagers knew him, the innkeepers harbored him when the soldiers gave chase, and, as it was discovered at his trial, he was born less than a mile from his favorite ambuscade.

"Unlike Turpin, however, Starlight ranges freely between five parishes and on the surface appears to have no favored hunting ground. Yet by his very cleverness he betrays an indisputable familiarity with the region. He also seems to have an uncanny instinct for survival. He has avoided every trap we have attempted to set thus far, leaving one to conclude his sources of information are astonishingly accurate and far-reaching. I have been here four months now, and in that same time, I have followed every accursed rumor, chased down every scant whisper waiting for him to make a mistake, and he has not obliged me. There has not been one single clue as to his identity, not one single witness who has been able to do so much as swear to the color of his hair, or his eyes, or say if half his face is covered in scars! There has not been one murmur of betrayal from men of his own ilk who would ordinarily bear witness against their own grandmothers if they thought it would put a few pennies in their pockets." He paused and curled his hand into a tight fist. "It has been like trying to catch air. And it has become a game to him. A cat and mouse game in which, thus far, he has managed to stay one leap ahead. Well, not for much longer, my dear. Not for much longer. I have vowed to catch him, and catch him I will, by God."

"The man who preceded you had been trying to do so for six years, had he not?"

"Colonel Lewis?" Roth spat out the name with a measure of venom. "He should have been forced to resign his post a dozen years ago, and would have if they could have lifted his head out of the ale barrels long enough to win his signature. For five of those six years the reward on Starlight's head did not go above thirty pounds. Who among the local peasantry would betray one of their heroes and legends for a meager thirty pounds?"

"Another Judas, perhaps?"

Roth's eyes flashed his contempt. "Need I remind you that however romantic and daring the tales of his escapades might seem to you, he has murdered three men—*in cold blood*—that we know of, and would not have hesitated to blow the top off of your Mr. Finnerty's fine gray head—or yours, for that matter—if he had seen the old man reach for a pistol tonight."

"I have told you, I will do what I can to help you catch him," she said carefully. "*Vraiment*, it does not mean I have to take pleasure in what I do, m'sieur."

Having allowed an uncharacteristic spark of temper to show, he forced himself to settle back against the wooden riser and to fold his hands together in his lap. "No, you do not have to enjoy it, but I do expect your full and absolute cooperation. Starlight will most assuredly be convinced he is being led into a trap and I will expect you to do whatever is necessary to convince our noble prince of thieves otherwise, for I am determined nothing will rouse his suspicions this time."

"May I know what I am to tell him when he asks about the time and place for the robbery?"

"When the time is right, you will know enough to whet his appetite."

"You do not trust me, m'sieur?" she asked mockingly.

"Not as far as one foot outside that door," he replied smoothly. "But I do have faith in the fact that you love your brother. I believe you love him enough, for instance, that if I were to tell you to stand up right now, walk up those stairs to my room, and prepare to receive me, naked, on your knees . . . you would do so. Moreover, you would do so with such enthusiasm, your lovely mouth would be kept far too busy to annoy me with your witticisms. Indeed"—he reached over and curled his fingers around her wrist, drawing her hand over the bulge at his groin—"see how your drollery has affected me already?"

＊ ☽

# Chapter 3

*A*s hot as it was in front of the fire, Renée felt herself go stone cold inside. Her hand turned to ice where he held it over his lap, and even though her fingers shrank back in revulsion, his grip was firm enough for him to rub the heel of her palm back and forth across his hardened flesh.

"There are four rooms at the top of the stairs," he said matter-of-factly. "Mine is on the left, at the rear. You should have no trouble finding it."

Renée's mouth went dry and her skin clammy. The filthy vermin was calling her bluff, smiling his mirthless smile and watching her reaction in a way that suggested he would not hesitate to follow through his threat and punish Antoine for her stubbornness.

He tilted his head a few degrees, feigning astonishment at her hesitation. "I confess your curious sense of loyalty does fatigue me at times, my dear. You express feelings of remorse over a murderous highwayman and seem almost unwilling to help your own brother. I warrant there are dozens of beautiful women in Warwickshire alone who would beg for the opportunity to keep their loved ones out of gaol."

"Then by all means, invite one of them to take my place. I am sure Captain Starlight will not question the substitution."

"And your brother?" Roth's eyes glittered. "When he

feels the coarseness of the noose tightening around his neck, will he not be somewhat bewildered as well?"

Renée felt the blood pounding in her temples. Some-where—it sounded as if it came from the end of a very long tunnel—she heard a door slam and a volley of rau-cous laughter and stamping boots. A moment later, the privacy of the common room was shattered as four young gentlemen, drunk as owls, staggered through the door-way, their shoulders bumping off the walls and each other as they struggled to hold one another up.

Startled, Renée jumped to her feet. The toe of her shoe caught the edge of the small table beside the settle and overturned it, sending her goblet into the stone hearth with a loud metallic *clan-n-ng*. Behind her, high beaver hats were being flung aside and clouds of dust slapped from the sleeves of elegantly tailored jackets, and in the midst of boisterous shouting for fresh bottles of wine, one of the gentlemen heard the crash and spun unsteadily around to stare at the cloaked and hooded fig-ure silhouetted in front of the fire.

At almost the same instant, Mrs. Ogilvie came hurrying out of the back room, demanding an explanation for all the noise.

" 'Twas an unblessedly long ride from Meriden an' my companions an' I'r parched with thirst!" said one of the newcomers.

"P-positively p-parched!" Another agreed through a rapid spitfire of hiccups. He grinned and tried to lean on the first man for support, missed, and crashed into a third, who happily spun him around and pointed to the silent figure standing behind the settle. Drawing himself up-right, the hiccupping man fumbled to straighten his cra-vat. "D-damm my eyes if they l-lie, gents, but I believe we have a l-lady in our midst."

"Did I not tell you she would be here?" exclaimed a blond, round-faced member of the group. "Lizbeth, my

peach! My swan! My light o' love! Come let me introduce
you to my very good fren's!''

Bertrand Roth, concealed until then by the solid
wooden back of the settle, shot to his feet beside Renée
and made his presence known with a scowl. "I am afraid
you gentlemen are mistaken in your expectations. The
lovely Lizbeth is *not* in attendance this evening."

The blond stopped cold in his tracks. He stood swaying on the balls of his feet a moment, peering from one
shadowy face to the other, then retreated the two steps he
had taken. "Beg pardon, m'lady. Beg pardon, sir. An honest mistake."

Two of his three companions welcomed him back into
their midst with a snort and a round of tippled laughter,
while the third simply stood and hiccupped and stared
raptly at Renée as she started to adjust her hood forward
again over her face.

On further thought, she pushed the satin dome back
off her head, baring her face and the surrounding cloud of
golden curls to the light. A second man joined the first in
staring, and to insure she drew the attention of the remaining pair, Renée unfastened the lace frog at her throat
and ran her hands across the nape of her neck to lift the
long, gleaming mass of curls free from the collar of the
cloak. Like liquid sunlight it spilled around her shoulders, the waves and spirals catching the firelight behind
her and glowing like a halo around her head.

The dazzling display drew Roth's sharp glance and his
hand grasped her upper arm. "What the devil do you
think you are doing?"

She looked first at his hand, then at his face.

"Do you not find it warm standing by the fire, m'sieur?
Since you have invited me to stay for supper, I thought I
would make myself more comfortable."

Roth's gaze flicked down. The act of disentangling her
hair, combined with the weight of the heavy cloak had
caused the latter to slip back off her shoulders and fall to

the floor. The plain white muslin gown she wore beneath was sashed high beneath the breasts and cut low across the bodice, and because there were no formfitting corsets or multiple layers of petticoats between her body and the sheer layers of her chemise and gown, the four pairs of owlish eyes were now focused intently on the general area between her neck and knees.

This was one of those times, she hoped desperately, when beauty had its purpose. It had been at Roth's insistence that their meetings take place as far away from the public eye as possible. His obsession with catching Captain Starlight and his conviction that the highwayman had eyes and ears everywhere—even in the regimental headquarters—made it imperative to avoid becoming the objects of anyone's curiosity. Coventry was a large city of some seventeen thousand inhabitants, most of whom kept up the pretense of a London society, with those of the upper class thriving on gossip and speculation and eager to spread rumors of romantic liaisons. Since the outset of the war between France and England, regiments of local militia had been conscripted and trained against a possible threat of invasion, and nothing tickled the gossips more than seeing virtuous young ladies being swept off their feet by the uniformed gallants. By tomorrow, at least one of these four leering lords would be sober enough to remember a tall, slim Française with striking blond hair and startling blue eyes engaged in a secret tryst at the Fox and Hound Inn. And if he did not move quickly to prevent it, someone would be able to identify Colonel Bertrand Roth by the equally memorable flaming redness of his hair and the accompanying hot flush of crimson that flooded his face.

With a softly snarled curse, he snatched up the fallen cloak and draped it back around Renée's shoulders. Grabbing her by the elbow, he ushered her across the room and out the door. He glared back into the far corner of the room which caused the four gentlemen to avert their eyes, though they were not sufficiently chastised out of nudging and winking among themselves. One even took the liberty of clearing his throat as Mrs. Ogilvie returned with an armload of bottles, complimenting her on the long-standing tradition of discretion at her fine establishment.

"That was extremely foolish, my dear," Roth hissed as he led her into the shadows of the outer hallway.

"I am sure I do not know what you mean, m'sieur."

"Do you not?" He swung her roughly around and pushed her back into the corner, crowding in close with his body. "I am not entirely familiar with French manners, but in any language, a blatant challenge demands an equally blatant response."

Renée tried to twist herself free, but his hands were on her shoulders, pinning her flat against the wall. "Let me go. Let me go at once, do you hear?"

"My hearing is quite excellent, I assure you. It is your ability to grasp and understand a situation that appears to be in some doubt, so if you will bear with me, Mademoiselle d'Anton, I will repeat this only one more time." He pressed his mouth next to her ear so she could feel the moist heat of each whispered word tingle ominously down the length of her neck. "Should anything—*anything*—go wrong between now and the fourteenth, I will not hesitate to clap you in irons and see you dragged before the courts to stand trial alongside your brother as an accomplice to attempted murder. Moreover, I will personally choose your gaol cell, my sweet, to be the one with the fattest rats, the sourest stink, and the filthiest guards to seek your company at night."

"Take your hands off me," she gasped. "Take them off or I shall scream!"

"Will you indeed?" he asked, cocking his head to one side. "Then by all means—scream away."

Renée opened her mouth to draw a breath, but before she could do anything with it, Roth's left hand shifted upward and something hard stabbed her in the tender junction of her neck and jaw, just below the ear. Once the initial shearing of white-hot pain had cut off every other thought she possessed, his thumb gouged deeper into the cluster of nerves and she found she could not move, could not blink, could not even breathe through the solid wall of blinding agony.

His head tilted to the other side, and the amber eyes glittered with amusement as he watched the successive waves of pain alter the expression on her face. "You do invite these things upon yourself, you know. You persist in throwing these little defiances in my face, as if I have not yet risen to the response you seek. Is that it? Do you prefer a more *violent* display of passion? Your own countryman, the Marquis de Sade, has written extensively on the subject of women who crave to be broken before they can feel truly fulfilled. Is it the same with you? Is it a *penchant* you French have acquired through the years of rampant decadence?"

Renée's eyes blurred with tears. The pain was excruciating and she could do nothing as he bent his head forward and thrust his tongue into the curl of her ear. Great pooling splotches of darkness began to cloud her vision; her lungs were on fire, her heart was pounding like a fist inside her chest though the blood seemed to have nowhere to go.

She felt Roth's mouth slide wetly down the curve of her throat, and she felt the sudden intrusion of his hand beneath her cloak. He grunted appreciatively when he encountered the fullness of her breast and with a rough jerk, he pulled the fabric down and brought her naked flesh into his palm.

Through the pounding of her fear, Renée could hear the four young lords laughing and clinking glasses inside the common room. They were less than twenty paces away, yet they might as well be twenty miles. So overcome was she by the pain Roth was inflicting on her neck and jaw that he was able to brutalize her with complete impunity.

"I think," he murmured, "it would be rather ungallant of me not to escort you home, certainly not with a dangerous highwayman on the loose."

Renée managed a strangled, choking sound in her throat. Out of nowhere, it seemed, a tall black shape loomed up behind them. She could not be sure it was not her eyes playing tricks, for they were so distorted by tears and pain she could see very little at all, but in the next instant, she heard a dull thud and the pressure on her throat was suddenly broken. Roth's head snapped to one side and remained that way for a long moment, his eyes glazed with confusion and not a little surprise. Then he was crumpling down onto his knees in front of her, his hands clutching at her skirts in a frantic, but ultimately futile, effort to retain his balance.

Finn raised his hand to swing again and Renée saw the glint of a heavy iron candlestick clutched in his fist. Before he could strike the second blow, however, Roth was on his face, his arms and legs spread in an ungainly sprawl across the floor.

Finn snorted once to express his satisfaction and replaced the candlestick.

"Are you all right, mad'moiselle?" he asked gently in French.

With the pressure on her throat eased, Renée was able to breathe again and she did so in great gulping mouthfuls as she clutched at Finn's arm and nodded. "Yes. Yes, I am all right. He—he was trying to make me . . ."

"I can well imagine what he was trying to make you do," Finn said with disdain, "and I would suggest—if we do not wish the rest of the patrons of this wretched little hostel to know it as well—that we remove ourselves as quickly as possible."

"But . . . we cannot just leave him here."

He glanced down and, after a brief hesitation, reached

to an inside pocket of his livery jacket and withdrew a slim silver flask. Unstoppering it with his teeth, he dribbled a fine stream of brandy over Roth's neck and collar, then fit the emptied flask into the unconscious man's hand. When he straightened, he saw the look on Renée's face and arched a wiry eyebrow.

"Strictly medicinal, I assure you. I anticipated it would be a cold evening."

She glanced back down at Roth. "Will he not be angry?"

"Furious, I warrant. But unless he wishes to face a very public charge of attempted rape, which would not only bring the wrath of the crown down upon his head, but the outrage of every officer and gentleman in the parish, I rather think he will bear his humiliation in silence and do nothing."

Renée shivered and fumbled to draw the edges of her cloak together.

"Come," he said. "Before I am tempted to throft him again on principle."

Her feeble attempt at a smile spurred Finn into stepping over Roth's splayed legs and hastening Renée out the door to where the coach stood, black and gleaming against the night sky. When she was seated inside with the rug pulled high under her chin, Finn climbed up into the driver's box and whistled the horses to attention. A grinding spin of the wheels and they were away, the glare from the coach lamp dwindling quickly into the distance.

Neither Finn nor Renée looked back at the inn, therefore neither one saw the sliver of light cut into the gloom as the door opened and closed to emit the tall, dark silhouette of a man.

He stood a moment in the cool night air and stared thoughtfully after the fading coach lamp. Then he, too, was gone, the wide black wings of his greatcoat curling back in his wake.

✳ ☽

# Chapter 4

The locals referred to Harwood House as the Gloomy Retreat. Built of gray stone, it stood isolated and forlorn against a bleak landscape, its ancient gables and lichen-covered walls exposed to fierce and unpredictable winds that blew off a nearby heath. A depleted stand of elm and yew marked the approach to what had once been the defensive outpost of a Norman baron; the round tower belonging to the original keep still marked the far end of the east wing. Only this ancient structure boasted a flat lead roof and crenellated stone teeth. Successive generations had added formal rooms and galleries and a second full wing of guest apartments, the whole surmounted by steeply pitched slate roofs.

These newer additions boasted long, mullioned windows, most of which had long ago lost the strength to do battle with the elements. The rooms were drafty and cold in the winter months, airless and musty in summer. The upper apartments suffered most from the strain of the heavy slate tiles exerting pressure on the rafters, and most of the ceilings leaked in anything more than a light fog. Dour and penurious, Lord Charles Finchworth Holstead, earl of Paxton, had inherited well on paper, but most of his estates were heavily mortgaged and his finances stretched too thin to justify squandering any coin on repairs or upkeep. At Harwood House, there were birds nesting in the eves and the windows rattled loose in their centuries-old cuspings and traceries.

Renée and her brother had taken bedrooms in the older wing, near the blocked stone walls of the old keep. Neither of them minded that the housekeeper, Mrs. Pigeon, and the rest of the meager staff of servants preferred to make their quarters in the sounder structure of the west wing. The isolation suited Renée, especially when the sky was as bleak as her mood and the possibility of sunshine seemed hopeless.

There was no one waiting up for her, no one standing attendance on the front door to greet her or take her cloak. She would have felt honored that someone had thought to leave a candle burning in the hall sconce if she had not known it was more for the benefit of the dragoon who normally slept through his watch in a comfortable chair in the foyer. That he was not in evidence now, either meant he was in the pantry sharing a bottle of red wine with the scullery maid, or that the wine was finished and he was sharing something else with the dull-witted chit.

The chore of tending to Renée's needs usually fell to Jenny, a slender, round-faced girl from the village who tried to do the best she could for her young mistress with the few resources at hand. But she would be long abed-by now. And while there were likely to be logs in the woodbox and kindling in the grate, there would be no fire blazing in her bedchamber to burn off the damp chill. Such an extravagance would be considered wasteful by Mrs. Pigeon, since there had been no one in the room all evening to enjoy either the heat or the light.

When Renée, Antoine, and Finn had arrived at Harwood House a fortnight ago, they had been presented with a lengthy list of what was permitted and what was generally discouraged. Great, glowering emphasis had been placed on the fact that whatever grand style to which she and her brother may have been accustomed while growing up in their gilded chateau in France, they were in England now; they were living off the grace and goodness of their uncle's charity and there would be neither waste nor willful excess, not so long as Ephemerty Pigeon's fist was clamped around the household keys.

A large, bellicose woman, Mrs. Pigeon had a face like one of the cement gargoyles that crouched over the battlements of the old tower, and footsteps heavy enough to rouse dust from the cracks between the floorboards. She had been in Lord Paxton's service for twenty-five years and was well acquainted with the ways of stretching a penny into a pound. She did not like Renée and made no secret about it. Any questions Renée asked were answered in snorts or grunts and any requests met with glaring belligerence. It was usually left to Finn, in his capacity as valet, coachman, servant, and guardian angel to find extra wood, extra candles, and even to charm an extra cup of chocolate out of the cook if it was required.

Just as there was no one waiting up for Renée, there would be no groomsmen waiting to unhitch the horses or stable them for the night. Finn would have to see to it himself—which he would, for he would no more consider leaving the tired animals in their traces until morning than he would admit to being too old and too weary to be carrying on so in the middle of the night.

Renée was more than tired herself. She was drained and depleted and had felt physically ill after leaving the inn. Those last few minutes with Roth had made her frighteningly aware of just how vulnerable a position she and Antoine were in. The story she had told the highwayman tonight was not a complete fraud. If anything, with a charge of attempted murder hanging over her brother's head, her position was worse than she had represented it. Roth had assigned four of his dragoons to remain in residence at all times, to watch and report every sneeze, every scratch, every walk or morning ride. They had no friends, no other family to whom they could appeal for help or refuge. Renée was afraid—no, terrified—to trust anyone other than Finn, and although she knew he would tear his heart from his chest if she asked him to, he *was* old, sixty, and not in the best of health despite his strident claims otherwise. He slept next to Antoine's room in adjoining valet's quarters, and there were nights she could hear him across the hall, coughing so hard, she expected to find his lungs on the floor the next morning.

Renée lit a second candle from the sconce and cupped her hand around the flame to guard it against the draft as she walked along the gallery toward the east wing. There were tall windows with many mullioned lights running the full length of the gallery, and as she moved past each pane she trod in the squares of moonlight that patterned the wood floor. The hem of her skirt and cloak whispered softly with each step, but otherwise she made no sound as she reached the end and turned to ascend the narrow, curved staircase that led to the upper floors. Because this was where the old keep was adjoined to the newer sections of the house, the stairs followed the rounded shape of the wall, and without windows, it was as black as sin. A thick and musty tapestry hung over the stones, concealing a small arched door that led into the tower of the keep. Antoine had discovered it one day quite by accident, and his curiosity had taken him as far as the first thick veil of cobwebs inside.

At his insistence, she had asked Jenny about it, but the serving girl had quickly crossed herself and spat over her left shoulder to ward off evil spirits. According to local lore, the ghost of the original owner still resided in the keep. He had been starved to death in the dungeons by a raiding party of Welsh barbarians and was known to roam the upper battlements, wailing and rattling his chains in hunger. It was another one of the reasons why the servants avoided the east wing and rarely ventured there after dark. And while Renée did not believe in ghosts, there were times, like now, when she felt an eerie sensation of fingers plucking at her hems that kept her moving smartly to the top of the landing.

Arriving at the second floor, she paused again, for there were no candles and the only window, large as it was, was near the middle of the hallway where a second corridor led back into the middle section of the house crossing above the gallery. Her bedchamber was on the right, and, after taking a moment to divest herself of her cloak and light the kindling in the fireplace, she moved quietly back across the hall to the room opposite hers and listened a moment before she eased her way inside.

The room was much like her own, square and utilitarian. The bed sat like a sacrificial altar on a raised dais, boasting four fat posts at the corners and a canopy overhead. Sturdy velvet draperies were swagged around each post and could be loosened to enclose the occupant in a warm cocoon at night. Heavy carpets covered most of the bare floorboards and tall, floor to ceiling curtains hung over the window. With the fire glowing robustly in the hearth and shadows reflecting off the writing table and chair, the blanket box at the foot of the bed, the two night tables with their pewter candelabra . . . it almost looked cozy.

Renée tiptoed to the side of the bed and experienced a momentary flutter of panic when she did not see the familiar pale splash of yellow hair on the pillow. She quickly dropped to her knees and lifted the bedskirt, and there he was, curled tightly in a ball, his arms hugging his shoulders, his eyes wide and staring out at her like a wounded creature trapped in the dark.

"Antoine," she whispered. "It is only me." She drew another breath to ease the tightness in her chest and added in as calm a voice as she could muster, "Come out of there now, my darling, before you catch your death of a cold."

With pitifully slow and halting movements, he unwound his arms and stretched his legs, using them to wriggle his way out from under the bed.

"*Mon Dieu,*" she scolded, "look at the dust. I vow the

floor under there has not been swept for a hundred years or more. Was I so late in coming home that you thought to frighten me and disguise yourself as a mole?"

He stood still as she batted away the cloudy wads of dust that clung to his nightshirt. He was trembling and his hands were cold as she took them into hers and raised them to her lips. "I did not plan to stay out so long, but look . . . it is barely midnight and I said I would be back by then. Into bed with you, goose, quickly before Finn comes up and sees what a fuss you have made."

*Did you see him?*

The words had no sounds, but after more than a year of silence, Renée had become proficient at reading his lips.

"Yes," she sighed. "I saw him."

His eyes brightened for a moment, but she pointed sternly to the bed. "If you get into bed and fall asleep right away, I promise to tell you all about it in the morning. *No*, not now," she added before his lips could form the words. "I am so tired my knees are weak."

Even so, Antoine raised his hand, folded his two fingers against the palm and raised his thumb like a cocked hammer. *Did he shoot at you? Were you very frightened? Was he mean and ugly and did he smell very bad?*

"No. He did not shoot at us. He was . . . quite civil, actually, far more so than Finn will be if you waken in the morning with a red nose and a rattling chest."

Antoine kissed her swiftly on the cheek to placate her, but he only took two small steps toward the bed before he was turning to look at her again, and the gleam was gone, leaving only the haunting darkness of his fears clouding his eyes.

*I was afraid you would not come back. I was afraid the soldiers would come and take me away where you would not be able to find me.*

Renée shook her head and opened her arms, and when he came into them, she hugged him so tightly she could feel his heart beating against her own.

"Never *ever* think I would leave you, *mon coeur*," she whispered. "Never believe *for one instant* that I would leave this place and not take you with me, or that I would not come back when I promised you I would."

She smoothed her hand across his brow, pushing back the silky strands of yellow hair. They shared their mother's fair coloring and startling blue eyes, although the structure of Antoine's face was all their father. The angular jaw, the high cheekbones, the strong nose, and wide, scholarly brow represented the last of a noble line that stretched back to the days of Charlemagne. Everyone else—uncles, aunts, cousins, nieces, and nephews—all had come to an abrupt and bloody end on a raised platform in the *Place de la Revolution*, and four months shy of his fourteenth birthday, Antoine was now the twelfth Duc d'Orlôns. His shoulders were still slender and his legs lanky, but the promise was there for breadth and power, and some day, if the madness in France subsided and the monarchy was restored, he would claim his place in the royal court with the authority and stature he deserved.

For the moment, he was a frightened boy who could not speak, who had witnessed more terror and suffering in his young life than men four and five times his age.

"Into bed with you now," she said, kissing his forehead, "or Finn will blame me for coming in here and waking you up just to get a hug."

The huge, solemn eyes regarded her unblinkingly for a long moment. Then as suddenly as it had disappeared a moment ago, his smile was back, wide and mischievous. He cocked both thumbs of both imaginary pistols and shot his way into bed, burrowing under the thick mound of quilts and blankets until only the top of his head showed above the bedding. Renée leaned over to ruffle the bright gold curls, and with a last stern warning issued through the pressure of a forefinger against his lips, she retraced her steps to the hall, then back across to her own room.

Once there, she closed the door and leaned heavily against it, her eyes shut, her throat burning with the need to scream. They had come to England thinking they would be safe here, thinking their uncle would offer them refuge from the horror in France, thinking they would be free of the tyranny, oppression, and fear that had governed their every waking and sleeping hour. But all they had encountered so far was more treachery. Their uncle was greedy and manipulative; he had wasted no time putting Renée on the auction block and selling her to the highest bidder. Her fiancé, Edgar Vincent, was a large brute of a man with ham-like hands and dirty leers, and though she suspected he thought it a form of flattery, he was usually visibly aroused when he stared at her for any length of time. He was also, purportedly, good friends with Roth, which made the colonel's behavior at the inn all the more repulsive. She had no reason to doubt Roth would have forced himself on her tonight had Finn not come to her rescue with the candlestick.

She groaned and pushed away from the door.

Roth would not let that pass. Finn would pay for his chivalry and Roth would delight in exacting his retribution. She felt like a fly caught in a spider's web, and if they did not find some way to tear free, the threads would tighten around them and they would be devoured inch by inch until there was nothing left but empty shells.

Lighting a second candle off the one she had left sputtering on the nightstand, Renée stripped off her shoes and stockings and left them where they fell as she walked into the adjoining dressing room. It was not very large. A hip tub sat in the corner nearest the door, where it could easily be dragged out and placed in front of the fire. A washstand, mirror, and cabinet commode accounted for the rest of the space on one side of the room, while the opposite wall was lined with shelves, barely a quarter of them filled with neatly folded garments. Her four pairs of shoes looked sadly overwhelmed on the long rack, as did her meager collection of gowns. If she were in Paris, and if there had been no revolution to destroy her life, her undergarments alone would have filled two rooms this size with floor to ceiling shelves and wall to wall compartments. She would have had four *hundred* pairs of shoes, in colors to match every gown, every mood, every change of weather.

Setting the candle on the washstand, she poured water into the stained porcelain bowl, and it was only when she was about to raise a dripping handful to her face that she dared meet her reflection for the first time. What she saw in the mottled glass of the mirror caused her to stare into her own eyes for a long, still moment before she could confront the angry red imprints left on her throat by Bertrand Roth's grasping fingers. Thankfully, the light had been too dim in Antoine's room for him to have noticed, but here, in the close circle of the candle flame, she could see where each individual finger had left an impression. And when she angled her chin upward, the spot where his thumb had gouged into her nerves was already an angry blue.

She let her gaze wander critically over her face. To her, it was just a nose like any other nose, a mouth that suffered from an overly generous lower lip, and eyes that seemed too large and dark and direct to ever master the art of subtle flirtation. Her lashes and brows were the color of tarnished gold, thick enough to give her eyes definition but not nearly as exotic as the lush, dark coloring of most Englishwomen.

Her mother had been an exceptionally beautiful woman, with silvery blonde hair and pale, soft skin. When the young and dashing Marquis de Mar had been introduced to Celia Holstead on a trip to London, it had been love from the very first moment they met. It did not matter that Celia's father had already chosen her future husband, or that her brother was outraged at the very notion of her wanting to marry a *Frenchman*. When every last avenue of appeal had failed, they had eloped, vowing to love each other all the more for the fact her father—a cold and brutish man at the best of times—had gone to his grave without ever speaking to her again, or that her brother refused thereafter to acknowledge her existence. They had each other and their love proved to be as strong two decades later as it had been the day they wed.

If she closed her eyes, Renée could still see her father's handsome smile, still hear the echo of his laughter and the way it always seemed to fill the rooms of their magnificent château outside Paris. She could even remember the scent of his skin, for although it was an outrageous notion that a man should still love his wife to distraction after so many years of marriage, Sebastien d'Anton always had about him a faint hint of her perfume, as if they had bathed together, dressed together, spent the night locked in each other's arms.

Renée stared at the blonde, curly hair that fell past her shoulders, remembering how her mother used to come to her room at night, glittering head to toe in silks and jewels. She would take the brush from the maid's hands and together she and Renée would count the strokes she made through the luxuriously heavy mass while they discussed their hopes and dreams for the future. They had laughed over the dozens of suitors, young and old, who had already expressed an interest in uniting their two powerful families; they had giggled over the anticipated bevy of young heirs who would strut before her like peacocks in all their finery. And because Celia d'Anton had married for love, not money, they also whispered about the one man who would eventually stand apart from all the others, the one who would take her in his arms and dance a single dance with her and sweep her heart away.

All of those fantasies ended the day the angry citizens

of Paris stormed the Bastille. The very next night the maid, who had been a part of the household for almost thirty years, spat in Celia d'Anton's face and declared herself free of the oppressive tyranny that had kept her a slave to the aristocracy all that time.

Within a year, Louis XVI had been forced to sign a newly drafted constitution granting every citizen of France *liberté*, *égalité*, and *fraternité*. Within two years all hereditary titles and estates were forfeited to the state, and many members of the aristocracy had begun making arrangements to remove themselves and their wealth to other countries. When the white flag of the Bourbon dynasty was trampled underfoot and replaced with the bloodied tricolor of the people's militia, the number of these émigrés grew. Four years after the revolutionaries had taken control of the government, when the king and queen were caught at the border trying to escape to Prussia, the trickle of fleeing aristocrats turned into a flood of terrified men and women who were thankful just to escape with their lives.

As the former Duc d'Orlôns, Renée's grandfather had been arrested along with his sons and a thousand others suspected of trying to help the king escape. Within a few short months, Louis XVI was found guilty of treason and executed on the guillotine, and the Committee of Public Safety had become the ruling voice of Terror throughout the new republic. The tyrant Maximilien de Robespierre had come into power and under the Jacobin leader's fanatical zeal, the freed citizens of France were encouraged to identify and condemn all aristocrats and monarchists suspected of plotting against the Republic of Virtue. If a man walked too fast or was seen talking too long with a neighbor, he could be accused of scheming against the glorious revolution. If he wore a hat with a brim that was too round, he was sure to be a monarchist; if he tied his cravat with too many folds, he exemplified the vanity of the privileged class. The wearing of powders or perfumes could be cited as treasonable acts, as could bathing too often or chewing fennel to clean the breath.

To no one's surprise, clothing with ruffles, lace, and trim vanished from the streets of Paris, as did wigs and panniers and petticoats of extravagant widths. White became the approved color for women's dresses while drab black coats and trousers became the standard for men. Hair was braided and confined beneath plain white caps or cropped short so as not to foster the sin of vanity.

The guillotines began to labor from dawn to dusk in their efforts to purify the new régime.

One morning Renée and her family awoke to see a pall of thick black smoke hanging over Paris and when Celia d'Anton asked a passerby what was burning, she was informed with a casual shrug that Citizen Robespierre had declared the prisons were too full. Two thousand *aristos* had lost their heads during the night and now, because the cemeteries were also too full, the tumbrils were lined up ten and twenty deep, piled high with their headless corpses waiting to be burned in a mass pit.

In a death-like panic, Celia had ordered Renée and Antoine to remain at home with the doors locked and barred. Finn had gone out earlier to see if he could trade a hoarded jewel for bread and eggs, and when he returned, neither Renée nor her brother would obey his orders to stay behind again. All three ran through the rain-drenched streets to the prison where their father had been taken almost a year before. Celia was at the guardhouse, begging one of the guards for information about her husband. He was the same guard she had bribed in the past so that she might be allowed to carry food and clothes to Sebastien d'Anton, but the *gendarme* only laughed this time and pointed to the column of ugly black smoke that scrolled over the city, telling her the former *duc* and his sons were no longer receiving visitors. They had been declared traitors to the republic and executed by order of the Committee.

Celia had collapsed on the rough cobblestones and Antoine had broken away from Finn to run out and help her. The guard was still laughing, calling to his comrades, nudging the dazed woman with the toe of his boot. The other guards had gathered around, kicking and spitting, taking long pulls out of the bottles of sour wine that gave them so much courage. Antoine had tried to reach his mother, but he was roughly shoved aside. He tried again but one of the men shattered a bottle over his head and when Celia saw him staggering back with blood streaking down his face, she screamed and lunged at the guard, her nails gouging at his eyes and throat.

A crowd had begun to gather, and now that they had an audience to impress, the guards took turns kicking her and beating her and inviting the onlookers to vent their anger on the filthy *aristo*. The cheering citizens picked up stones and threw them. Some carried pikes and clubs, and they joined the guards in beating the crumpled, bloodied form until it lay still and lifeless at their feet.

When there was no more sport to be had beating a dead woman, they remembered Antoine, but where they had left him there was only a guardsman writhing on the stones, his hands clutched around a knife protruding from his belly. Someone reported seeing a tall, skinny old man half dragging the boy down the street . . . and the chase was on.

The three could not return to their house on Rue Dupont and they dared not appeal for help from anyone who might be greedy to collect the reward that would soon be on their heads. Being English had kept Celia and her children safe up to then, but with her husband branded a traitor and a guard dead by Finn's hand, they would be taken directly to the guillotine if they were caught. Hoarding his own grief for a later time, the resourceful Finn stole a gun and some ragged clothing into which they could change, and, convincing a dung collector he was an expert shot, forced the terrified peasant to carry them out of the city in his stinking cart.

Much of what followed ran together in a blur of freezing nights and days when they were too exhausted and too hungry to do more than huddle together under a pile of hay, numbed by a sense of loss so deep and chilling Renée feared she would never know the pleasure of feeling warm again. When they reached the coast, it had been no simple matter to find someone willing to ferry them across the Channel or, once they were in London, to present Renée and Antoine—half-starved and lice-infested— to Charles Holstead, Lord Paxton, as the children of his estranged sister.

They had not expected him to welcome them with open arms and an open heart. It had been thirty years since he had seen his sister, and no less than thirty days since he had received a letter from the French government informing him the entire family of the *ci-devant* Duc d'Orlôns had perished. At first Renée had thought her uncle was just shocked to see them alive, but she soon came to understand that it was the shock of having to assume the burden of their welfare that had sent him staggering back, his hand clutched over his heart. With almost indecent haste he had proposed her marriage to Edgar Vincent, showing a callous indifference to the fact that she was still in mourning for her parents.

She had refused, initially, to even consider the marriage. For the first four and a half months they had lived in London, nothing, not the hostile isolation she endured in her uncle's town house, not the accusations of ingratitude, nor the endless lectures on obligation could have made her agree to marry Edgar Vincent of her own free will. This coming January she would be twenty-one and of legal age to make her own choice in the matter of marriage, but four weeks ago in London someone had shot her uncle. Antoine had been accused of the crime, and Renée had found herself with no choice but to agree to the marriage, agree to help Roth, agree to do anything necessary to prevent her brother from being arrested for attempted murder.

Renée opened her eyes. Her gaze fell unerringly to the small sandlewood box that contained the tiny vial of rose-scented oil she rationed out a drop at a time for her bathwater, the larger bottle of bluish laudanum she took to ease her monthly cramps, and the folded paper packets of powdered opiate that were sometimes required to ease the blinding pain of a migraine headache. The latter two, she had been warned by the physician in London, could be lethal if taken together in large doses. More than once she had been tempted to do just that, and if not for Antoine and Finn, she might well have succumbed to the idyll of a deep, dreamless sleep.

She stared into the mirror again. Her tears had left two shiny streaks on her cheeks, and she wet the small square of flannel that was folded over the rim of the washbowl, scrubbing her face until it glowed a resentful pink. She started to bathe the bruise marks on her throat when her gaze stalled again. There were more marks lower down where Roth's fingers had dug beneath the edge of her bodice, and, disgusted at the thought that there might still be some of his sweat or spittle on her flesh, she unfastened the wide ribbon beneath her breasts and shrugged the gown to the floor, chasing the slippery sheath of her silk petticoat after it.

Dressed only in her chemise, she soaped and scoured her flesh, untying the row of tiny bows in front so that she could wash her breasts and remove the lingering taint of his hands and mouth. There was one mark that would never come off, no matter how hard she rubbed, and in the end she cursed it for what it was: a harlot's brand. A wine-colored mole, perfectly heart shaped, it was seated above her left breast, high enough to be visible over the edge of all but the most modest of necklines. More than one pair of lecherous eyes had settled on it, bright and hard, assuming it was a cosmetic patch, glued there to invite attention.

She threw the cloth aside and reached for her dressing gown but it was not on the shelf beside her. With a sigh, she recalled seeing it draped neatly across the foot of the bed and guessed that Jenny had laid it out earlier.

The bedroom was dark and she paused a moment at the dressing room door, letting her eyes adjust to the gloom. The kindling she had set alight earlier had smoldered down to a listless pile of ash. The candle on the nightstand had succumbed to a draft and was sending a thin finger of smoke trailing through the stream of blue-white moonlight that poured through the window. One of the panes had swung open, and she cursed the lack of a sturdy latch that could keep the windows closed against more than a halfhearted breeze.

A shiver sent her in that direction first. Barefoot, her hair flowing over her shoulders, and her chemise gaping open halfway to her waist, she went to the window and closed the pane. She stood there a moment, her hand still pressed to the glass as she gazed out over the brightly moonlit landscape. A new and unbidden image filled her mind—that of a black-clad highwayman racing across the open fields, free to come and go where he pleased. The image swept her away and she closed her eyes, envisioning herself riding into the wind with him, her arms tight around his chest, her face pressed against his back, her hair fanning out like silvered waves of silk behind them.

She had ridden out on that dark stretch of road tonight not knowing what to expect. A thief was a thief; they had sly, shifting eyes and half-rotted teeth. They were brutish and coarse; they smelled of ale and sweat and debauchery, with the grime embedded so deeply into their flesh, it corrupted their souls. They were cowards and murderers who deserved to be put behind bars, and she had been able to ease her conscience somewhat by convincing herself this highwayman was no different. He was a thief and a criminal, and, as Roth had so brusquely pointed out, whether she helped capture him or not, his life was fated to end on a noose, hanging from Tyburn Tree.

Yet she had been startled almost beyond breath when she had seen the tall, mist clad highwayman emerge from the shadows behind the coach. Sly he may have been, and certainly cunning enough to have eluded his hunters for six years, but his demeanor was not that of a common drayman. His laugh had been deep and rich, and when he had extended his hand to seal their pact, his grip had been firm and strong, the gesture almost courtly in manner.

Renée tipped her head up and stared at the luminous circle of the moon.

She had thought—seriously thought—of attempting to steal the jewels herself, but Edgar Vincent was not the kind of man who let anyone who picked his pockets get away unscathed. He had given her the rubies in London when their engagement had been announced, and for the following fortnight had allowed her to wear them in his presence. But he always reclaimed them the instant they boarded the coach for home and whisked them away somewhere safe until the next occasion arose when he wanted to display his vulgar extravagance. When Roth had come to her with his proposition—to elicit her help in setting a trap for the elusive Captain Starlight—she had thought it pure fantasy to use the jewels as bait. Madness, even. But now she wondered.

Could a man who had outfoxed and outmaneuvered the king's men for all these years manage to slip through the teeth of a trap one more time? She was certain Roth would plan for every possible contingency, but . . .

What if the legendary Captain Starlight could actually steal the gems? The suite was worth over fifty thousand pounds, and with that much money she and Finn could take Antoine far away from Roth and his false warrants.

They could go to America. To New Orleans. Her father had been there just after the American revolution and . . .

Her breath fogged the glass pane and she placed her fingertips over the dampness. She was not staring at the moon anymore. Her gaze had been drawn to the reflected glare of candlelight that originated inside the dressing room. She had deliberately left the door ajar to let some of the light spill into the darkened bedroom, but over the course of the past few moments, the gap had grown narrower and narrower, the movement gradual enough for her to have credited it to an errant draft pushing the door slowly closed. Now, however, with only inches of light to go, she knew the door was being pushed by something far more ominous than a ghostly current of air. Something . . . someone was standing beside the door deliberately cutting off the light and plunging the room into darkness again.

The skin across her breasts tightened and a fine spray of gooseflesh rippled up her arms. She turned and searched the shadows, but they were too dark and her eyes too disbelieving to discern more than a vague shape against the wall.

It was not possible. She had imagined him only a moment ago galloping free across the open fields, yet there was no mistaking the configuration of the tricorn and the multi-collared greatcoat. And no mistaking the silver scrollwork on the brace of snaphaunce pistols that were leveled at her chest.

# Chapter 5

"*You!*" she gasped.

"Don't be frightened, mam'selle. I am not here to harm you."

It was hardly a reassuring statement with the two pistols glinting in the moonlight. She needed a moment to catch hold of her wits. "Then . . . may I ask why you are here?"

"I wanted to know a little more about you. It isn't every night I am stopped on the road and hired to commit a robbery."

"But . . . h—how did you find me? And"—she glanced at the window and could not remember any vines or latticework attached to the outside walls—"and how did you get in here?"

"I followed the coach," he said simply. "And there is a rather convenient drainpipe running down the wall beside your window. As to how I knew which room was yours, well . . . that was sheer guesswork on my part, but the sudden appearance of candlelight made for a good start."

Renée felt a strange sensation flowing down her body, as if there were rivulets of water sliding over her skin, and she glanced down, startled into realizing the skimpy state of her dress. She had not retied the bows on her chemise and where it gaped open in front, the valley between her breasts was visible, laid bare almost to the waist. Where the linen had been splashed with water, it clung to her skin, clearly revealing the shape of everything not already glowing white in the moonlight. The lower edge of the hem barely reached the tops of her thighs to safeguard her modesty, and below that, her legs gleamed pale and translucent against the shadows. As casually as she could, she pulled the halves of her chemise together.

"I was not expecting guests. May I at least put on my robe?"

"I was actually enjoying the view. But if it would make you feel more comfortable, by all means do so."

She had to pass through the shaft of moonlight to retrieve the garment, with every step under the vigilant eye of the highwayman, and to her credit, she was able to accomplish it without tripping over her feet. Roth had certainly not planned for this contingency. Who, indeed, would have expected such audacity?

When the robe was belted snugly about her waist, she turned and stared into the barrels of the guns again.

"Are they absolutely necessary, m'sieur? As you must have clearly seen, I have no weapons."

There was another pause, followed by a soft, husky laugh as he tucked the snaphaunces beneath his coat. "I would not be too sure of that, mam'selle."

His laughter caused another flush of warm sensations to ripple through her body, and she pointed at the nightstand. "May I light the candle again?"

"No. I like it fine the way it is."

"That you should know me, but I not know you?"

"An unfortunate necessity in my profession."

For the second time that night, she found herself asking, "You do not trust me?"

"No." After a pause he added, "Is there any reason why I should?"

"I have hired you to commit a crime," she said slowly. "Does that not make me an—an *auxiliaire*?"

"An accomplice? Only if you stand up in court and confess that you hired me. Otherwise it is your word against mine—if I am caught—and my word, I'm afraid, does not carry much weight with the local magistrates these days."

The wash of warm prickles she experienced this time went all the way to her knees, leaving them perilously unsteady. "Do you have any objections if I sit down?"

"As it happens, I was going to invite you to do just that."

The only available seat, aside from the bed, put her directly in the beam of moonlight and she recognized the disadvantage at once. If she thought about it, of course, there was not much about this unplanned meeting that was not appallingly to her *dis*advantage. She was alone in her bedroom, in her bedclothes, with an armed and dangerous man who thrived on flaunting convention. Rape, she imagined, would likely not strain the dictums of his conscience, nor would the use of violence to get what he wanted.

With the skirt of her wrapper belling softly behind her, she went back to the window and took a seat, noting that he moved as well, guarding against the possibility of any reflected light betraying his features.

"And so, m'sieur, have you thought about our arrangement and reconsidered?"

"Have you?"

"No," she said calmly. "I have not changed my mind. If anything, I am even more determined to see this thing done and leave this England of yours far behind."

"You dislike our country, mam'selle?"

"I have found nothing here to commend it, m'sieur. The weather is foul, the people stare and whisper and act as if I am here to steal the food off their plates."

"You do not seem to be lacking too much in the way of creature comforts. Harwood House is not exactly a stew."

"*Qu' est-ce que c'est* . . . stew?" she asked with a frown.

"A brothel. A place where strumpets sell their wares to the highest bidder."

There was a serrated edge of sarcasm to his voice, and it sent yet another rush of nervous flutters through her body. That he knew the name of the manor came as no surprise; Roth had said the highwayman was familiar with the parish. It stood to reason, then, if he knew the name of the house, he most assuredly knew who owned it.

She ran the tip of her tongue across her lips to moisten them.

"Perhaps to you it looks respectable, but the rooms, the furniture, the bedding always smell of mould and mustiness. There are beetles in the kitchen and mice in the walls; the windows are cracked and the wind howls through at night bringing in the rain and dampness. My toes, my fingers have not been warm since leaving Calais."

She realized too late it was a shockingly guileless invitation for him to inspect the slender and very bare feet that peeked out from beneath the hem of her wrapper. She held her breath a moment, wondering as she did, if Finn had returned from the stables yet and if so, would he hear the low murmur of their voices as he passed by her door? With her visitor's next words, however, she forgot her feet, forgot Finn, forgot everything but the two cocked pistols that were no less a threat for not being visible.

"Perhaps you have been looking in the wrong places for heat and succour. The Fox and Hound, for instance, is hardly where one might expect to find such creature comforts . . . unless of course, you stopped there seeking a more immediate form of heated gratification."

Renée stared at the shadow within the shadow and felt the blood drain to her feet out of sheer foolishness this time. If he had followed her home, it was only logical to assume he had seen her stop at the inn. And if he was but a fraction as clever and resourceful a thief as he was reputed to be, he would undoubtedly have discovered why she had stopped and who she had met.

Though she willed herself not to react outwardly, inwardly she was one thudding heartbeat after another. She wanted desperately to bolt for the door, but she knew she would never make it. Similarly, she wanted to look anywhere but at the looming shadow in the corner, but she could not seem to tear her eyes away from him. She dared not. He was waiting for her response and if she gave him the wrong one she was quite certain his reaction would be swift and violent. The warning he had given her on the hillside came back to her in a rush, and she knew it to be true: He would not hesitate to wring her neck if he thought she was lying to him.

"You seem to have gone to a good deal of trouble, m'sieur, just to refuse me my request."

"Only fair, since you seem to have gone through a good deal of trouble to make it. And like you, I prefer to communicate any information I have—good or bad—face to face."

It was an odd time to do so, with her heart pounding and ice flowing through her veins, but she thought of the jungle cat again. Sleek, black, and deadly, it had prowled constantly from one end of his cage to the other just hoping for some sign of weakness in the bars, some flamboyant indiscretion on the part of the onlookers that would bring one within range of the razor sharp claws.

"You are referring, of course, to my meeting with Colonel Roth," she said quietly. "No doubt you are curious to know what we discussed."

The silence stretched past half a minute, then a minute. She was suffocatingly aware of his intense scrutiny, and somewhere in the pit of her stomach, butterflies were starting to beat their wings and fly in panicked circles.

"Do go on, mam'selle," Tyrone invited quietly. "You have my full attention."

She bit her lip nervously before she complied. "We discussed you, of course. He is quite obsessed with the idea of capturing you. In fact it—it was his idea that I meet with you tonight. Everything," she admitted, "the robbery, everything was his idea in the beginning. He ordered me to ride out tonight, as he had on the three previous nights, with instructions for me to make contact, to appeal to your mercenary nature, or, if need be, your—your 'cavalier sense of self-indulgence'—those were his exact words—whichever I thought would be more likely to succeed in winning you over to my cause."

Renée saw the seemingly casual movement as he folded his arms across his chest and propped a shoulder against the wall. "Dare I ask which one you felt was more *apropos*?"

"To be perfectly honest, m'sieur: neither. Almost everything I told you was the truth."

"Almost?"

What she said next, the sound of the words themselves coming out of her mouth, was as strange and startling to her as if she were sitting at a distance, hearing someone else speak. The idea, the outrageous notion, had been there all along, lurking at the back of her mind, but to actually *say* the words, and to say them with such astonishing confidence . . .

"What I did not tell you, m'sieur, was that although the colonel may think he is being clever and cunning using me this way, it is I who hope to be able to turn this trap he wishes to set for *you* . . . against *him*."

Again he said nothing through a long, throbbing pause, and somewhere out in the darkness a dog began to bay at the moon. It was a hollow and mournful howl laden with scorn for all of man's more foolish machinations, prime among them being the thought that Renée d'Anton could place her fate, and very likely her life, in the hands of a thief, a murderer, a phantom of the mist.

\*

Tyrone Hart was not a man given to overt displays of emotion. He prided himself, for that matter, on his ability to show absolutely no reaction whatsoever, be it rage, contempt, hatred . . . or surprise. In this instance, however, he was grateful for the darkness, for he was certain his eyes had widened and his jaw had gone slack and his face had warmed a shade or two beyond ruddy.

He had come to confront her about her meeting with Roth at the inn, but he had not expected her to admit it so casually, nor to neatly turn the tables by suggesting it was her intention all along to double-cross the colonel.

If Dudley had been standing there to give him advice, Tyrone suspected it would be to climb out the window and ride away without looking back, and frankly, he could think of no logical reason not to do exactly that. It had not required a smack in the head with an iron pan to figure out the French minx had been part of some elaborate trap from the outset—for the two thousand pound reward if nothing else. Equally obvious to him was the likelihood that the jewels did not exist and that the coach she wanted him to stop would be carrying a swarm of eager Coventry Volunteers with their muskets primed and loaded.

Just because the invitation had come wrapped in satin and moonlight did not mean the devil had not sent it.

Devil indeed. He had not known what he had expected to discover hiding beneath the cloak and shadows, but a tangled waterfall of silvery curls had not been of the first order. Nor would he have foreseen legs as long as sin, skin as pale as moonlight, and everything displayed before him in a shape-molding wisp of silken nothingness that had had a distinct effect on the way his blood had altered its course through his veins. Even now it was difficult to keep his thoughts focused above her chin, and harder still not to acknowledge the heat that was building in places that should have been able to show better restraint under the circumstances.

"I must confess, mam'selle," he murmured finally, "you have left me somewhat bereft of words."

"It is quite simple, *Capitaine*. I still wish to hire you—for the amount agreed upon—to steal the rubies."

Tyrone gave in to the temptation and contemplated the shimmer of cloth where it molded around her breasts. Five of his six senses were warning him against listening to anything more she had to say. It was the sixth, located somewhere in the region of his groin, that imprudently encouraged him to let her go on.

"I am still listening, mam'selle."

Very deliberately Renée unclasped her hands and positioned them on the arms of the chair. It was madness, pure and simple, and if Finn were here, he would tell her so to her face, sparing nothing in the way of deference to her gender or social rank. He would point out, quite emphatically and quite rightly so, the sheer insanity of trusting a rogue and freebooter. Nor would he hesitate to mention the thousand and one things that could go wrong, the very least of which would be Roth discovering her duplicity.

*But what if this rogue and freebooter could do it?*

He was obviously not afraid to take risks, not afraid of the night or the shadows. He was cunning and clever and handsome—yes, he was handsome behind all that darkness, she had determined it must be so. He was also bold and daring and probably as eager to humiliate Roth as Roth was to see him caged and humbled.

*What if he could really do it?*

"Colonel Roth has great respect for your skill as an adversary, m'sieur, and it would appear to be well deserved. This was something I did not realize until tonight. In truth, I thought you were nothing more than a common, petty thief who had merely been lucky in managing to elude capture thus far."

"Is that an attempt to flatter me, mam'selle?"

"Flatter you? No, m'sieur. I only wish you to know that I agreed to do this thing in the first place because I believed you *were* petty and common, and that you would be caught eventually, if not with my help then surely someone else's. Two thousand pounds is a great deal of money to someone who does not have two *livres* to spare."

"It still is."

"Yes," she conceded, "and I would not blame you if you walked away and never looked back."

"The urge, I will admit, is quite strong. I would have to have a damned good reason to ignore it. And an even better one to believe or trust anything you say from here on out."

He was right. Of course he was right. Renée could scarcely believe what she was saying herself, let alone that she should be convincing enough for him to believe her. And yet, if there was the smallest chance it could succeed, it would be worth the risk, would it not? She was so tired of being afraid, so tired of being pushed and pulled and bullied and threatened. She was tired of seeing the haunted look on Antoine's face, tired of finding him cringing beneath the bed or huddled in a corner waiting for the next person to betray him. Tired of feeling like crawling into a dark space herself.

"I agree completely, m'sieur," she said quietly. "We must be able to trust each other before we can go any further."

Without taking her eyes off him, she rose and took several tentative steps toward the shadows where he stood. When she was as close to him as she dared go, she reached up and very deliberately gathered her hair in two glossy fistfuls, pushing it into a haphazard mass on the crown of her head.

Shutting her eyes, she tilted her chin up and exposed the slender arch of her neck. "You did warn me, did you not m'sieur, what you would do if I lied to you again?"

Tyrone's throat swelled shut. She was a glowing, gossamer figure bathed in the shimmering moonlight, and she was close enough to touch. With her arms raised, the sheer fabric of her robe molded snugly to the underside of her breasts, drawing his attention to just how lush and full and infinitely touchable they were. With her fair coloring, he knew her nipples would be as pink as a blush, the skin supple and smooth and warm. Even more tantalizing— and when he saw it, it was all he could do not to come out of his own skin—was the tiny heart-shaped mole that rode one soft white swell, rising and falling with each shallow breath, teasing him with dangerous thoughts of other luscious secrets that might be hidden in the pearly shadows.

If the devil had indeed sent her, he was a canny old bastard, Tyrone thought, for he had not been tempted with such a succulent offering in a long time.

He was quiet and still for so long, Renée risked a peek through her lashes. Seated with her back to the light, her eyes had gradually adjusted to the darkness, and whether it was because of this or because her robe was reflecting some of the light, creating its own glow to penetrate the shadows, she could see vaguely defined contours of his face. The topmost collar of his greatcoat was no longer raised like a shield to hide his features, and his jaw appeared to be square and clean-shaven. His eyes were wide and deep-set beneath an unbroken slash of dark eyebrows, his nose straight and firm, and although it was impossible to prove by these few blurred impressions, he *was* handsome. Shockingly, dangerously handsome.

Something stirred against Renée's sleeve and the butterflies in her belly took a sharp swoop en masse downward. His hand had plucked a few hanging strands of her hair, and he was watching the sparklets of moonlight dance off the gleaming threads as he fed them through his fingers. At some point he had removed his gloves, and she could see his hands were masculine and well formed, with long tapered fingers. One of them, she suspected, could crush more flesh and bone than two of Roth's, with half the effort.

Once, twice he wound the curl around the palm of his hand, drawing so close she could smell the lingering scent of leather and horseflesh that clung to his greatcoat. When the slack and the distance between them was taken up, he paused. His long fingers stretched out to touch the bruise at the juncture of her jaw and neck, and, almost as an afterthought, he traced a featherlight line from her ear down to her collarbone. There, he followed along the collar of her robe, pausing to edge it aside so that his thumb might caress the dark blush of the mole and verify it was real.

His hand radiated heat like the intense warmth from a candle flame held too close, and she was aware of her flesh responding. There were tremors racing through her belly and the skin across her breasts had tightened with each careless stroke. Her nipples had risen taut and erect beneath the satin, their impertinence as obvious as the quivering folds of her robe where the satin shivered and shimmered around her legs. She had struck a brazen pose, hoping to assure him of her sincerity, but instead she was melting in waves, trembling like a loosely set syllabub inside and out, and if he did not say or do something soon to ease the tension, her knees were likely to buckle beneath her.

"I do not recall seeing any other lights on this floor," he murmured. "You have no maid?"

She had to swallow before she could answer, and even then the words came out dry and thready. "Finn has a room across the hall. The—the housekeeper and the rest of the servants are all in the west wing."

"*All* of them?"

She stared at his hand. No more than the width of a drawn breath was separating it from her breast. The palm and fingers had already assumed a curved shape, as if he meant to cradle her flesh to test the firmness and weight, but at the last possible instant before contact, he lifted it away, and his thumb retraced the route from her breastbone to her collar, up to where the fine blue veins below her ear betrayed the erratic flutter of her pulse.

"There is no one else?" he asked again.

The thought came on a rush of hot and cold sensations: Did he know about Antoine? Was this a test of her commitment to the truth?

Before she could debate the wisdom of answering one way or the other, he was leaning closer, his breath warming her ear. "This Mr. Finn of yours . . . is he a sound sleeper?"

It was then, between one heartbeat and the next, before the last breath and the one not yet taken that she remembered something else she had told him—something she had declared so offhandedly he might think it meant nothing to her. She had told him she was no longer a virgin, and that no price was too steep to pay in order to win her freedom.

His fingers caressed her neck and she raised her lashes, shocked to see his face was only an inch or two from hers. She could see the shape of his eyes, quite clearly; they were large and thickly lashed and glittered with pinpoints of light.

"He hears me when I cry out, m'sieur."

"When you cry out?"

"I . . . often have nightmares," she whispered. "I dream I am back in the streets of Paris, in the *Place de la Revolution* where they took my father to be executed. I see the guillotine, standing so tall and thin against the sky, and I see the blood that drips from the blade and runs in rivers from under the stock to stain the feet of the citizens who have gathered to watch and cheer."

She saw no reason to confide any more of the horror that waited for her in the dark, and he held her gaze for what seemed like half an eternity before he straightened and started untangling the captive curl from around his hand. He seemed reluctant to let it go, but even as the last glossy strands slithered out of his fingers, he had retreated several steps into the shadows again, turning his face from the light.

"Exactly how much do you estimate these rubies are worth?"

The question, coming while her body was still taut and vibrating, produced answers that did not have the benefit of thought or subtlety. "Fifty thousand pounds, perhaps more."

"Fifty thousand?" He whistled softly under his breath. "For a few pieces of jewelry?"

She sensed more than just doubt in his voice now and she let her hair drop back around her shoulders.

"They are not just any jewels, m'sieur. They are known as the Dragon's Blood rubies."

"For fifty thousand pounds, they should be Christ's blood."

She ignored the blasphemy and pushed aside a lock of hair that had fallen over her cheek. "They belonged to a very old and very noble family of France, one whose bloodlines were founded on the courage of those who conquered this damp and miserable island of yours. Like so many others who began to fear they could lose everything to the revolution, the Duc de Blois made arrangements to transfer much of his family's wealth out of harm's way. The Dragon's Blood rubies, along with other irreplaceable heirlooms, were smuggled out of France and were to be kept safe in a bank vault until the *duc* or his heirs could escape and claim them."

"I gather the *duc* did not escape?"

"He was betrayed to the Committee and executed for treason, as were his wife, his sons, his grandchildren, even a baby who could have been no more than a month old at the time. Robespierre," she added tautly, "was very thorough."

"How did the rubies come to be in your fiancé's possession?"

"He was the one who arranged to take the jewels, the

hoards of gold and silver—not just from the Duc de Blois, but from several others—and promised he would safeguard their wealth until they could escape with their families. Indeed, he safeguarded it in the vaults of his own bank until he received word they were imprisoned and executed, then it was a simple matter to claim the treasures as his own."

"How enterprising of him," Tyrone mused.

"Enterprising," she agreed, "if it does not trouble your conscience that your profits are stained with blood."

Wary of her growing agitation, Tyrone raised his hands in a gesture meant to placate. "I am hardly in the position to offer any defense on your fiancé's behalf, but—"

"There is no defense," she snapped. "These men and women trusted him to secure their future, to protect their family's heritage. They paid him enormous sums to smuggle their wealth out of France before Robespierre and his greedy minions confiscated it in the name of *liberté*, *égalité*, and *fraternité*, and then he turned around and stole it out of their graves."

"And now you plan to steal it from him?"

"If I can, yes."

"And the, ah, moral ambiguity does not trouble you at all?"

"*Que est-ce que c'est dit . . . ?*"

"Ambiguity? In this instance it means condemning someone for doing something you are about to do yourself. But never mind, you don't have to answer that. I am more curious about something you said earlier tonight, that you can sell the rubies without suffering any loss of value?"

"There are people in London loyal to France, to the monarchy, who would willingly pay to see the rubies safely back where they belong and to insure they do not fall into the hands of someone like Edgar Vincent again."

"Edgar Vincent? What the devil does he have to do with this?"

She gave a brusque, disparaging sigh. "He is my fiancé. He is the man I am to marry on the fourteenth."

Safe in his shadows, Tyrone could not resist a wide grin. "The hell you say!"

"Does this make a difference, m'sieur? Do you know him?"

"We have crossed paths before—and swords. And no, it did not matter when I robbed him five months ago; it should not matter now."

"You have robbed him before?"

Another low, throaty laugh came out of the darkness. "Indeed I have. And if memory serves, among the generous contributions donated by him and his female companion, there was a particularly fine trinket. A brooch"—his words slowed thoughtfully as he made the mental connection—"made of rubies and diamonds . . . and a pearl the size of a small fist."

"Please tell me," she said on an indrawn breath. "Were the rubies coiled around the pearl like a serpent? A serpent with a golden body and diamonds for eyes?"

"It was an unusually exquisite piece," he agreed. "So much so the, ah, gentleman with whom I have a long-standing association refused point blank to deal with it. As I recall, he muttered something about my bringing constabulary hellfire down around his shoulders should he even attempt to sell it through his normal contacts."

Renée was almost afraid to ask. "Does that mean you still have it?"

"If I do?"

"If you do . . . it would increase the value of the suite immeasurably."

"This would not be another blatant appeal to my crude instinct for profit, would it?"

"I doubt the instinct is a crude one, m'sieur. Practical, perhaps, yes? And to that I would gladly pay whatever price you ask for the brooch."

"Any price? A dangerous offer, mam'selle. An unscrupulous rogue might be tempted to take advantage."

She stared into the vicinity of his eyes and said softly, "I do not think you are as unscrupulous as you would wish me to believe."

"Why? Because you still have your clothes on? Or because I have not tried to kiss you yet?"

The bluntness of the question startled her, but he did not allow her time to recover. In two swift strides he loomed before her again, his one hand raking deep into the silvery cloud of her hair to tilt her mouth up to his, his other slipping around her waist and drawing her hard against his body. The embrace was like the man himself, forthright and audacious, with no time wasted on flattery or finesse. He ignored the startled cry of protest that sounded in her throat, and with quick, efficient thrusts, won his way past the barrier of her lips and sent his tongue plunging hotly into her mouth, swirling to the deepest recesses, laying waste to any and all perceptions she may have had as to what a kiss entailed. It was more an invasion than a caress, and when it ended, when he withdrew the heat and the bold, lashing wetness, she continued to gape up at him, her mouth open, her lips feeling blushed and bruised, and, to her profound disbelief, craving more.

"You would do well to heed a small piece of advice, mam'selle," he said in a silky murmur. "I am neither a saint nor a savior, and any youthful inclinations I may have had toward monkhood are well and far behind me. Do not tempt me with more than you are prepared to give. Or lose."

He released her as suddenly as he had taken her captive. "How was Roth planning to spring his trap?"

The rapid change in subject and in his demeanor left her stammering. "I—I do not know the d—details, m'sieur, he did not tell me. This is the truth, I swear it.

But," she added on a faintly guilty note, "he knows I am to meet you again in three days' time."

He considered this a moment before asking. "You do realize what will happen to you if Roth finds out you are planning to double-cross him?"

"I am aware of the colonel's temper."

"His temper? Mam'selle, you have not yet seen his temper. You have seen his greed and deviousness, perhaps, but you have not had but a sampling of his predilection for cruelty and violence. If I were you, I would endeavor to avoid being caught alone with him again. You were lucky tonight, for he has a rather unsavory reputation where women are concerned . . . both the willing and the unwilling kind."

Renée's lips were still wet and tingling from his assault as she twisted them into a wry smile. "More so than yours, m'sieur?"

"I have never forced a woman to do anything she did not want to do," he countered smoothly. "I may have had to rise to a challenge a time or two, but I have never forced my attentions where they were not wanted. And certainly not in any manner"—his fingers brushed gently over the angry red marks that striated her throat—"that might bruise something so . . . delicate."

Renée's eyes widened. "You were there? You saw what he did?"

"Let's just say your Mr. Finn's filibuster with the candlestick came half a moment before my own. And I would not have stopped at merely knocking the bastard out cold."

Renée thought back, but her memory of the darkened hallway was vague at best, blurred by pain and fear. If he had been concealed in the shadows, watching, she had not seen him, although the greater irony might be that Roth had been standing less than a few feet from his quarry and not known it.

"If you saw what happened, m'sieur, then you must know I am not his willing associate."

"By the same token, I'm certain you can appreciate that I will still have to give your request some thought. Roth is a clever bastard. Stupid in some ways, but"—his gaze rested briefly on her lips—"very clever in others. We will meet again, as planned, in three days' time, and I will give you my decision then."

"But Roth knows where we are to meet. Will he not send his soldiers there to try to catch you?"

"I would be extremely surprised if he did not."

He dismissed the concern so casually, she was dumb-founded for the moment or two it took her to realize he had returned to the window. "You are leaving?"

He swung open the pane and glanced over his shoulder. She had spun around and was standing in the full beam of moonlight, her face and body awash in its luminescence.

"Mam'selle," he warned her quietly, "if I were to stay any longer, it would not be for the purpose of talking."

She swayed slightly at the flagrant implication behind his words and clasped her hands tightly together at her waist. "What if something happens before the three days are out and I must get in touch with you?"

He slung one leg over the sill and perched there a moment while he drew on his gloves.

"If you need me," he said slowly, "for any reason . . . go to the post in Coventry. Speak to the clerk who writes letters for people who cannot write themselves. Have him put up a notice on the public board addressed to Jeffrey Bartholemew, advising him to collect his carriage wheels at once or they will be sold to recompense his debt."

"Jeffrey . . . is that your name?"

"No."

"May I *know* your name, m'sieur?" she asked in a whisper.

"May I know yours?"

She hesitated only fractionally. He knew the house, he knew who owned it; it would only take a question or two to discover the identity of the *Française* in residence.

"It is d'Anton. Renée d'Anton."

"Then I bid you keep well, Renée d'Anton, until we meet again."

He gave a small salute and with a swirl of dark wool, he was over the ledge and gone. She hurried to the window and looked out over the sill, but managed only to catch a fleeting glimpse of the bat-winged shape after he reached the ground and vanished into the darkness below.

She continued to search the shadows, trying to track his movements, but her efforts were in vain. There was nothing to see but the patterned dappling of moonlight where it sliced through the gently swaying boughs of the trees.

The press of cool, damp air on the flimsy satin of her robe spurred her into shutting and latching the window behind him, but she leaned against it for several more minutes waiting for her heartbeat to slow, for her pulse to stop racing, for the warm and insistent throbbing in her lips to fade.

## Chapter 6

Robert Dudley was waiting with the horses and muttering under his breath when Tyrone appeared suddenly at his side.

"High bloody time," he protested, relinquishing Ares' reins to Hart's outstretched hand. "I wasn't sure whether I should storm the bastions or simply give you up as lost."

"We had an interesting chat. It went on a good deal longer than I expected, is all."

"A chat? As in . . . conversation? Social discourse? An exchange of pleasantries? Or did you actually find out what you wanted to know?"

Tyrone glanced up through the trees to the barely visible outline of Harwood's steep roofs and slanted gables. "I found out . . . she is an exceptionally fetching creature without her clothes on."

Dudley's eyes narrowed. "You couldn't possibly have had time to—"

"Haul your mind out of the gutter, Robbie. I only meant she had dispensed with the heavy cloak and hood. Mind you," he cast a crooked grin over his shoulder as he steered Ares back through the woods toward the open road, "another five minutes or so and I might have been able to impress you with my prowess."

"You impress me every day," Dudley said dryly, following close behind. "Dare I ask what you talked about?"

"Her upcoming marriage to Edgar Vincent, among other things."

Dudley, who had been concentrating on the ground to steer his horse around a knot of roots, looked up so suddenly, the branch skimmed the top of his head and would have carried off his hat if he had not reached up in time to grab it. His horse, startled by the sudden struggle for balance, danced forward several steps before being reined to an abrupt halt.

"Did you say Edgar Vincent?"

"I did. Apparently he is the lucky groom our lovely little French minx plans to leave standing at the altar with nothing but his hat in his hand."

Dudley muttered, "Christ," then swiveled around in his saddle and said, "*Christ*!" again as if it was just occurring to him who owned the Gloomy Retreat.

"Exactly," Tyrone murmured. "She claims to be Lord Paxton's niece; she is engaged to Edgar Vincent; and she is apparently helping Colonel Bertrand Roth set a trap for us. Do you still wonder what kept me from sliding down the drainpipe sooner?"

Dudley turned slowly back around, the leather in his saddle creaking as his weight settled again. "Naturally, she denied seeing the good colonel at the inn?"

Hart shook his head. "As a matter of fact, she admitted the meeting outright. She also told me he had set the whole thing up, that he had sent her out on three previous evenings in the hope of luring us out of hiding."

"And . . . ?"

"And . . . she seems to think it is a fine plan and still wants me to steal the rubies out from under Roth's nose."

"She thinks . . . *what*?" Dudley strained forward, as if his ears had played him false. "She wants to double-cross Roth?"

"It would appear so."

"Surely you don't believe her?"

Hart frowned. He believed the ugly bruises Roth had left on her throat and he believed the loathing and fear he had seen in her eyes at the inn. Lord Paxton's part in all this, Tyrone could readily understand, for the earl was a gambler, heavily in debt, and if he had indeed betrothed her to Edgar Vincent, he had either done so for a price or to settle an outstanding wager. Vincent, on the other hand, was a fishmonger, a commoner who had started out selling carp pies out of a London gutter. How he had become one of the wealthiest merchants in London was a mystery to some, but to those in the trade, his was a familiar name in the black market. Dealing with the disposable wealth of dead French aristocrats sounded loathsome enough and profitable enough for Vincent to have his hand well in it.

All the money in the world could not buy a gutter rat what he wanted most, however, and that was respectability. Marriage to Paxton's niece would give Vincent that, especially if there were some further considerations due upon the earl's death. Paxton's only son had died of a childhood fever and should a marriage between Vincent and Renée d'Anton produce a male heir, the boy would likely inherit the titles and estates.

As for Roth, the man was arrogant and ambitious, determined to make a name for himself. He would use any means at hand to further his purpose . . . women, children, dogs if they could be trained to betray their masters. If he had some kind of hold over Renée d' Anton, something devastating enough to make her a participant in his scheming, Tyrone would have to find out what it was before he even considered meeting her again.

"You have that look on your face again," Dudley remarked warily. "The one where we usually wind up neck deep in shit, skinning our arses on the steps of the Old Bailey."

"Your skin is safe. I haven't agreed to anything yet."

"You haven't told her to fall on her own sword yet either, have you?"

"I will admit," Hart nodded thoughtfully, "to being curious enough to see where this might lead."

Robert Dudley sighed. "There, you see? I can feel the noose slipping around my neck already."

"For fifty thousand pounds, suffer the discomfort a little longer."

"Fifty thousand?" Dudley whistled softly under his breath. "And our cut?"

"The full fifty thousand, naturally." Tyrone nudged Ares forward again. "Kindly show a *little* faith in me, old friend. Have I ever let a woman interfere with business before?"

"No, but there is always a first time. And in your case, the first time could be fatal."

"Believe me, I am as fond of my neck as you are of yours and I won't be agreeing to anything unless I am convinced the profits are worth the risk."

Dudley snorted. "Aye, now if we could only agree on our definitions of the word 'risk.'"

Tyrone only laughed. "Risk, my good man, is what keeps the blood flowing hot and fast through the veins."

His companion did not sound convinced. "How did you leave it with her?"

"I told her I had to think about her proposition. That we would meet in three days, as planned, and I would give her my decision then."

"Three days . . . it isn't a lot of time."

"She also told Roth about the meeting, so we can expect him to be there as well."

"Of course," Dudley said wryly. "Why would I even doubt it?"

"If I altered the arrangements in any way, and if Roth is watching her, then he would know something is amiss. That fine pointed nose of his would start twitching like a bloodhound in heat and we might lose the advantage."

"We have an advantage?"

Tyrone leaned over and slapped Dudley on the arm. "We have you. In three days' time, you could find out why the king's piss is blue and if the queen's lover dresses to the right or the left. In this case, all you have to do is find out everything you can about the girl, what hold Roth has over her, and how we can turn it around to use it against them."

Dudley glared. "Is that all?"

"Since you asked: you might want to post a discreet question or two about the rubies. She called them the Dragon's Blood suite and implied there were exiles from Louis' court who would pay an exorbitant amount to keep them from falling into the hands of a London fishmonger. That should keep you busy for a day or two anyway. Meanwhile"—Hart settled back and looked thoughtfully out over the darkness—"a visit to Doris Riley might be in order. If anyone knows anything about Edgar Vincent's upcoming nuptials, it would be the madam of his favorite whorehouse."

"You to a brothel and me to the town gossips? It hardly seems a fair apportioning of tasks."

Tyrone laughed. "Fine. You call on Doris and I will ride back to Priory Lane and explain to the very pregnant lass waiting in your bed for you that you are in Berkswell gathering information."

"Aye." Dudley crammed his hat back on his head. "I see your point."

"The point Robbie, is not to let a woman get so far under your skin that you feel guilty looking at another pair of ankles."

"My fondest wish is to be able to quote those words to you one day."

"It will never happen. My skin is far too thick and I enjoy the view too much."

\*

As soon as they were clear of the trees, Tyrone gave Ares his head and they streaked away across the open fields like a bolt of dark lightning. In less time than it took for either of them to become winded, low clusters of outlying cottages came into view, marking the approach to the village of Berkswell. Hart veered east, careful to keep a line of trees and hedgerows between himself and the winding ribbon of road, circling well around the town itself until he reached the westerly limits and came upon a tall, stately home set back a ways and surrounded by a low stone wall.

To a casual visitor, it looked like any one of a dozen elegant homes situated along the riverbank. To the local residents—the men in particular—it was one of the most exclusive brothels between Coventry and Birmingham.

It was not an unusual sight to see men coming and going from the house at all hours and Tyrone was cautious enough to keep to the trees. Doris had four girls working for her at the moment—Laura, Cathy, and two Judys—and Tyrone was no stranger to any of them. They were beautiful and energetic and only too happy to provide him with an evening's diversion when it was warranted.

At twenty-nine years of age Doris was the matriarch, the Queen as her girls called her. She entertained who she wanted and did not give a fig how many black-busked matrons flared their nostrils and crossed the street to give her a wide berth. For that matter, if it ever came to a spitting match, she was quite capable of telling the rich and noble ladies of the parish exactly what they deserved to know, for she knew by name how many of their husbands were faithful and how many of them lavished expensive gifts on their mistresses. She was mature, sinfully uninhibited, and shared Tyrone's need, every once in a while, not to seduce or flirt, not to plead, cajole, or make excuses. Not to talk at all. Just to strip and soak the bedsheets with sweat and waken in the morning with a clear head and a fine sense of accomplishment.

It had happened almost four years ago, after a particularly close call with a patrol of militiamen, that Tyrone had found himself at the Berkswell house, badly winded and bleeding from a saber wound. Doris had asked no questions. She had simply peeled off his clothes, ushered him into bed, and when the lobsterbacks demanded to search the premises, they found Tyrone and Doris engaged in activities that had sent *them* away red-faced and sweating.

In the intervening years, she had become one of his best sources of information. Among her own personal clientele she numbered army officers, local magistrates, bankers, and merchants who were not above bragging how much money they had, how much they carried to and from their places of business, and what manner of precautions they used to safeguard it. Periodically, she would send a card or a note inviting Tyrone to dine and over the course of the evening, would let slip a remark pertaining to what so and so might be carrying on his person when he left for London the next day, or where, sneaky devil that he was, the burgher hid his tax collections. Sometimes she would elude to one of her own evening entertainments, and in whose company she might be found, and at the call to stand and deliver, she acted suitably surprised and indignant, never revealing by a glance or a gesture that she knew who might be behind the collar and tricorn.

On one such occasion, when he had followed her advice to stop a certain conveyance on the Narborough turnpike, it was Tyrone who'd had difficulty controlling his expression, for Doris Riley had emerged from the coach wearing nothing but a blush and a diamond pendant. Her male companion, prompted by the threat of the snaphaunces, had stumbled into the moonlight in a similar state of flagrante delicto, his only accessory a festoon of red ribbons knotted around his nether region.

Tyrone had recognized Edgar Vincent at once, despite his ridiculous appearance. A tall, bull-necked man in his mid-thirties, he had the solid upper body of a wrestler and the belligerent nature of someone not accustomed to having either his privacy or his personal possessions violated. A wise thief, upon discovering who he had inadvertently chosen to rob, would have apologized profusely, hastened them back into the coach, and ridden away, not stopping until he had put half of Britain's width and dust behind him.

Tyrone had only laughed.

In truth, he laughed every time he thought of the burly fishmonger standing there too drunk to utter anything more coherent than threats, too tightly bound in his silken torment to allow for any noticeable decrease in the pain or size of his tumescence. Vincent had vowed to bring ten kinds of hellfire down on Tyrone's head but so far only one had taken shape. Colonel Bertrand Roth had arrived in Coventry within a week of the robbery, and in that time, had trebled the patrols on the roads at night, had issued standing orders to stop and question any lone horsemen out on the roads after dark and if they refused to comply or attempted to run, they were to be shot out of hand. It was a nuisance and an inconvenience, but, so far, he had not had any more success than his predecessor, Colonel Lewis, who had been quite happy to turn the task of capturing the elusive Captain Starlight over to Roth.

It was lucrative work, and exciting. There were nights Tyrone felt like throwing his head back and howling at the moon. Nights when every moment was crystal-clear perfection, when drawing each mist-laden breath was a deliberate and conscious act, when the effect was felt deep and cold in the lungs and his entire body vibrated with the thrill of being alive.

Those were the nights he had no regrets, no pangs of guilt for the course he had chosen to take through life, nothing but complete and absolute acceptance of who and what he was: a thief, a scoundrel, a rogue. It was better than anything fate might have had in store for him had he kept on a straight path and followed a preordained destiny as his father and his grandfather had before him. Both had been game wardens, descended from a proud line of foresters dating back to a time when nine tenths of England was greenwood and a man could lose his hands and his life for daring to raise a bow against a royal deer.

Tyrone would not have had much hope of rising to anything grander in life had sheer luck not brought him into the world the same week a son and heir was born to the lord of the manor. Because his mother had shared her milk as a wetnurse, Tyrone had spent his first few years as playmate and companion to the fat young Reginald Braithwaite, a spoiled and truculent child given to tantrums and fits of foaming apoplexy if he did not get his way. Reginald hated school and insisted he would only agree to tolerate a tutor if Tyrone shared the classroom with him. Although he sat ignored in a back corner for the most part, Hart learned from watching and listening. He possessed a quick wit and a keen intelligence and once he realized the symbols on a page could be transformed into knowledge and adventure and romance, he would steal into the big library at night and read, devouring as many words as he could cram into his hungry mind. While the little lord cursed and spit over endless rounds of deciphering and translations, Tyrone learned French and Latin and Greek. He proved to be a fine mimic with an ear for accents and provided no end of amusement for the Braithwaite heir by strutting about the classroom imitating the speech patterns of the latest Oxford dean sent to drum knowledge into his head.

He was also a tall and strappingly handsome youth, all sleek muscle and latent virility, which in turn amused the young lord's vivacious older sister to no end. It was not always by accident she would appear in the stables when Tyrone was stripped to the waist helping his father birth a foal or train dogs for the hunt. And it was not without enthusiasm that she introduced him to the pleasures of a woman's body at the tender age of fifteen.

When he was sixteen, the duke decided it was time for his son to take a tour of Europe. With a little sly persuasion and subtle goading, Reginald refused to even consider it without Tyrone to act as companion and bodyguard. They were away six months longer than originally planned, mainly because Tyrone had wanted to see the pyramids and the Parthenon and to hear the poets in Italy and to listen to piano concertos in Frankfurt. It was there, in the summer of his seventeenth year, that Reginald contracted the throat inflammation that forced the two weary travelers to return home. They were not back in England a week when the young lord died from an inability to swallow, and without preamble, Tyrone found himself back in the stables, sunk up to his ankles in ripe horse manure, mucking out the stalls.

Compounding his difficulties, when he offered a smile to the duke's daughter as he helped her mount her horse, he was lashed across the face with a riding crop and accused of daring to make lewd advances to his betters. He was ordered off the estate at once and with no money, no true sense of where he belonged, he eventually found himself wandering along the London waterfront, where he signed on board the first vessel that looked as if its cannons were used for more than just hunting whales.

Life aboard a successful privateer had opened his eyes to the many wonders that lay beyond the far edge of the horizon. It had also opened the skin on his back on more occasions than he cared to remember, and he still bore a crisscross pattern of scars on his shoulders from a heavy-handed boatswain who decided a sailor had no business quoting from the Greek classics. Hart served three years as a gunner's mate before a drunken dispute on shore with that same oafish boatswain fixed the first charge of murder on his head. Deciding he had had enough of the sea anyway, he headed north, into Scotland, where he joined a band of reivers and learned from those master thieves how to steal and rustle and outfox the British soldiers who had been keeping the Highlands under severe military rule since the failed rebellion of '45.

That two-year escapade earned him more lashmarks and a stint in a British gaol. It was there he had met Robert Dudley, the victim of an unlucky tumble off a wagon running barrels of Scots liquid gold—*uisque baugh*—across the border into England. Robbie had been thrown into Tyrone's cell with the broken bones of his left leg protruding out the skin, denied the services of a doctor because, according to the guards, he would likely be hung before they could justify the expense of needle and thread to stitch the wound closed.

Having learned a little about tending wounds on board the privateer, Tyrone set the bones as best he could and tore strips from his own clothes to bind it in a makeshift splint. Hart had not been in the best shape himself, for his gaolers were convinced he knew the location of the reivers' hoard of stolen goods, and were as liberal with the lash as they were with their fists hoping to persuade him to reveal it. By the end of two weeks' confinement, it was Robert Dudley who was dragging himself across the cell to tend the most recent battery of bruises and bloody flaymarks on Tyrone's nearly lifeless body.

The night before Dudley was scheduled to hang, he badgered the guards to come and get Tyrone. Hart had suffered a particularly brutal beating the previous morning and he was, Dudley claimed, quite dead and beginning to stink, which, for a condemned man's last night on this earth, was too much to have to endure. One of the guards, tired of listening to Dudley's protests, came alone and unwisely into the cell, ostensibly to break Dudley's other leg and shut him up until the hangmen came to fetch him at dawn. He got no farther than the initial threat before Tyrone, rising miraculously from his mouldy straw deathbed, lunged from behind and slammed the guard into the stone wall with such force, his skull cracked open like a ripe walnut.

Using the guard's keys, and a confiscated blunderbuss, Hart and Dudley were able to escape, and, deciding Scotland had become too warm for both of them, rode south in search of good English ale again. It was on a dark stretch of road outside of Exeter that they came across a richly appointed coach waylaid with a broken axle. The owner of the coach had been in the process of collecting a stallion he had won as a wager, and when the axle broke, he had attempted to mount the stallion and ride it the rest of the way home. The beast, black as night with sparks of fury blazing out of his eyes, had refused to oblige and was being whipped so savagely by the young lord, his flanks were covered with blood.

Tyrone had ridden straight for the owner and knocked him half senseless on the first punch. While Dudley occupied the driver and the groomsmen's attention with the blunderbuss, Tyrone had taken the leather whip and thrashed the young man's flanks equally bloody. Leaving him screaming by the side of the road, they had ridden away with the stallion, a hefty purse full of gold, and a fine new sense of purpose.

That had been six years ago, and neither Dudley nor Hart had been given cause yet to regret the path they had taken. They chose their victims and their turnpikes with equal care, mapping out ten ways of escaping any particular stretch of road before they even ventured into the moonlight. Despite denying the fact to Renée d'Anton, they were careful never to rob from those who could not afford it, which meant they stayed away from the local post coaches and only stopped the smuggler's wagons to purchase—at a fair price, negotiated with thieves' honor—some of the black market goods. There were others, like Doris Riley, who were not reluctant to share information if a little profit was to be had, and innkeepers who thought it a fine joke to see the lobsterbacks chasing after their own shadows.

At the same time, Tyrone did not try to fool himself

into believing he was infallible. He could make a mistake, or one of Roth's tin soldiers could get lucky. That day might even be coming soon when the temptation of a two thousand pounds reward would prove to be too much for those innkeepers to resist. Even so, if the rope were to tighten around Tyrone's throat on the morrow, he could still laugh and say he'd had a damn good run at life, beholden unto no one but himself, grudging himself nothing he wanted, nothing that might otherwise have been forbidden him because of his lowborn station in life.

A rare, boyish smile crept across Tyrone's face as he stopped with his foot on Doris Riley's porch and watched the last sliver of the waning moon sink below the distant treetops. In his mind's eye, he could still see it riding high and swollen in the night sky, casting a luminous stream of light through an open window to render a scanty, damp chemise all but transparent around the curves of a silver-haired beauty. Renée d'Anton. Even her name was exotic and ethereal. Her eyes, when she had discovered him there in the shadows, had been positively luminous, and her mouth had simply proved to be too much of a temptation to stare at too long without doing something about it. Her lips had been warm and sleek, as velvety as he imagined the rest of her body would be, and he could not help but wonder, had he held that kiss a moment longer, or let his hand caress the provocative fullness of her breast . . . would he be standing on Doris's doorstep contemplating the mist and the darkness?

The sliver of moon disappeared in a wink, leaving him with the image of a man and woman straining together in a crumple of satin bedsheets. He felt a pleasantly heated rush of blood to his extremities and was starting to climb the last few steps when his smile began to fade and the faces of the two imaginary lovers became clear. One of them was undoubtedly the French beauty, but the other belonged to Edgar Vincent, and Renée was not writhing

beneath him in pleasure, but pain. He was forcing himself
between her thighs and she could do nothing to stop him,
for her wrists and ankles were bound to the bed with
blood red ribbons.

Tyrone drew a deep, startled breath. At almost the
same moment, a very real sound intruded on his thoughts
and he melted quickly into the deeper shadows that
flanked either side of the doorway. He reached instinctively for one of the snaphaunces, but remembered too
late he had left them in his saddlebag. With scarcely a
second to spare, he vaulted over the low wooden rail and
crouched down beneath the level of the shrubbery, barely
avoiding the wide swath of light that shattered the darkness as the door swung open to a tinkle of feminine
laughter.

"Enough," the voice cried. "You've already torn one of
my best gowns tonight, you lusty brute."

"I'll happily tear a dozen and replace them with a
dozen more."

Tyrone felt the fine hairs across the nape of his neck
bristle end to end as he saw a tall, burly man step out onto
the veranda, his hands dragging a reluctant but laughing
Doris Riley into the evening air. Her laughter was briefly
muffled beneath a wide-mouthed kiss, and there was the
distinct sound of a seam parting as her companion
squeezed and kneaded the voluptuous shape of her
breasts.

Her groan was half appreciative, half seductively chas-
tising as she twisted expertly out of his grasp. "You were
the one who said you had to leave," she reminded him
through a pout. "And that was two hours ago. Won't the
colonel wonder what has become of you?"

The bulge in the man's breeches was massive, testing
the strength of his own seams as he apparently weighed
the importance of whatever appointment he had been
resigned to keep against the thin, transparent veil of

Doris's gown where it parted in the breeze, revealing the long slender legs and lush round hips beneath.

"What the hell," he grinned. "The bastard isn't even expecting me in Coventry until tomorrow night. Why should he have all the fun?"

Doris laughed and welcomed her eager lover back into her arms, squealing with delight as he scooped her up and carried her back inside, slamming the door behind them.

Tyrone waited, his palms cool and clammy, his pulse racing. The brief glimpse he'd had of the man's face had been enough to stiffen his spine and set the muscles in his jaw into a square ridge.

It was Edgar Vincent. Real. Not just a ghostly illusion. And nothing—not even the memory of the fishmonger standing naked on a moonlit road—could evoke a smile now.

*✻ ☽*

# Chapter 7

*R*enée stared, transfixed, at the candle flame. Vaporous blue at the heart, it expanded to tarnished yellow, then fiery orange before the scorched tip sent a thin, dark pencil of smoke curling upward. Made of tallow, it gave off the unpleasantly murky scent of unwashed sheep. Although the odor eventually permeated the air, curtains, fabric, and clothing, Mrs Pigeon would sooner have danced naked on shards of broken glass than squander the extra pennies it cost to burn candles made of beeswax.

Distracted from the game of chess she was playing with Antoine, Renée glanced, at the clock on the mantelpiece, certain it must be gone midnight. It was barely ten. The last time she had looked, the ornately scrolled minute hand had been standing straight up and down. Now, as she stared in disbelief, it was just creeping past the numeral one. She knew it was working; she could hear the faint *ticka tocka ticka* over the low hiss of the fire. She could also hear the wind rattling against a loose pane of glass, and the little *snaps* the tallow made when the flame encountered dampness in the wick. Every now and then she could even hear the faint *gurgle* and *burp* from Antoine's stomach as it protested the remnants of the evening meal.

In the five and a half months she and Antoine had been in England, Renée had yet to eat a meal seasoned by a spice other than mustard. The cook at Harwood

House rarely ventured beyond the extravagance of boiled meat and cabbage, mashed turnips, and some round green légume of unknown and unpalatable origin. Renée could weep when she thought back to the meals her mother used to design. The d'Anton household had once boasted six chefs, four *pâtissiers*, and a bevy of cooks' apprentices all of whom conspired each night to provide meals of eight and nine full courses, each with different tastes and textures, some sweet, some light, some so rich and frothy the sauce alone made the mouth water.

Nothing, so far, in English cuisine made anything but her eyes water.

It did not help that the air in Antoine's bedroom was tainted with the smell of a mustard poultice. The morning after Renée had found him shivering under the bed, he had wakened with a slight fever and a dry, raw cough. For the past two days he had been kept abed with plasters and hot bricks, and while the fever had met defeat against Finn's battlefield regiment of broth and strong herbal teas, the cough was persisting and Renée was worried his lungs might fill with the rattling, hacking malady he had suffered as a child.

Antoine tapped a finger on the edge of the chessboard to draw her attention.

*If you insist on leaving your queen unguarded, I will take her, make no mistake.*

They were sitting in his bed with the game board between them and although he had been tolerant of her frequent distractions, there was a limit to how much he would endure. In this instance, she had only one move possible: to save her queen she had to sacrifice her knight. Even then, it was only a temporary reprieve, for the queen was still vulnerable to attack on three sides and the checkmate would come within the next two moves.

Renée sighed but just as she leaned forward to reach for the poor, doomed knight, a trick of the candlelight changed the ebony armor, shield, and lance it carried to a multi-collared greatcoat and tricorn. Her fingers recoiled without touching it and, despite the fire blazing in the hearth behind them, she felt a chill ripple across her skin.

What had seemed like such a brilliant, clever scheme two days ago now seemed ludicrous and foolhardy in the extreme. What had seemed daring and bold and romantic was just plain suicidal. Hire a highwayman to steal the Dragon's Blood suite? Double-cross Roth and expect to get away unscathed?

It was madness. Madness to assume she had the courage to carry off the charade, and madness to put her faith in a shadowy villain who, regardless of if he was as handsome as Lucifer and twice as cunning, offered no guarantees she and Antoine would be left any better off than they were now, nor any assurances they would not be a good deal worse.

What did she know about him? Starlight was a thief and a murderer and had not troubled himself to deny either charge.

Two brief encounters hardly qualified her as an expert on his character and a single incident of reckless bravado—lifting her hair and offering him her throat to throttle—scarcely proved she was his equal in nerve or courage. The fact that he spoke well-mannered English instead of broken cockney and offered his hand in a gentleman's agreement did not signify anything other than a refined sense of humor and an ability to imitate his betters. How did she know *he* would not set a trap of his own to outwit Roth and double-cross her in the process? What did he care if she was forced to marry a man against her will or choice?

It was not without some grave misgivings that she had earnestly begun to believe her early impressions of the intrepid Captain Starlight had been tainted by the moonlight and shadows. Since then she'd had two long days and nights to rethink her position, weigh her chances, recognize her limits. She'd had Finn's reprobation to contend with too. The doughty old valet had turned scarlet when she had told him about her late night visitor. He had been all in favor of packing up what little they had and leaving then and there, taking their chances with a fast coach and an open road. They had eluded Robespierre's bloodhounds, he had declared, surely they could evade Roth and his damp-behind-the-ears Volunteers.

Any further debate they might have had was rendered moot when Antoine woke up with his fever.

"You can hardly keep your eyes open anyway," Renée said to her brother, forfeiting the game of chess with a dismissive sweep of her hand. "I am surprised Finn has not come to chase me away."

*He has gone to fetch more broth,* Antoine mouthed through a wrinkling of his nose. *Perhaps he could not find enough bat wings and chicken toes to boil in the pot.*

Renée smiled. "It is making you feel better, is it not?"

The only answer was another crinkle in the nose and, as if on cue, the door to the bedchamber opened. Finn entered carrying a tray laden with a small bowl of steaming liquid and a fresh poultice.

At the potent influx of mustard vapor, Antoine rolled his eyes imploringly in his sister's direction, searching for a reprieve.

*Can you not tell him I am much better now?*

She shook her head. "In this, we must bow to Finn's knowledge. He has been treating your coughs and runny noses since you were in baby linens and I would not dare risk his wrath to interfere."

*I am not coughing, and my nose is perfectly dry. Look.*

He angled his face toward her, but Renée only smiled. "Perhaps tomorrow I will save you from the bat wings, *mon coeur.* Tonight you still belong to Finn."

She stood and gathered up the scattered chess pieces. Even though Antoine flung himself back against the pillows in abject despair, he did not look all that sorry to see the game ended. His eyes were heavy, the lids drooping with weariness.

When Finn had finished laying the fresh plaster on Antoine's chest, Renée leaned over the side of the bed and kissed him tenderly on the cheek.

"Goodnight. Sleep well. Know that I love you with all my heart. If you need anything at all . . ." She left the sentence unfinished, for she knew Finn would not leave his side until he was asleep.

Escorting her as far as the hallway, Finn was quick to assure her. "I shall also leave the adjoining door open tonight, although I cannot say it is beneficial to my own state of repose. The young master snores almost as loudly as that Pigeon woman, but I shall endeavour to persevere."

Renée smiled her thanks, and shared a wink with Antoine, for they both knew Finn should not have invited comparisons on whose snoring was the loudest.

"Goodnight, then."

"Goodnight mad'moiselle. If *you* need anything—"

"I am quite capable of fetching it myself. You must not fuss over me so."

"Indeed I must. No one else in this godforsaken travesty of a household appears willing or able to do so with the exception of young Jenny, and she has had her hands full today preparing rooms in the west wing."

Renée bit down on the pad of her lip. Mrs. Pigeon had received a note from Lord and Lady Paxton instructing her to clean and air out the large bedrooms in anticipation of their arrival at the end of the week. They would be bringing several guests and could expect more as the day of the wedding, now less than two weeks hence, drew closer. For the most part, Renée had managed to push the unsavory event to the back of her mind, never really thinking the day might actually arrive, never really believing she might have to go through with it.

Finn interpreted her expression correctly and shook

his head gravely. "I promised both your mother and your father—"

"Yes," she said softly, laying her hand on his arm. "Yes, I know. You promised you would look after Antoine and me until you drew your last breath."

"It was not an idle promise, though I seem to have failed somewhat in the execution."

"You have not failed at all. Antoine owes you his life— we both do, many times over. And without you by my side, I should have gone mad long before now. I may still go mad, of course," she added in a whisper, "but not because of anything you have failed to do."

He opened his mouth to question the odd remark but remembered Antoine behind them and settled for clearing his throat. "My last breath is a long way away yet, mad'moiselle. We *shall* endure."

Renée blew a final kiss in Antoine's direction and retreated across the hall to her own room. There, she found the fire had been stoked early enough to make the air nearly as warm and dry as in Antoine's room. Two fat logs were glowing a brilliant red in the grate, with tiny wavelets of yellow flame licking across the tops. None of the tallow candles was lit, and for that she was grateful, enjoying the clean smell of wood smoke.

Sighing, she rubbed her hand across the knotted muscles at the back of her neck and crossed over to the window. The skies had been overcast and bleak for the past two days, and there was nothing to see through the pane of glass but darkness. The nearest neighbor was four miles down a long, winding road, so there was not even the twinkle of a distant light to relieve the blackness and sense of isolation. Her gaze touched briefly on the scrolled latch, reassuring herself it was locked as tightly as she had left it several hours ago.

Finn, bless him, had left a decanter of wine on the nightstand and she poured herself a glass, draining half of it in the first few swallows. It was heavy and left a musty, iron taste at the back of her throat, but it was strong; she could feel its effects almost immediately in the warm rush that filled her belly. She forced down the second half and poured another glassful before replacing the stopper in the decanter, determined, if nothing else, to get a few hours of sleep tonight. She still had decisions to make and was no closer to a solution than she feared she would be an hour before the appointed rendezvous.

If she went.

Still at the window, she reached up and pulled the pins and delicate silver *peignes* from her hair. Setting the combs aside, she used her fingers to loosen the thick knot of curls, kneading her scalp at the same time, hoping to massage away the strange, restless feeling that had begun to seep through her body. It was the same every night. Regardless of how tired she was, as soon as she was alone in the darkness of her room, her eyes refused to close, her body refused to relax. She was lucky if she slept more than a few sporadic minutes at a time, luckier still if those minutes were not filled with horrific images from the past.

She had another sip of wine and unfastened the ribbon belt beneath her waist, then shook out the folds of white muslin to let the gauzy fabric hang free and straight. Thinking the numbness that was still spreading through her limbs was caused by the wine, she debated downing the rest of the second glass of wine as recklessly as the first, but then—whether it was because it was so unbelievably impossible it just had to be true, or because somewhere in the back of her mind she had almost been expecting it—she lowered her arms and stood as motionless as the shadowy figure in the corner.

He had not moved or betrayed his presence in any way. Perhaps it had been a subtle flaring of the flames in the hearth that had given him a hint of substance for a fleeting moment, or perhaps it had been the faint scent of mist and saddle leather and damp wool that had betrayed him. In any case she knew, suddenly, and without having to turn to confirm his presence, that the phantom who had been plaguing her every waking and sleeping moment for the past two days and nights was standing less than ten feet from her side.

She closed her eyes and swayed briefly with the flush of icy prickles that melted down her spine. "What are you doing here, m'sieur? Why have you come again?"

"I have been wondering that myself, mam'selle. The only answer I have been able to come up with is . . . curiosity."

"Curiosity?"

She heard the soft crush of his boots on the carpet as he moved out of the corner and came up behind her. He stopped short of touching her, but she was acutely aware of his solid and imposing presence at her back.

"Curious," he said again, "to know if you really understand how dangerous a game you are playing . . . or if it is just that you thought I would be easier to manipulate than Roth."

"I do not think either one of you is easy to manipulate, m'sieur, nor am I trying to do this."

"No?"

A black gloved hand reached past her shoulder and she half expected to see the glint of a pistol in its grip. There was no gun, however, and the only sparkle came from her wine glass as he plucked it out of her fingers and lifted it to his mouth.

When he swallowed, it was a hard, male sound, as abrupt and harsh as the curse that accompanied the glass to the table. "Personally, I have always found brandy to be more effective for keeping demons at bay, but I suppose an immature, rusty claret has its uses."

"You have demons, m'sieur?"

"We are all a little afraid of what lurks in the dark, mam'selle."

His answer, murmured close to her ear, set a small eddy of sensations whirling into motion between her thighs, and in the next instant, the eddy turned into a strong current, for his hand was at her shoulder, shifting the heavy golden mass of her hair to one side, exposing the curve of her throat.

"Curious," he said again, as if their conversation had not taken a brief detour. "You said yourself you had heard the stories about how clever I am"—he paused to trace a gloved fingertip along the sloping line of her shoulder—"surely you must have known I would check your story."

"I did not lie to you, m'sieur," she said through a shiver.

"You did not tell the whole truth either. Or did you just *forget* you had a brother?"

"Antoine?" she whispered. "He is just a boy. He is not yet fourteen—"

"And already accused of murder. How industrious."

"H—how did you know—?"

"My dear Mam'selle d'Anton—" his voice caressed her nape, the words spiraled down her spine, the drag of his finger caused her flesh to tighten across her breasts and belly. "I have had two days to discover what would make a beautiful woman like yourself bow to the demands of a bastard like Roth. It might interest you to know I have even seen the warrant."

Renée was stunned. Maximilien de Robespierre had once bragged of having the most extensive spy network in all the world, but he and his revolutionary tribunal would have been put to shame by the seemingly casual efforts of this English highwayman.

"The charge is false," she said, trying to regain a measure of composure. "Antoine did not attempt to murder anyone. He heard a shot and ran to help, and when he found my uncle, Lord Paxton was already senseless. He claimed he was shot from behind and could not identify his attacker. I do not think even he believes it was Antoine, but Colonel Roth persuaded him to sign the warrant and to act upon it if I did not agree to help them."

"They went to all that trouble just to force you to cooperate?"

"I do not understand it either, m'sieur, for I have no doubt there are a thousand women who would gladly ride the roads at night hoping to make your acquaintance."

He was mildly surprised but obviously not amused by her sarcasm, for when she tried to turn her head, his left hand was suddenly there, cupping her chin, holding her firmly in place. At the same time, his right arm circled her waist, drawing her back against his body. It was, Renée realized at once, the perfect position for snapping her neck should the occasion warrant it. And although she stood tense and trembling in his ominous embrace, she did not attempt to resist the intimacy nor did she provoke him into tightening it.

"Two thousand pounds is a lot of money," he said slowly.

"Fifty thousand is a good deal more. If I were only doing it to collect the reward, m'sieur, I would have screamed the first night you came into my room and Roth's soldiers would have come at the run."

"Yes," he murmured, "do tell me more about the guards."

"There are usually two on duty at any given time. One watches the front entrance, one patrols the stables and courtyard." She glanced again at the securely bolted window latch. "How did you get in here, m'sieur? Finn has been extra diligent at locking the windows at night."

"I am a thief, remember. I make my living going where I am not wanted, taking things that are supposedly placed under heavy guard." His hand shifted down from her chin, fitting itself more snugly to the curve of her throat. "Locks only make the challenge more interesting."

Renée suffered a small wave of lightheadedness. His voice was a soft snarl in her ear, his body was a heated wall behind her, his arm an immovable band of muscle and sinew around her waist. His gloved fingers were fitted firmly enough around her neck that he was surely able to feel her pulse racing along her throat, and try as she might, she was not able to take anything but rapid, shallow breaths.

"Have you any other little secrets you are keeping from me? Any more brothers? A lover, perhaps?"

"Antoine is my only brother. And . . ." Renée swallowed against the pressure of his hand, "my former fiancé died in Paris. He was executed the same day as my father."

"An *aristo*, naturally?"

She bristled instinctively at the note of condescension in his voice. "He was the son of one of the most powerful and noble houses of France, m'sieur, but he was also kind and gentle, compassionate and honorable, if such things are important to you."

"They are not, mam'selle. Kindness and gentleness will get you killed in this business just as surely as compassion and honor, and right now, the only thing that is important to me is determining whether or not I should trust you."

"*Vraiment*. And if you hold these qualities in such contempt, how am I to determine if I can trust *you*?"

"I should think my position is a little more precarious than yours. If I get caught, I hang. If you get caught, you will likely spend a night or two in Roth's bed by way of punishment, but at least you will be able to get up and walk away when he is finished with you."

"I would rather die," she declared tersely, "than have him touch me. I would rather take my own life than submit, willingly or otherwise, to either Colonel Roth or Edgar Vincent."

His fingers remained curved around her throat another full minute while he likely tried to determine if her outrage was genuine or staged for his benefit. When he finally relented, the dragging motion he used to take his hand away was almost a caress. "Why don't we find out together, mam'selle, exactly what risks we are willing to take and just how much we can trust one another."

She turned her head slightly, waiting.

"Does your door have a lock?"

There was the smallest hesitation. "Yes."

"Then lock it. And bring me the key."

He withdrew his arm from around her waist and the immediate absence of warmth from his body sent a shiver across Renée's skin, another through her limbs.

For several moments she continued to stand and stare at the two dark reflections of their silhouettes in the window. The fire threw just enough light to define the angles of the tricorn, the breadth of his shoulders, the standing upper collar. By contrast, she was a head shorter and her outline was blurred by the tumbled waves of her hair, some of which were still clinging to the wool nubs on his greatcoat as she turned.

She did not look up at his face. She walked past him and went to the door, knowing he had turned as well and his eyes were following her every step. If she did as he commanded and locked herself inside the room with him, it would take several minutes for Finn—or anyone for that matter—to break the door down and come to her aid. On the other hand, if she ran screaming into the hallway he would be out the window and vanished into the night before Finn or any of the guards below could catch him.

Either way, it would be over. Roth would know his trap had been discovered and there would be no further meetings tomorrow or any other night. He could hardly hold her to blame for an armed highwayman breaking into her room and terrifying her half to death.

She reached for the brass latch. It was cool to the touch as she fitted her hand around it, so was the key as she grasped it between her thumb and forefinger and gave it two slow, complete turns. She drew it out of the slot and closed her fingers around it, waiting for her knees to stop shaking before she turned and pressed her back briefly against the carved wood to lend her support. He had not moved. He stood where she had left him by the window, his eyes glittering faintly where the firelight reached beneath the brim of his tricorn. Was he surprised? She could not tell. Was he satisfied? She could not determine that either. Was that the test? She did not think so.

# ✴ ☽

# *Chapter 8*

$W$hen Renée was halfway back to the window Tyrone held up his hand to stop her. He was not exactly certain if this was a test of her willpower or his, but he needed a moment just to *think*. He had not been able to do much of that when she was in his arms. Her hair had smelled like flowers—roses—and felt like silk against his cheek. It was spilling around her shoulders now like a silvery halo, burnished russet by the glow of the fire. Without the belt gathering the folds of her gown at her waist, the muslin hung straight from the edge of her bodice to the floor and there, too, the firelight was playing havoc with his powers of concentration, teasing its way through the sheer fabric to reveal the shapely contours beneath. It did not require a vigorous strain on his powers of recall to remember how she looked in just a skimpy, water-dampened chemise, how long and slender her legs were, how trim her waist, how soft and round and firm her breasts. Roses aside, the scent of her skin alone was as subtle as the drift of exotic spices that warned a sailor of a tropical island just below the horizon, and it had the same effect on the way his blood altered its course through his veins.

"Perhaps it is simply too dangerous to do this thing, m'sieur," she whispered. "Perhaps it *was* a foolish idea, *sans connaissance*, and—and I do not think I could bear it if . . ."

Tyrone moved a measured step closer to her, closer to the glow of the fire. "If . . . what?"

Renée watched, dumbfounded, as he casually peeled off his gloves then reached up and removed his tricorn. With seemingly familiar ease, he tossed both onto the seat of the chair and advanced another step toward her.

"What is it you could not bear, mam'selle?" He asked again, unfastening the top three buttons on his greatcoat. Loosened, the tension fell out of the standing collar and it began to fold back around his shoulders as the remaining buttons were worked free. The fire was bright enough to reveal wide, deep-set eyes and boldly slanted eyebrows. His hair was thick and fell from a central parting over his collar, laying dark as ink against his cheeks and throat. His nose was straight and forthright, his jaw square, and his chin somewhat blunted with the hint of a cleft, or a scar, marking the midpoint.

It was, as she had guessed, a handsome face. Devastatingly more so than she had imagined it would be. There was also a careless nobility about his features, as if he was well aware of the effect it would have on most people to know this common thief was not so common after all.

He shrugged the greatcoat off his shoulders and draped it over the foot of the bed before he moved another step closer to her.

The coat had added breadth to his form, but not so much so that he was reduced to a spindled weakling when he took it off. There were a good many muscles beneath the fashionable cut of his jacket giving bulk to his chest and arms, tapering down to a trim, lean waist and legs that needed no false padding to convey strength and power. His boots were tall, made of soft leather with a folded cuff below the knee; his neck was bare and his shirt open at the throat revealing the faintest hint of dark hairs curling over the top of his breastbone. That he wore no neck stock or cravat came as no surprise, for the whiteness would have shone like a beacon against the unrelieved darkness of the rest of his clothing. What did surprise her was the richness of each garment. The skin tight breeches were fine merino wool, his jacket exquisitely tailored broadcloth, his waistcoat black silk brocade embroidered with gold thread.

When he was close enough, he tucked a finger under her chin and tipped it upward, forcing her to meet his gaze. His eyes were paler than she had expected, of no distinguishable color in the uncertain light, but she felt more danger staring into them than she had into the twin barrels of his pistols. The glow that came from their depths rivaled that of the fire and was far more unnerving than any phantom starlight.

"Tell me," he murmured. "What is it you do not think you could bear?"

"I . . ." Her lips remained parted, but the word hung in the air as a faint sound for a moment before she could force more to take shape. "I do not think I could bear the thought of you being hung for something I had persuaded you to do."

"You do not even know me."

"But I would be responsible for betraying you, m'sieur, and I do not think I could live with that."

"You were prepared to live with it two days ago. What happened between then and now to change your mind?"

"Nothing happened, m'sieur."

"Nothing?"

She watched the play of firelight in his eyes and suffered another prickling rush of sensations through her body. How could she explain? When he had just been a faceless, shapeless name bandied about in a parlor, he had been just that: a stranger, a shadow, a phantom. Exactly when he had turned into a flesh and blood man, she could not say for certain. On the hillside? In her room afterward? Or just now, when he had stood behind her at the window and held her in his arms and not every part of her had been anxious for him to let go? Whenever it had happened, he was real to her now, and if he did this thing, if he was caught . . . or killed . . . she would be no better than the good citizens of Paris who testified against their neighbors for an extra crust of bread.

"Nothing happened," she repeated in a whisper. "I just feel . . . perhaps it is too dangerous."

He sighed and his fingers, which were still lightly propped beneath her chin, brushed thoughtfully down the curve of her throat. "Life is dangerous, *ma petite*."

"But Roth—"

His eyes, which had been following the path his fingers had taken, snapped up again. "Roth is *moin que rien*," he insisted. "Less than nothing."

"Nevertheless, he wishes to make himself something by capturing you, m'sieur, for he has vowed to watch you hang."

He continued to stare at her for a long, throbbing moment and when he finally relented, the slow smile that spread across his face almost caused her knees to buckle. "I assure you, mam'selle, I am a grown man capable of making my own choices and decisions and would no more consider you to be responsible for any of my actions than I would wholly accept the blame for yours, regardless if those actions led to the gallow"—he bowed his head and replaced his roving fingertips with the press of his lips— "or to the bed."

Renée was shocked to utter stillness. His words shivered down her spine leaving her flesh tight and tingling in their wake. The skin across her breasts seemed to shrink and pull itself into taut little peaks, while the spot on her shoulder where his lips were working their mischief became warm and loose, almost buttery—as if the flesh would slide away from the bones. Her heart began to beat like a wild thing, her legs felt weak, her belly watery. A soft gasp marked the shudder of sheer erotic pleasure as his lips and tongue began to plunder a determined path from the curve of her neck to the edge of the muslin sleeve.

"*Capitaine*—"

His fingers ignored her airless protest and eased aside the muslin to bare the round, satiny ball of her shoulder. His lips descended again, exploring the exposed flesh with a thoroughness that left her dangerously bereft of will or reason.

"*Capitaine*, please," she whispered. "You must not do this."

"By *this*," he inquired with a frown, "do you mean this"—he kissed her shoulder and retraced the path he had taken from the tender crook of her neck—"or do you mean this?" He threaded his hands into her hair and held her while his mouth moved boldly to claim hers.

The memory of his first kiss caused her to stiffen briefly, but there was none of the anger or violence he had demonstrated before, none of the defiance or the need to master and control. He covered her lips with teasing gentleness, and if there was any challenge in them now, it was the challenge to deny the bright wash of pleasure that came on every languid swirl of his tongue.

She made a small sound in her throat, but he only pushed his fingers deeper into her hair and held her closer. His tongue coaxed her lips apart and traced their sleek, soft contours, but he ventured no farther than her guarded gasps allowed. When he lifted his head, she was more confused than ever, more bewildered over his restraint than she would have been had he flung her over his arm and kissed her like a ravening madman.

"As I said," he murmured, "life is full of dangers. It should be lived to the fullest while we have the chance because it could all be taken away from us tomorrow."

Her eyes were huge and round and dark, her lips were moist with the taste of him, and her body was so tightly strung she was not certain she could have moved had she wanted to.

"Do you say this because you truly believe it, m'sieur," she asked breathlessly, "or because you wish to take me to bed?"

This time his smile was slow to form and somewhat startled at her candor, but entirely, heart-stoppingly genuine. "I am saying it because it is the rule I live by . . . and because I want very much to take you to bed."

Still wide-eyed, she watched him bow his head toward her, his mouth warm and indulgently patient as it moved over hers; each suckling caress was delivered with a tender invitation for her to respond, for her to part her lips and share the pleasure of the moment. And it would just be for the moment, she thought wildly. Letting him seduce her would be even more insane than hiring him to commit a robbery. It would be shocking and shameless. All other implausibilities aside, she was the daughter of a *duc*! The royal blood of France's nobility flowed in her veins while he was just a thief. A man who lived without any thought to the future . . . who had no future. She had Antoine to think about. Antoine and Finn . . .

Her hands clutched at the folds of his jacket and she fully intended to push him away, but somewhere between a caress and a corresponding whimper the perilously fine line between what was instinctively right and what was outrageously wrong seemed to become blurred. She did not want to think about what she *should* be doing, only what she *wanted* to do, here, now, with this man, these fleeting few moments they would have together.

Her conscience lost whatever final chance it might have had to save her as she leaned fully into his heat and felt the thrill of desire burst like a flame deep down inside of her. The way her legs were shaking, they would not have supported her any longer on their own anyway, she reasoned, and since her hands were already twisted into the loose folds of his shirt, it was a small matter to slide them upward and wrap them around his shoulders. She heard him acknowledge her capitulation with a low groan and felt his hands shift down and circle her waist, pulling her closer, almost lifting her against him while his tongue began to plunge boldly, deeply into her mouth.

Here was the madness, she thought. Here, as she opened her mouth to him and greeted each sleek, silky thrust with a broken whimper of pleasure. Hot, bright sparks of hunger raced down her spine, and the weakness that had begun in her limbs spread upward to engulf her whole body. She tightened her arms around him, pressed her body closer to his, yielding to the promise of his embrace, and with an urgency unlike anything she had ever experienced before, she eagerly returned his kiss thrust for thrust. And when she felt his flesh rising swift and hard between them, it was as if she had known all along there would be something even more momentous to come, something as wild and reckless and dangerously unpredictable as the man himself.

She had spoken the truth when she had told him she was no longer a virgin, but her first and only lover had been as innocent as she. Their couplings had been hasty and furtive, prompted more by patriotic desperation than any real sense of lust or desire. Jean-Louis de Blois had been young and handsome and as loyal to her father as to his own blood, and she had loved him for that. She would have been content to marry him, happy to live out her days surrounded by his warm, gentle passion.

But this. This was nothing warm and gentle. It was hunger, raw and explosive, and if there was any manner of desperation fueling her responses, it was driven by a need to feel all that heat and power naked in her arms, naked inside her—to feel his strength and reckless courage and have something strong and totally fearless to cling to in the darkness.

Her reaction was more than Tyrone had expected, and while he obliged her with all the gallantry and skill at his disposal, his own response was another matter entirely. He had already known her lips were lush and pliant, but he had not expected them to be so deliciously capable of matching his ardor. He had also known she would be willowy and soft in all the right places, but he had not anticipated his own casual flagrancy would surge into an instant and blood-pounding arousal the moment she pressed her sweet body against his. Moreover, he had only meant, initially, to teach her a lesson about playing dangerous games with dangerous men, but instead, he had heard himself confessing quite truthfully that he *wanted* her. At the first shy flicker of her tongue in his mouth, his body had hardened and all he could think of was plunging himself inside her, feeling her body tighten and shiver around him. And where there had previously been smug satisfaction over her capitulation, there was now a solid, throbbing urgency straining to reach her through the layers of their clothing—layers which seemed to be vanishing as quickly as his hands could remove them.

His jacket and waistcoat were cast into the shadows. His shirttails were pulled from the waist of his breeches almost in the same feverish motion that he peeled the shoulders of her muslin gown down off her arms to expose the sheer layer of her chemise beneath. His mouth left hers to blaze a fiery hot trail down to the ribboned front closure, only to be distracted by the fullness of her breasts pushing over the upper edge. When the chemise was banished into the darkness, he bowed his head again, capturing each hard-peaked nipple and drawing as much of the silky flesh into his mouth as her cries of pleasure would bear. At the same time, he skimmed his hands down the satiny length of her thighs, parting them slightly and fitting her over the bulge at his groin so she could feel exactly how much he wanted her, how much she had affected him.

With a deep and husky sound that was half groan, half growl, he swung her up into his arms and carried her to the bed, his mouth never leaving her flesh, his hands tearing at the last few buttons and bindings that kept him confined.

Renée's newfound rashness almost faltered when she felt his hands, trembling and eager on her knees, urging them apart. It all but deserted her entirely when his weight settled between her thighs and the formidable strain of his flesh began pushing forward. The initial thrust, delivered without preamble, was bold and invasive and startled her so completely with its depth and fullness that she did not even have the breath or wit to cry out. The second brought a groan to her lips when there seemed to be too much—too much flesh, too much heat, too many muscles in his back, his shoulders, his arms, his thighs. He was too big and she felt a momentary clutch of fear as he began to thrust hard and deep, seemingly oblivious to the differences in size and shape of their bodies. His hands even plunged beneath her hips to angle her higher into each vigorous stroke, and she had no choice but to move with him, to reach down and hold fast to the rapid rise and fall of his hips and to arch herself upward that she might be more easily able to bear the force of each thrust.

Her first orgasm took her by swift surprise, bursting like a sudden flaring of heat and bright light throughout the length and breadth of her body. She gasped and stiffened beneath him, but when the wave passed, her flesh was still tight around him, gripping him with an eagerness that had become acutely sensitive to the heat and friction of moving flesh. She tried, through a series of breathless pleas, to pull him even harder and deeper inside, and he obliged her every cry, shifting his hands, his hips, his body to chase after every clenching spasm, groaning when her pleasure brought her rising desperately, frantically up beneath him.

A moan, involuntary and uncomprehending, marked new levels of sensation for Tyrone as well. Feeling her squeeze around him, hearing her awe and disbelief as each wave was prolonged beyond any previous limits, he had to fight to catch each breath. It was not supposed to happen like this. He was not supposed to feel so out of control. His body was one massive raw nerve being teased and tormented by muscles so tight and wet and greedy he could feel the effects tingling in the tips of his toes. Even worse, he was displaying as much skill and savoir faire as a—as a fishmonger, for pity's sake, but he could not help it. Not when she was beginning to shiver around him again and her cries were in his ears. Not when her hands, her body was begging him, urging him, demanding more. . . .

His groan was couched in an oath as he rolled, first onto his side, then onto his back, thinking the shock alone might delay the inevitable. But it was worse, not better, feeling the silken drag of her hair across his chest, the startled clenching of her thighs as she straddled him, the near catastrophic eagerness of her body curling forward to take him so deep inside, he could feel her heartbeat thudding around him. She was shuddering, shivering, squeezing him in a constantly moving sheath, and he groaned with the pressure, with the compelling, rippling suction that seemed determined to draw his whole body inside out. He rolled again, while she was in the throes of yet another orgasm, and his passion swept through him with the power of a gale force wind. His body arched with one mighty thrust and the pressure flooded out of him in throbbing bursts, the ecstasy raw and savage and white-hot in its intensity.

\*

Tyrone continued to hold her and to shudder deep inside her, his flesh acutely sensitive to each lingering tremor as it dissipated within the velvety warmth of her body. She was still quaking beneath him, still panting, weak with disbelief, and he rested his head in the crook of her neck, his mind stunned by the total betrayal of his

body. Even his hands seemed not to want to leave her as
they stroked her hair, her arm, the smooth length of her
thigh.

Renée focused on each gentle caress as if it was a life-
line to reality, the only thing that kept her from drifting
away. His flesh, she thought, was the only solid thing left
inside her, for the rest of her body had become completely fluid, without strength or substance. Her legs
were hooked up and over his but she did not have the
energy to untangle them. Her arms were locked around
his shoulders, her hands still clutched the muscles of his
back, and although her fingers were beginning to slip on
the dampness, they did not possess the initiative to let go
on their own. It was just as well. She did not have the
faintest notion what she was expected to say or do now
that the fury of the moment had passed.

She had just allowed a complete stranger to bed her.
She had not only allowed it, she had been a willing participant, encouraging him to such haste he had not even
taken the time to remove his breeches. They had been
unbuttoned and pushed down just far enough to clear his
hips and lay bunched around his knees. To her further
mortification she realized she still had her stockings and
garters on, and if she was not mistaken, her right slipper
was dangling from her toe.

It was surely the heat of a full body blush that brought
his head up off her shoulder. The dark locks of his hair
were flung forward over his cheeks, obscuring what little
of his face might have caught the glow of the fire. He did
not seem the least disconcerted by their haste or state of
semi-undress. If anything, she could swear he was smiling
as he elevated himself onto his elbows and forearms and
stared down at her.

"I must say, mam'selle," he murmured. "You do surprise me."

A thin, silvery line of wetness shimmered along her
lashes and collected at the corners of her eyes, slipping in

two shiny streaks down her temples. He watched them
trickle into her hair and saw the quiver in her chin, and he
sighed.

"That was meant in a most complimentary way, I assure you. If I were to mock anyone's behavior tonight it
would be my own, for I am not usually so . . . undisciplined." He shifted an arm slightly and one of his
thumbs brushed away the wetness at her temple. "I am
not usually so blind either, mam'selle," he added quietly.
"You were not a virgin, but I think you were not so vastly
experienced as you would have led me to believe."

She flushed again, from the tips of her toes to the verge
of her hairline and tried to turn her head to avoid his gaze,
but he would not allow it. "This . . . former fiancé. He
was the only one?"

"If he was?"

He drew a breath and kissed her—kissed her deeply
enough and thoroughly enough to convince her the question was not asked out of any sense of disappointment.

When he lifted his head again, his hands continued to
cradle her face between them. Her hair lay in scattered
gold waves across the bedding, and his skin bristled with
the memory of it sweeping across his chest. His gaze followed the slender arch of her throat down to where her
breasts lay ripe and full beneath him, their whiteness a
stark contrast to the dark hair that covered his chest. He
had guessed her nipples would be palest pink, and so
they were in repose: pale as rose dust, soft as velvet. They
looked every bit as chafed and reddened as her mouth
now, however, and while he was not a man given to making apologies for too many of his sins, he regretted his
haste, his crudeness, his lack of delicacy. Not that he
could have done anything about it at the time. He had
definitely *not* been in full command of his senses, nor had
he expected to be so utterly enthralled with the feel of
her in his arms, the taste of her in his mouth. Even now,
he could feel himself stirring again, wanting to know if it

had just been an aberration inspired by the firelight and the honesty of her passion, or if he had indeed unleashed something here that was both unique and dangerous.

"Dangerous," he decided in a whisper. "I would definitely call this dangerous, mam'selle. And foolhardy and . . ."

"Undisciplined?"

He stared at the lusciously moist pout of her lips and allowed a wry smile to curve his own. "Definitely undisciplined."

"*Indécent aussi*," she added through a small catch in her voice. "For I do not even know your name, m'sieur."

His thumb curved down onto her cheek. "It is Tyrone."

"Tyrone . . . ?"

"Which you may call me instead of '*m'sieur*' or '*capitaine*.' Both seem rather formal under the circumstances, would you not agree?"

"I suppose. Yes."

"And I will call you Renée, if I am permitted?"

She hesitated a moment, then nodded. "Yes."

"Have we decided then, that we can trust each other?"

"Yes."

"Completely? Absolutely?"

She searched his eyes a moment. "I trust no one completely or absolutely. Only Antoine and Finn."

"Ahh. The stalwart Finn." He smiled and his lips brushed hers on their way down to claim the bewitching, wine-red mole on her breast. "I have a feeling his conduct would not be too exemplary at the moment if he knew I was here."

Renée closed her eyes against the sensation of his lips roving down to her nipple. He drew it with almost apologetic tenderness into the suckling warmth of his mouth, and she wanted to stretch like a cat and purr beneath him. "He would not be happy, no."

"I imagine"—his mouth slid to her other breast and he

lavished the same care and attention that had brought the first peaking to attention—"he would be quite incensed at the impropriety, and I do not mean only the fact that you are naked in bed with a man less than a fortnight before your wedding—though from what I have seen, I believe that would be enough in itself to cause the old fellow to inhale all the air in the room."

Renée had no doubt he would, but she also knew precisely what Tyrone meant. Even through the initial, blinding rush of desire, she had paused a moment to remind herself how shockingly inappropriate such a liaison was, however brief and passion-driven it might be. To a servant, whose opinions on class and social distinctions were often more rigid and unbending than those they served, such a lapse of judgment would be an affront in itself.

"If you are worried about what Finn would say or do if he found out, rest assured, m'sieur, he would not betray you. Not if it meant betraying me or hurting me in any way."

His mouth released her nipple with a soft, wet *fwithp* and, after a long, considering look into her eyes, he shifted his body lower and ran his lips along the smooth, flat surface of her belly. His hands skimmed down to remove her stockings and garters and, after a brief tussle with linen and tapered wool, he cast his breeches away into the shadows. "M'sieur!" Her eyes widened as she realized his intent. "Do you think it wise—?"

"No. I do not think it wise at all, mam'selle. In fact, I think it very *un*wise for me to stay here one moment longer than necessary. On the other hand," his hands coaxed her legs apart then slid around to cradle her bottom while he bowed his dark head between her thighs, "there is the matter of defining what is necessary."

Renée's mouth fell open. He was the cat now and she felt his tongue lapping her like a bowl of cream. Instinct bade her to try to wriggle herself higher on the bed, but his hands were firm, his tongue devilish as it mocked her efforts to escape him. "M'sieur—! You mustn't—!"

He lifted his head a moment. "You did say you trusted me, didn't you?"

"Y—yes," she stammered, "but . . ."

The unruly waves of his hair brushed the skin on her inner thighs as he murmured something against her flesh. She thought he said something about discipline and fishmongers, but then it was nearly impossible to think at all. It was enough just to be able to twist her hands into the bedsheets and hold on for dear life.

✷ ☽

# Chapter 9

Renée felt the bedding rustle and the mattress jostle slightly beside her. She was incredibly content, drifting in a state of semi-sleep, and resented the need to open her eyes. But then she remembered . . . and came awake so fast, she almost gasped out loud.

The room was dark. The fire was reduced to a bed of glowing red cinders and did not allow for much more than a vague impression of a shadowy figure moving to and fro, gathering up scattered articles of clothing. Renée was sprawled naked, facedown on the bed, half blinded by the veil of thick blond hair that was scattered over her eyes.

Careful not to move anything other than her hand, she pushed the hair off her face, tucking it behind her ear. Even so small a gesture made her aware of subtle changes elsewhere in her body. She felt flushed and warm, her skin so keenly sensitive she could identify every fold and crease in the bedsheets. The flesh across her breasts felt deliciously chafed, her inner thighs were wondrously achey, and deep inside, she was all soft and slippery and still throbbed tenderly with the lingering effects of expended passion.

*Mon Dieu*, she thought, but he had certainly made up for his initial haste and lack of control a hundred times over. Subsequent lovings had been exercises in sensual torment, lasting half an eternity and culminating in such prolonged and protracted torrents of pleasure, she had very nearly fainted from the excess. There was not one square inch of her body he had not explored with meticulous care, not one sensation he had left a guarded secret, not a single cry or gasp or plea he had not obliged with chivalrous extravagance.

If she thought about it, she should resent the fact that he could still stand and walk and dress as if nothing untoward had happened. On the other hand, if she thought about the things he had done, the things she had allowed him to do, she would surely melt into a puddle of shame and never be able to lift her head again.

She squeezed her eyes tightly shut and did not open them again until she was able to focus on the moment at hand.

A surreptitious peek at the window confirmed it was still dark outside. He would, naturally, want to be away before any hint of dawn light betrayed his presence to any servants rising early to tend their chores. She could have set his mind at ease somewhat by assuring him that none of the servants at Harwood House was overly conscientious. Not even Jenny ventured up the stairs with hot water or a pot of chocolate before mid-morning.

Renée turned her head slightly, repositioning her cheek on a fresh puff of feathers in the pillow. There was, she realized, another pillow under her hips, but she curled her hand into a small, embarrassed fist and refused to dwell on how it came to be there, or why.

Tyrone moved in front of the remnants of the fire and bent over to pull on his drawers. She had never watched a man dress before. Granted, it was difficult to see now, but there was enough of a glow behind him to gild the taut muscles of his thighs and buttocks as he drew the linen garment up his legs and tightened the drawstring around his waist. The muscles in his arms bulged and the veins stood out in prominent relief; the lean and tempered plane of his belly folded in hard, layered bands as he bent over again to repeat the motion with his breeches.

His chest was a magnificently sculpted display of curves and contours, and her hands tingled with the memory of running through the forest of crisp, dark hairs, of feeling the thunder of his heartbeat beneath her fingertips. He had encouraged her to explore his body as thoroughly as he had explored hers and she had done so, shyly in the beginning, but then with increasingly bold strokes and forays that had revealed some breathtaking pleasures . . . and some unsettling surprises. The number of scars he bore had disturbed her. Marring the broad plates of muscle across his back and shoulders were varying levels of raised welts, suggesting he had been subjected to a lash on more than one occasion. There was an ugly, round pucker on his thigh and another shiny trough on his arm, the results of a bullet and sword respectively, she guessed, for he had not answered her questions when she had asked how he had come by the marks. He had deftly distracted her with his hands and his mouth instead, branding her body in ways that would be invisible, but no less indelible.

Tyrone's movements startled her thoughts back to his dark silhouette. He stood in his breeches and boots and was shaking the folds out of his shirt to separate the tails from the collar. Pulling it over his head gave him substance, made him a ghostly white blot against the darkness, and when he started groping about him, searching for something else in the shadows, she bestirred herself to sit upright.

"You may light the candle, m'sieur, if you are having difficulty finding everything."

He straightened slowly and turned his head toward the bed.

"I am managing. But thank you."

She did not give voice to her suspicions, but it occurred to her that he likely had a great deal of experience locating his clothes in the dark.

"Actually . . . I am glad you are awake," he said. "I have been giving the matter some thought and—"

"And you have decided to turn down my request?" She dragged the sheets up over her breasts and curled her legs beneath her hips. "I have been thinking the same thing, m'sieur, and I believe it is for the best. Roth is determined to catch you and I fear he will succeed if you go through with this thing."

"You appear to have lost a great deal of faith in my abilities over the past two days."

"It is not your abilities I doubt. I have known men like Roth before; the leaders, the ruling parties of the revolutionary government changed three times in four years and Paris was infested with *citizens* who would sell their souls, betray their closest friends in their hunger for power. Roth is a little man who strives to be more than he is. He will kill you if he has the chance."

"Assuming I don't kill him first, of course."

She regarded him with huge, solemn eyes. "If you had wanted to kill Roth, you could have done so long before now. This time, I think it is you who wishes to make me believe you are more than what you are."

His soft laugh came out of the shadows. "So now my abilities *exceed* your expectations?"

He was mocking her, gently to be sure, but it stung all the same. "I simply do not want the burden of your death on my conscience."

"And I have told you, mam'selle, I am not your burden to bear. With Roth on one side of you and Edgar Vincent on the other, I would think you have enough to worry about already."

"Until now, I have been too afraid of my own shadow to do much more than run and hide. Or to obey like a meek lamb and always do what is expected of me."

"Running has merit, mam'selle," he said, sobering. "So does hiding. But nothing feels quite as good as beating a bastard at his own game."

She shook her head. "*Non.* I release you from the agreement we made, *capitaine.* You are free to—to practice your trade elsewhere."

The blur of white moved closer to the bed. "Are you *firing* me?"

Her cheeks warmed, but her mind was made up. "Yes. Yes, I am."

"Just like that."

"*Oui.*"

"This"—he spread a hand to indicate the bed— "wouldn't have anything to do with your decision, would it?"

She looked up at him and frowned. "If you recall, I had all but made up my mind before this happened."

"Ahh. Yes." He drew his arm back and folded it, along with the other, across his chest. "We were discussing the comparative values of our necks. But what will you tell Colonel Roth?"

"I will not have to tell him anything. When you do not show up tonight for our meeting, he will correctly assume you became suspicious of a trap and changed your mind."

"Frankly, I have learned never to assume anything where Roth is concerned. But what about your marriage to Edgar Vincent?"

She clutched the sheets closer to her chest. "I told you, m'sieur, I have no intentions of marrying a man who has blood on his hands. What he does is of no further concern to me. I will not be here one way or the other to know."

His head tilted thoughtfully to the side. "Where will you be?"

"As far away as Finn can take us."

"You are not worried about the warrant Roth holds for your brother's arrest?"

"The warrant was to be destroyed if I cooperated. He cannot possibly blame me if his scheme does not work."

"*Ma pauvre innocente,*" he murmured. "Do you honestly think that is all Roth wants from you? Did his behavior at the Fox and Hound *suggest* that was all he wanted?"

Renée felt a chill that had nothing to do with the fact the fire was a smoldering ruin. "But he and Edgar Vincent are friends."

"Roth has no friends."

"And you do, m'sieur?"

"I have acquaintances with mutual interests," he said after a brief hesitation. "And the name is Tyrone."

*"Pardon?"*

"My name is Tyrone. Surely you have not forgotten it already?"

This time the edge in his voice left a hot blaze of color on her cheeks. "I have not forgotten. But since I will never see you again after you leave here, and you will never again see me, I think it best if we return to being . . . formal."

At that, Tyrone's irritation was defused and he could not resist a smile. There she sat in her crumpled nest of bedsheets, gloriously naked and gleaming in her dishevelment, her skin still rosy from their lovemaking, her thighs undoubtedly as sleek as butter and reminding her why on each indrawn breath . . . and there she was dismissing him like a servant, telling him she never wanted to see him again.

By the same measure, here he stood under the mistaken impression his sense of imperviousness and self-assurance had been fully restored, feeling his flesh thicken and throb as painfully as if he had never touched her.

"Before I do leave," he asked wanly, "may I ask how you intend to get away from here? You said Roth has men watching you, and I doubt if he has assigned fools to guard the coop. Roth himself is no half-brain, though it bears arguing at times. If the meeting tonight does not go off as planned, he'll not simply shrug his shoulders and walk away. He has gone to an inordinate amount of trouble to bring this together and if he even suspects you have had thoughts of doubledealing, you will see a side of him that will keep you screaming through nightmares the rest of your life."

"But I have done my part. I have done all he has asked me to do. He has no reason to suspect me of anything."

"Until the jewels go missing."

"What?"

"I said"—he leaned slightly forward—"until the jewels go missing. Then he will most assuredly suspect you of something."

"I do not understand."

"It is quite simple, really. I think the risk is worth taking. I think we should meet tonight, as planned, and I think we should steal the jewels as per our agreement. That was what I was about to say before you interrupted me with your cavalier order of dismissal, and that is what I plan to do, with or without your help."

The sheet slipped unnoticed from her hands as she gaped at him. "You would do that? You would go through with the robbery anyway?"

"Why not? They *have* gone to a lot of trouble to get my attention. And I would be a damned poor thief to let fifty thousand pounds' worth of jewels go wanting. By the same token, I can understand why you would want no further part in it."

"I have to think of Antoine's safety," she whispered.

"Of course you do."

"If it was just me . . ."

"You would don a greatcoat and tricorn and rob him yourself?"

The teasing note of mockery was back in his voice, but Renée did not care. He could laugh out loud at her cowardice and she would not care.

"Roth will be furious."

"Furious men make careless mistakes."

"And you never do, m'sieur?"

"Oh, I make my share of mistakes, mam'selle. I am only human, after all." His words faded to a murmur as his gaze strayed to the pale mounds of her breasts. The extremely human part of him wanted to reach out and take her into his arms again, but that would be breaking nearly every hard and fast rule he had set for himself, prime among them being to encourage no emotional attachments. Friendship, affection, obligations, ties of any kind, were dangerous things, best avoided. And to that end, he was glad the fire had faded and the light was gone, for he had the very real sense, looking into her eyes, that a man could drown in their depths and never even know he was even sinking until it was too late.

"Well, mam'selle," his voice was brusque and businesslike again as he pushed away from the bedpost. "As I said, the decision is yours whether you stay in the game or not. If you choose not to, I would suggest you finalize your plans to leave here as soon as possible. If you run into any difficulty, you might want to remember the name I gave you the other night: Jeffrey Bartholemew. Aside from writing letters for the post, he also owns a small livery. He was an old shipmate of mine and while he is not much younger than your Mr. Finn, he is a hapless witling when it comes to beautiful women. For the promise of a smile, he will get you safely—and discreetly—to London, or anywhere else you care to go. To that end, I wish you the very best of luck in your future endeavors."

Renée watched him tuck his shirt in his breeches and pull on his waistcoat and jacket. His movements seemed to be less precise than before, as if he was in a sudden, pressing hurry to get away.

"M'sieur?"

Tyrone was in his greatcoat and halfway to the window when her voice stopped him. He heard the drag of bed-sheets as she stood up and brought them with her, using the linen to shield her nakedness. It was such an innocently modest gesture, he almost groaned and banged his head on the wall.

"I would like to wish you the very best of luck *aussi*," she whispered.

He looked down at where her hand was suddenly resting on his sleeve. Pale and white, the fingers were so long and delicate and soft, his flesh surged again at the memory of them exploring the shapes and textures of his body.

He dug his bootheels into the floor and moved purposely forward to the window.

Renée watched as he unlatched the pane and swung it open. He settled his tricorn firmly on his head and glanced back one last time, and while he looked as if he wanted to say something more, he did not. Without a further word or glance he swung himself over the sill and was gone, vanished into the cool night air.

## Chapter 10

*A*n hour later, when the utter blackness of the night began to give way to a watery pink dawn, Renée was still standing by the window. She had been there, wrapped in the bedsheet, since Tyrone left, only vaguely aware of the light growing stronger, giving shape to the trees and fields, burning away the wispy layers of mist that hovered over the ground.

He had not even kissed her goodbye.

She had not expected him to, of course. He had taken what he wanted from her and now it was back to business. The business of robbing coaches and waylaying travelers, of living by his guns and his wits, flaunting danger, defying fate and death and anything else that appealed to his macabre sense of humor. He was going to rob Edgar Vincent whether she helped him or not, and she was going to have to get away from here whether she had the means and motivation to do it or not. And the sooner the better before Roth or Vincent or her uncle—or all three—began to suspect her of dealing *with* the enemy, not against him.

A faint buzzing sound drew her attention to the top of the eight foot window where a fat, green fly was beating itself into a frenzy as it circled the pane of glass looking for a way out. She would gladly have opened the window and chased it out to put it out of its misery, but she had no time for such small mercies as she hurried into the dressing room. When she emerged a few minutes later she had exchanged the bedsheet for a robe and tamed the wild tangle of her hair into a tail at the nape of her neck.

Kneeling in front of the hearth, she stirred the high mound of ash enough to uncover the red coals beneath. She lit an oil-soaked rush and touched the flame to a candlewick, then, as an afterthought, tossed some kindling and fresh wood on the grate to revive the fire. The warmth and languor she had been feeling a short time ago had vanished out the window with *le capitaine.* She was cold. Her body was beginning to feel more battered than deliciously bruised, and although she had been vigorous with the soap and washcloth, she still wore the scent of him on her skin like an emblazoned brand.

With the fire catching nicely, she took up the candle and went to the door, intending to go below and see if anyone was awake enough to bring hot water to her room for a bath. She was also, oddly enough, ravenously hungry and, because they had consumed the rest of the wine last night, thirsty for something that did not taste tepid or rusty—which ruled out any water left in her pitcher overnight.

The latch, when she twisted it, did not turn, and she remembered, after a brief flash of panic, that she had locked it herself and removed the key from the plate.

It had been clutched in her hand at one point last night, but then he had kissed her, and she had forgotten all about it.

She knelt and searched the area of floor where they had been standing. The candle, held high over her head, cast a wide enough halo of light that she found the key on the first pass. It was when she was gathering up her chemise and dress and stockings that a second wink of light caught her eye.

It was a jeweled cravat pin. Tyrone had not been wearing a cravat, but he had been dressed formally otherwise and might have removed it earlier, tucking the pin in a pocket or sticking it in a lapel for safekeeping. Consequently, it must have fallen or been sprung loose in the frenzied haste to remove and discard clothing.

She cradled the pin in her hand and examined it under the glare of the candle flame. It was no tinker's piece, that much was a certainty. The shaft was gold and the head embossed with a crest and shield, the latter divided into quadrants with three of the four sitting diamonds no less than a full carat in size. The fourth held a sapphire. It was exquisitely detailed work and she had no doubt that if the light was stronger and her eyes less bleary, she could have read the tiny print in the motto scrolled along the lower edge of the shield. But it was the diamonds that caught and held her attention. They were of the very best cut and quality, the facets reflecting myriad brilliant points of light.

He had obviously stolen it from a very wealthy patron.

Her blood was coursing with decidedly more confidence as she secured the pin to the underside of her collar and hurried out of the room. The hallway outside was silent as a tomb and dark, save for the yellow circle of light thrown off by her candle. She went instinctively to Antoine's door first, but changed her mind at the last instant. If he was asleep, she should leave him as long as possible. He would need all the rest he could get over the next few days.

Padding barefoot along the hall, she went to Finn's room instead, and, after sparing a cautious glance along both ends of the hallway, tapped her knuckles softly on the door.

There was no answer, no light showing below the door, and no sounds from within as she knocked again and put her ear to the polished wood.

"Finn? *M'sieur Finn?*"

Nothing.

She glanced over both shoulders again and turned the door knob, opening it just enough to press a whisper through the gap. "Finn? *Es-tu ici?*"

Pushing the door wider, she lifted the flickering stub of tallow over her head. The dull glow reached as far as the empty, rumpled bed, and she eased the door wider, slipping inside. Easily a quarter of the size of her own, the chamber and its contents were spartan and neat, like the man who slept there. The furnishings were plain, the bed narrow and utilitarian with a single flat bolster and a spare woolen blanket folded across the foot. One thin window was covered by a single panel of curtain, and a connecting door that led through the dressing room to Antoine's bedroom allowed just enough space beside it for a sturdy armoire.

Like her own room, there were no personal touches. There were no family mementos, no cameos, nothing to indicate over sixty years of life, half of them spent in the most luxurious, decadent country in the world. It was odd, but until this very moment, Renée had not given much thought to Finn's first thirty years. He was an Englishman, after all. Did he still have family on this side of the Channel? If so, had he tried to contact them at all since their return to England?

"Did you want something, mad'moiselle?"

Finn's voice, coming from over her shoulder, nearly startled the candle out of Renée's hand. As it was, the melted tallow came dangerously close to drowning the flame before it splashed over onto her fingers.

Finn stood in the doorway to the dressing room wearing only his nightshirt and cap. The shirt was shapeless and fell well short of covering his bony ankles and bare feet, the peak of the nightcap was folded over and hung in front of one ear. In his left hand he carried a tallow candle, in his right, a porcelain chamber pot.

"Is there something you require, mad'moiselle?"

She glanced over his shoulder. "How is Antoine? Did he sleep well? Is his cough any better?"

Finn arched a silvery brow. "His chest has been quiet

tonight and he has slept the sleep of the innocent . . . something that, if I may dare to suggest, you have not?"

For the span of a heartbeat, she thought he was making a veiled reference to her late-night visitor, but with the next, she realized he looked too rumpled and sleep-creased for subtlety.

"I have not had much sleep, no," she admitted honestly enough. "And . . . I have been thinking that I cannot go through with this. I thought I could, but I simply cannot go through with it."

He opened his mouth to comment, but remembered the pot in his hand and turned aside to dispose of it. When he straightened again, she was no longer standing in front of him, but had crossed over to the window.

"Mad'moiselle—"

"I cannot do it, Finn. It is too dangerous. A thousand things could go wrong and Antoine would be made to pay for my foolishness."

Finn's eyebrow inched upward. "I gather you are referring to your arrangement with Colonel Roth?"

She nodded. "Yes. I have thought about it for two days, thought of nothing else, in fact, and—and I know I cannot go through with it."

"Well, thank God for that, mad'moiselle!" His shoulders, his entire body seemed to sag with relief. "I know it is not my place to interfere, but I was truly beginning to fear I would have to do something drastic to bring you to your senses. Roth is vermin, not to be trusted, and this rogue highwayman is . . . well, he is a criminal. A thief and murderer and likely to end his days on a gallows if he is not shot out of hand first."

"The good citizens of Paris branded my father a thief and a murderer. Does that absolve the man who betrayed him to the tribunal?"

"You must not confuse crimes invented by political zealots with crimes committed against the laws of God. This scoundrel steals honest coin from honest people—

well, for the most part, honest people. He has multiple charges of murder laid against him, at least a dozen or more according to the latest warrant I saw posted."

"And we both know English warrants contain nothing but the truth," she retorted bitterly.

He frowned and compressed his lips into a thin line. "Has he said or done anything that would lead you to believe the charges are false?"

"No, he has not denied he is a thief."

"A damned clever thief who has already been fore-warned that a trap is being set. I dare say you have given him more than a fair chance to save his neck being stretched this time and that alone should clear your conscience of any culpability." There was more than a hint of sharpness in his voice, for Finn had not been at all pleased to learn of the captain's first visit to her room. What his reaction would be if he knew she had just spent the better part of the night in his arms did not bear speculation. "Moreover," he was saying, "I should think that if he is fool enough to rendezvous on the turnpike tonight, he rather deserves whatever fate lies in store."

She turned to the window and eased the curtain aside with her finger. She stared out across the bleak landscape and somewhere in the back of her mind she saw the image of the horse and rider streaking away in the distance, his laughter echoing softly on the wind.

"He is anything but a fool," she decided quietly. "Neither is Roth. But I have no intentions of being caught up in the middle of their little games anymore."

She dropped the curtain back in place as she turned around. "For that matter, I have no intention of being anywhere near any turnpikes tonight unless they are well away from here and pointing the way to London."

"London, mad'moiselle?"

"They have ships leaving from there and sailing to America, do they not?"

"*America*?"

"They have no guillotines in America, Finn. And no love of British soldiers. Papa spoke often of New Orleans. He said it was a gracious and elegant city, too far to be corrupted by the royal court, too closely allied with the American colonies to be influenced by the politics of the revolution. We would be safe there, would we not?"

"As safe as one could be, I suppose, in a land of red-skinned savages and bloodthirsty pirates."

"Would you prefer to remain here where the savages are white and the pirates are no less bloodthirsty for being called family and friends?"

Having no immediate response, Finn pursed his lips. "There is still the matter of getting there. Apart from the financial requirements, I understand it is an arduous voyage of several weeks' duration, which might be unpleasantly extended to *months* if one's vessel is blown off course or encounters foul elements."

Renée curled her lower lip between her teeth and bit down. Finn had been green for most of the Channel crossing, with his head bowed over the rails. His relief at having safely escaped France had been surpassed only by his joy at reaching solid land again.

"I am sorry, Finn. It is the only place I can think of where we will be safe from my uncle's influence, Roth's anger, and the nightmares of the revolution. Antoine will be safe there. He will be able to grow into a strong, fine young man and perhaps . . . in a place that is new and strange and wonderful, he will even be able to put the horror of *maman*'s death behind him."

Finn nodded slowly, if somewhat reluctantly, in agreement. "Of course, you are absolutely right, mad'moiselle. We must think of what is best for the young master. I am still at a small loss as to how we might achieve our ends with so little at hand, but I am certain, if the will is strong, the way will prevail. I have," he added with a slight clearing of his throat, "already checked Lord Paxton's silver drawers and plate cabinets and found them sadly lacking.

If there is anything of any value to be found on the premises, I have no doubt that Pigeon woman keeps it under tight lock and key."

Renée chewed her lip again and beckoned for him to follow her back across the hall to her own room. While he held the candle, she knelt beside her bed and located a section of seam in the mattress ticking that had been unstitched and hastily tacked closed again. She pulled the threads apart without much care for the feathers that puffed into her face and thrust her fingers inside, pulling out a small cloth pouch. Inside the pouch there were two gold coins and a meager handful of silver *livres*—all that remained of the hoard she had brought away from Paris sewn into the hem of her chemise.

Finn was not looking at the coins in her hand, however. He was looking at the bed, at the blankets and pillows that were tossed every which way, some of the latter thrown halfway across the floor. She was normally a light sleeper who rarely left a dent to show where she had lain, and by the time Finn's startled blue eyes arrived back at her face, her cheeks were a deep burning red and her fingers had curled over the coins to form a small defensive fist where she held it clutched against her breast.

"Mary and Joseph," he whispered. "He was here again, wasn't he?"

There was no point denying the obvious, not when he lifted his candle and brought it closer so that he might see the condition of her hair, the pinkness of her skin, the shine of culpability in her eyes.

"Good God," he rasped. "Did he . . . did he force himself upon you?"

It took what little strength she had left not to lie and save herself a further, painful surge of hot blood up her throat and cheeks. "No. No, he did not force me," she said quietly. "I was quite willing to steal what I could from him."

"*Steal*, mad'moiselle? I'm sure I do not understand what *you* could possibly steal from *him*."

"Some of his courage, perhaps. Some of his boldness. Some of his fearlessness. And this," she added, remembering the diamond cravat pin. With trembling fingers she plucked it off the underside of her lapel and held it out. "It must have fallen when he . . . when he was leaving and he did not see it. I did not see it either, although I might not have returned it to him even if I had. It is very valuable, is it not? Surely worth three fares to America?"

Finn stared at the glittering diamond pin but he did not touch it. He took several steps backward and sat heavily in the chair, looking suddenly very much his age, thin and frail in the oversized nightshirt.

"I . . . never thought it would come to this. Being forced to sell yourself to this—this road hawk. Where have I failed you?"

"I did not sell myself," she insisted quietly. "Nor did I plan to give myself either, it—it just happened. And I have never been forced to do anything other than live when I would have preferred to die."

Finn's gaze rose slowly to hers. "What do you mean?"

She shook her head and sank down onto her knees before him. "I was standing in the same square as you and Antoine when *maman* was attacked by the soldiers. I did not run forward to try to help her because I was too frightened. I saw them beating her, kicking her, laughing at her, and I wanted to scream as loudly as Antoine, but . . . I was too frightened. I could not move. I saw it, I heard it, I knew there must be something I could do to help, but . . . I could not move. Afterward, I wanted to die. I just wanted to die, but you would not let me. You made me run and you made me think of Antoine, and you made me come here, to this place, when all I really wanted to do was go back and be with *maman* and *papa*, Jean-Louis . . . the others. Without you by my side I should have gone mad long before now. *Vraiment*, I may still go mad, but not because of any promises you have failed to keep. If anything, it is I who have failed you."

One of Finn's bony hands stretched out, the fingers trembling, and stroked a length of the long golden hair. "How?" he asked with a frown. "How have you possibly failed me?"

"By not being more like my mother. By not having her courage, her strength."

"Good God, child. Is that what has been laying so heavily on your mind all these months? Is that why"—he leaned forward suddenly and gripped her shoulders tightly—"is that why you agreed to cooperate with Colonel Roth? Is that why you agreed to this abominable marriage? Because you were not able to sacrifice yourself in Paris? Because you are alive and your mother is dead and—" he had to stop himself again, for the words, the sentiments were as thick in his throat as they were in Renée's.

Thirty years earlier he had helped Celia Holstead escape her family's clutches to flee London and elope with Sebastien d'Anton. The escape had required courage and precise timing, for the old earl had kept his daughter under lock and key, watched day and night by servants as well as family members until such time as she could be whisked to the altar and safely married to the aged and gout-ridden Duke of Leicester. On the day of her wedding, Finn had taken his place as usual in the driver's box, but instead of going to the church, he had ridden hard and fast for the coast, where Sebastien had a ship standing by and ready to set sail the moment she set foot on board. It had not been in Finn's original plans to depart England himself, but with the earl's retainers in hot pursuit, and shots being exchanged ship to shore, he was easily persuaded to make France his new home.

He had remained a steadfast and loyal member of the d'Anton household ever since, yet no one had ever suspected the real reason why he had stayed. No one but

Renée, who had only understood herself after witnessing his utter devastation following her mother's death. He had loved her as deeply, as honorably, as nobly as any man could love a woman, and had borne it in his heart with silent dignity for over four decades.

"Never," he said raggedly, "never let me hear you say such a thing again. Never let me believe you are even thinking it, for if you regret a single day that you are alive, then her death, your father's death, would have been in vain. We might well all have offered ourselves to the guillotine and shouted, while we did so, that all our lives, all *their* lives had just been a waste. That they had no meaning, no purpose. That neither you nor your brother should have been born, that you should never have survived to provide living proof that your mother and father had lived, had loved, had left a part of themselves behind. If nothing else, child, you are proof of that. You are proof they existed and so long as you keep them alive in your memory, all the blades in all the town squares cannot eradicate that."

The tears Renée had been fighting so valiantly to suppress welled along her lower lashes and splashed free on the first blink. Seeing them, Finn cleared his throat again and pushed to his feet.

"I agree: hang the rubies. It was a fanciful notion at best and the sooner we are away from this place, the better. The guards have become lax although discretion, of course, must still be our tantamount concern; we must not give cause for anyone to raise an alarm. I dare say Colonel Roth will not take kindly to being cheated of his entertainment."

Renée dashed the back of her hand across her cheeks and stood beside him. "I hope he chews his fingers raw with frustration."

"Yes. Well. I have been giving the matter some thought and"—he paused and glanced around the room—"how did he get in here, anyway? The doors are guarded and I was most thorough in locking and bolting all of the windows."

"I do not know how he got in," she admitted. "He was just . . . here. He said it was how he made his living, going places he was not wanted, taking things he was not supposed to take. Locks, he said, only made the challenge more interesting."

Her voice trailed away and Finn snorted. "One can only hope he is as resourceful when he finds himself challenged by the stout locks on a gaol cell. In the meantime, we shall benefit from his example and simply leave by the main door. In order to avoid suspicion, we shall have to forgo the taking of any baggage save for what can be carried in a single valise. When it is ready, I should be able to remove it to the coach house without too much difficulty, but it will fall upon you, I am afraid, to find some excuse to drive into town. That Pigeon woman will insist on accompanying you, as usual, but . . ." He stopped and frowned. "Do you still have those packets of sleeping powders the doctor in London gave you?"

Renée nodded and went to retrieve three small envelopes from the sandalwood box in her dressing room. When she returned, Finn's shoulders had a determined squareness to them again. He took one of the packets, then muttering a comment about the housekeeper's vast bulk, took another. "We will stop first at a pastry shop and suggest a treat of something particularly sweet and cloying—she thrives on those little white cakes soaked in porter and cream. While you peruse the next shop, I shall sweeten her cream further"—he wiggled one of the packets—"and if her past behavior holds true, she will endure perhaps one additional stop before remaining behind to devour her cake and sip an ale. As soon as she is asleep, we can drive the coach to some secluded street and hire another from the public livery. By the time her head clears, we should be halfway to Manchester."

"Manchester? Not London?"

"London, I rather think, will be the first direction they search, and without the rubies, we have no real reason to go there. I imagine the hounds will be loosed on all points as soon as it is discovered the hares have escaped the warren, but I believe the greater concentration of efforts will be to the south, not north." He paused, and noting that her eyes had not lost any of their haunted look, he attempted to reassure her with a brief smile. "Granted, the plan is not without its flaws, but then neither is Colonel Roth as skilled a huntsman as he boasts, despite his endless, tedious declarations to the contrary. If he were, he would not have required your assistance with the redoubtable Captain Starlight in the first place."

He took the cravat pin out of Renée's fingers and held it up to the light. "Indeed. A particularly fine piece. The gems should easily fetch enough to pay for three passages to America. One can only hope the cost of buckskins and beaver hats is not too dear."

"He gave me the name of someone who might help us."

"Who did?"

"M'sieur Tyrone. That is Captain Starlight's name," she added in a whisper. "Tyrone."

Finn's nostrils flared slightly in disdain. "Irish. Hardly a surprise."

Renée gave the old butler an odd look. "Are you not part Irish yourself?"

He arched an eyebrow and gave his nightshirt a tug to straighten it. "It is not something I am wont to brag about, mad'moiselle. They are a mad, unpredictable race of people who lack any self-discipline and adhere to wild notions of independence."

At the mention of the word discipline, Renée's cheeks flushed and her belly fluttered. Her gaze strayed to the bed, to the tumble of sheets and pillows where, for a few brief hours, she had felt as bold and unafraid as the man who had held her in his arms.

"Waken Antoine," she said quietly. "Then inform Mrs. Pigeon we will be driving into town this morning."

* ☽

## Chapter 11

$\mathcal{F}$inn excused himself to dress and within the half hour, Jenny was at the door carrying two steaming bucketsful of water. The tub was dragged out of the dressing room and set in front of the fire and while the maid hastened away to fetch more water, Renée finished packing a tapestry valise.

The small pouch containing most of the coins went in first, muffled inside stockings and spare underpinnings. The cravat pin remained on the collar of her robe until such time as she was able to dress and clip it safely to the underside of her chemise. Apart from her small box of medicines, her brushes and combs, there was not much else she considered a necessity. Finn was right. Aside from the sheer impossibility of removing trunks and boxes, too much baggage would slow them down as well as make her a more easily identifiable traveler for anyone who sought to give chase.

For such an auspicious occasion as flight, she also chose to wear an English style skirt and fitted bodice. The whalebone corset would pinch her waist and push her breasts upward and outward like the prow of a ship, but again, the gown was an unremarkable style, almost matronly, with wrist length sleeves and a modest neckline. The skirt was cut from an overabundance of blue velvet that flared from the waist over a stiff layer of petticoats, but it would be warm and sturdy for traveling and, with the addition of a plain riding coat, buttoned high to the neck, ought not to raise a curious eyebrow anywhere along the way.

Jenny returned with more buckets of water and a cup of thick chocolate that would serve to curb her appetite until she descended to the breakfast room. It was a gritty and bitter drink, very nearly unpalatable, having not been beaten or frothed long enough to remove all the lumps of cocoa butter. But she choked it down anyway, once again obeying Finn's orders to take in as much nourishment as she could, for there were no guarantees what or when they would eat again after today.

The logic extended to more than food, Renée reasoned as she stepped gingerly into the tub of hot water. Most inns and posting houses looked at a guest as if they had three ears if they requested a bath, and she was almost certain such luxuries were unheard of on board ocean-going vessels. Her present hip tub was enameled tin and did not allow for much more than sitting with the knees bent up to the chin, but at least the water was hot and the soap smelled clean and she was able to soak away a few more memories of the night.

Of course, the bed was there in full view to remind her. She had tidied the sheets and blankets and returned the pillows to their proper places, but each strayed glance produced a vivid image of two naked bodies entwined together, moving and writhing and straining to the urgent rhythms of passion. She could feel his hands on her hips and his mouth on her breasts, and she could close her eyes and relive the sensation of each full-blooded thrust, when all the world was reduced to brilliant flashpoints of pleasure.

"Ma'am?"

Jenny was standing by the tub holding up a towel, waiting for Renée to stand so she could dry her body and hair. The water had cooled quickly and she was shivering as she rose, her body white and glistening in the mix of sun and firelight. Finn would be happy to see the hazy light streaming through the windows; it would make for better haste on the roads.

"Ye want the blue?" the maid asked, indicating the gown Renée had laid across the bed.

"Yes, I think so. I was planning to drive into Coventry today to do some shopping."

"Ooo, gar, there's a fair goin' on in Spon. All the ribbon makers'll be out to show their wares." She sighed, picking at a particularly stubborn tangle in Renée's damp hair. "Wish't I were goin', but Mrs. Pigeon, she says we 'ave no time for such doin's. Trollops put stock in ribbons, she says. Trollops an' 'hores an' Frenchies what need to catch themselves a rich hus—" She stopped with her mouth still open around the word, then clamped her lips tightly shut. "Sorry, m'um," she murmured a few seconds later. "I mean, yer are Lord Paxton's niece an' all, so yer not exactly all French, are ye? An' ye can't 'elp it if yer' air al'us looks ever so nice in ribbons, an' men look at ye all the time. S'trowth, they'd look at ye if ye wore a sack over yer 'ead and dressed in woolies."

Renée glanced sidelong into the mirror that hung from the back of the tub. Her hair was almost dry, flying and crackling in all directions as Jenny brushed it in the heat of the fire. It truly was a luxuriant detriment to anonymity and her gaze flicked again, this time to the tray of crimping irons Jenny had set by the fire. The scissors gleamed dully in their midst and she was tempted, sorely tempted, to just take them up and start cutting. There wasn't time now, but perhaps later, when they were stopped somewhere for the night, a drastic change in appearance might be warranted.

For the time being, she bade Jenny plait it into a thick rope and coil it on the crown of her head. There were enough short sprigs and wisps around her face to satisfy the maid's need to ply the heated irons and the result was simple, yet pleasing. The corset was another matter but Renée grit her teeth and allowed herself to be laced to within a breath of torment before the bodice was fastened overtop. Stockings, petticoat, and overskirt were added, the tapes tied, the folds fussed and fretted over until she was pronounced "awesome luvly."

While Jenny was occupied with the task of emptying the tub water out the window, Renée returned the tray of brushes and combs to the dressing room, slipping one of each into the tapestry bag before she set it unobtrusively in the corner. She also retrieved the cravat pin from her robe and transferred it to the inside of her chemise, tucking it securely between her breasts.

After a final look around, she walked across the hallway to Antoine's room. The door opened before she had a chance to knock and both she and Finn jumped back in surprise.

"Beg pardon," he said at once. Recovering, he glanced past her shoulder and frowned when he saw Jenny through the open door to her room. "His Grace is not with you?"

"No. I was coming to see if he was well enough to go down to breakfast today. In fact," she paused and moistened her lips, equally aware of the maid behind them, "I was hoping he was well enough to accompany me into town later this morning. I have some errands to run and I thought, if he was feeling better, he might enjoy the fresh air. It looks so warm and sunny," she finished lamely.

Finn barely glanced over as Jenny exited the room carrying the empty buckets and wet towels. "I am certain he would, mad'moiselle. Shall I bring the carriage around?"

"Please. Eleven o'clock should be soon enough."

He offered a slight bow. "As you wish."

Nodding, Renée turned and, with a creditable lack of haste, followed the wide, main corridor down to the central stairway. Sunlight was streaming brightly through the two-storey window lights that flanked the main entrance, and as she passed by the stairs, she glanced down over the main foyer. The guard at the bottom must have heard the soft whisper of her skirts, for he turned and stared back, his eyes following her progress as she crossed from one wing of the house into the other.

The morning room was located at the far end of the west wing, above the kitchens. The walls had been painted garish yellow by some former resident who had decided the windows did not allow for enough light or cheer. The combined effect of the sunlight and the glare off the walls was temporarily blinding when she opened the door and stepped inside; her subsequent relief at seeing Antoine seated at one end of the cherrywood dining table lasted only as long as it took to blink the stars out of her eyes.

He was not alone. There were four other men in the room with him, one of whom shot instantly to his feet and blushed as deep a red as his tunic when he saw Renée standing in the doorway. Even before her eyes adjusted to the light and her heart to the shock, she recognized Corporal Chase Marlborough of the Coventry Volunteers, the young and painfully earnest militia officer who was acting adjutant to Colonel Bertrand Roth.

Roth was sitting with his back to the glare of the window, but there was no mistaking the stilted arrogance of his profile. He was in his regimental uniform, a splash of crimson against the flaring light. The redness of his hair was dampened under a white military wig, but his smile, when he drew his lips back over the double rack of over-sized, misaligned teeth, gleamed with the same delighted malice she had last seen at the Fox and Hound Inn.

"Ahh. Mademoiselle d'Anton. A pleasure indeed to see you up and about so early. We were just discussing the lay-about habits of most beautiful young women who think nothing of sleeping half the day away. What do you think, Edgar? Will you be encouraging or discouraging such energetic vigor in a new wife?"

Slowly Renée turned her shocked regard to the third

man in the room who was only now following Roth's tardy example and pushing to his feet. Edgar Vincent was a tall man, easily six feet in height, with the broad shoulders and solid, bullish neck of a man who had spent more years at hard labor than behind the desk of an exporting office. His features were thick and blunt; a single black slash crossed his forehead in lieu of separate eyebrows and the eyes beneath were a dull, flat brown. A far cry from ugly, he was also well beyond the reach of friendly. His manners were forced, as if he resented having to possess any, and his speech was often coarse, respecting neither the age nor tender sensibilities of anyone who happened to be in his company.

Renée felt their chilly assessment as he looked with obvious disappointment at her choice of attire. At their first meeting he had inspected her like a man buying a show horse, falling short of checking her teeth and testing the firmness of her calves, but not by much. Successive meetings had produced little more than a curt nod if he approved or a slight curl in his lip if he disdained. The lip was nearly folded in half now over the severity of her hair, the modesty of her neckline, the primness of the blue velvet, and she felt a flush of resentment stain her cheeks. He was peasant stock, a *bourgeoisie* graveyard thief, yet he had the effrontery to sit in judgment on others.

The fourth man was at the server, helping himself from the contents of several chafing dishes. Renée could only see the side of his face, for he seemed more intent on the food than the company, but he appeared to be as tall as Edgar Vincent, the impression heightened by the addition of a powdered wig. His breeches and swallow-tail coat were charcoal gray, styled at the extreme end of fashion with indulgently high, molded lapels on his jacket and a neckcloth wound so tight, pleated so precisely, it was a wonder he could move his chin at all as he inspected the various dishes.

"Do come and join us, my dear," Roth said, indicating

the empty seat opposite him. "We have just won a minor victory over Mrs. Pigeon's niggardly disposition, managing to badger her into providing something more substantial than gruel and green ham. Wretched creature. I must say I'm surprised Paxton has not had her shot and spitted years ago. Not nearly as accommodating or resourceful as your own Mr. Finn, I warrant?"

The color Renée had so recently won in her cheeks drained away again with the speed of an opened vein. She had not seen or heard from Roth since their meeting at the Fox and Hound. While she had been grateful for the reprieve, she could see by the hard light in the amber eyes that he had neither forgotten nor dismissed the incident, and the fact it was far too early in the morning for a social visit, despite her fiancé's unexpected appearance in Coventry, pressed in upon her breast with the strength of a second corset.

"Yes, do join us," Vincent said, waving a hand impatiently.

She looked up into the flat, brown eyes and willed the revulsion she was feeling not to come through her voice. "I . . . have just come to fetch Antoine. Finn is bringing the coach around to take us into town. I have some errands to run and—"

"They can wait, I am sure." Roth interrupted, frowning. "We have come on errands of our own that merit far more consideration than gadding about town on a shopping adventure. Marlborough, for heaven's sake, if you are going to hold your breath to the point of asphyxia will you at least do the honors first before you swoon away?"

The corporal was indeed suffering an excess of adoration as he stumbled in his haste to pull out the high-backed chair for Renée. He looked almost too young to be in uniform—eighteen or nineteen at most—with round, puppy eyes and smooth cheeks devoid of the faintest hint of stubble. He stood perhaps an inch taller than Renée, but looked as if he would gladly have knelt at her feet if she requested it.

"Mam'selle," he said, his voice a reverent whisper.

She willed her legs to carry her forward as far as the chair and was not quite there when the man at the server cursed through a nasal whine and started rubbing at a speck of fat that had splashed on his cuff.

"Blast it, anyway! The devil take whoever left the sodding spoon at such an angle. Look here, now. A sleeve ruined and the hour not yet gone ten."

Roth cast a droll glance in his direction. "And you already in your third costume this morning."

"The gray I selected initially was decidedly too pale for the weather. The brown did not show well with these boots, and the black was simply a travesty. Threads loose everywhere. A pucker in the seam, no less. Had I been given more warning of your arrival—" The chastisement was left to hang in the air as he turned around and tipped his head smartly to acknowledge Renée's presence for the first time. "Mam'selle. You must excuse our boorish behavior. I, for one, was roused quite before any civil hour and ordered into a coach without benefit of a biscuit or tea—both of which, I might add, I was in dire need of to combat an entirely sleepless night. Demmed tooth, if you must know. Refused to give me any peace, not even when I attempted to chew a clove. Blast me if I wasn't getting quite desperate enough to send my man out to the river to catch a frog that I might bind it to the top of my head."

A noticeably prolonged silence stretched until Vincent's curiosity got the better of him.

"Why in God's name would you tie a frog to your head?"

"Why, I have it on very good authority it takes the pain of a toothache—or a megrim headache—instantly away."

Renée felt her heart drop lower in her chest, felt the beating slow to a near deathly halt. Luckily hers was not the only startled gaze that followed the gentleman as he carried his plate around to the far side of the table, for as he walked, he continued to expound upon the medicinal properties of frogs and toads.

She was, in the end, thankful for the long-windedness of his dissertation, for the distraction it caused around the table gave her time to at least partially recover from yet another shock.

Not that there had been anything immediately familiar about him. If she had passed him in the street she might never have taken a second look. Nor would she have ever associated such a prim and prancing fop with the darkly handsome, broodingly dangerous man she had last seen exiting her bedroom window.

It was the way he had said "mam'selle" that had sent a spray of gooseflesh down her arms. The pronunciation was distinct and softly slurred in a way no two men could duplicate. Here was Captain Starlight, her phantom midnight lover who had left her with the indelible impression of gleaming muscles, raw power, and unquestionable masculinity.

In the garish sunlight of the breakfast room, Tyrone's jaw was still chiseled and lean, but his complexion had been lightened by cosmetics, the brows dulled by chalk. His hair—that gloriously unruly mane of dark waves—was confined beneath a wig dominated by a series of manicured sausages from the temples to the ears. Even his eyes, so large and bold and thrillingly seductive in the half-light, were kept in a pretentious squint so that she could not immediately discern their color a table's width away.

What was he doing here? Why was he with Roth and Vincent? Why, in the name of all the saints, was he staring at her, smiling a simpering smile as if he was seeking her approval for something he had said?

In a mild panic she looked around the table, coming perilously close to suffering asphyxia herself as one by one the other pairs of eyes in the room turned to stare at her.

"You do not have to answer that, of course," Roth mused. "Endless pontifications on the merits of frogs and other such inane incidentals have become a common, if somewhat tiresome, affliction some of us must endure for the sake of working together in harmony. But, alas, I do not believe you have had the pleasure of making this gentleman's acquaintance. Mademoiselle Renée d'Anton, I have the . . . honor of presenting Mr. Tyrone Hart, Esquire."

Later she would swear that his steps were minced as he came around the end of the table again to execute a graciously low bow over her hand.

"Mam'selle," he said, brushing his lips over the backs of her fingers. "While the pleasure and the honor is all mine, I assure you, the weight of shocking incivility may be credited solely to these two gentlemen. What is more, if they find it inane of me to point out the total unreasonableness of being roused at such an ungodly hour, well, it is to the further default of their own characters. I expect we have quite unsettled you by appearing like a band of pillaging vagabonds at your breakfast table, and without so much as a card delivered beforehand by way of warning. I beg you accept my apologies, mam'selle. I should never have countenanced such behavior had I discerned their intentions ahead of time."

Though the words sounded stilted and were delivered in a petulant tone, Renée had recovered enough of her wits to sense the apology was sincere, meant to convey the fact that he was as ill at ease with the situation as she. His eyes, when she dared look into them, came briefly out of their squint, and she imagined she could see in their clear gray depths the encouragement she needed to regain control over the wild beating of her heart.

"There is no need to apologize, m'sieur," she said quietly, determined to keep her voice from breaking. "I am sure it could not be helped."

Something flickered briefly in his eyes—was it relief or admiration? A moment later he executed another, less flamboyant bow and returned to his seat. As she watched him retreat, her fingers throbbed, and she realized there had been an ungovernable tautness in his grip. He had been wound as tightly as a spring beneath the calm facade, not at all certain what her reaction was going to be.

Knowing this, knowing she was not alone in her confusion and panic, she was able to hold her trembling hands folded in her lap, and even to muster a polite smile as she turned to Vincent.

"You must forgive my own lack of manners, m'sieur, for we were not expecting you until week's end."

"I had business in Warwick. It brought me away from London sooner than expected."

"I see." She moistened her lips. "And my uncle?"

"I am told Lord Paxton's gout has flared up again," Roth provided, "giving him an excuse to remove himself from the emergency House debates, so it should not surprise you to see him as early as tomorrow or the day after."

"Is it true," Hart inquired, dabbing his mouth with the napkin, "there is nothing but squabbling and bickering going on in political circles these days? I have heard that Fox stands on one side of the floor demanding our armies be brought home from France, while Mr. William Pitt has braced himself on the other insisting we must dispatch our navy to the Mediterranean at once before this upstart Napoleon takes all of Italy and seriously threatens our trading routes."

"I would not have guessed you to be political, sir," Vincent declared. "Or to give a fig's ass what our armies do."

"I'll have you know, sir, I care very much indeed, and am in complete agreement with Mr. Pitt."

Even Roth looked surprised. "You condone our making war on two fronts? Of leaving our coastlines vulnerable to attack while the navy is sent off to defend a strip of land a thousand miles away?"

"Not just the land, dear chap. He who commands Italy, commands the Mediterranean, and I would condone anything that would preclude the necessity of doing without our India trade for any length of time. Can you imagine not being able to procure the most basic staples? Why, at the very least we could expect to fall an entire year out of fashion for every shipload of silks waylaid by some devilish French blockade. I swear it is enough of a travesty to discover we are already lagging far behind the Italians and Spaniards in their quality of lace and silver. You need only look here, at this flounce"—he thumbed the cuff of lace that jutted from his coat sleeve—"made not ten miles from here and so unremarkable in quality and character as to verge on an embarrassment." He clucked his tongue in disdain and this time, in the absolute silence that followed, Renée could hear little more than the sound of her own blood rushing past her ears.

Vincent glared at Roth. "Is this absolutely necessary?"

"I'm afraid so, especially if we expect to have any success in our efforts to capture Captain Starlight. To date, we have not had many volunteers in that respect, and it would be foolish to refuse even a modicum of expertise if offered."

Renée could not help the bewildered look she sent along the table this time, but Tyrone deferred again to Roth by way of a waved fork, indicating that his mouth was too full of buttered parsnips to offer an explanation.

"It appears I am once more guilty of the error of omission," Roth sighed. "I neglected to mention Mr. Hart is our esteemed Surveyor of turnpikes, and to that end, with the possible exception of Starlight himself, there is no other man in the five parishes as familiar with every hill and dale, every patch of gorse and stretch of bog along every turnpike between here and London."

*✴ ☽*

# Chapter 12

Renée's sense of reality took another swift, unsettling spin. The Surveyor of turnpikes? The man in charge of designing, laying, and overseeing the construction and repair of roads throughout the parish was the same man who took apparent delight in robbing the travelers who used them?

The buzzing in her ears seemed to have grown louder as she turned to Roth. "I beg your pardon, m'sieur?"

"I said: You mentioned you had errands to run today. Nothing too urgent, I trust?"

"No." She swallowed hard to clear her throat and sat a little straighter. "No, I—I had heard there was a fair in town today and thought Antoine would like to see it. He has not been feeling well these past few days and—"

"And you were intending to go alone? Without an escort?"

"Mrs. Pigeon would be with us. And Finn, of course."

"Of course." Roth's smile was slow to form. "I only ask because there has been another incident."

"A coach was waylaid on the Lutterworth turnpike early last evening," Corporal Marlborough explained. "Some of the evidence indicates it may have been the work of Captain Starlight."

"*May* have been?" Roth arched a brow.

The young officer flushed. "There is some room to doubt he was the true culprit. The robbery was particularly brutal in nature and did not follow the pattern of any of his former outings."

"In *your* opinion."

"In m—my opinion, yes sir."

"Which I do not recall soliciting."

Marlborough's flush darkened and he sat stiffer in the chair.

"He viciously pistol-whipped one of the passengers," Roth continued, "and shot another outright in the leg. All for a meager profit of three guineas and a cheap cravat pin."

"How appalling," Tyrone exclaimed. "Early evening, you say? Are we not even safe venturing forth for dinner or a social game of whist without having to fear being dented on the head?"

"I have increased the patrols," Roth assured him. "Moreover, my men have been ordered to challenge their own fathers should they be found out at night without a reasonable explanation."

"I was accosted last night myself," Vincent grunted. "By a brigade of your overenthusiastic militiamen on the road to Berkswell."

"Barely a company of ten men," Roth countered wanly, "who were merely doing their duty. Had you troubled yourself to inform me you had arrived in Coventry early, it might have spared you the inconvenience of being brought to headquarters, where I, as it happens, was already inundated with half a dozen *gentlemen* all proclaiming their innocence and outrage at being waylaid."

"If you think I am going to account to you for every damned waking moment I am in this farmer's market"— his gaze followed Roth's as it flicked in Renée's direction and the hand he had been about to slam on the table was withdrawn—"you have a deal of re-thinking to do."

Roth only smiled. "Speaking of heads being dented"—he leaned forward and set a silver flask on the table in front of him—"you would not happen to know to whom this belongs, would you?"

Renée called upon every last ounce of will she possessed to keep her expression blank. She was still feeling faint from the corporal's revelation that there had been another robbery—a brutal robbery—last night and wondering how to discreetly tear the cravat pin out of her chemise and fling it on the floor before it burned a hole in her skin. She did not need to be confronted with the silver flask Finn had left behind at the Fox and Hound Inn after knocking Roth over the head with the candlestick.

"If you do," Roth was saying, "I should dearly like to return it to the owner with my compliments."

"No," she murmured. "I am afraid I do not recognize it, m'sieur."

He tapped his badly gnawed fingertips on the silver and glanced thoughtfully in Antoine's direction. "You boy? Do you recollect seeing it before?"

Startled that someone should have noticed him sitting so quietly at the end of the table, Antoine's clear blue eyes lifted from the object he had seen too many times to recount and gazed steadily back at the colonel.

*Stick pins under my fingernails and tear out my toenails and I would not tell you.*

"What did he say?" Roth looked politely at Renée.

"He said no, m'sieur. It is not familiar to him."

"Well, blast me if it isn't a fine piece of work," Tyrone declared. He reached over and plucked the flask out of Roth's hand, angling it into the sunlight to peer at the guild mark. "English made, I vow. Wickes . . . or possibly Netherton. Sure you didn't win it in a game of chance, Colonel?"

"I prefer to make my own luck, thank you, not rely on a toss of cards or dice."

"Pity, that. I fancy m'self quite the deft hand at trumps. But pray tell me you've not forgotten about the soirée this evening at Fairleigh Hall?" He glanced across the table at Renée. "I beg you say you will be attending, mam'selle, for I should so like to know there will be a friendly hand there I can rely upon to rescue me."

"Rescue you from what?" Vincent asked gruffly.

"Well, it seems Lady Wooleridge is determined to pair me off with her daughter—you must know the one: she sports as fine a mustache as my great-uncle Horatio. At any rate, her dear mama—who is not so dreadfully shy of nasal fleece herself—seems to think if we stroll the gardens together it must result in breathless infatuation and an immediate betrothal." He shuddered delicately and rolled his eyes. "Can you imagine?"

Renée had not been aware of any invitation, and started to say as much, but her reply was cut short by Roth. "Indeed, Edgar was just telling me he was looking forward to sampling Lord Wooleridge's cellar tonight. And to winning back the thousand guineas he lost the last time they played hazard together."

"Gad, yes." Tyrone widened his eyes appreciably in Vincent's direction. "His tables have been known to go on for days at a time. Thank heaven I have never acquired a fondness for dicing games, although," he waffled his wrist as if he was shaking invisible cubes, "it does show off one's cuffs to good effect."

Roth's teeth ground together momentarily before he turned to Renée. "You needn't worry that you will be held hostage at the Wooleridge estate until the dice have lost their spots. I doubt Edgar would expect you to endure much past, oh, midnight or thereabout."

Renée's heart gave one last resounding beat before it quieted to a dull thud. So that was why they were here, she thought. To make sure she kept her rendezvous with Captain Starlight.

She thought of her valise packed and ready for flight, and she remembered the fly she had seen that morning trapped against the windowpane, the open air and freedom within sight but impossible to reach. Foolish as it was, she felt a pang of guilt now for not having taken the time to open the window and let it out.

"I should probably find Finn and tell him our plans have changed," she said quietly.

"Mmm." Roth had to swallow a mouthful of hot tea before he could speak. "Let the boy go instead; he appears to be finished with his meal, and I'm certain our conversation will do little more than bore him. Marlborough may go with him. Take the boy outside and . . . show him the horses, or . . . whatever."

Antoine waited for his sister's nod then quit the room with as much subtlety as a cat running from a bucketful of scalding water. The corporal rose at a much more sedate pace, obviously resenting the perfunctory dismissal. When he was gone and the door closed behind him, Hart sighed extravagantly.

"I am still somewhat in the dark as to why *I* have been included in this early morning concourse. Surely—ha, ha—you do not envision me hoisting a petard and joining the hunt for this rogue Starbright? Dash me if I can even recall the last time I held a pistol, much less hoped to fire one."

"You prefer swords, do you?" Vincent asked dryly.

"I agree the rapier is by far and away the gentleman's weapon of choice. Alas, I cannot profess to any excess of skill m'self, more's the pity." A pained expression came over his face as he massaged his wrist. "An unfortunate breakage in childhood left me with a lamentable weakness in the bone. Still and all," he added, brightening, "I attend fencing instruction every month to keep apprised of the latest techniques and style. Only last week Lord Cavendish claimed it to be strictly de rigueur to keep one's waistcoat buttoned fully to the throat while dueling, and that the proper footwear must include no less than a three-inch cuff on the boot. There was quite a heated debate on that point. The gallery, m'self included, was clearly in favor of two."

Vincent shifted in his seat and shot another bristling glance in Roth's direction, but the colonel only laughed.

"Have no fear, Hart. The only assistance we require from you is in the form of your maps. I confess I would not even have thought of you had an aide not mentioned the repairs you made recently on the Birmingham turnpike."

"*Augh*, yes. A frightful mess that was too. Holes large enough to swallow a coach-and-four whole, but not a spare pence to be found for new gravel until the earl of Kenilworth put his teeth through his tongue driving along it one rainy Sunday. Suddenly, they were all a-froth to have the workers conscripted, the gravel hauled, and the pocks filled. Gad. I had to use convicts to supplement the work force. But m' maps"—his powdered lashes swept down in a gesture of false modesty—"they are admittedly the best to be had anywhere and should tell you all that you desire to know, not only about the road, but the surrounding terrain. Had you permitted me to stop in at my office first, of course, they would have been here now and I there, but you insisted on rushing about"—he emphasized the words by waving his fork in a figure eight—"and thus I had to dispatch my man Dudley to fetch them."

"The cripple?" Vincent asked.

"He has a slight limp," Hart acknowledged, glaring down his nose. "Which in no way impedes his mental abilities. And if I do say so m'self, his artistic touches allow us to command the top prices for our designs and reproductions. You will not find a more meticulous eye or a more skilled hand for capturing the wonders of nature in paint and ink."

"I am counting on that, sir, for our goal is to capture Captain Starlight," Roth declared. "To do this we have to know every copse of trees, every outcrop of rock, every potential hazard or hiding place ahead of time."

"Indeed." Tyrone looked more interested in the apple he was dissecting, and Renée suffered through another wave of lightheadedness. Roth was once again two feet from his quarry, blithely unaware he was about to discuss how best to catch him unawares in a trap.

"And where, might I inquire, were you anticipating this final dénouement to take place?"

"I cannot be specific," Roth said, "but I would hazard to say—and you can lay a heavy wager on it if you like—he will be caught somewhere within the boundaries of this parish, before the fortnight is up."

"How intriguing. And how teasingly vague."

"Necessarily vague, I'm afraid. Any one of a score of places within a five-mile radius of Harwood House and a ten-mile radius of Coventry offer the perfect conditions for an ambuscade. What we need to know from your maps and your intimate knowledge of the area, is which ones he is most likely to favor, affording the best chance of success and the most avenues of escape."

"But why the deuce do you suppose he would attack a particular coach on a particular road, on any particular night? His success, as I understand it, is mainly due to his extremely annoying lack of predictability—is it not?"

"I am confident his sense of greed will win out over caution this time. The bait we are offering up should prove to be too tempting to resist."

"Ah. I see. Well, of course," Tyrone paused long enough to run his tongue along the inside of his cheek to dislodge a small piece of apple, "naturally I will do what I can to help. I shall try m' very best to think like a nefarious highwayman."

"A strain, I realize," Roth said, smiling again. "But perhaps if you approach it like more of a game—"

"A game?" The powdered eyebrows shot upward and the buffed fingertips danced together with delight. "If I predict correctly, shall I win a prize?"

Vincent cursed and scraped suddenly to his feet. "I'll

give you a prize, you bloody ponce! I'll let you keep your teeth." He tossed his linen napkin on the table and glared at Roth. "I want a word with you. In private."

"Can it not wait five more minutes?"

"No. It can't."

Roth watched him stride angrily out of the breakfast room then carefully set his fork and knife aside. "Forgive me. I suspect we are all suffering from a lack of sleep last night. This should not take long."

He did not look at all pleased as he took his leave, following Vincent out into the hallway. Not more than a second or two passed before the door was yanked shut behind them and angry footsteps could be heard echoing along the length of the wood floor. While the sounds grew fainter, neither Renée nor Tyrone moved so much as a muscle. His eyes remained fixed on the door; hers stayed fastened to his face, fascinated to watch his features ease out of their pinched affectations. A clock nearby ticked off the seconds it took for her to rouse the ability to speak, and when she did, the words came out strained, cracking with anger and amazement.

"I cannot believe your audacity, m'sieur," she hissed. "Coming here like this. Posing as the Surveyor of turn-pikes. Has no one guessed?"

"No one in the past four years since I purchased the appointment," he admitted grimly. "And it was not my idea to come here today, mam'selle. I had barely made it home through my back door when they were pounding at the front. I lost another five years of my life when the coach turned into your lane, for they did not tell me ahead of time where we were bound and by the time I guessed, it was too late to do anything without raising any suspicions. I am"—he paused for emphasis—"truly sorry, Renée. If I could have spared you this, I would have. Although I must confess, you did very well. Better than me, I warrant, since I fear I have sweated rings down past my breeches."

"I could have fainted dead away. Or screamed. Or given you up a hundred different ways."

"But you didn't," he murmured. "You were very brave and I find myself with a desperate craving to kiss you right now."

She looked at him in horror. "You must not say such things. Or even think them. It is difficult enough sitting here looking at you and knowing . . ." She swallowed a small gasp and squeezed her lashes tightly shut.

"I meant what I said, Renée. I had no way of warning you." He waited a moment, and when she still had not opened her eyes he edged forward slightly. "*Courage, ma petite*. You are not going to faint on me now, are you?"

She opened her eyes and looked at him. Sunlight was striking the side of his face, making the ridiculous carousel of rolled curls glow like a bubbled halo, but all she saw was a mad, reckless fool who did not have the sense or sensibility to be frightened. She tried to draw a deep breath, but her corset was binding, the sun was hot, and the room stifling. Any air to be had was stale with the smell of cooked mutton and pooling grease.

"Did you rob that coach last night?"

His face hardened a moment. "I beg your pardon?"

"Did you do it?"

"You mean, did I pistol-whip one man, shoot another, then come here and make love to you all night? I would have to be a pretty cold-blooded bastard to do that, don't you think?"

Her hand was pressed against her bodice, the fingers splayed like a pale star over the blue velvet. The cravat pin was biting into the tender flesh of her breast and she could not think at all.

He was suddenly standing, towering over her. "Come. Walk with me."

"Wh—here?"

"Anywhere; it doesn't matter."

He did not give her the opportunity to balk as he

tucked a hand beneath her elbow and levered her firmly to her feet.

Once out of the sickly yellow glare of the breakfast room, the air was noticeably cooler and less cloying, and Renée was able to hold a breath long enough to bring some color back into her cheeks. Tyrone's supporting hand remained rigid under her arm as they walked along the hallway, his long strides forcing her to take two steps for every one of his.

Halfway along the corridor he steered her toward a set of closed doors and after a quick glance in both directions, ushered her inside. Renée opened her mouth to speak, but he held up a forefinger, cautioning her to silence until he quickly assured himself there was no clear view into the room from the terrace outside or gardens below. Satisfied they could not be seen by any prying eyes, he retraced his steps to where Renée stood trembling by the door, and with the softest of muttered oaths, crowded her gently up against the wall, took her face between his hands, and kissed her.

\*

"Pretend it is a game, by God?" Vincent's boots made angry crunching sounds on the gravel drive as he approached his carriage. "That bloody ponce has enough difficulty pretending he is a man!"

Roth paused a moment at the door of the coach, then climbed the step and joined Vincent inside. It was an enormous berline built for comfort, made of black mahogany, its surfaces varnished to a mirror gleam. Large enough to travel six, the seats were padded leather and sank pleasantly beneath his weight. There were windows on each side panel as well as the doors, making the interior as bright as the grounds outside and as Roth watched, Vincent leaned forward and pushed a hidden clasp beneath the lip of the seat opposite them. A wooden panel slid open to reveal a cupboard containing gold-rimmed glasses and a bottle.

"Cognac," Vincent grunted. "New shipment in last week. The real stuff, straight from France. Strong as hell and just as necessary if I am not to smash that bloody fool to pulp the next time he flutters at me."

"I shall endeavor to keep him at a safe distance," Roth mused. "But you must also promise not to commit any violent acts, at least until he has served his purpose. Delicious," he agreed, sampling the liquor. "Trust the Frenchies not to let anything so trivial as seven years of revolution deter them from making the finest spirits this side of sin."

Vincent swallowed the brandy then wiped his mouth with the back of his hand. "The girl looks nervous. Are you sure she is going to hold up?"

"She will do just fine. She loves her brother very much."

Vincent's lip curled at the corner. "I still don't see why you wouldn't let me bring in some of my people. A few broken bones, a few twisted titties, and we would not only find this Captain Starlight, but we would have the pleasure of dealing with him ourselves instead of having to hand him off to the courts."

Roth glared at Vincent, finding it a drain on his patience to have to explain yet again why a private manhunt, complete with broken bones and twisted body parts would only draw unwanted attention to themselves.

"You will still have your chance to slit his throat and knot his tongue into a cravat, if that is the vengeance you crave. But in the meantime, we have a militia three hundred strong at our disposal and the righteous indignation of the wealthy citizens of Warwickshire to help us flush this rogue from his lair and bring him to justice."

"Your brand of justice, maybe," Vincent muttered. "But there isn't another bastard within five hundred miles stupid enough to rob me and think he can live to laugh about it."

"Well, this one is still living and thriving five months after he undoubtedly laughed himself all the way home. Bound up in red ribbons, indeed. I won't even hazard a guess as to which head you were thinking with when you thought to dally naked in a coach with a whore or to lavish jewels upon her."

Vincent drained his glass and poured himself a second. "I wasn't *lavishing*. I was merely amusing her with a few trinkets."

"Yes, and to this day, I am still amused, still wondering why our property was not safely locked away"—he tipped his head to indicate the hidden compartment—"where a man with several hours on his hands would never have found them, let alone a road thief with minutes to spare at most."

"I had made the trip before and never met with any trouble."

"Next you are going to tell me you have never met a whore like Doris Riley, either?"

Vincent looked him straight in the eye. "Frankly, no. I haven't. Given the right incentive, she could suck the skin off a green apple."

"A commendable talent, I am sure. Had I known an avid pair of lips could make such short work of your common sense, I would have found another way of transporting our goods out of London. Now we are short nearly ten thousand pounds' worth of gems and jewelry, and you sit there with a lewd grin on your face reminiscing about green apples."

Vincent's ham-like fist closed around the brandy glass, looking for all the world like he would have liked to smash it into Roth's face, and for a moment, the colonel's amber eyes glittered, hoping the arrogant oaf would give him an excuse to draw his sword. Vincent was not quite that stupid, however, and Roth was almost disappointed when the glass went to the thick lips instead and shot back the contents.

"I gather you have not heard from any of your contacts about anyone attempting to sell any more of the gems Starlight stole from you that night?"

Vincent shook his head. "There are so many damned Frenchmen pawning their family heirlooms these days it is difficult to keep track of who is selling what, but no; nothing else has turned up apart from the one necklace, and we were lucky at that. Starlight appears to be rather well-connected himself."

"And clever," Roth mused. "He has probably broken most of the settings down by now; if that is the case, he could sell the jewels one at a time as the need warranted and live comfortably on the profits for years."

"If that *is* the case," Vincent muttered, "no one would be able to trace the stones back to us or connect them to the unclaimed treasures of dead aristocrats."

"In most instances, I would agree, and for that we can be somewhat grateful. But eventually, Starlight will have to find buyers for the bigger pieces, and when he does—"

"The thefts will still be traced back to him," Vincent argued. "He will take the blame, not us."

"No," Roth murmured with disdain. "Not us. Not unless—and until—he tries to hawk a certain brooch that belongs to a certain suite of rubies that half of London saw you string around your fiancée's neck."

"I had no idea at the time—"

"You had no idea, period. You acted without thinking in another moment of flagrant, misguided braggadocio, the ultimate example of which—dare I call it inept lunacy—was to present your fiancée with jewels she and half the displaced émigrés in England would readily recognize as having once been the property of the late Duc de Blois." Roth glanced sidelong at Vincent. "Did you bring them?"

Vincent set his empty glass aside and leaned forward

again, feeling behind the alcove that had held the bottle for a second catch concealed at the back of the cupboard. When it sprang open, he reached inside and withdrew a blue velvet case. A flick of one blunt-tipped finger released the tiny gold hasp, and as he lifted the lid, the light fell on a glittering bed of rubies and diamonds.

Roth's reptilian eyes widened in appreciation. The necklace was displayed in the center of the box around a mound of more crushed velvet. Seven rows of rubies, each circled by a ring of tiny diamonds, were strung on gold wire, the links of which had been fashioned to resemble overlapping scales. Each row of stones was progressively larger and heavier than the one above, descending to a deep vee in front where a single ruby the size of a robin's egg hung suspended from what looked like the jaws of a dragon. Earrings were pinned to the velvet above the necklace and a matching bejeweled bracelet was tacked across the bottom.

"Exquisite," Roth breathed. "Truly priceless."

Vincent only chuckled. "If you think so, then you reveal your own ignorance, Roth, for *these* gems are only worth about . . . oh, a hundred guineas or so, all told."

Roth glanced at him sharply. "What do you mean? These are the Dragon's Blood rubies, are they not?"

Instead of answering, Vincent fished beneath his coat to an inside pocket, and a moment later held up an unmounted gemstone.

Setting it on the floor of the coach, he struck it hard with the heel of his boot and ground the residue beneath three, four twists. When he moved his foot, the "ruby" had disintegrated into a coarse pink powder.

"Glass," he announced smugly. "On their own, they pass well enough, but next to the genuine stones, they look as real as red carbuncles." When he saw the look on Roth's face his lip curled up at the corner. "Surely you didn't think I was going to put the real suite at risk?"

"But you were, of course, going to tell me."

"I'm telling you now, aren't I?" He snatched up the bottle and poured himself another healthy portion of brandy.

"You *might* have told me before."

"And spoil the surprise? What difference would it have made anyway? You weren't planning to steal them for yourself, were you?"

"Don't be ridiculous. What need would I have to steal a single set of jewels that I dare swear I could never reveal in public anyway—or sell in private—without waking up one morning to find a fish hook through my spine?" He paused a moment to regain his composure and offered a wan smile. "And the real stones?"

Vincent pursed his lips and swirled the brandy around his glass. He tilted his head to indicate the compartment beneath the seat, and this time it was Roth who leaned forward and reached inside, withdrawing a second, identical square case, this one in black velvet. He sat back and balanced it on his knee while he unsnapped the clasp and lifted the lid.

The three pieces were identical to the first suite with the exception that these stones, when he tilted the box to catch the sunlight, came alive. The diamonds threw sparklets of reflected light onto the ceiling and walls of the coach, while the rubies glittered in every hue and intensity of red imaginable. He laid the box flat a moment and snatched up the first set of jewels, holding them side by side, angling them this way and that, noting the now-obvious differences.

"Like I said," Vincent used his glass to point to the fakes. "They will hold up on their own. And if anyone cares to look close enough, the Jew who made them for me even duplicated the patterns in the gold scales."

"Amazing," Roth murmured, looking from one suite to the other. "They are perfect. Almost *too* perfect. But by God, this could prove to be an exceptional stroke of good luck. Only last week Paxton was caterwauling in a panic because he had heard someone was making inquiries. An agent for the French government, a man by the name of Dupardier had heard a rumor that the Dragon's Blood suite had surfaced in London."

"Well, we have the fake gems to display now."

"Indeed, and if anyone asks to examine them, we will encourage them to do so to their heart's content."

Vincent grimaced. "Is that why you summoned me here like a stableyard lackey? On the off chance that someone in this"—he searched for the appropriately derogatory words—"blazing hotbed of society will come at us with a quizzing glass and an overabundance of curiosity?"

"I summoned you here," Roth said tersely, "because I have only just discovered that we have another problem."

Vincent sighed. "What now?"

"Well, as you can appreciate, when Dupardier started asking questions, I thought it prudent to make some of my own inquiries and it seems the estimated value the Jew gave you for the rubies was somewhat in error."

"In error? How?"

"Apparently he did not take into account the long and somewhat illustrious history of the jewels or the family dynasty to which they belonged. Sold individually, the bracelet, necklace, earrings, and brooch would indeed fetch a combined sum of perhaps forty or fifty thousand pounds. Sold as a complete suite however"—he paused and gave his head a small shake of disbelief—"I have been told it could easily bring four times that amount."

"Two hundred thousand pounds?" Vincent's brows crushed together in a frown. "For a few strings of rubies?"

"Ahh, but it seems these are not just any rubies, dear fellow; evidently they date back to the Crusades. The unmounted stones were captured in the fall of Jerusalem and presented to Eleanor of Aquitaine by her son, Richard the Lionheart. They were eventually given to her champion, a dark knight of some repute, in payment for a lifetime of loyal service. The knight then bequeathed them to one of his sons, Eduard FitzRandwulf de Blois, who eventually had them fashioned into the suite you possess today."

"So they're old, is that what you're telling me?"

Roth's fine rack of teeth made a disdainful appearance. "They were called the Dragon's Blood suite after some dark family secret, lost to the ages, but they are considered to be one of France's most important treasures because of the pearl."

"The pearl?" Vincent's frown deepened as he looked into both boxes, seeing only rubies and diamonds.

"It was mounted in the brooch," Roth explained patiently. "It was a gift from Aquitaine to her granddaughter, Eleanor of Brittany, who in turn presented it as a token of gratitude and affection to the same Eduard FitzRandwulf de Blois after he staged a daring rescue to save her from certain death at the hands of her uncle, King John. There is a further rumor concerning a son born to Eleanor of Brittany, who eventually married one of the de Blois offspring, but—"

"You are losing me quickly, Roth. Is there a point to all of this?"

"The *point* is that the value lies solely with the one piece, and more specifically, with the pearl, named after the princess—the Pearl of Brittany. It is, I am told, of such a unique color and size, there is no other like it and without the brooch to prove the provenance of the suite we might just as well have a boxful of pretty glass."

Vincent's frown deepened. "I don't even remember seeing the damned thing."

"I do. It was quite exquisite."

Vincent blew out a brandy-soaked breath. "So now you're saying we not only have to catch this bloody highwayman, we have to find the brooch?"

"Precisely."

"And if he refuses to cooperate, or he tells us he has already disposed of it?"

"Then we shall give him two hundred thousand slow, painful reasons to regret he ever crossed our path."

Vincent pondered this a moment before he reached down and pulled a thin, razor sharp knife from a sheath secreted in the top of his boot. "It will be my pleasure," he grinned, "to filet the bastard like a fish, layer by layer until he is a mass of screaming jelly. He will end up telling us things we never wanted to know."

Roth, who had seen his companion's handiwork on more than one occasion, offered up another wan smile. "Yes, well, keep the blade well honed because I made the same promise to Paxton if he attempts to double-cross us again."

Vincent chuckled and returned the knife to its sheath. "I would have thought you, of all people, would have considered greed to be one of the stronger virtues in a man."

"Greed, yes. Stupidity no, although I am surprised his spine turned out to be stiff enough to try cutting us out of the d'Orlôns fortune."

"Could be he just turned sentimental on us," Vincent snorted derisively, "thinking they were all dead. I wager you could have blown him over with a feather when his poor dead sister's children appeared on his doorstep."

"It was a full year's work convincing the Duc d'Orlôns and his sons to trust our network of couriers. And with what he finally put into our vaults, we could have lived like kings the rest of our natural lives. We still can if you do your part and put a brat in her belly right away."

Vincent spread his hands. "I shall give it my best effort, you may be sure. But what if the brat is a girl?"

"You can drown her, like a kitten, and try again. We need our own legitimate heir and the sooner the better. I don't trust Paxton to keep to his end of the deal, not when he has already tried once to cut us out."

"It's a good thing you found those papers in his office."

Roth nodded. "If he had successfully applied to make himself the boy's legal guardian, he would have had sole control over the estate until the boy came of age. When I confronted him with it, the bulbous bastard actually found the ballocks to say he saw no reason why he should have to share with us anyway, since he was, as his dead sister's only living relative, the legitimate trustee. I tell you"—Roth clenched his jaw at the memory—"he is lucky I did not put the bullet through his ear instead of just taking off the lobe. Lucky for him as well that I was content—for the time being, anyway—just to see him piss himself yellow and beg for mercy."

"*Un*lucky for the boy to have come running into the library when he did."

"On the contrary, if we had not found a use for him, he would be long dead by now. This way, the boy shouldered the blame for the shooting and the girl proved willing to do whatever it took to keep him out of gaol. Even marry you," he added sardonically, "despite the lingering odor of the waterfront that clings to you. Once you have your own legitimate heir, however, all three of them become expendable. The treasure in the vaults will be discovered and the lineage traced to the fruit of your loins"—he raised his glass in a mock toast—"grandson to the late, lamented Sebastien d'Anton and the newest little Duc d'Orlôns."

Vincent frowned. "You said all three?"

Roth glared at him. "Good God. You are not going soft on me as well, are you?"

"She is a very beautiful woman. I could be content taking her to my bed every night."

"You will be bored within the month. Ladies of the nobility are not inclined to get down on all fours or suffer splinters in the back from being slammed up against a stable wall. And I warrant the only thing she knows to do with an apple is eat it. Of course, you could always use a little gentle persuasion on her, but bruises tend to attract unwanted gossip."

"You would know this firsthand, of course. What was that woman's name, now? Angelina? Ernestina? Was there even enough left of her face for a proper identification when you got finished with her?"

Roth's eyes glowered a warning. "That was ten years ago, and she was a whore."

"It was seven years ago and she was the daughter of a prominent magistrate. You are forgetting, Roth, I know all of your dirty secrets. I even know where some of the bodies are buried—the ones who couldn't quite bear up to your demands."

Roth flushed as red as the rubies and Vincent was about to laugh at his own wit when the soft crunch of gravel outside the window forestalled any movement or sound from either man. Roth, with his hand already curling around the hilt of his sword, reacted first. He was on his feet and out of the door before Vincent could heave himself off the seat, and by the time he did, the colonel already had the point of his blade against the throat of a man pinned to the side of the coach.

"Who the devil is he and why is he sneaking around like a cur?"

"I was just about to ask the same question," Roth said on a snarl, edging his blade upward, forcing the man up on tiptoes.

"Weren't doin' nothing', sar. Weren't sneakin' nowheres neither. Were just walkin' up to the 'ouse, is all."

"Do I know you?" Roth demanded, his eyes screwing down to slits.

"Th—the name's Dudley, sar. Robert Dudley. Mister Tyrone, sar, 'ee said as 'ow I were to fetch 'is maps an' bring 'em 'ere, an' fetch 'em I 'ave. Right 'ere, sar, see?" He fumbled to point at a bulging leather pouch slung over his hip. "Tied my 'orse to the post, I did, an' were just tryin' to walk past quiet-like is all. I 'eard voices, ye see, an' didn't want to disturb no one."

"So you stood here eavesdropping on our conversation instead?"

Dudley's jaw dropped. "*No sar*! Never 'eard owt. Only 'ears in one ear anyroad, sar, since I fell off'n me 'orse an' 'ee kicked me in the nog."

Roth bared his teeth in another snarl and Vincent sighed from the door of the coach.

"For God's sake, man, let the dog go on his way. You truly are becoming annoyingly obsessed with this Starlight business, imagining spies behind every bush, a thief lurking in the guise of every twisted drudge. I, for one, will happily launch a display of Chinese rockets when you finally catch the bastard and hang him."

Roth's arm lost some of its belligerence and with a snap of the wrist, the sword was returned to its sheath. "Go on then," he said to Dudley. "Get about your business."

"Aye sar. Yes sar. Thank 'ee, sar."

Dudley limped past, his stride broken and uneven, his body slanting drastically to the left each time he put his weight upon the poorly mended leg. Roth continued to glare after him, watching the seesaw gait and bristling under Vincent's coarse chuckle.

"Indeed, a dangerous-looking villain. Another moment and I have no doubt he would have knocked us cold with a roll of maps and stolen the teeth out of our heads."

Roth eyed the bottle in Vincent's hand. "Do you really think it wise to drink yourself into a stupor this early in the day? We still have a great deal to do and it would help to keep *all* of our wits about us."

"*You* still have a great deal to do," Vincent countered with a sneer. "My part doesn't begin until the wedding night."

*  ☽

## Chapter 13

𝒯yrone had his head tipped forward and his eyes closed. His body swayed gently while his hands caressed and seduced, and Renée found herself breathless again, her eyes scalded by a rush of unexpected and unwanted tears.

The room they had slipped into was the conservatory. It was as neglected and musty as the rest of the house, with paneled walls and poorly painted depictions of various musical instruments scattered about to provide the proper atmosphere. Tyrone was at the piano, his profile etched darkly against the glare from the window behind him. Renée was seated on one of the chaises beside him, her back stiff, her head bowed, her hands clasped tightly in her lap as she listened to the sweet, melancholy chords of a sonata. Her father used to say her mother played *forcer les anges de pleurer*—to make the angels weep—and it had been one of Renée's early disappointments in life to discover she had no natural musical talent and embarrassingly little coordination when it came to playing the piano. She used to listen, however. With her eyes closed, she would be transported as Celia d'Anton played to drown out the sounds of looting and shouting in the streets of Paris.

Tyrone had called her brave, but she was not. He had told her to have courage but that, too, was an easy commodity for a reckless man to summon. He had held her and kissed her and comforted her but when she would have asked him a hundred, a thousand, questions, he had set her aside like a child whose bruises have been soothed and taken a seat at the piano, looking for all the world as if it were just another act of another play being staged for the benefit of an invisible audience.

Was that all it was to him? An act? A play? A game of chance? He was a man of so many contradictions she doubted she would understand the rules if he sought to explain them. She was still astounded by the heights of his audacity. Surveyor of turnpikes! A public servant constantly under the eye of town authorities, the military, the wealthy merchants, and the citizens of the parish who paid heavy tolls to the same man who donned a cloak and tricorn by night and robbed them of their profits. How did he do it? Where did he come by the nerve? How did he maintain two such different identities without losing himself completely?

And which part of which impersonation was she seeing now? Thieves did not learn to play the piano or speak in cultured overtones, nor did well-paid civil servants learn how to clamber up vine-covered drainpipes in the dead of night.

As if to chastise her for her thoughts, one of the long, tapered fingers struck an errant note on the keys and the music ended with an abrupt curse. Renée's head tipped up almost at the precise moment Colonel Roth pushed the doors to the conservatory open and struck the bare flooring with the heel of his boot.

"Dash me if I am not saved," Hart declared on an irritated sigh. "I vow m' timing is all wrong today and there must be lead weights in m' fingertips. The right hand is apparently blissfully ignorant of what the left is doing and the exposition is so muddled, the poor composer should have perished from mortification were he not spared the indignity of being dead already. I do most humbly apologize for the cacophony, mam'selle, but I did warn you my interpretation of Chopin's muse was far superior to my rendering of Mozart."

"I thought it was very beautifully rendered, m'sieur," she said with quiet honesty.

He sniffed a dismissal and turned to Roth. "And you, sir! Could you not have stamped your heel any harder in remonstration?"

"A moment more," Roth said wanly, "and I would surely have been inspired to start a country dance."

"Quite so." Hart rebutted the cut with a flick of his wrist. "I dare say you would, having no better knowledge of where to put your feet in genteel company."

"One or two places come to mind as we speak," Roth murmured.

"Dash me. A wit and not yet noon. But I see you have managed to find Dudley, so the day is not entirely lost."

Renée had not noticed the second figure standing in the doorway, a man of medium height and slender build who instantly snatched the felt cap off his head, dislodging a thick lock of sand-colored hair in the process.

"You brought the maps, I presume?" Hart asked in a lazy drawl.

"Aye, sar. Right y'ere." Dudley kept his gaze fixed on the floor until he had limped his way safely past Roth. After a brief, intent look into Hart's face, he glanced cautiously around the room, skipping past Renée several times before finally seeming to muster the boldness to take a hard, lingering look.

"Must I invite the colonel to wrestle you to the ground?"

Dudley blinked and his gaze shot back to Tyrone. "Eh?"

"The maps, m' good man." He pointed. "Do you intend to just stand there clutching them to your bosom or do you imagine you might be persuaded to relinquish them into my care?"

"Oh. Oh, aye sar. Aye. Beggin' yer pardon sar. Y'ere they be."

Tyrone took the pouch and started pulling rolled sheets of parchment onto the piano. There were a score, all neatly bound with ribbon and labeled with a small wax disc. He looked at one or two, discarded another, then threw his hands up in a gesture of impatience. "Well. I simply cannot be expected to make sense of geography on the top of a pianoforte. And good heavens"—he cocked his head as a clock began chiming the hour—"you did say this would not take too long. I've an appointment with m' tailor this afternoon and he can be deuced prickly if he is kept waiting. He sold me a new bolt of Banbury silk, still warm off the loom, so to speak. Seventeen guineas for the lot, but I bought every thread of it despite the extravagance. Simply would not do—would not do at all to have someone like Lord Gravenhurst with his great larded belly walking about in the same toggery. Can you imagine it?"

Roth's teeth gleamed through a fixed smile. "It would be a veritable travesty of fashion I'm sure. Miss d'Anton"—he turned to her and tilted his head slightly through a request—"if it would not be too dreadful an imposition, might we avail ourselves of Lord Paxton's library for an hour or so?"

"Of course." She started to stand up, but Roth held up his hand.

"Do not trouble yourself, my dear. I know the way. I also took the liberty of telling Mrs. Pigeon we would be sequestered there and to bring us some fresh tea. If you will excuse us then?"

Hart gathered up his maps and the two men exited the room, each pausing at the door to vie for the honor of allowing the other to pass first. When they were through it, Renée continued to stare at the space they had vacated, while two paces away, Dudley stared long and hard at her.

*

What he saw was not exactly comforting. He had expected her to be beautiful, for Tyrone rarely stayed out the entire night for anything less. The vaguely dismissive descriptions of yellow hair and blue eyes, however, had only made Robert Dudley curious to know what had sent the usually confident and complacent swordsman reaching for the bottle of brandy so early in the morning. He'd had no chance to ask, what with Roth pounding on the front door scant moments after the first swallow, but being neither blind nor celibate, he suspected the reason was shimmering softly in front of him now.

Calling her hair yellow did not do justice to the silky, silver blond clusters of curls that surrounded the pale oval of her face, and using the word blue to characterize the color of her eyes was like describing the sky as being big. Yet beauty alone was not enough to affect a man like Tyrone. She could have been the homeliest creature in twelve parishes and it would still have been the *look* in those eyes that would have given a man pause. Dark and quiet and haunted, it was the look of a wounded doe trapped in the sightlines of a hunter's musket.

Dudley had not known what he would find at Harwood House and he had made his approach cautiously through the woods hoping to avoid being caught in a trap if one had indeed been sprung. He certainly had not expected to find Tyrone tinkling a sonata on the piano. The *piano* for God's sake. The complete incongruousness of the situation aside, they had been together seven years and in all that time, Dudley had never once known Tyrone Hart even to admit to possessing the ability, much less to play the instrument for anyone outside his own four walls. It was an intensely private passion, his only connection to a past he had forsaken along with the name he had used for the first twenty-one years of his life. The fact that he had been playing Mozart here, now, for her, was nearly as staggering as the announcement he had made while he had been *pouring* the brandy that morning. He had said they were going to steal the rubies anyway, despite the fact Roth would likely be ready and waiting for them.

He, Robert Dudley, was getting too damned old for personal vendettas. This business between Roth and Tyrone had definitely become personal, and if Hart wanted to torment and humiliate Bertrand Roth, that was his prerogative, of course, but Dudley had responsibilities now. He had a wife—well, he would as soon as he and Maggie Smallwood could say the proper words in front of a priest—and in a few months, he would have a child. They certainly did not need the money the rubies would bring; they had acquired more than enough lucre to live out the rest of their days in luxury. Although he did not think it likely he would hear the words from Tyrone's mouth any too soon, it was well past time for both of them to retire. It was only a matter of time before Roth's sheer, dog-like persistence paid off. He was arrogant and cocky and too brutish for subtlety, but he had been in the military longer than Tyrone had been on the highways. He had seen service in Austria and Flanders and had returned to England a wounded hero, lauded for his victories in the war with France.

And while Tyrone had certainly modified his activities in the past months since Roth had come to Coventry, he had only laughed at the colonel's open declaration that he would not rest until Captain Starlight was caught, hung, and his corpse left to rot on the gibbet as a warning to all who sought to follow in his footsteps.

Over the past seven years, Robert Dudley had come to know Tyrone as well as anyone could. As well as anyone was *allowed* to know him, which was not admitting to a great deal. Tyrone Hart was as much an enigma now in his clownish wigs and powdered eyebrows as he had been the first time Dudley had seen him curled on a bed of mouldering hay in a fetid, stinking gaol cell in Aberdeen.

He was as capable of cold, killing violence, as he was of dancing a gavotte with the proper turn of ankle. He could drink his way to the bottom of a rum barrel without batting an eye, or he could nibble on crumb cakes and crook a delicate pinky while sipping tea. He fit everywhere, like a chameleon, yet belonged nowhere, and he seemed content to live for the day, cavalierly dismissing the likelihood that he had no place to go when it was all over and done, except a gibbet and a shallow grave.

Dudley himself had almost had his heart stop when an ebullient Tyrone Hart, newly fitted out in satin breeches and a tailored coat had blown through the door of their rented rooms and announced he had purchased the position of Surveyor of turnpikes for the shire of Warwick. The gold they had taken from the young whiplashed lord, combined with the results of several profitable robberies had not only provided enough cash to deck himself out like a proper gentleman, it had given him the wherewithal and brashness to bribe his way into the coveted appointment as Surveyor of roads. For the ludicrous sum of a hundred pounds a year, he had been given free reign to chart every road, every hill, every forest, every stream, and in return was not only paid a portion of the tolls collected along the turnpikes that crossed his territory, but in his guise as the supposedly bored scion of a distant and disapproving nobleman, he was welcomed into society with the gaiety and oblivion that seemed to be a singular trademark of the aristocracy.

It had been as ridiculously easy, in his paints and powders, to ingratiate himself with the lords and ladies of Warwickshire, as it had been in his greatcoat and tricorn to win the sly cooperation of innkeepers and courtesans.

Dudley felt a cool prickle down his spine and realized Renée was staring at him.

"Have you . . . worked . . . for m'sieur Hart very long?"

"Seven years, miss." He raised a hand and respectfully touched his forelock.

He saw her eyes widen slightly and the blue actually deepen as she stared at the shiny stub where his baby finger used to be. His face had been hidden behind a mask the first time she had seen him on the moonlit road, but he had made a point of drawing her attention to the stub and she had marked it then the way she marked it now.

"I see. And has he always been this . . . foolhardy?"

"Foolhardy, miss?" There was a surprising lightness in his step as he walked back to the door. At the threshold he paused and glanced over his shoulder. "Up to today, I would have said there wasn't a foolhardy bone in his body."

# Chapter 14

$R$enée noted the decreasing rumble of the wheels as the coach began to slow. She suspected Finn would have preferred to keep the horses at full gallop and not stop until they were on the docks of Manchester, but Antoine was still at Harwood House and even though Roth and Edgar Vincent had remained behind at Fairleigh Hall, Renée had no choice but to go through the motions of keeping her meeting with Captain Starlight tonight.

Tyrone Hart had been much in evidence at the soirée this evening. A blaze of silver satin and fountainous lace, he had managed to amuse nearly everyone with his antics, instigating a game of charades after supper that had rendered most of the ladies insensible with laughter. The men had, for the most part, tolerated him and were content to entrust their wives to his company while they focused their attentions on card tables or dicing boards.

Fools, Renée had thought. They considered him a harmless buffoon, yet she could clearly see the rapt look in several of the women's eyes that suggested they knew better. Just how much better, Renée did not want to speculate. She deliberately avoided whatever corner of the room he was in and, apart from the odd, fleeting glance she sent his way, attempted to ignore him as thoroughly as he ignored her.

Not that he would have had much opportunity to approach her. When Roth was not by her side, Vincent's eyes and hands were on her. He acted as if she were already his wife, his property, his chattel, and led her around like a dog on a leash. When the clock passed eleven and chimed the half hour, she was thankful it was time for her to make her excuses. She left Vincent settling into a game of cards and Roth debating politics with their host. Her last glimpse of Tyrone Hart, taken while she waited for Finn to bring around the coach, put him strolling quite casually on the terrace with the buxom and flirtatious Lady Victoria Roswell.

No one had considered it unusual for Renée to depart early or alone. Apart from a few perfunctory invitations to join in on a conversation, most of the ladies had preferred to treat her as if she only spoke French and understood no English words above a single syllable. If it wasn't for the fact that Edgar Vincent's black market trade supplied their husbands with contraband wines and cognac, she likely would have been snubbed as a common whore. And in truth, she probably would not mean much more than that to him if she married him.

Renée drew the lap robe high under her shoulders. The windows were locked against the rush of cool night air but she was chilled to the bone anyway. She had not eaten anything all day. Wine, on the other hand, had taken a smooth and willing path down her throat and the combination of too many glasses of burgundy together with an excess of forced civility had left her feeling on edge. And cold enough to wish she were burrowed under a mound of warm blankets.

This was undoubtedly the most foolish charade of the night, riding out to meet a man who would not be there. They had said all there was to say last night. Moreover, he would not risk drawing attention to himself by leaving the party so soon after her. His nose was probably nestled snugly in the cleft between Victoria Roswell's bosoms by now, resentful of any interruption that might delay his next conquest.

Just as two warm spots of anger started to prickle in her

cheeks, she heard Finn call to the horses and felt a noticeable change in the speed of the coach. It was slowing.
The churning of wheels rolled to a deliberate halt and a
second voice, deep and bristling with authority, advised
the driver to remain in his box and do nothing that might
invite an unpleasant expenditure of a bullet.

Renée peered anxiously out the window but could see
nothing through the distortion of the thick glass. It wasn't
possible, was it?

As the brisk crunch of footsteps approached the side of
the coach, she shrank back against the cushions and
stared at the door. A moment later the latch turned and
the panel swung open to her soft gasp, for she was half
expecting to see a man standing there dressed in a powdered wig and silver satin. Instead, she saw only somber
darkness. It was him; she recognized the scent of wind
and moonlight and saddle leather. But he looked much
like he had the first time she had seen him, his tricorn
pulled low over his forehead, the upper collar of his greatcoat standing tall against his cheeks to guard against any
stray light from the riding lamp.

"I see you came alone. Very good."

His words were crisp and businesslike. When a black
gloved hand reached inside the coach she recoiled as if it
were a snake, for in the other gloved hand he brandished
one of the snaphaunces.

"What are you doing? Why are you here?"

"We arranged to meet tonight, did we not?"

"Well . . . yes, but—"

"Then meet we shall." A mildly impatient wagging of
the gloved fingers invited her to disembark. "If you have
no objections, mam'selle, I still prefer to keep my view of
the surroundings unimpeded."

"But I do object. This is not necessary."

He sighed, releasing a surly breath of alcoholic vapors
past her face. His fingers closed around her wrist and he

all but dragged her out of the seat and down the step to stand beside him.

"I have had a very long and tiring day, mam'selle. Kindly oblige me by sharing a few final moments of your company. Oh, and Mr. Finn"—as he led her away from the coach, he aimed the gun warningly at the silent figure perched in the driver's box—"I would advise you to keep your eyes straight ahead and your ears tuned to the sound of the wind in the grasses."

Renée heard a grumbled retort from the driver's box and saw Finn's shoulders stiffen at the threat. They had been as stiff as his upper lip all day, for he had not taken the news of Roth's visit well. Her valise was still packed, however, and Antoine had been told to be ready and waiting when they arrived home. If it was true her uncle was arriving within the next day or two, they could not afford to delay their departure any longer.

Thus, it was with a small pang of guilt that she felt the sharp facets of the cravat pin dig into her flesh as she walked. She had not dared leave it behind where a snooping Mrs. Pigeon might find it, and although she had exchanged the blue velvet for a softer evening gown of pale pink muslin, the pin was snuggled beneath her breast and she could feel it pressing with each step.

"I did not think you would come, m'sieur," she said, panting slightly at the haste with which he distanced them from the coach. "I thought we had decided there was no further reason to meet."

"It would have been rather ungallant of me to leave you sitting out here in the dark on your own, would it not?"

"You took a terrible risk, m'sieur. Will you not be missed? Will no one wonder where you have gone in such a hurry?"

"Who the devil would wonder? The mustachioed Miss Wooleridge? Had you been paying attention, you might have noticed that I deftly deferred her into the hands of young Winston St Clair, the earl of Kenilworth's nephew—addled as a newt, but by far a better catch."

"And Lady Roswell? Did you defer her as well?"

He stopped abruptly and swung around to face her. "So you *were* paying attention?"

"Do not flatter yourself, m'sieur. It was simply difficult not to notice the two of you laughing and playing together all evening."

"Playing?"

"Charades. Whist. Commerce." Her voice trailed away, taking the unexpected flare of resentment with it. "She is a very beautiful woman. I am sure everyone noticed you together."

"She was only hoping her lover would."

Renée tipped her face up.

"They had a spat," he explained. "She wanted to annoy him."

"By making love with you?"

"I would hardly consider a game of charades to be *making love*."

She waved a hand to disparage the differentiation. "M'sieur, please. Who you walk with, who you talk with, who you take to your bed is none of my affair. I am only questioning why you would come all this way to meet me when it was not the least bit necessary. Nor," she added tautly, "is the gun."

"Force of habit," he muttered, tucking the weapon beneath his coat. "And as it happens, I thought the meeting *was* necessary. In fact," he paused and cast a glance along the empty ribbon of road, "I have absolutely no doubt whatsoever that Roth would know within the hour if the coach was not intercepted."

"You could have arranged to have someone else meet it."

"I could have," he agreed.

Renée looked away. "If Colonel Roth does have someone watching us, he will now be able to report all has gone as planned, yes? There is no further reason to stand out here in the cold."

Tyrone released another huff of breath. Her cloak was glowing pale against the darkness, outlining the slender shape of her shoulders. Wisps of gold escaped the confines of the hood and it took all his willpower not to reach out and push back the offending garment, to remove the pins and combs that held the curls so tightly in place, and to run his fingers through the silky mass until it was free and tumbling over her shoulders like liquid moonlight.

It was indeed dangerous to remain a moment longer than was absolutely necessary. But he had been in a decidedly dangerous mood all evening long watching how Roth and Vincent had hovered over her like hawks. Vincent in particular had put his big possessive paws on her every opportunity that availed itself, and while Tyrone normally paid little heed to mismatched couples other than to decide if the wife was amenable to a night or two of diversion, it put a knot in his gut to think of Renée pinned beneath Vincent's sweating hulk. He had tried to ease the knot by drinking too much and making too much noise and yes, by giving serious consideration to losing himself in Victoria Roswell's soft and opulent body. But every time Renée d'Anton had moved so much as a hand he had noted it. And every time Edgar Vincent had leered into her bodice, he had wanted to take up a board studded with nails and smash it across his face.

After another long moment of inner debate, he reached beneath his greatcoat again and withdrew a small, cloth-wrapped packet. He cradled it in his palm and traced his thumb back and forth over the bumpy surface, then, with a soft soundless oath, he held it out to her.

"Here. Take this."

He heard a soft whisper of silk as she faced him again. "What is it?"

"Just take it. Use it to buy yourself a fresh start somewhere."

Her eyes searched through the gloom for his. She did not make any move to accept the packet and after several more thunderous heartbeats, he swore again and unfolded the layers of overlapped velvet. Nestled at the heart was the brooch containing the Pearl of Brittany.

Even in the poor light, the luster of the pearl shone against the velvet. Daylight would reveal it to be a uniquely pale and iridescent dun color, larger than a hen's egg, mounted in a nest of gold. Coiled around it was a serpent made of rubies, with jeweled claws and two carat-sized diamonds for eyes.

Renée had been but a child of four or five when she had first seen the brooch. The serpent had quivered and glittered in the candlelight and seemed poised to breathe flames, and she had stared so long and hard at it, waiting for it to do just that, the aging Duchesse de Blois had wondered aloud if her eyes were going to pop out.

"Take it," Tyrone said again, his voice gruff at the edges. "Get yourself the hell away from here and sell it for what you can."

Her eyes rose to his again and he sighed, folding the corners of velvet over the brooch, smothering the glittering gems a quadrant at a time. When it was secure, he pressed it into her hand and curled her slender fingers around the bundle of velvet.

"Do not take less than five thousand; anyone who claims it is not worth at least that much is a thief."

Such advice, considering the source, would have made her smile if she were not so overwhelmed. She looked down at the bundle in her hand, then back up at Tyrone. "I do not know what to say, m'sieur. Or how to thank you."

"Just get safely away from here, and from Roth. That will be thanks enough."

Tyrone's keen eyesight picked out the brightness welling along her lashes. With a flush of genuine discomfort, he started to turn back toward the coach, careful to keep his own gaze deliberately averted, but Renée's hand stopped him. She reached out and caught his sleeve, freezing him to a block of stone.

"You did not have to do this."

"It . . . was just a trinket to me. When you asked me about it the other night, it sounded like it meant something to you."

"I knew the Duc and Duchesse de Blois very well," she whispered. "It was their son, Jean-Louis, who—who . . ."

He turned his head slightly.

"I would have married," she finished lamely.

He did not want to look at her. Every shred of common sense remaining, every instinct of self-preservation was screaming at him not to look at her, not to acknowledge the two enormous drowning pools that shimmered in her eyes.

But Renée foiled his good intentions again by sliding her hand up from his sleeve to his cheek and easing aside the staunch wool of his collar enough to press her lips to the muscles that had turned so rigid in his jaw. It was surely one of the most modest and proprietary kisses Tyrone had experienced in many a long year, yet he closed his eyes and felt the effect of it ripple to the soles of his feet. The contact was fleeting, meant only as a gesture of gratitude, but if there had been room in his boots, he was certain his toes would have curled in boyish ecstasy.

It was too much. And it was not nearly enough when what he really wanted to do was hold her and crawl inside her skin and hear her cry out his name like she had last night. She had not called him m'sieur or *capitaine*. She had cried out his name, Tyrone, over and over, her voice so soft and shy and full of wonder it had only encouraged him to do things to make her cry it more.

With a groan he turned, deliberately replacing his

cheek with his mouth. He captured her lips with his, smothering her small, startled gasp. His arm went around her waist, drawing her close and hard against his body. His tongue trailed fire along her lips, then between them, plunging deeply and possessively into the sweet recesses, until she was moaning and trembling and her arms were creeping up and around his neck and she was pulling herself shamelessly into his heat.

This was not supposed to have happened. Renée had been so proud of herself for remaining so calm and cool in his presence. She had dismissed their one night together as just that: one night, with no possibility or probability of ever feeling herself enveloped so passionately in his arms again. Yet here she was being kissed half senseless and seeking to burrow her way, somehow, beneath the bulky folds of his greatcoat so that their bodies might once again thrill to the heat and pleasure discovered there.

Tyrone made it easier for her by opening the wide woolen wings and enfolding her inside, and when he felt her softness press urgently against him, he shuddered like an unseasoned youthling. His blood began to rage and his heart was pounding in his ears. His arms were shaking and his body had grown so hard and tense he came perilously close to pushing her down on the grass beneath him. It took more strength than he thought he possessed to grasp hold of his failing wits and ease her to arms' length, to hold her away in an effort just to *think*.

In the next instant, it was not his conscience screaming at him but the insistent jangle of an alarm going off at the back of his mind. Too late he saw the telltale flash of powder igniting in a firing pan, and far too late he heard the muted *pooft*, followed a fraction of a second later by the loud explosion of a gunshot. He shoved Renée to one side and flung himself in the opposite direction, rolling catlike onto his feet again with both pistols drawn and cocked. The shot had come from the front of the coach, and Tyrone barely had time to bring his guns to bear on the crouched target before there was a second flash of sparks and another thunderous explosion of powder and shot.

*  ☽

# Chapter 15

"*F*inn! No! *Mon dieu* . . . no!" Renée struggled to
her knees, then her feet, cursing the tangle of skirts
around her ankles. Tyrone had pushed her clear and she
had sprawled painfully onto the wet grass, but the shock
and hurt was nothing compared to the fear she felt as she
saw the second shot fired from the coach and heard the
two returning blasts from the darkness beside her. With
both shots, Tyrone's dark shape was briefly illuminated in
the flare of the firing pans and she could plainly see the
rage on his face. His lips were drawn back in a roared
curse and his eyebrows were crushed together in a single
dark line; he had lost his tricorn when he'd somersaulted
and his hair was flown wildly about his face, obscuring
everything but the snarl and the disbelieving fury in his
eyes.

Then she looked at the coach. Finn must have been
watching, must have seen Tyrone pull her into his arms,
and thought . . . oh God, she did not know what he
thought! She only knew she had to stop him!

She started to run back toward the road, hoping to
reach Finn before he could reload and fire again. At the
same time, she heard the snaphaunces being cocked behind her and remembered they were double-barreled.
The second volley of shots tore across the blackness and
thudded into the side of the coach like blows from an axe,
scattering wood chips a dozen feet and blowing the door
clear off its hinge.

Finn was nowhere to be seen and she ran forward again, shouting his name. Behind her, she heard a shrill whistle and the pounding of hoofbeats, and she turned in time to see Tyrone's huge black stallion skid to a halt beside his master and pause long enough for the caped figure to swing himself into the saddle.

"No! Wait!"

But he was already spurring the beast to a gallop, tearing away across the rolling field.

"No," she sobbed quietly. "Wait . . ."

She watched him disappear in the distance and whirled around, remembering the four shots he had fired at the coach.

"Finn! Finn, where are you?"

"Here, dammit. Over here."

She followed the voice to the front of the coach and saw him emerging from under the protective breastwork that curved below the driver's box. His head was bowed and he was cupping the side of his face, and as he took his hand away, she felt something warm and wet splash her cheek.

"You are hurt! You have been shot!"

"The bastard damn near took my eye out!" he screamed. He staggered into the light and when he saw the amount of blood dripping from his hand, he swore again. "Christ Jesus, but he will pay for this! If it is the last thing I do on this earth, I will make him pay for this!"

Renée gasped and stumbled back a half step. The hunched shoulders were no longer hunched, the gray wig had been cast aside somewhere in the exchange of gunfire, and Colonel Bertrand Roth looked every bit as enraged as Tyrone had in the eerie burst of igniting gunpowder.

"*You!*" she gasped. "But where is Finn?"

"Probably at Harwood House by now," Roth growled, pushing past her as he walked to the rear of the coach. He raised the lid of the boot and reached inside, pulling out two more pistols, powder and shot, and his swordbelt. These he set briefly to one side as he tore off the livery coat and replaced it with his scarlet tunic.

"Did you honestly think I would let an opportunity like this pass? Jesus *Christ*!" he swore again, pressing a linen handkerchief to his face.

Renée was stunned. Granted, her departure from the party tonight had been hasty and she had been preoccupied worrying about the meeting ahead, yet she could have sworn it was Finn she had seen sitting high in the driver's box. Roth had been nowhere in sight, but for that she had been grateful, not suspicious.

"Why did you not tell me? I thought it was Finn who was shooting. I thought it was Finn who was shot!"

Roth paused in the act of blotting the blood on his face and, with biting, cruel fingers, grasped her by the arms and swung her around so that she came up hard against the side of the coach.

"And just what the bloody hell were *you* doing? I tried to get a clear shot but it was impossible to see who was who, you were standing so close together. Incredibly close together," he added with a snarl.

Renée fought to keep hold of her senses. How much had he seen? How much had he heard? They had been twenty paces from the coach at the very least and whispering. And it was dark. The moon was just a faint suggestion of illumination above heavy banks of cloud and the lamp had been deliberately hooded.

"I . . . w—was only following your orders," she stammered. "You told me to do whatever was necessary to win his confidence."

"So you *kissed* him?"

"H—he was going to leave, you must have seen that. He was angry. You must have seen that, too, when he pulled me from the coach. H—he suspected it was a trap, that I w—was doing it for the reward. He had only come to tell me he was not going to go through with the robbery, that it was too dangerous."

"And you thought a *kiss* would change his mind?"

"I did not know what else to do. Use every means at my disposal, was that not what you told me?"

He crowded her painfully close against the side of the coach. "And if that hadn't worked, what else would you have done to persuade him? Would you have dropped to your knees and kissed him somewhere else?"

Whether it was just a reaction to the recent, explosive violence, or because she was Renée Marie Emanuelle d'Anton and he had finally pushed her too far, she swung her arm up sharp and fast, slapping him across the cheek with the flat of her hand.

The crack of flesh on flesh was as loud as one of the gunshots and Roth jerked back, startled as much by her audacity as by the strength behind the blow. He was also, clearly, not accustomed to being struck by anyone, let alone a woman supposedly at his mercy. His reaction was instinctive and savage, and he returned with a vicious backhand, catching Renée on the side of her jaw with enough force to send her reeling sidelong into the enormous rear wheel of the coach.

Up to that moment, she had forgotten the velvet-wrapped bundle she clutched in her hand. Thrown against the spokes, she reached out to save herself from the fall and the bundle went flying out of her fingers, landing in the gravel at her feet. The velvet had not been bound tightly around the brooch, and she stared in horror at the winking sparks of the serpent's bright eyes where they glittered in the pool of lantern light.

The next instant, Roth was spinning her again, shoving her back against the coach. His hand was under her chin, his fingers were digging into her throat, and his face was close enough to spray hers with spittle as he spoke.

"I believe I warned you once before about testing the limits of my patience."

She tensed her body in anticipation of another blow and was convinced it would have come had they both not been distracted by the rumble of approaching hoofbeats. Within moments, a full patrol of dragoons emerged from the darkness behind them and halted abruptly enough to cloud the road with rolls of dust.

Roth leaned forward and hissed at her one last time. "We are not finished with this conversation, madam. Not by a far cry."

He thrust her aside and stepped back just as Corporal Marlborough dismounted beside them and offered a smart salute.

"We heard shots and came at once, sir. Good God . . . your face!" He started forward, but a glare from the amber eyes stopped him cold. "Are you all right, sir?"

"Fine, blast you. Did you see him?"

"No, sir. We were less than a quarter mile back and saw no one. Was it him? Was it Captain Starlight?"

"It was him," Roth said, staring over the officer's shoulder.

Renée, pressed against the spoke of the wheel, edged her toe forward so that the hem of her skirt smothered the sparkle of the brooch. She dragged it back, careful not to look down or to draw the attention of any of the dragoons, but she needn't have worried; most of them were waiting for Roth to speak again.

"Are the rest of the men in position?"

"Aye, sir." Marlborough nodded curtly. "As per your orders, there are pickets set up every fifty yards from the crossroads forward, encompassing a two square mile perimeter. A flea could not pass through the line without us knowing it."

Roth's grin, stained red with blood, was pure malice. "So much for the wisdom and advantage of choosing flat terrain. Remember, I want him alive. Wound him if you have to bring him to ground, but I want the bastard alive!"

He walked to the closest dragoon and without preamble, reached up and pulled the man out of the saddle. "I want you, Marlborough, and four men to escort Miss d'Anton back to Harwood House. You are to remain there, alert and on guard, until further notice. As for you, my dear," he swung himself up on the horse and turned to glare down at Renée, "be *assured* we will continue our discussion when this is over."

He offered a brusque, insolent bow and jerked the reins around. A shout started the horses racing away in another boil of dust, into the same darkness that had swallowed the fleeing highwayman.

Corporal Marlborough, his shoulders easing slightly out of their enforced stiffness, looked decidedly uncomfortable when he glanced at Renée. She took a step toward the broken door of the coach, seemed to stumble a moment, but when the young officer rushed forward to assist, she straightened and glared away his offer of help.

"I am quite all right," she said coldly, tucking her own hand beneath the folds of her cloak. "It was just a pebble under my shoe."

∗

As cold as Renée had been on her way to the rendezvous, she was twice as chilled on the seemingly endless ride to Harwood House, not the least because of the shattered coach door. She had nearly fainted before boarding the coach, certain Marlborough had seen her retrieve and conceal the brooch. Her jaw ached where Roth had struck her, and while it came as no surprise that he was an animal and a brute, it was still a shocking blow to what few shreds remained of her composure. She had never, in all her twenty years, been struck or manhandled and Roth had done it twice now. She had no reason to doubt he would do it again, or to doubt Tyrone Hart's warning that if Roth suspected her of double-crossing him, she would see a side of him that would make his previous acts of brutality look mild by comparison.

When the coach rolled to a halt in front of Harwood House, Finn was there, lantern in hand, waiting anxiously to greet her. From the look of utter and abject mortification on his face, she guessed he had been almost beside himself with guilt, and worry. From the wide gash on his temple, she assumed he had not agreed to the substitution peacefully.

"Mad'moiselle, I had no idea—" he began.

"It is all right, Finn. It is over and done, and everything is all right. Where is Antoine?"

"In his room, asleep. I thought it best not to worry him unnecessarily."

She nodded, grateful for at least one small mercy, and started toward the door.

"Miss d'Anton—?"

She stopped and stiffened but did no more than tilt her head to aknowledge Corporal Marlborough's address.

The young officer moved haltingly forward, daunted as much by the small, square shoulders as he was by the threat of murder on Finn's face. "I . . . would just like to say that I—I am sorry if you were inconvenienced in any way tonight. I disagree wholeheartedly with Colonel Roth's methods. He is *not* representative of His Majesty's government and—and if you were insulted in any way or if he said or did anything untoward, I swear on my sword and on my family's honor . . ."

Renée whirled on him so unexpectedly, it was a wonder he did not damage himself snapping to attention. She said nothing, however. There was nothing she could say, either to express the full measure of the contempt she was feeling or to alleviate the young corporal's indignation.

Finn did so with a righteous sniff as he turned and followed Renée into the house. He took the lead when they reached the stairs, exchanging the lamp for a candelabra as they walked down the long corridor to the east wing. Without waiting to be asked, he lit additional candles in her room and added another fat log to the fire blazing in the hearth.

Only then, when it was bright enough to see the dried streaking of tears on her cheeks, did he notice and dare to question the fine drops of blood on the front of her cloak.

"It . . . is not yours, is it mad'moiselle?"

Her eyes required a moment to focus. *"Pardon?"*

He pointed tentatively to the blood. "Not yours?"

She looked down as if seeing the droplets for the first time. *"Non. N'est pas à moi."*

The whisper was more unnerving than the sight of the blood, and Finn quickly assisted her out of the cloak and bade her sit by the fire. He fetched a glass of wine from the sideboard and forced it into her chilled fingers.

"I can only hazard a guess as to what happened after that insufferable Colonel Roth had me manhandled to a back room."

"He took your place," she said quietly. "He wore your coat and a gray wig. Even I thought it was you, and *le capitaine* . . . he would have had but a brief glimpse and assumed it to be you as well."

Finn's upper lip twitched. "We should have anticipated something like this. Roth is definitely not a gentleman, not in any sense of the word." He paused discreetly to refill the glass. "And the captain?"

"We were talking, and—and he must have seen something, for the next thing I knew he was pushing me aside and drawing his guns, and—and . . ." She looked up into the craggy old face. "He must have thought you were attempting to defend my honor, for I do not think he aimed his shots to kill, not at first. But then you . . . Roth . . . fired again, and he—he . . ."

"Assumed, perhaps, that it was not your honor I was attempting to defend, but rather the reward of two thousand pounds I was hoping to gain?"

She swallowed hard and nodded. "The look on his face in that last moment . . . it was very terrible to see."

"Dear me." Finn straightened and ran a finger around his collar to loosen it. "I can well imagine. Lucky for both of us, then, that he is dead."

Her head jerked up. "The *capitaine* is dead? How do you know this?"

"Did you not just say he had a—a 'last moment.' "

"*Oui*, before he called to his horse and rode away."

"He rode away?"

"*Oui*. He fired his guns and forced Roth to duck behind the coach, then called his horse and escaped." Her shoulders sagged forward again. "Of course, I do not know how far he went, for Roth had men waiting all around the fields. They seemed quite confident he would not be able to get past them."

"Then that should teach you not to put too much stock in the British army," said a voice from behind them. "They were equally confident they could defeat Napoleon in Flanders and look what happened."

Finn jumped, sloshing wine out of the decanter as he spun around. Renée dropped her goblet on the floor, scarcely able to believe her eyes as the door to the dressing room was nudged open by a tall black boot and Tyrone Hart stood facing them, the twin snaphaunces primed and cocked in his hands.

"*M'sieur*!" She gasped and leaped to her feet. "What are you doing here? How did you get past the soldiers?"

"I am sorry to see you *have* lost all faith in me, mam'selle. Or did you think I would be so distracted by your sincerity and innocence that I would fail to take the simplest precautions?"

She did not know what to say. The multiple collars of his greatcoat were folded back, the closure itself flung wide to reveal the silver-gray waistcoat and loosened jabot of frothing lace he had worn so primly at the soirée tonight. His face had been wiped hastily clean of cosmetics, but the swarthy, sun-bronzed complexion only served to emphasize the overall menace in the squared jaw and pale, blazing eyes. Once before Renée had compared him to a jungle-cat and the image was even stronger now, only this time, the jungle-cat was on the loose and in a full rage.

"I did not betray you, m'sieur," she whispered. "Neither Finn nor I knew what Roth was planning to do tonight; you must believe that."

Dark, thickly lashed eyes held hers for a moment, then flicked to the elderly valet. When they focused on the gash in his temple, Finn touched it gingerly with a forefinger and scowled.

"Mad'moiselle speaks the truth, sir. I was silenced and brought back here without so much as a by-your-leave."

Tyrone glared a moment longer then aimed one of the snaphaunces at the decanter in Finn's hand. "Is there another glass?"

"Yes, sir. Right away, sir."

"Why have you come here?" Renée asked again. "There are soldiers downstairs and likely to be more on the way when Roth discovers you have escaped his trap."

Tyrone cast a stony glance in her direction. "He could not set a trap to catch himself. And I came here, mam'selle . . . to have another taste of Lord Paxton's fine wine. If you object to my company, you need only scream to bring young Marlborough here at a run."

She blanched at his sarcasm but did not back down from his steady gaze. His face was glistening with sweat and as she watched, a slick, fat bead ran from his temple to the collar of his coat. Where his hair curled forward over his brow and cheeks, it formed damp black corkscrews against the bronzed skin.

"Mad'moiselle—" Finn hastened to rid himself of the decanter just as Tyrone's legs started to buckle beneath him. "I do believe he's about to—"

He caught the highwayman high under the arms as

Tyrone pitched forward. A groan that sounded as if it came from the bottom of Hart's belly lasted until the wiry valet managed to ease his bulk to a less painful landing on the floor. The guns clattered to either side and the pale eyes rolled back until only the whites were showing.

"Finn?" Renée rushed forward. "What is it? What is wrong?"

"Oh dear gracious me."

The valet moved to one side as Renée knelt beside him. He pulled open the upper lapel of the greatcoat, showing her the huge red stain that had soaked most of the lower half of the silver waistcoat.

"I fear he has been shot, mad'moiselle."

"*Shot!*"

"Indeed." He leaned over the unmoving body and thrust a gnarled finger through a hole in the front of the waistcoat. He ran his hand around behind the bloodied silk, removing it a moment later, his fingers smeared red. "I can feel a second hole, suggesting the bullet has passed cleanly through."

"What should we do?"

"Do?" Finn stared at his hand, then at the highwayman again. "Well, I suppose we should attempt to staunch the flow of blood first. He seems to be leaking rather a great deal."

Renée ran into the dressing room and gathered up all the towels and linens she could find. Finn placed a thick wadding over the front of the oozing wound, but when he sought to do the same to the back, the bulk of the greatcoat hindered him.

"We shall have to get him undressed—remove the coat, anyway."

While he worked to free Tyrone's arms from the heavy woolen garment, Renée stripped the counterpane and blankets on her bed and tossed most of the pillows aside.

"I would hasten to offer a word of caution, mad'moiselle," Finn advised, not even looking up.

"While I realize the servants are by no means the epitome of efficiency, it would not do for one of them to accidentally stumble upon an injured man in your bed. Indeed, it would not do to find him anywhere in the house at all."

"You are not suggesting we turn him out the window!"

"I doubt he would survive the fall," Finn remarked dryly. "At the same time, we cannot leave him here. If we knew how the blazes he got past the guards! Have you any scissors?"

"*Quoi?*"

"*Ciseaux.* He was jostled quite enough in removing the outer garment; I shall have to cut away the rest to save him giving up another pint of blood."

To judge by the quantity soaking his clothes and beginning to seep onto the floor, it did not look to Renée as if he had another pint to spare. She fetched the scissors and watched anxiously as Finn sliced through the elegant silk waistcoat and fine linen shirt beneath. A bright bubble of fresh blood welled up in the candlelight and in an attempt to keep her stomach from rebelling against the sight of the blackened, ravaged flesh, she focused her attention elsewhere—on his face as it happened. Where his hair had fallen away from his brow she could see a fine rim of white following his hairline, chalking the dark roots in places where the hairs extended too far down onto his forehead. He must have left the party shortly after she did and raced like the wind to make the rendezvous on time.

Remembering something else, she reached awkwardly under the hem of her gown and removed the velvet-wrapped bundle from where she had tucked it into the top of her stocking. She unwrapped the brooch and cradled it in the palm of her hand, her gaze blurring as she realized he had taken this terrible risk just to give her her freedom.

"Dear foolish m'sieur Hart," she whispered.

"Luckily, no. The shot missed the heart, mad'moiselle, though I warrant not by much."

She blinked and looked up. "*Non*. Hart is his name. M'sieur Tyrone Hart."

Finn's eyes widened out of their creases. "Surely not the same Mr. Tyrone Hart who was here today with the colonel and Mr. Vincent? I only had a brief glimpse, but nonetheless—"

"*Regardez*. Imagine a powdered wig and white face paint. Put lace at his throat and a foolish pout on his lips and . . . *voilà*! He plays the perfect fool to make fools of them all! And look what he has given me tonight!" She held out her hand and uncurled her fingers, letting the soft luste of the pearl shine in the firelight. "He gave it to me so we could sell it and have enough money to sail away to America."

"How extraordinary," Finn murmured.

"That is why we cannot let Roth's men find him. We cannot. We must hide him and keep him safe until he is well enough to look out for himself."

"Hide him, mad'moiselle?" Finn was shocked. "Keep him safe until he is well? Do you have any idea what that would entail? The man needs a doctor. Even if we stop the flow of blood, the wound requires stitching and dressing. And then there is the small matter of your own safety, and Antoine's."

"I have thought of little else these past few weeks," she said softly. "But I cannot run away now and leave him here to die."

"Are you forgetting your uncle is due to arrive shortly? He will be bringing guests and more servants."

She dismissed it with a small shake. "They will all be kept too busy in the family wing to trouble themselves over us. There are four perfectly good rooms at the end of our hall that no one would think to use—"

"You cannot rely on that, child."

Renée sat back on her heels. "Then he will stay here

and I will lock the door and claim I have caught the plague.''

Finn sighed wearily but knew there was no point in arguing. He cast a sullen eye around the bedroom, thought of his own, thought of the small storage closet at the end of the corridor, but dismissed them all as not being completely safe from unwanted intrusions. He looked down at the highwayman again and suspected his concerns were quite possibly premature. The rogue would likely be dead by morning anyway and the dilemma they would be facing then would be how best to dispose of the body.

A sudden, startling crack of thunder had both Finn and Renée jumping and staring at the window. Fat, glistening drops of rain began to splatter against the glass but they barely had time to recover their wits from the one shock when a second, equally ominous pounding began to rattle the bedroom door.

*★ ☽*

# Chapter 16

$R$obert Dudley did not start to worry until the chimes on the library clock tolled five times. He had dozed off in front of the fire, a glass of brandy in his hand, and wakened with a start, dropping the glass and its remaining contents on the hearth. With a muttered curse, he noticed the time. Then, with a hasty glance at the empty desk behind him, realized he was alone.

Tyrone's town house was an unremarkable three-storey building located at the outermost end of the socially acceptable district of Coventry. The decor and furnishings on the first two levels were suited to a bachelor who preferred to take his entertainment away from home. The library was cluttered with books and maps and drawing boards; an adjoining parlor was slightly more presentable, but lacking any personal tastes or touches. Visitors to #33 Priory Lane saw nothing to suggest Tyrone Hart was anything but a bored public servant who worked at overseeing the maintenance and repair of local transportation routes.

The upper level was rarely, if ever, violated by guests. Here were located the private quarters—a massive, darkly furnished bedroom, dressing room, and study. An expensive and exquisitely cut crystal decanter held the finest French cognac north of the Channel, which he could sip while playing the piano in his study, or while lounging in the full-length, waist-high copper and enamel bathtub he'd had imported from the Far East. The bed was a large four-posted tester hung with heavy velvet draperies; the carpets underfoot were plush and thick, covering all but a few strips of the polished oak flooring.

Robert Dudley's quarters, though somewhat less spacious, were no less comfortable despite being located below the main level. He had a large, private bedroom and sitting room situated conveniently close to the kitchens, pantry, and wine cellar. A cook and maid came in every day but the only other servant living in residence was Maggie Smallwood, a petite, dark-haired Irish lass who had arrived at their back door one evening with a note from Jeffrey Bartholomew—a man who'd had his own reasons for wanting to start over in an new, anonymous life—asking if she might be taken on as a housekeeper. The local scrivener had vouched for her character and added further that she was fleeing from a brutish husband who beat her senseless for his amusement, and that any help they might provide would be regarded as a personal favor. As good as his word, Bartholomew had become a profitable source of information for Captain Starlight, while Maggie, after only a month in residence, had won herself a permanent place in Dudley's heart and bed.

He heard her telltale soft footfall behind him now as he was struggling to get down on his good knee to pick up the pieces of broken glass.

"Mr. Tyrone did not come home yet?" she asked.

"Apparently not, though I suppose he could have come in while I was asleep and gone straight up the stairs."

She looked as dubious as he sounded and touched him gently on the shoulder, ordering him aside as she knelt and gathered up the scattered bits of glass. Dudley's eyes softened, as they often did these days when they settled on the growing swell of her belly. There was not much to see through the shapelessness of her nightdress and robe, but he smiled anyway and his hand strayed over to stroke the surprisingly hard bulge.

"You should be in bed."

"So should you," she said. "He's not a lad who needs a candle kept alight in the window anymore."

"He doesn't like to think so, but I still have my doubts." He glanced toward the window, his frown returning when he saw the dull gray light beginning to define shapes and colors outside. "He should have been back long before now."

"Perhaps he got . . . distracted. Perhaps one thing led to another and"—she stopped and leaned into the pressure of his hand—"and well you know how that can happen," she added softly.

He let his fingers drift up until they were caressing the distinct thrust of her nipple. When she had first come to Priory Lane, she had been thin and gaunt, hardly beautiful in any sense of the way with stringy, filthy hair and a bruised look in her eyes. She had kept to herself, working quietly and diligently, and Dudley had pretty much avoided her as well, embarrassed by his limp, self-conscious of the ugly, lava-like scars that ran from his thigh to his ankle. A few mornings of seeing him fight the pain of a leg that had stiffened overnight brought her into his room one night with a salve she had made from herbs and camphor and in spite of his protests, she had insisted on him letting her massage it into the knee. While his recovery was not miraculous, there was a marked improvement in mobility and pain-free mornings. And each night thereafter, as he watched her work her fingers through the corded, mangled muscles, he began to notice how her hair glowed a soft chestnut in the firelight, how her cheeks had filled out and dimpled around each smile, how her eyes sparkled like polished emeralds.

"Yes," he murmured, bending forward to kiss her. "I do know how that can happen—"

A sharp and intrusive rapping on the front door caught them both by surprise. Maggie dropped the shards of glass and Dudley spun around, nearly losing what little balance he had.

"Who do you suppose it could be?"

"Shh." He pressed a finger over her lips and after a moment, struggled awkwardly to his feet. His knee protested the sudden urgency as he limped over to the desk and opened a bottom drawer, withdrawing a long-nosed pistol and checking it quickly to insure it was primed and loaded.

"Get back down the stairs," he ordered quietly, "and stay out of sight."

"But Robbie—"

"Do it, love. Now. I doubt if Roth or any of his lobsterbacks would show the courtesy of knocking, but all the same, it's a hell of a time for honest folk to come calling. Down you go now. Bolt the door behind you and find Bess."

Maggie nodded, her eyes wide but showing only trust, not fear.

Dudley waited until he heard the rasp of the bolt being drawn across the door before he carried a light out to the foyer. Whoever it was knocked again as if to confirm to a half-asleep servant that he had not been hearing things.

Dudley set the lamp on a side table and tucked the gun into his belt at the small of his back. He ruffled his hair and loosened the front of his shirt, and when he opened the heavy oak door, he was stifling a yawn.

" 'Oo the bluddy 'ell—?"

"Are you Mr. Dudley?"

It was raining hard and Robbie had to squint to see beneath the drooping brim of a wide felt hat. "If I yam?"

"If you are," Finn dragged the waterlogged hat off his head, "Mr. Hart is in dire need of your assistance."

Dudley came instantly alert. Finn's hair hung like gray icicles to his collar and beneath his coat, he wore what looked like a nightshirt hastily tucked into the top of his breeches. Behind him, early morning pedestrians, servants and clerks, mingled with farmers hauling goods to the market. None of them passed so much as a glance at the house as they hurried through the heavy downpour, but Dudley pulled Finn hastily inside and closed the door behind him.

"What happened? Where is he?"

"At the moment, I am afraid, he is in a dungeon."

"*What?*"

"Well, an archaic old tower room, actually, but it brings to mind a dungeon. It was, I fear, the best place we could think to hide him."

"What happened? Start at the beginning and leave nothing out."

"Indeed, well . . . the, er, captain kept his rendezvous with mad'moiselle d'Anton last night, only instead of my driving her to the meeting place, I was summarily dragged off to one side and Colonel Roth—cleverly disguised in a wig and livery—took my place. There was a confrontation and shots were exchanged. The captain managed to elude capture though there were several dozen of Roth's men waiting in ambush. He found his way to Harwood Hall and before he could shoot us, he collapsed on the bedroom floor."

"Collapsed?"

"Did I not mention he was shot? Rather a nasty wound, too, I must say, though I am not an expert by any means. Mad'moiselle Renée was absolutely beside herself wondering what to do when young master Antoine came barging into the bedroom, frightened by the storm. He has dreadful nightmares, you know. They both do, actually, though I would hasten to suggest the young master is—"

"Tyrone," Dudley interrupted. "What about Tyrone?"

Finn quirked an eyebrow. "You did say to leave nothing out."

Dudley glared and he continued. "Yes, well, the young master was equally distraught, what with seeing all the blood and the body, but he came around quite admirably, however, and it was he who suggested the old tower room. I must confess neither Mad'moiselle Renée or myself would have thought of it. In truth, we pass by it every day, three and four times to be sure, but there is a rather sizeable tapestry hung over the entryway and one just never thinks of it being there. Indeed, if not for master Antoine's curiosity—apparently he stumbled into the tapestry one day quite by accident and discovered the niche behind it—I doubt we would even have known there was access to it from the main house. At any rate, it seemed the perfect solution last night and by dint of the three of us exerting a considerable effort, we managed to move Mr. Tyrone into the tower room. Unfortunately, we are none of us experienced in the carrying and moving of somewhat large, insensible bodies, and I regret to say he was bleeding again, rather persistently, right up until I left. We did what we could, of course, but a doctor's services are most urgently required, or I shouldn't hold much hope of him seeing out the day."

Dudley blew out a long breath. It had always been a possibility, of course, that one or both of them could be shot, or even killed, but it was not something one could accept like a report of the weather.

"Mad'moiselle d'Anton hoped you would be able to help. We have a somewhat pressing need of our own to be away from Coventry, but she refuses to leave until the captain is seen into safe hands."

"This happened last night, you say?"

Finn drew himself upright. "I assure you, Mad'moiselle d'Anton dispatched me as soon as it was reasonably safe to do so. As I mentioned, the countryside is swarming with Volunteers. Harwood itself is under intense scrutiny and I was forced to take my leave in a *dairy* cart. I had to bribe the boy with five shillings in order to have him drive me directly to the edge of town, whereupon I walked the rest of the way, not entirely certain of the distance required or exactly which house I was seeking. Indeed, it cost me an additional two shillings to win directions from a grimy-faced urchin relieving himself in a gutter!"

Dudley held up his hand. "I'm sorry. I wasn't thinking. You were right, of course, to be cautious. Where is he wounded—an arm? A leg?"

"Just about here—" Finn pointed to the spot on his ribs. "Thankfully the bullet appears to have gone cleanly through, but he *has* lost an inordinate amount of blood and will undoubtedly lose more if a doctor does not attend him at once."

Dudley thought fast. There was old doc Brockman, but he was too fond of his wine to be reliable. Bartholomew probably knew someone, but that would entail another delay and another outsider knowing. . . .

"If you give me ten minutes to dress and gather up my herbs," Maggie came quietly up behind them, "I can stitch a wound as good as any butcher you might find willing to help at this hour."

Dudley started to refuse the suggestion before it was even fully out, but she silenced him with a small but emphatic *thump* as she set down the stock of the huge Brown Bess she carried. Holding it by the muzzle, she placed her other hand on her hip.

"And if you're after saying no, Robert Dudley, 'tis too dangerous, I'll be reminding you how much I owe Mr. Tyrone and I'll just be going along anyway with or without your say so."

Dudley studied the defiant little jut to her chin and nodded. "You have five minutes. That should be long enough for us to rig out the cart." Maggie returned his nod and hurried away, and Dudley shook his head as he looked at Finn. "You say he's in the old tower?"

"It is the only place neither the soldiers nor the servants venture near."

"Good. There is an underground passage that leads

from the tower to the banks of the canal; it should be easy enough to drive the cart along the river and carry him out."

Finn was genuinely surprised. "A passage, you say?"

"Most of the old castles hereabout have them. Coventry was a Parliamentary town during the civil war, but there were a few Royalist sympathizers, none of whom went without a secret back door, especially if it was near a river. And then there are the smugglers and black market dealers. Tyrone has surveyed most of these canals and roadways and knows most of the popular routes and transfer points. He also knows most of the secret ways in and out of these old manor houses, especially, er . . ."

"When there might be a need to steal into a lady's boudoir?" Finn's mouth curled with distaste. "We were wondering how he managed to get inside, past the guards and patrols."

Dudley threw the bolt across the front door and beckoned for Finn to follow him along the foyer, down to his own quarters. There he fetched a heavy woolen coat and wide-brimmed hat, and added two more pistols along with powder and shot to his personal arsenal before leading the way again out a rear door to the stables and coach house. By the time Maggie joined them, he had hitched a horse to a small cart and saddled his own mount.

A low, sullen mass of cloud glowered overhead, rumbling like an old man's belly and pelting them with a steady downpour as they drove out of Coventry. They stayed on the main road until they reached the edge of the heath, then went by smaller, less traveled roads and paths to the banks of the canal. Within the hour they were coaxing the reluctant horse and cart down the steep incline and rattling along the rocky ledge, and likely would have driven right past the hidden entrance of the passage had a familiar head not poked out of the tangled greenery guarding the approach.

It was Dudley's horse who caught the scent and nickered a soft greeting to Tyrone's huge black stallion. Ares was too well-trained to respond until he heard Dudley whistle a command, but then he came through the bushes at a sedate trot, blowing and rolling his eyes to express his displeasure at being abandoned for so long.

"There, old fella." Dudley dismounted and ran his hands down the gleaming neck and withers, checking the animal's legs for any signs of damage. "You thought we forgot about you, did you? Good boy. Damned good boy." He produced an apple from his coat pocket and it disappeared in a single bite. "Just a wee bit longer then, eh? And you'll have company this time."

He waved to Finn, who drove the cart through the low archway of branches and found himself under an umbrella of rock twelve or so paces deep, wide enough to shelter the horses and wagon from the rain. Dudley helped Maggie to disembark, then all three hurried into the passageway, pausing only once to light the lantern they had brought with them.

The tunnel was long and cluttered with debris. It smelled of damp earth and bat droppings and moved upward at a gradual angle for a hundred yards or more before taking a sharp elbow turn and sloping down. All three had to walk stooped over, their pace governed by Dudley's limp. No one spoke or remarked over the occasional pile of dried bones they passed, but they were all relieved when the ceiling began to rise and the pebbled floor ended at a steep set of stone block stairs.

The door at the top scraped open on rusted hinges, and after raising the lantern and throwing a circle of light around the small chamber, Dudley cautioned them to watch their footing. There was a gaping hole in the middle of the floor, a reminder of even earlier times when the original keep had been built as a defense against raiders from the north. Dudley kicked a stone over the lip of the old cistern and counted slowly to three before he heard a splash, then took Maggie by the hand and led the way to a second door set on the far side. This opened into yet another chamber, larger and circular in shape, with vaulted stone arches supporting the ceiling and an array of more recently abandoned debris including, Finn noted with some surprise, canvas sacking, crates, lanterns, and a supply of candles.

"You implied earlier that Lord Paxton deals with smugglers?"

Dudley snorted. "He's one of the biggest thieves in Warwickshire. How do you think he and Edgar Vincent became so friendly?"

"I confess, the association did puzzle me," Finn muttered. "I knew him when he was much younger, of course. Thirty years ago, to be precise, and he always did keep rather unsavory company."

Dudley pointed to a pair of iron rings bolted to the wall with a length of chain hanging from each. "Care to speculate when they were last used?"

Maggie shivered and poked his arm. "Just go."

The exit to this chamber was little more than a square panel of heavily strapped planking with several wrist-thick iron bars lying alongside that could be fed through corresponding fittings in the mortar to prevent it from being opened from the other side. There were scratches in the dirt, indicating it had been used recently and when they swung it outward, they emerged at the base of the tower, in a dark well at the bottom of a circular stone staircase. The other side of the panel had been built to resemble a prayer nave, a place where the chatelaine of the castle might have come to receive evening benediction. Beneath it was a shelf that held more candles, tapers, and an old iron key long ago rusted into the wood. Clearly winded from his exertions thus far, Finn managed to regain some spark when he realized where they stood.

"There," he exclaimed in mild amazement, pointing to a narrow arched door facing the bottom of the stairs. "That leads into the main house. That is the door master

Antoine found when he leaned against the tapestry. We carried Mr. Tyrone in this way."

With Dudley's permission, he led them up the last flight of steep, winding steps. At the top he tapped twice, softly, on the door, and a moment later heard the shuffle of footsteps on the other side. When it opened, he flinched back, splashing his fingers with the hot wax.

Renée was standing less than five feet away, her body lit from the side by lantern light. Her arms were held straight out in front. Her hands, trembling visibly with the unaccustomed weight, were clutched around one of Tyrone Hart's primed and loaded flintlocks.

\*

*"Mon dieu!"* Renée lowered the heavy gun. "I could have shot you."

Dudley pushed his way through the door and went straight to the pallet where Tyrone was lying. Maggie nodded briefly at Renée as she passed and while she was removing her cloak and mittens, Robbie lowered himself awkwardly onto one knee.

Tyrone might well have been mistaken for dead already if not for the shallow rise and fall of his chest beneath the blankets. His complexion, normally a robust, weathered bronze, had taken on the yellowish cast of old wax. His skin was clammy, wet to the touch, and when Robbie peeled back the blankets, the wad of linen over his ribs was an ominous red.

Behind them, Renée touched Finn's arm. "We thought you would never come back. We thought—"

"It is raining like the very devil out there," Finn explained, "and the roads are becoming quite treacherous. Surely you have not been up here all this time?"

"Antoine and I"—she turned to acknowledge her brother, who was standing in the shadows against the far wall—"have been taking turns sitting with M'sieur Hart. I went back to my room and waited for Jenny to come with my morning chocolate, and when she did, I told her I was not feeling well and would likely remain abed all day."

"She noticed nothing amiss?"

Renée shook her head. "I cleaned everything as best I could and put a rug over the stain on the floor. I did not know what to do with his clothes and the soiled towels, so Antoine brought them here."

Finn's gaze skimmed past the bundled rags in the corner. "Indeed, you seem to have been busy since I left."

Beside the pallet, which he had carried up himself, there was now a low wooden table and a straight-backed chair. An iron brazier was glowing against one wall and beside it, a tin crib half full of coal. The room was oppressively damp and dusty, but an effort had been made to clear a reasonably clean circle around the bed. A water pitcher and basin—the contents pink—sat on the table beside a lamp and several fat sticks of tallow.

"We will need more light, more blankets," he said almost to himself. "I should also make an appearance in the kitchens to forestall any unwanted curiosity, at which time I can fetch up some food, a pot of tea perhaps, some biscuits. Master Antoine, heaven help us, you should not be here in this ill-humored air else you suffer a relapse in your lungs. And—and oh! Good sweet merciful Jesus!"

The oath was emphatic enough to draw Dudley's attention. "What is it? What's wrong?"

Finn was staring aghast at the bruise on Renée's jaw. It had darkened considerably over the past few hours and was swollen as badly as if she had an abscessed tooth.

He turned to Dudley, who limped over with the lantern. "Do you look at that, sir! This is the second time Colonel Roth has dared to raise his hand against Mad'moiselle d'Anton, and I vow it has gone beyond all my endurance! I shall impale the bastard on his own sword, I swear it!"

Dudley inspected the bruise despite Renée's protests.

"The skin isn't broken. My Maggie will have some salve you can use; it should disappear within a day or two."

"I can only wish the same fate on Colonel Roth," Finn declared. "Him and that blunt-nosed swine Vincent, and yes, I declare it: upon Lord Paxton as well, for the part he has played in this—this abomination!"

At the mention of her uncle, Renée started, remembering something else Jenny had told her. "My aunt and uncle spent the night at Stoney Stratford. A rider brought word ahead that they might be expected either late to-night or early tomorrow."

"Not if this rain holds up, they won't," Dudley said through a frown. "That's thirty, thirty-five miles of slippery roads to cover, and from what I know of Paxton, he does not like to inconvenience himself overmuch."

"M'sieur Vincent also sent word that he is enjoying Lord Wooleridge's hospitality another day, and Corporal Marlborough"—Renée paused a moment as her voice grew unsteady—"was called back to Coventry because the patrols captured five men out on their own during the night, three of whom had been shot dead and identified as possibly being Captain Starlight."

Finn's brow arched. "The devil you say."

"Two thousand pounds is a lot of money to a common soldier," Dudley remarked dryly. "And the greedier ones don't necessarily care if the body they produce is dead or alive, so long as it fits the general size and description. With any luck at all, Roth should be kept busy for a while identifying them. And if this storm gets any worse—"

As if on cue, the walls of the old tower trembled under a long cannonade of thunder. From somewhere high in the gloom above their heads, a cold gust of wind blew through the recessed archery slits and set the yards upon yards of drifting cobwebs into motion.

"I was about to say, if this storm gets any worse, the good colonel and his Coventry Volunteers will find themselves waist deep in mud trying to keep the bridges clear."

Maggie's voice called softly from the pallet. "Just as well it keeps raining then, for we can't be moving Mr. Tyrone just yet. I'm not even sure if I can—" The words were cut off as she bit her lip and Dudley hastened back to her side.

"Tell us what you need."

She looked helplessly at the senseless form as if she did not even know where to begin. "More blankets. Water. And something in which to boil and steep herbs. I have needle and thread, but we will need a knife with a wide blade. And more coal. We're going to have to make this fire very hot, for I fear simple stitches are not going to be enough to stop the wound bleeding. It will have to be seared." She laid her hand across Tyrone's brow and shook her head. "He's lost so much blood, there'll be a fever, sure."

Antoine, who had remained back in the shadows until now came forward and tugged at Renée's sleeve. *Is he going to die?*

She looked at the solemn faces one by one before answering. "I hope not. But if he is to get well, we must all do what we can to help."

*Me too?*

"You most of all, *ma petite souris*, for like a mouse you must scurry about without anyone seeing you and find blankets, quilts, more candles, soap, sheets to tear into bandages, a broom if it can be found. And you must go with Finn *immédiatement* and see that he changes into clean, dry clothing. See how his teeth chatter! He should not be worrying about your lungs, so much as his own."

Antoine's eyes lit with a brief, mischievous spark. *I know how to make a mustard plaster.*

"*Vraiment*, we may all need them if we cannot bring more warmth into this room," she said, rubbing her arms. "Go now. And be very careful no one sees you leaving."

Proud to have been given such an important task, Antoine pointed Finn sternly toward the door. When they were gone, Renée moved closer into the light and stood quietly at the foot of the bed. Maggie was checking through the canvas sack she had brought with her, laying out needles, thread, small pots, and packets of herbs and medicines. At one point she raised a hand to chase back the damp lock of hair that had fallen over her eyes, and Renée noticed her condition for the first time.

"You will tell me, please, if there is something I can do to help?"

Dudley looked up. "A prayer wouldn't hurt, miss."

"A prayer," Maggie whispered. "And the luck of all the saints."

* ☽

# Chapter 17

 Tyrone wakened to the muted rumble of thunder. He became aware of distant sensations in his feet and hands first, the confining press of bedsheets and quilting, then the smell of something stale and unpleasant in the air around him—an underlying stench of mustiness and decay that could not be completely overwhelmed by the sickly sweetness of camphor.

He tried to open his eyes, but the effort proved too costly. He searched with his senses instead, feeling pressure now over his chest and thighs, a lumpy softness beneath him. He had no idea if it was day or night, no memory to offer a clue as to where he might be or how he had come to be there.

His mouth tasted foul, his tongue was thick and furred with the kind of taste that usually came on the heels of a hard night of drinking and carousing, but for some reason, he did not think his lethargy was alcohol-induced. And while there was no doubt he was lying naked in a strange bed, there was no lingering redolence of female musk to suggest recent companionship.

It was safe to assume, then, that he was not in a woman's bed. Nor were his chest, thighs, and ankles strapped down with the intentions of immobilizing him for pleasurable reasons.

His heart quickened and the sting of sudden tension stiffened his spine.

So where was he? And why was he tied to a bed?

Why could he not remember anything? *Think. Think!*
He had survived the shock of being driven to Harwood
House in the company of Colonel Roth and Edgar Vincent, and he had managed, remarkably, to keep his wits
when he had first seen Renée d'Anton walk into the
breakfast room. He remembered feeling his heart take an
odd turn in the conservatory when he had gathered her
into his arms to comfort her, and he remembered trying to
cover his own sense of inadequacy by playing the piano
for her—the piano, for pity's sakes!—like a cowering
mongrel seeking approval. Then Roth had walked in and
saved him, for his fingers had turned to lead and the
music sounded stiff and forced and she was likely thinking him the biggest fool on this earth.

Unfortunately, he had been acting like a fool. He
should have known Roth would have some trick in mind.
He should have known—he *had* known—and yet . . .
he had let himself be distracted. He had been reckless
and careless, breaking another one of the major rules in
the game: never think with anything other than your
head! He was a thief, and a damned good one, and if he
started to succumb to every pair of big blue eyes that
looked his way, he might as well place the noose around
his neck himself.

His eyes needed no further coaxing to open but a
mildly panicked search of his surroundings had them
popping even wider. He was indeed lying in a bed—a
thing of rough wooden sides slung with ropes for supporting a narrow, lumpy mattress filled with hay. He was naked save for a thin coverlet, with bindings keeping him
flat on his back, alone in a chamber that could have come
out of a medieval nightmare. The walls were made of
stone blocks, the ceiling crisscrossed with thick wooden
beams that, at first glance, looked shrouded in a haze of
mist or smoke, but were in reality spun with thick layers
of cobwebs. The door was made of rough wood planking
cut in a gothic arch and strapped with bands of iron.

There was a single, narrow window cut high into the wall near the ceiling. As he stared at it, he could see the erratic flicker of lightning coming from the storm outside, but the blocks were set too deep and the source was too far to penetrate the gloom above the beams. Apart from the bed there was only a table and two chairs, the former cluttered with washbasin, towels, and an apothecary's delight of bottles, unguents, and tinctures. One of the chairs was wooden and functional, the other sent Tyrone's head on another disoriented spin, for it was upholstered in silk brocade and looked as if it had come out of a nobleman's parlor. Two tallow candles burned in barbaric iron cressets on the wall and another on the table. Beside him, tucked back into a corner of the room, was a pot-shaped brazier, its bed of coals glowing red but barely throwing off enough heat to counteract the drafts that moved the cobwebs back and forth like ghostly veils above him.

He had never been inside the gaol in Coventry, but he could well imagine it must look and smell this way. Yet if he had been caught, why could he not remember? Surely the shock alone would have left an imprint somewhere in the fog that was clouding his brain.

He had been shot, he could certainly feel that well enough. He also remembered the flashes of gunpowder in the dark, a sensation like being kicked in the side, and a fury so great he could feel it boiling in his veins. Part of the general aura of rankness was coming from the thick wadding of bandages wound around his ribs, and as he lifted his head to have a better look, he could feel the pain throb to life in the torn muscles. He tried to move a hand, but whoever had strapped him to the bed had known his business and bound each wrist flat to the slats. His ankles were similarly immobilized and even as he looked around again, searching this time for something, anything, that might be used to cut himself free, he heard the scraping sound of a foot outside the door and an instant later, saw it swing open as someone came into the room.

*

Renée peered gingerly at the still form on the bed. He had not moved, as far as she could tell, since she had checked in on him an hour or so ago. Nothing much had changed for that matter, except perhaps the level of noise coming from the storm outside. She supposed they should all be thankful for small mercies. Apart from one hasty visit the afternoon following the ambush on the road three days ago, the weather had been keeping Colonel Roth busy elsewhere. High, fierce winds and unseasonably violent squalls had caused flooding on most major roads and turnpikes, and the militia had been called out to assist in one emergency after another.

Harwood House had not been abandoned altogether, however. Twice, a sodden and miserable-looking Chase Marlborough had stood dripping in the front hall while he paid his respects and conveyed messages to and from Fairleigh Hall. Lord and Lady Paxton had stopped there to rest before making the last leg of the journey to Harwood and, discovering Edgar Vincent to be in residence, had decided to partake of the Wooleridge's hospitality until the roads were passable.

Tyrone Hart had spent the three days he'd been a guest in the old tower thrashing in the delirium of a high fever. Finn's ingenuity had come to the rescue and he had bound long strips of braided linen around the injured man's wrists and ankles and while Hart had twisted and writhed and strained the cords to their limit, he had not worked them free. The fever had broken some time during the night and he had not moved since. Not a finger, not an eyelash. Now Renée found herself worrying that the next time she came into the room, she would not even see the steady rise and fall of his chest.

Something made her look at the thick crescents of his

lashes, certain she had detected a flicker of movement . . . but there was nothing. He lay as still as stone, his head propped on a double layer of pillows, his feet tenting the covers at the end of the cot. He was almost too long to fit the mattress, and there was barely an inch of space to spare on either side of his broad shoulders.

It was a wonder he was alive at all.

Maggie Smallwood had worked quickly and efficiently to seal Hart's wounds, then had bandaged the ribs with a vile-smelling poultice of turpentine, crushed wild carrot, and flax seed. By then he was already showing signs of fever and moving him from the tower was no longer a subject for debate even though Dudley and Finn were still of a mind to try getting him to the cart. Maggie stated flatly that he would be dead before they reached the exit of the passage, and Renée had once again been forced to make a perilous decision.

Her gaze drifted back to Tyrone's face. It seemed strange to see him without some protective mask of cosmetics or shadow. Each time she came she wanted to bring the light closer, to study the features of the man who knew her so intimately yet had never fully revealed himself. Each time she did, it was surprising and unsettling to see how truly beautiful he was. He had fine, high cheekbones and a well-defined brow. His lips were full and cast with careless sensuality, his jaw was lean and square, his eyes cloaked behind long, dark lashes. She was already shockingly aware of the strength molded into those arms and shoulders, but to see the power in the sinews that shaped the hard, flat belly and long legs was to acknowledge the sheer splendor of a body created under the exacting eye of a master sculptor—a sculptor who surely would not have wasted such a masterpiece on a man destined to hang as a mere road thief and murderer.

There had to be more to Captain Starlight than an intimate knowledge of the back roads and gutters. Those fine, tapered fingers had not learned to play the piano with such skill and emotion in a common taproom, nor had the manners, the bearing, the inherent qualities of an aristocrat been acquired merely through mimicking his betters. His French was flawless, and his back, beneath the scars of punishment and hard labor, was straight and strong and proud.

The overall impression he gave, in fact, was one of nobility gone awry. A blending of blue blood with that of a heathen gypsy, the courtly bearing of a gentleman with the wild sensuality of a barefooted Romany.

A fine sheen of moisture glistened at his temples, and Renée first touched the backs of her fingers to the soft prickle of three days' beard stubble, then gently rested the flat of her hand across his forehead. There was no sign of fever. The dreadful, dry heat was gone, taking with it the unnatural flush that had burned through his complexion and cracked the skin across his lips.

There was a folded cloth on the table and she dampened it in clean water, wringing it nearly dry before she blotted his brow and cheeks and throat. Deciding it would be remiss of her not to check the bandaging on his wound, Renée set the cloth aside, freeing both hands to peel back the layers of bedding. His chest, from just below his breasts, was bandaged in strips of linen, and, leaning slightly forward across his body, she searched for any signs of weepage through the poultice. But the bandages were clean and dry and smelled of nothing more sinister than the moist, mealy mass used to make the dressing.

She straightened and started to draw the covers up again, but paused. She had been to Rome once and been transfixed by a statue carved by Michaelangelo. The biblical David had possessed the same latent virility, the same breathtaking blend of power and beauty as the man before her, but while Michaelangelo's creation had been made of cold and inflexible marble, Tyrone Hart's flesh was warm and satiny. When she touched it, as she did now, it lured the fingers to explore further, to trail into the tangle of dark fur on his chest and feel where his heart beat strongly beneath.

The curious pads of her fingertips skimmed over the strip of bandages and picked up the swirl of dark hairs where they thinned to a fine line over the flat, washboard belly. She remembered, with shocking clarity, following that same taunting line with her lips, exploring every curve and plane as thoroughly as he had explored each of hers. With delicious impudence, she had discovered his nipples reacted much the same way hers did and she had teased them with a similar mercilessness until they grew as dark and taut as they were now.

*As they were now!*

Startled, she looked up at his face and saw that his eyes were open. Clear and remarkably direct, they met hers over a devastatingly charming smile.

"Please mam'selle," he murmured, "do not stop on my account."

*☽

## Chapter 18

Renée's lips parted around a small gasp as she snatched her hand away. "You are awake, m'sieur."

"And a more pleasant method of being roused, I could not imagine."

She opened her mouth, but closed it again on the next breath for there was certainly no excuse she could give—or any that he would believe—to explain why she had been running her fingers across his belly.

For Tyrone's part, it had taken every ounce of will-power he could muster to remain as still as he had as long as he had, although he doubted he could have borne one more soft stroke of her fingertips without giving rise to something that would have shocked her beyond the warm flush that was flooding her cheeks now.

She was a welcome sight to his muddled senses, for it was a certainty she would not be in a gaol cell hovering over him like a guardian angel. She looked clean and cool in a simple white muslin gown. Her hair was loose, held back off her face by a narrow silk ribbon that was success-ful for the most part, save for the tiny spray of fine blond curls that clung to her temples. Having been inspected so closely himself, Tyrone had no qualms about doing like-wise, retracing the soft line of her jaw, the smooth arch of her throat.

His gaze came to rest on the enticing mole that rode high over her left breast, and it took a moment or two for him to realize she was speaking.

". . . said you should have died."

"Who said that?"

"Finn and Maggie Smallwood were both of the opinion you should have bled to death on my bedroom floor."

"Maggie is here?"

"Was, m'sieur. I sent her home, mmm, yesterday. Yes. It was yesterday. We agreed she was in too delicate of a condition to be sitting here in the cold tending a sick man."

"If it is not too ungracious of me to ask: where exactly is *here*?"

"The ghost tower . . . or at least that is what Antoine calls it."

His eyes narrowed through a guarded frown. "So I haven't been flung back through time? There are no fire-breathing dragons waiting outside the door to be slain?"

Renée followed his glance up to the cobwebs. "It was the only place we could think of to hide you, m'sieur. And at least you *have* wakened, something I was beginning to believe would not happen."

His brows crushed together in a frown. "How long have I been here?"

"You were shot three nights ago. Do you remember nothing at all?"

"Nothing," he said honestly. "Pain, maybe. Like someone was holding a torch to my side."

"Someone did," she admitted with a hesitant smile. "Maggie feared the stitches alone would not stop the bleeding so she—she heated up a knife and . . ." Renée finished the explanation by gesturing lamely toward the brazier. "But she assured M'sieur Dudley, if you survived the fever, the wound would heal much faster."

"Robbie—?"

"Finn fetched him as soon as we thought it was safe to do so. He stayed through the first day, hoping you might improve enough to withstand being carried down to the canal, but then you became feverish and—and he agreed he had no choice but to leave you here. Maggie sent him back for more medicines and herbs, and by then the storm was much worse. He said there were already several angry notes at your house summoning you to help with flooded roads."

"Christ—"

"It was M'sieur Dudley's intention to go in your place, and if someone asked where you were, he would tell them you were somewhere else tending to another emergency. Then, of course, he would go to the second place and tell them you were at a third."

Tyrone swore again and went to lift his hand but found the action cut short by the linen cords. "Are these absolutely necessary?"

She flushed again. "You were very . . . active . . . m'sieur, in your fever. We were afraid you would hurt yourself further."

"And if I promise to behave?"

"We can remove them, of course," she said, setting her fingers nervously to the task.

He watched her, his eyes intent upon the small dimple in her cheek caused by her efforts to concentrate on the strips of linen. It felt strange being told so much had happened when he could remember so little.

"I think I recall waking once," he said slowly. "I saw a face—yours, but not yours. Big blue eyes and short yellow curls, like a cherub."

"That was Antoine," she told him with a smile. "He said you stared at him a moment then started shouting and cursing at the devil."

"I must have thought I had been sent to the wrong place. Everything else, however, seems to be a blur."

"You do not remember being shot?"

"I remember thinking I'd had too much of Lord Wooleridge's fine claret at dinner."

"You must have had a great deal of Lord Wooleridge's claret," she corrected as she circled the bed to untie his other wrist, "for you came here afterward, waving your guns, threatening to shoot me for betraying you."

He blinked once to help focus his thoughts. "I threatened to shoot you?"

"Finn and I both. You thought—or assumed—we knew about Colonel Roth taking Finn's place in the coach."

There was a tightness in her voice that suggested some lingering resentment and when the binding was loose enough, he twisted his hand and caught hers gently by the wrist. "Renée, if I said or did anything—"

"You were very angry," she murmured. "But of course, you were wounded."

She was staring at his hand but did nothing to attempt to pull free and seeing this, he slid his hand down until he was no longer holding her wrist, but had twined his fingers through hers. "Has no one ever told you wounded animals are at their most dangerous when they feel trapped—or betrayed."

Huge, solemn blue eyes met and held his for a long moment. "The circumstances are dangerous for all of us, m'sieur. We have been exceedingly lucky so far, but when the storm ends the servants will put aside their fear of the tower ghost and—"

"Tower ghost?"

She flushed even darker and Tyrone wondered that he had never noticed how many shades of pink a blush entailed. He stroked his thumb across the back of her hand and was fascinated to see an almost instantaneous, deeper rose warm the roundest part of her cheeks.

"You were very loud in your fever," she was saying. "And since there is already the rumor of a ghost haunting the old battlements, Finn went up to the roof in a white sheet and rattled chains."

"Stalwart Mr. Finn?"

"He is not without a sense of humor, m'sieur."

A slow, sinfully handsome smile crept across his face,

and Renée felt a corresponding tightness in her belly, warming her in a way that made her aware of subtle changes taking place elsewhere in her body. Her breasts grew exquisitely taut, chafing against the linen of her chemise on every breath. The gentle strokes of his thumb were causing tremors of sensation to coil through her limbs, between her thighs, and she was afraid to move in case she dissolved beside him.

"It . . . was quite a dreadful sound," she added haltingly. "It sent Jenny running belowstairs, where she has remained ever since. None of the other servants have dared to venture too far from their beds either, not even Mrs. Pigeon."

"I shall have to remember to compliment Mr. Finn on his ingenuity."

"It was Antoine's idea, actually." She curled her lower lip between her teeth and tried to casually extricate her hand. "I remember him playing a similar prank on our cousin when—when we were all younger."

"Does anyone *else* know I am here?"

She looked up and frowned. "Neither Finn nor Antoine would betray your presence, m'sieur. And if you still believe I am doing this only to collect the reward—"

Tyrone laced his fingers more possessively through hers. "No. No, I do not believe that at all. It's just that your brother is young, he might inadvertently say something—"

"If he did, it would indeed be a miracle, m'sieur," she whispered, "for he has said nothing for over a year."

He felt himself drawn into the haunting blue of her eyes and did not fight it through a long moment of silence. "Nothing at all?"

"*Rien*," she breathed. "He . . . we both saw my mother beaten to death by the soldiers outside the gates of Temple Prison in Paris. She had just found out my father had been executed and . . ." She shook her head, unable to continue.

"I'm sorry. I did not know."

"How could you, m'sieur? How could anyone know how terrible it was to see the men, the women, the *children* taken away in carts like animals, crying and holding each other, holding strangers for courage, knowing there was no hope, not even knowing what crime they had committed to deserve such a dreadful punishment."

This time, when she twisted her hand free, he did not try to stop her, and she walked around to the foot of the bed, embarrassed and bewildered as to why she would have shared such a private pain.

"I am sorry, Renée. Roth never said anything and I thought the boy was simply shy—or overwhelmed—at the breakfast table the other day."

"He was not just overwhelmed, m'sieur, he was frightened half to death. For this reason as much as any other, you must see why you have to leave this place as soon as possible."

She could see the narrowing of his eyes as another memory was jolted free. "You said I've been here three days? What is the date?"

"The ninth, m'sieur."

"The ninth? Christ! And you are supposed to be getting married on the fourteenth? Why in blazes are you still here?"

The last binding around his ankle fell slack and she looked at him. "We did not have much choice, m'sieur. You could not be moved and we could not leave you here alone."

"Well by God if you will just help me find my clothes—"

He started to push himself upright but the movement, along with any noble intentions, ended on an abruptly savage stab of pain. His right hand flew to cradle his ribs, an act that put him off balance and sent him arching back against the pillows with a second jolt. The stab in his side became a breathtaking flare of agony, one that stiffened his whole body and brought Renée rushing to his side.

"You must not move yet, m'sieur! You are not strong enough."

Tyrone clenched his teeth against the sudden wave of nausea that rose in his throat and managed to gasp out a hoarse request for water.

Renée reached quickly for the pitcher and poured a glassful, then supported him firmly under the neck while he gulped the contents. His hand closed over hers again while she held the glass and did not let go, not even when his head fell back against the pillows and some of the tension around his lips started to relax.

"Take the bandages off," he gasped.

"What?"

"Take the bandages off. I want to see how bad it is."

"I do not think—"

His hand squeezed hers hard enough she feared the glass might break under the pressure. "Please."

"*Bien*," she whispered. "I will have to cut through the bindings and then rewrap them again."

He nodded and pushed her hand away. Renée fetched the scissors and cut through the strips that held the wadded poultice in place, then carefully lifted the lot away until the wound was laid bare. This time Tyrone braced himself before he raised his head and with Renée's help was able to angle himself forward enough to see the extent of the damage. He was relieved to see it was not the deep and mangled twist of lacerated flesh he half expected to see, although it was certainly ugly enough to draw a curse from his throat. The hole in his flesh had been sewn closed with thick black thread, then the raw edges seared with the red-hot blade of the knife. The surrounding flesh was blue and purple, with splotches of yellow spreading out from his ribs.

"It looks much better than it did three days ago," she assured him. "And at least the bullet passed cleanly between two ribs. There were no pieces of bone or bullet to cut out."

Tyrone offered up a snorted *hmphf* and laid his head back on the pillows. "You will have to forgive me if I sound less than deliriously grateful, but the last time I was flat on my back and incapable of tending myself, I was a child and my mother was holding my head while I puked my toes into a bucket."

"Do you have to puke, m'sieur?"

"No, dammit." He waited a moment before adding, "But I do have to do something else."

She followed his gaze to the china thunderpot set in the corner. She retrieved it and removed the lid but when she would have lifted the edge of the blanket, his hand shot out yet again.

"I do not think I am that helpless yet, mam'selle."

"You have been considerably more so these past few days," she pointed out.

It was Tyrone's turn to flush and when he did, it was with all the heat and magnificence of a male in his prime forced to acknowledge a basic weakness. He glowed from the bottom of his throat to the verge of his hairline and his eyes, normally so pale a pewter gray as to be almost colorless, burned with flecks of blue chagrin.

"Be that as it may, mam'selle," he said tersely, "I was also oblivious."

She handed him the pot. "Shall I wait outside?"

"Please," he said through his teeth.

Renée was halfway to the door when a thought struck her. "You have a mother, m'sieur?"

"Had. She died when I was eight." His head tilted on a wry angle. "You say that with such astonishment in your voice: did you think I was hatched from an egg?"

"No, of course not. I was merely inquiring in case she lived close by. You might be more comfortable being cared for by someone you know, like a mother or a— a . . ."

"Wife?" A frown supplemented the tilt. "I promise you, my status as an affirmed bachelor is well known throughout the parish."

"I think it would be safe to say, *capitaine*, that you are not exactly what you appear to be to everyone in the parish. For all that you caper and mince about like a marionette, you might well have a wife and ten children hidden away somewhere."

"I might," he agreed with a belligerent scowl. "But I do not. Apart from my unchanging pleasure at being unfettered by hearth and home, a family would be somewhat more of a burden than a comfort to a man in my line of work. In fact, a commitment to anything or anyone who sought to rely on my being there every night to offer stability and succour would be rather selfish of me, would it not?"

Renée pondered this as she waited outside the room, giving him more than what she considered ample time to complete his task. He must have thought it overly generous as well, for she heard him clear his throat loudly several times before she finally obliged him by returning.

She replaced the lid on the pot and set it back in the corner, then went through the motions of straightening the blankets around his feet.

"Surely you must have cared for someone at some time," she said from behind the shield of her lashes.

"Is that what you want to believe, mam'selle? That I am the result of some tragic affair gone awry? That instead of throwing myself off the nearest cliff in irreparable despondency over some lost love, I chose instead to avenge myself through a life of crime and dissolution?" He sighed and shook his head. "I am exceedingly sorry to have to disappoint you, Renée, but there was no woman involved in my fall from grace. There were no amorous tragedies in my past, no doomed love affairs to haunt me, no fists beating on the chest in despair, no injustices crying out for revenge."

"Then why do you do what you do, m'sieur? Why do you kill and steal and taunt men like Colonel Roth until they become obsessed with catching you?"

"In the first place, I have only killed two men deliberately, and both were in the process of doing their best to kill me." He watched her adjust the blanket for the tenth time and waited for her gaze to come to him. "Secondly, I do what I do . . . because I find it exciting. And because I am good at it. And, odd as it may sound, because it suits my bourgeois sense of humor to watch dolts like Bertrand Roth chase their tails in circles. What about you?"

"Me?"

"I should think marriage—not to a bastard like Vincent, of course—would solve a good many of your problems. Have you no wifely urges? No desire to have the security of a husband and protector? No pressing need to go to nest and produce a houseful of your own little goslings?"

"I used to think that was what I wanted, yes."

"And now?"

"Now?" Her voice softened and her eyes seemed to lose their focus. "Now I would just like to feel warm again. I would like to find a place where I belong, where Antoine could learn to laugh and Finn could let us take care of him for a change." A distinctly moist shiver reminded her of where she was and whose pale eyes were watching every change in her expression. To cover her uneasiness, she took up a roll of clean bandaging. "We should replace the poultice, *capitaine*. Do you think you can sit up or shall I fetch Finn to lift you?"

"I can sit up," he said grimly and stretched out his right arm. "If you will help me."

With his arm slung around her shoulder and Renée supporting him, he was able to sit upright and to his credit, there was only relief in the hiss of air he let out between his teeth.

"It gets easier every time," he said, panting slightly into the crook of her neck.

"You speak from experience, m'sieur?"

A grunt was her only answer and, working as quickly as she could, she wound the roll of bandaging around his ribs to hold the poultice in place. He was leaning awkwardly against her and it was not easy to balance while her hands went round and round with the roll of linen. His face was pressed into the curve of her shoulder, and while she suspected he was, perhaps, just a little too dependent on her for support, there was not much she could do to lessen the intimacy.

"Speaking purely as a cad and a rogue," he murmured, "I have to say I thought you were exceptionally warm the other night. Any warmer, in fact, and I would have had to douse us both in cold water."

The roll slipped out of her hand and she had to fumble a moment in the blankets to keep it from unraveling over the side of the bed.

"I—I thought you said your memory was in a blur, m'sieur."

"After Roth shot me. Before, however"—his fingers curled around a silky crush of blond hair and pushed it to one side, baring her nape—"everything is quite clear."

She turned her head, intending to censure him, but that was a mistake. Their eyes, their mouths were level; strands of his dark hair had become tangled with hers to fashion a veil of gold and black threads between them.

"I even remember you kissing me by the coach," he murmured.

"You remember it wrong, m'sieur. *You* were kissing *me*!"

"You invited it."

"I was . . . merely attempting to express my gratitude. For the brooch. It is the custom in France," she added, hastily turning her attention back to the bandages, "to thank someone in this way for a kindness."

"Really?" His thumb stroked the downy softness along her hairline. "Then I would, indeed, be remiss if I did not thank you properly for all you have done for me."

Renée froze as she felt his lips press into the sensitive hollow just below her ear. Her eyes quivered shut under the immediate rash of cool, tingling goose bumps that rippled down her arms and legs and it was all she could do to keep her knees from buckling beneath her.

"Please, m'sieur . . ."

"I am only trying to express my gratitude, mam'selle, as feeble an effort as it may be."

The murmured words vibrated against her skin. His lips, dry and rough though they were, were also bold enough to shock her into twisting free. He remained sitting upright for a long moment, a lopsided grin on his face—a grin that rapidly turned to panic when he realized he no longer had her support. Renée was able to catch him as he fell back, saving him from the worst of the jolt, but the amorous bravado had cost him. His mouth went white and beads of moisture broke out across his lip and brow, and he did not move or speak again until she was finished tying off the ends of bandage.

"And so you have proved what, *capitaine*?" She reached for the washcloth with brisk efficiency and plunged it in the basin again. "That you would make love to me now and kill yourself in the process, just to demonstrate your *virilité*?"

"An interesting proposition, mam'selle," he rasped. "You would naturally have to allow for some minor adjustments in technique."

"*Imbécile*," she muttered. She wrung out the cloth and laid it across his forehead, then, fearful of the fever returning, drew the blankets high under his chin and forced him to drink another glass of water, this one laced with a healthy dose of laudanum.

For the hundredth time—the thousandth—she found herself wondering what manner of senseless whim had prompted her to hide the wounded highwayman in the tower room. To hide him anywhere, for that matter. She had the brooch and her miserable hoard of money. She could have been hundreds of miles away from Coventry by now. Perhaps even on board a ship bound for America. Capitaine Clair d'Etoile was enterprising and resourceful and as she had suspected earlier, just too damned stubborn to die. Given no other choice, Robert Dudley could have found a way to carry him home. She should have insisted on it, but no. She was here, nursing a hunted man, threatening to melt into helpless little puddles every time he looked at her. Or touched her.

"I will have Finn bring you some broth. You must try to get your strength back, m'sieur, and then you must leave this place as quickly as possible."

"Believe me, mam'selle, I have no more wish to remain trapped here than you do. As soon as Robbie returns, I will be off your hands."

Renée said nothing and when he saw the dubious look on her face he scowled. "In the meantime, I would appreciate some clothes. And my guns. Where the devil are my guns?"

"They are here, m'sieur. Directly beside you on the floor."

She leaned over, intending to produce one to set his mind at ease, but the motion was halted when his hand closed around a bunch of golden curls and pushed it back off her shoulder, baring the faded blue bruise that marked her jaw.

"How did that happen?"

"It . . . was nothing. A clumsy mistake in the dark."

The backs of his fingers brushed lightly along her jaw and ended beneath her chin, angling it toward him again, his touch not quite as gentle as it had been. "You have not yet mentioned Roth's reaction to all of this."

"He was angry, naturally, that you escaped."

Tyrone rolled his thumb carefully over the bruise. "How angry?"

When she did not immediately answer he drew a slow breath and his jaw hardened. "It seems I may just have to kill him after all."

"Get well first, m'sieur. Then worry about who you may or may not wish to kill."

His hand dropped down onto his chest and although she could see he was fighting hard to keep his eyes open, the laudanum was starting to take effect.

"I am sorry, Renée. Truly sorry for all the trouble I have caused and sorry for waving my guns and frightening you the way I did. Sorry for . . . doubting you. Most of all, I am sorry for keeping you here when I'm sure you would rather be anywhere else."

His words were beginning to slur and on impulse, she leaned over and kissed him gently on the lips. "You are indeed a good deal of trouble, m'sieur, and I do wish I were anywhere else but here. But perhaps not entirely for the reasons you think," she added softly.

"Can't think," he murmured. "Can't see you either . . ."

"Because your eyes are closed."

"Ah. That's okay, then."

The tightness around his mouth went slack and his entire body began to sag, as if everything of substance was draining out of him. His breathing slowed, became shallow and measured, easy in sleep.

Renée studied him a moment, and experienced a further moment of panic, for she wanted nothing more at that moment than for him to be able to sit up straight and strong and take charge again. She wanted him to tell her everything was going to be all right. Most of all, to her abject dismay, she wanted to crawl into the bed beside him and feel his heat surrounding her. She *had* felt warm in his arms, warmer than she had believed it possible to feel again. At the time, she had blamed it on the wild, careless madness of the moment—on the utter improbability of their paths ever crossing again or of her ever having to look him in the eye and acknowledge how badly she longed to share his sense of reckless passion.

She lowered her lashes and stared at her hands. They were still trembling and had been since he had first wakened and twined his fingers through hers. It was not going to be so easy to forget him, she feared—and not at all easy to walk away the next time, knowing she would never see him again.

# *☽* Chapter 19

$\mathcal{I}$t rained all the next day. Torrents of it fell, washing out roads, bridges, turnpikes. Thunder and lightning came in sporadic bursts, accompanied by winds that bent trees in half and rattled furiously against the windowpanes. Dudley did not make an appearance until the following afternoon, and then only to report that although the rain had stopped, the banks of the canal were flooded and it was impossible to maneuver a cart to the entrance of the tunnel. Renée had not reacted at all when she heard this. She had begun to resign herself to expect the worst, and when she heard it, at least she was saved having to weather another disappointment.

To his credit, Tyrone was genuinely angry at the further delay. He had behaved like a model patient throughout the first day, drinking as much broth as he could hold, taking bread and a few pieces of meat in an effort to rebuild his strength. He insisted on taking short circuits around the tower room, refusing by sheer dint of will to admit he was too weak to do so. When evening came, Renée found him sitting at the edge of the bed, his face drenched in sweat, his body shaking like that of a newborn foal. Antoine confided that the captain had insisted on climbing up and down the tower stairs, not once but four times!

By the end of the second day, Antoine had carried up the chessboard, had stolen a plate of cold meat and cheese from the pantry, and provided Tyrone with shaving gear, soap, even an oiled cloth that he might clean and reload his pistols. Renée's temper, so carefully held in check until then, had flared when she found him showing Antoine how to hold and aim one of the snaphaunces. She had chased her brother from the room and stood glowering at the captain, who had the fine sense to put the guns out of sight.

Just looking at him, brawny and handsome, with his unruly mane of black hair and crooked, careless smile, she should have guessed Antoine would be struck with a wide-eyed sense of awe. Here was the epitome of danger and adventure in the flesh. Tyrone Hart thumbed his nose at everything from social conventions to the laws of the land and to a young, bruised soul who had known only fear of authority, just being in the same company as the legendary Captain Starlight would have been enough to strip him of his sensibilities.

"You must not encourage him so, m'sieur. He told me you were recounting stories about your various exploits this morning."

"I was only trying to pass the time," he protested.

"Such time could have been put to better use resting," she countered. "Look at you, m'sieur. You try to do too much too soon. The water drips off your hair! *Vraiment*! I vow if you invite your fever to return, the only one who will be listening to your stories is the tower ghost!"

To this point, Tyrone had been sitting with his head bowed and his arms bracing him upright at the side of the bed. At the sound of the threat, he tipped his head upward and gazed sheepishly through the shaggy mane of his hair.

"Be kind to me, mam'selle. I spent the latter part of the afternoon with your Mr. Finn. If his eyes were daggers I would have a thousand stabmarks in my body and be mutilated beyond recognition. I gather he knows we were together in your room the other night?"

All the stiffness in Renée's spine deserted her in a rush. "Yes," she admitted quietly, "he knows."

"He does not hide his feelings very well, does he? He made it quite clear I was thoroughly unworthy to touch so much as the hem of your skirt."

"Finn has been very . . . protective since *maman* and *papa* were killed."

"And so he should be. Your bloodlines alone should have been enough to curdle mine for even daring to look, never mind touch."

The pinkness in her cheeks indicated he had touched a nerve and he sighed through an apology. "If I swear to do nothing further to corrupt the moral fiber of your brother or test the patience of your valet, will you stay and talk with me for a while?"

"My uncle is expected to arrive in the morning. I must—"

"Just a little while. The atmosphere in here is a tad too reminiscent of a former gaol cell for comfort."

"So you *have* been in gaol before?"

"Once, in Aberdeen. It was a wretched experience I have vowed never to repeat. There, you see?" His mouth curved up at the corner. "If you stay and talk a while, you will discover all manner of things about me that I can tell you are bristling to know."

"I hardly think I am bristling, m'sieur."

"Not even mildly curious?"

She sighed with no small amount of exasperation. "Will you promise to lie down and rest?"

"Happily, mam'selle. If I could but have your steadying hand a moment—?"

She approached the side of the bed and he smiled again at the wariness written all over her face. "You and your Mr. Finn have more in common than you think," he mused. "I should like to sit in the shadows sometimes and watch your face while a room full of pretentiously silly geese debate the shattering impropriety of serving a course of sweetbreads before fish."

She assisted him to lie back down and fussed a moment straightening the blankets.

"Will you take more broth?"

He glanced at the tin pot propped over the brazier and grimaced. "No. Thank you. I have had enough broth today to launch a fleet of ships."

"Do you require—?"

"*No*. I mean, no thank you. I made good use of my freedom while I was up." A dark, thick lock of hair had fallen over his brow and in a gesture that was almost boyish, he swept it aside and scowled. "Please . . . bring the chair closer. You keep moving it back into the shadows and I cannot see your face."

The irony of the complaint was not lost on either of them and Renée almost smiled. "What need do you have to see my face, m'sieur? Surely you must be tired of it by now."

"I would have to be dead to admit to that," he answered. "And besides, it is your eyes I like to look at. They have this incomparable ability to call me a fool and rogue and a wastrel, yet always with such underlying tenderness, I am not without hope for redemption. Come. I promise no flamboyant displays of—of *virilité*. Not that you would have to worry anyway. Sad to say, I doubt I could rouse enough energy at the moment to impress a gnat."

Renée dragged the chair a scant few inches closer to the bed and sat on the edge, her back straight as a post, her hands folded primly in her lap.

"*Très formidable*," he murmured. "The same gnat would find more encouragement in a convent."

"I am not here to encourage you, m'sieur."

"No. And you do your job very well." He sighed and pressed his head back into the pillows. He closed his eyes, carefully regulating his breathing to compensate for the persistent throbs of pain in his side, and when he raised his lashes again, Renée had left the chair and was wringing water out of a fresh square of linen. He watched her while she bathed his face, noting how her eyes were determined not to make contact with his, how the blush ebbed and flowed in her cheeks when the cloth touched his neck, then the top of his chest. Finn had provided him with a nightshirt, large and shapeless, but the laces had come undone during his repeated forays around the room and gaped open to the top of the bandages. The water was cool and her touch so soothing he almost wished he had a fever again so he could rid himself of the shirt and lie there guiltlessly naked.

For that matter, he wished they were both naked, with the candlelight gilding her hair and the blush warming her entire body.

She straightened and he cleared his throat. "You said your uncle is arriving tomorrow?"

"Corporal Marlborough brought a note from Fairleigh earlier today. M'sieur Vincent is anxious to make preparations for the—the wedding."

He heard the catch in her voice when she said her fiancé's name. He compared it to the way she had said his, on long, shivering breaths while her body had arched up beneath him and her hands had clawed into his thighs, urging him deeper into the silky heat.

He closed his eyes, resolved to honor his promise of just a few moments ago; an impossible feat if he had to stare at the luscious pink bow of her mouth much longer. Impertinence had always been one of his first lines of defense, and he fell back on it now.

"Have you not asked yourself why Edgar Vincent is willing to go to such lengths to marry you? And please, I mean no offense, for I am sure there are scores of men who would gladly marry you on a wink, most of them, if not as wealthy, certainly far more respectable than Vincent."

"Perhaps it is that respectability he craves."

"I thought so, too, at first," he admitted.

"But then you thought there must be other heiresses, other daughters of English noblemen who could give him more respectability than a French *émigré*?"

He smiled at the faint edge of bitterness in her voice. "Never put words in my mouth, mam'selle. Especially if they are the wrong ones."

"Are you saying there are no English heiresses who would be of more value to him?"

"English heiresses are as rife as apples in September. It is purely a question of suitability. Would your father have let you marry a fishmonger?"

"If I loved him, yes."

Her answer—obviously not the one he expected—came so quickly and so honestly, Tyrone was taken aback. But only for a moment. "He must have been a very unique member of the aristocracy. The only way an Englishman would allow such a travesty of social mongrelism would be if the fishmonger was as rich as Croesus and the peer was so deep in debt his toes were touching hell."

"My uncle is in debt?"

"His estates are all heavily mortgaged. He has embezzled funds from the trusts and entailments to pay off his gaming debts, which are in turn, so steep they have fostered a separate wagering pool as to who, among his many creditors, will cut his losses and slit the old bastard's throat in a dark alley one night."

This was news to Renée, who had been given no indication her uncle was anything but miserly.

"But I have no money, no dowry. Would a man like Vincent not expect such a thing?"

"You underestimate the value of those good bloodlines, mam'selle. It is entirely possible the dowry has gone the other way in order for your fiancé to infuse a little noble blood into the veins of his heirs. As I said, that was what I assumed—before I discovered you had a brother lurking in the background."

Renée sank back into the chair. "And now?"

"Am I correct in presuming Antoine is the current duc d' Orlôns, regardless of whether the present government in France recognizes the validity of his claim or not?"

The subject was rather personal and wholly unsuitable for discussion, but she managed a nod.

"Then marrying you—and please correct me if I am wrong—would be of little direct benefit to Vincent's heirs, if there are any."

"You are not wrong. The title passed to my father on the death of his father and brothers. Had the revolution not happened, *papa* would not have inherited at all—well, nothing more than a small portion of the estates—for he was the youngest of four brothers, and there were several sons born to the eldest and the title would have passed to them. Robespierre was very thorough, however, he eliminated everyone whose claim might supersede my father's. It was his way," she added quietly. "Especially if he thought he could manipulate the remaining heir by fear or threats of execution. Fortunes that might have otherwise been hidden or smuggled out of France were added to the treasury of the new republic in this manner. Titles could be forfeited on the stroke of a pen, but jewels and gold buried in the forest could not."

"So he took hostages?"

"They were called dissidents."

"And they were held until the fortunes were turned over to the government?"

"Yes, and then often executed anyway, under a charge of treason."

"So much for politically pure motives," he murmured. "Did your grandfather have jewels and gold buried in the forest?"

She shook her head. "I do not know. Papa cared very little for baubles and trinkets and if he knew of anything grandpère had hidden away, he would happily have given it up to the tribunal in exchange for the guaranteed welfare and safety of his family. I suspect that was why Antoine and I were not arrested sooner, for the d'Orlôns fortune was quite considerable and they may have been convinced *papa* knew more than what he was telling them."

"Are you suggesting Robespierre never got his hands on it?"

Renée shrugged and sighed. "I honestly do not know, m'sieur. If it is buried under a tree somewhere in a forest, the truth of it went to the grave with *grandpère*."

Tyrone laid back and stared up at the drifts of cobwebs. He was missing something. There was a link somewhere and he was missing it. He tried to think back over everything Dudley had discovered about the honorable Lord Paxton's dirty linens and tried to fit the pieces together, beginning with the scandalous elopement of Celia Holstead thirty years ago. The father had betrothed her to the Duke of Leicester, an alliance intended to unite their two families as well as their two financial empires. But she had eloped, on the very day of her wedding, with a young and dashing Frenchman, causing one of the largest scandals of the decade, not to mention the complete dissolution of any business mergers that had been forthcoming. Without that infusion of money and prestige, the Holstead fortunes had plummeted. The father had disowned the daughter and never again acknowledged her existence until the day he died. The brother had refused any attempts at a reconciliation, despite the fact the groom turned out to be a member of one of the wealthiest and most influential families in France. Had he been the eldest son and heir to the vast fortune, there might have been some leeway for forgiveness, but Sebastien d'Anton had not been worth the earl of Paxton's notice or sympathy.

All that would have changed, of course, when the

revolution came along and the Duc d'Orlôns found more than just the lives of his family in jeopardy. He might have found the wisdom to seek, if not a reconciliation, at least a mutually beneficial business arrangement.

"What if that tree was in England?" Tyrone asked slowly.

"M'sieur?"

"Was your grandfather the kind of man who would bury old hatchets and ignore past insults to his family if the safety and well-being of its future was at stake?"

"I do not understand your question."

"The first night we met you told me your uncle had arranged your marriage to a man who profited from the blood of those who died on the guillotine."

"Yes. That is the truth."

"You also said there were a number of terrified aristocrats who paid him enormous sums to smuggle their wealth out of France before men like Robespierre could confiscate it in the name of *liberté*, *égalité*, and *fraternité*. According to you, he took their jewels and promised to safeguard their treasures until the arrangements were made for their escape."

Renée felt a chill brush down her spine. "Yes," she whispered. "That is the truth also."

"But then, you said he placed it in the vaults of his own bank until he received word the family was executed, and then he claimed it as his own."

"Forgive me if I do not understand, m'sieur, but—"

"Edgar Vincent is not the one who owns the bank. Your uncle does."

"My uncle?"

"It is not something he might brag about in genteel company, but Lord Charles Holstead, earl of Paxton, owns one of the larger banks in London. In his father's day it was also one of the most reputable, but after the merger with Leicester failed, it was forced to seek the business of a different kind of clientele. Slavers, black marketeers"—he had the grace to offer a rueful grin—"thieves. His managers ask no questions and tell no secrets . . . for a price of course."

Renée was mildly astonished. "And how do you know these things, m'sieur?"

"In my line of business, my life depends on what I know. For instance, I know Roth and Vincent go back a long way. There was some trouble when the colonel was younger—something to do with a young woman who was rather savagely beaten to death if I recall correctly—and his family bought him a commission in the army, hoping to hide him away for a while until the stink blew over. Vincent, who I suspect was somehow involved with procuring the evening's entertainment, suddenly found himself with a small windfall of cash—a payoff for his silence, perhaps—and was able to branch out to bigger and better things in the black market. Your uncle, meanwhile, was gambling away his fortune and running himself so far into debt he had no choice but to start stealing from some of his accounts. Vincent was one of them."

She looked about to interrupt again and Tyrone held up his hand. "Humor me a moment longer. Suppose, when Roth is sent to France to fight for the noble cause of preserving the monarchy, he finds himself in the midst of a flood of wealthy, panicking aristocrats willing to pay almost any amount to see themselves and their families out of Mme. Guillotine's reach. He talks to his old friend Vincent, who has smuggling barks that regularly cross the Channel carrying perfume and brandy. Subsequently, Vincent talks to Paxton, who has a bank with nice deep vaults and a larcenous weakness to exploit. It's a good scheme, charging a percentage of what they smuggle out, and provides a steady flow of money, even adding a bonus now and then when the aristocrat who hired them never makes it out to claim his treasure."

"But that is—"

"Thievery?" he provided, when she stopped to grope

for a word. "They probably viewed it as more of a finder's fee. I mean, really, what else are they to do with unclaimed gold? Give it back to the French government? Give it to our government? Either option would expose their tawdry little smuggling operation and while everyone knows it is happening, it would not do for Lord Paxton to appear to be profiting off the war in any way. Not with him being such a vocal ally of William Pitt. And probably, if not for my untimely appearance on that misty, moonlit road five months ago, they could have kept on smuggling and stealing with impunity."

Her eyes held his like magnets. Dark blue magnets that pulled the truths from him like little metal shavings. "The night I robbed your fiancé, you see, the brooch was not the only thing I took. He also had in his possession a rather impressive assortment of trinkets, gold and such, probably transporting them out of London to a safer place, away from the scrutiny of any agents who might be starting to wonder where all these unclaimed fortunes were vanishing. After the robbery, I tried to dispose of a few pieces and the next thing I knew, the dealer with whom I did business was dead and my intermediary, when he discovered it was Edgar Vincent who had the dealer 'questioned,' refused to handle any more of the jewels. Within the week Roth had himself transferred to Coventry, hell-bent on running me to ground, vowing to use any and all means at his disposal to rid the parish of the scourge known as Captain Starlight."

"And instead of staying out of his way, you torment and taunt him so that he becomes obsessed with catching you? So obsessed he threatens to hang my brother for a crime he did not commit and uses me to lure you out into the open so you can both try to kill each other. Very enlightening, m'sieur, as always, to know how much more civilized and mature you English are."

"Ouch," he murmured. "That is quite the dagger you wield, mam'selle. And me a mortally wounded man."

She glared at him as he held his hand over his heart and appealed for sympathy.

"If what you say about my uncle and the others is true, why can we not just go to the authorities and expose them?"

"*We?*"

"Me," she corrected hastily. "Antoine and I."

"What would you tell them? That you suspect your uncle, Lord Charles Holstead, the earl of Paxton, honorable member of Parliament, has been opening his bank vaults to French aristocrats attempting to prevent their worldly possessions from falling into the greedy coffers of the revolutionary government? Will you tell them Colonel Bertrand Roth, a wounded hero and veteran of the war in Flanders, has profited from the misery of fleeing émigrés? Or that Edgar Vincent, the man who insures a steady supply of French cognac and Lyons lace to half of London society, is guilty of wanting to marry you because you are destitute, orphaned, and beautiful beyond measure? Without proof, that is all they are guilty of, mam'selle. And even with proof, you would be hard-pressed to find too many juries—filled with men whose sons are most likely on a battlefield somewhere fighting and dying at the ends of French muskets—willing to convict. I could be wrong, but the law does seem to turn a blind eye to thieves who steal from enemies of the state. Some are even encouraged to do so—unofficially of course."

"Have you, m'sieur?"

"Have I what?"

"Been encouraged to steal from your country's enemies?"

"You mean has it been suggested—unofficially or otherwise—that to stop a French nobleman on the road and rob him down to his garters is not so dreadful a crime as halting some fat English burgher?" He smiled and his eyes glittered faintly. "No, mam'selle. I'm afraid I cannot even offer that as an excuse for my actions, regardless how determined you appear to be to find one, or"— his voice softened noticeably—"how much I would like to oblige you by providing it. God knows I haven't had this many appeals to my conscience in more years than I can recall, but the plain truth of it is, I am exactly what you see before you. Nothing more, nothing less."

"A thief who plays a piano *forcer les anges de pleurer*," she murmured as she stood. "A man who drinks fine Burgundy claret and plays the part of a buffoon because it suits his sense of humor to do so? If that is all you are and all you ever will be . . . then I pity you, m'sieur, for I have looked into *your* eyes and seen the possibility of so much more."

She turned and walked slowly to the door.

"It would be another grave mistake, mam'selle, to think you know me. Or to wish you could change me."

His voice halted her briefly and she looked back at where he lay, sprawled like a fallen archangel in a pool of candlelight.

"No, m'sieur." She smiled somewhat sadly. "I would never make that mistake, I promise you."

*☽

# Chapter 20

Renée had already closed the door behind her before she realized she had not brought a candle or taper with her to light the way down. She thought briefly about going back, but her exit had been made with such fine resolve, to return in search of a light to ward off castle ghosts would doubtless restore the mockery to his smile.

She had walked up and down the narrow corkscrew staircase a dozen times or more over the past few days, so there was no mystery as to what loomed below. Nor was it entirely pitch black, and she guessed that Antoine had left a candle burning in one of the sconces at the bottom. Nonetheless, it was a ghostly sort of glow that lost strength on every turn of the stairs and was thinned to a pale haze by the time it reached the landing where she stood. The more eerie darkness came from above and behind, from the additional turn that led up to the rooftop battlements. If there was an otherworldly being in residence, he was more than likely crouched up there in the utter blackness, his eyes glowing like two pinpricks of light, his breath cold and dank as it frosted out before him.

Renée started moving swiftly down the spiraling stairs, the muslin of her long skirt catching on the steps behind and belling out like a white cloud. Because she was so intent on ignoring the rasping breath of the specter, who was by now lunging down the stairs after her, she

rounded a turn and slammed fully into a tall, dark silhouette coming the other way.

The shriek she gave off startled Finn almost as much
as seeing a pale apparition floating down the stairs toward
him. He raised the hooded taper he was carrying and gave
them both a moment to verify the identity of the other
before lowering it to waist level again.

"Mad'moiselle Renée," he said on a gust of relief. "I
should think it a rather reckless business running down
these stairs in the darkness."

Her heart was still squeezed against her rib cage and
although she had a hand over her breast to keep it from
bursting through, she still slumped back and leaned a
shoulder against the wall.

"You were not in your room when I went to fetch you,
and Master Antoine implied you might still be here." He
paused to gulp at another breath. "There are carriages in
the drive, mad'moiselle. Five of them. Your aunt and uncle have arrived along with Mr. Vincent and at least a
dozen others I did not linger to identify. Lord Paxton was
howling for wine and brandy, while his lady wife was
giving instructions to that Pigeon woman to prepare a late
supper. Ten o'clock, she proposed, and it has just gone
eight now."

"But . . . they were not supposed to come until tomorrow."

"I gather your uncle decided the longer he had to partake of Lord Wooleridge's hospitality, the longer he
might have to offer it by way of reciprocation."

Renée turned so that her entire back was against the
wall, not just her shoulder, and from somewhere out of a
distant memory, she conjured an oath that was vulgar
enough to have Finn lifting the lamp again and peering
narrowly at her face.

"I believe both you and the young master have been
spending far too much time in that rogue's company." He

angled the light even closer. "Has he said—or done—something to upset you?"

"No. No," she said, frowning, "but he has given me something to think about."

Without preamble, she relayed Tyrone Hart's speculations concerning her uncle, Roth, and Edgar Vincent, and by the time she had finished, Finn was sitting on the step beside her, his brow similarly crumpled in a frown.

"Frankly, I never liked your uncle very much," he declared. "He was always sneaking about stealing coins from your grandfather's office or running up enormous debts his yearly annuity could not cover by a fourth. And yes, his friends and associates were a scurrilous lot. Dirty fingernails and eyes too close together to suggest any real intelligence. And manners—*faugh*! Better suited to a brothel or a pig sty. Why, I remember once . . . no, never mind. It hardly warrants repeating except to say I would not be entirely shocked to discover there is some foundation for Mr. Hart's speculations. After all, who better to judge a thief than another thief?"

Renée was quiet so long and her gaze remained so unfocused, he leaned forward to try to catch her eye. "Mad'moiselle?"

"Yes," she murmured. "I heard you. I just . . . find it hard to believe there is nothing we can do about it."

"Well." He sighed. "There, too, I find I must agree with the brigand. We cannot very well go to the authorities; it would be your uncle's word against ours, and ours I'm afraid, would be the more suspect, especially with the warrant outstanding for Master Antoine's arrest—counterfeit as it might be. Unfortunately the only way to punish men of this ilk in a way they understand is to strike where they would feel the pain the deepest—in the purse. And since our one attempt to do that appears to have failed so miserably, I would suggest we have no alternative now but to accept defeat, cut our losses, and leave this wretched place at the first opportunity."

"Or we could steal the rubies ourselves," she said slowly.

"I beg your pardon?"

"We could steal the rubies ourselves," she repeated and turned to look at him.

"Ourselves?"

"Why not?"

"Why *not*?"

"For heaven's sakes, Finn, if you are just going to repeat everything I say—!"

"If I am repeating it, mad'moiselle, it is because I cannot believe I am hearing you correctly. Steal the rubies ourselves? Have you been exposed to the noxious effects of camphor and mustard plaster too long? Or perhaps it is the air in this tower," he said, glancing warily around. "It was said all Royalists were slightly mad to defy Cromwell in the heart of England."

"Perhaps it is long past time I was exposed to something," she said. "Something that would not make me so afraid of my own shadow."

"Mary and Joseph," Finn muttered. "Where would you come by such an absurd notion? You are brave beyond measure!"

"I may act brave and bold in front of men like Roth and Vincent," She insisted, "but that is all it is: an act. Inside I am terrified. I tremble like a small child and wish only that I could crawl under the bed with Antoine to hide."

"Well, good sweet mercy, child, we all shake and tremble inside in the face of adversity. You would not be human if you did not. Even he"—Finn gave his head a belligerent jerk toward the top of the stairs—"has likely felt his heart palpitate a time or two, I warrant."

She glanced up at the darkness and very much doubted it. "Nevertheless, Finn, if we do nothing and simply run away again, I have a greater fear that we will just keep running for the rest of our lives."

"But . . . what you are suggesting—"

"What I am suggesting is that we cheat them at their own game. You say we have no way to prove they stole the gems, but if we had the rubies, we would *have* the proof, would we not? When he gave me the jewels in London, he made a great mistake by allowing me to wear them in public, for I know there were some *Françaises*, like the Comptesse de Trouville, who recognized the suite. If their testimony is not sufficient for the English authorities, it would surely be enough to interest the agents of the French government who care very little about English courts and laws."

"You would deal with those people? The same ones who persecuted your family and drove us out of our home?"

"If it were the only way to make them pay for their crimes, yes."

"You propose a dangerous game, mad'moiselle," he said quietly.

"Life is full of danger, Finn," she quoted softly. "And precious little justice. Even if we only manage to steal the rubies, we will have the satisfaction of cheating them out of the fifty thousand pounds they are worth."

"I would be happier cheating them out of our company," Finn said grimly. "Something that grows more difficult to do the longer we remain in residence here. The wedding, if I might remind you, is but three days hence."

"You stole my mother away from the altar an hour before the ceremony was to take place," she reminded him. "At any rate, we have a way out now—the passage—and can leave at a moment's notice, regardless how many soldiers Roth has watching the doors and windows. M'sieur Hart would even help us, I am sure."

"Has he offered?"

"N—no. Not exactly."

"Nor will he, not when his own neck is at risk. Rogues

like him are always chivalrous when they are at your mercy. For all that he appears to have the fortitude of an ox, however, I should not anticipate his gallantry lasting beyond the hour of his departure."

A faint hiss and sputter drew Finn's attention to the lamp. The candle had been barely more than a stub when he had lit it and they had been sitting in the stairwell a fair half hour now.

"It will be nearing nine o'clock. I was dispatched to inform you that your presence, and that of your brother, would be expected at supper."

She nodded and stood, and Finn shot to his feet beside her.

"Mr. Hart should be informed they are here," Finn said, handing her the lamp. "Take extra care when you are exiting below. There are sure to be additional maids and servants running about and it would not do to have one of them see you emerge from a presumably solid stone wall."

"I will hold the light while you go up."

"I am quite able—"

"To break your neck or your leg or both in the dark," she said flatly. "I will wait and hold the light. Tell *le capitaine* what he needs to know, then go to Antoine. See that he dresses in his very finest clothes. We must make a good and dutiful impression on our guests."

Finn hesitated a moment, then took the uncharacteristic liberty of placing both his hands on her shoulders. "I have not agreed to anything yet. And if, at any time, I feel there is danger—"

"You will have to pick up your heels and run fast to keep up with Antoine and me," she assured him. "Now go. Tell M'sieur Hart the ghost must be extremely quiet from now on."

✱

Renée followed her own advice and changed into a pale, rose-colored gown with a low-cut bodice and long fitted sleeves. Jenny arrived in time to dress her hair in a high crown of golden curls, and although Renée normally shunned the use of cosmetic aides, she dabbed a small amount of rouge on her cheeks and a touch more on her lips to relieve the bloodless cast of her skin.

It was precisely ten o'clock when she and Antoine descended the main staircase. While she had braced herself for the first meeting with her uncle in over five weeks, she faltered a moment on the landing when she heard a raucous burst of masculine laughter coming through the open doors of the main drawing room.

Antoine had stopped beside her. From his expression, she guessed he would rather run naked through a gauntlet than go any farther. He was wearing a light gray coat and dark breeches. His cravat was tied high and tight beneath his chin and his curls had been tamed into smooth blond waves. For the briefest of moments, she saw her father's face imposed over Antoine's, and as frightened as he was, she saw some of the same determination flex into the muscles of his jaw.

"Have courage, *mon coeur*," she whispered.

*I would rather have one of the captain's guns.*

She gave him a startled look but he only extended his arm and offered Renée a shaky smile.

Edgar Vincent was standing by the fireplace, a drink in his hand, looking like a large black hawk in dark wool and contrasting whites. He was talking to two other men, both of whom seemed vaguely familiar, though their names escaped her. Lord Paxton and his wife, Lady Penelope, were at the opposite end of the wide hearth; her aunt was sitting and conversing with another woman of similar starched qualities, while her uncle stood to one side in a stance that conveyed his best parliamentary mien. He was a large man with a forthright belly and short, thin legs, all of which was pinched, girded, and stuffed into peacock blue satin. His reddish brown hair framed his face in short, well-oiled waves that flowed down each heavy jowl to form thick muttonchops whiskers. In the early days of the revolution, when King George had been suffering one of his fits and the cry was out to install the Prince of Wales as regent, Lord Paxton had backed Charles Fox and his fellow radicals in Parliament. Later, when the tumbrils had begun to roll through the streets of Paris and Fox had been depicted as supporting regicide, Paxton had quickly declared himself for William Pitt—a change many of Fox's former compatriots had also made, but for valid political reasons.

If Tyrone Hart's suppositions were correct, Renée could see why—now looking at her uncle with a calm and dry eye—it would have been expeditious to declare himself a monarchist, sympathetic to the plight of the fleeing French aristocrats. Who, indeed, would put their family's welfare into the hands of a banker who believed in abolishing the crown?

"Mademoiselle d'Anton! How lovely to see you again!"

The shrill, nasal greeting had come from her left, where two younger women that Renée had not previously noticed were standing. She recognized the voice and the speaker at once, partly by the instant tightening of the skin across the nape of her neck and partly by the long, extraordinarily hooked nose that had earned Ruth Entwistle the unkind nickname of "Miss Beaker."

Having established the one identity, it helped put a name—Sir John Entwistle—to one of the gentlemen speaking with Edgar Vincent. And it was Dame Judith Entwistle, Miss Beaker's mother, who nudged Lady Paxton on the arm and whispered a less than discreet alert.

Noting her aunt's cool response, Renée smiled and offered Miss Beaker a polite curtsy.

"How nice to see you again, Miss Entwistle, and how

lovely of you and your family to visit. I trust the roads were not in too dreadful condition?"

"Oh my dear, they were simply appalling. I was just saying to my dear sister Phoebe that I have not been bounced around so much since I was an infant on papa's lap. Even so, we should not have missed the festivities for all the rain in the world." Small, feral eyes glinted in Antoine's direction. "Gracious! I had quite forgotten how handsome, and mature, is your brother." She dipped in a tastefully executed swirl of burgundy silk. "Your Grace. You do, of course, remember Phoebe?"

Renée could feel Antoine's body tensing beside her as Miss Beaker thrust her younger sister forward for his inspection. He might only have been thirteen, but he was a *duc* and would be regarded as a highly prized catch to a family consisting of eight other siblings, all girls.

"I am afraid you will have to excuse us a moment, Miss Entwistle, for we have not seen our aunt and uncle since their arrival in Coventry."

"Of course." When she smiled, the end of her nose hung well over her front teeth. "But we shall expect to monopolize your company at supper."

"Renée." Lord Paxton's voice was cold and dry, the nondescript blue of his eyes even more bland as he offered a perfunctory bow. "I trust you have been well these past weeks?"

"Thank you, yes." Unable to stop herself, Renée stared at the abbreviated nub of his left earlobe and the scar just visible beneath the carefully arranged waves of his hair.

"Colonel Roth told me your gout was causing you some discomfort," she murmured. "Was he mistaken?"

Paxton followed her gaze down to acknowledge the glaring lack of bandages or cane. "Bah. Sound as a tree stump, actually. It was all the braying and bleating in the House that began to wear on my patience. Shouting day and night. And all because this Napoleon fellow is scattering the Austrian army like skittles and putting Mr. Pitt in a righteous froth. Wants us to send troops to Italy, would you believe it? Wants to send Nelson and the whole bloody navy to the Mediterranean just to slap the wrist of some short-assed artillery commander who imagines himself a conqueror. I tell you it is enough to bring on a bout of gout, what with all the kicking and stamping and long-winded elocutions. I was thankful to have an excuse to come away."

Sir John and Edgar Vincent joined the circle, the latter coming up beside Renée. After studying the appreciable amount of cleavage revealed by the low-cut bodice, he slid his hand with possessive familiarity around her waist.

"I can sympathize with your feelings of impatience, Paxton. These last three days are going to seem like an eternity."

"You will be kept too busy to notice the time," Lady Penelope promised, her smile as pretentious as the eyebrow that arched in Renée's direction. "We will be hosting a small party here tomorrow evening. Nothing too elaborate on such short notice, of course, but it seems to be expected, so we must comply. Just a few neighbors and close acquaintants, some political associates, the like. The invitations were dispatched this morning from Fairleigh Hall before we departed, but if there is anyone you especially wished to include. A new friend you have made, or some such . . . ?"

"I did not have many opportunities to socialize," Renée said quietly.

"No, indeed." Her aunt offered another pinched smile. "Mrs. Pigeon tells me you have been quite the ideal houseguest. She claims she rarely saw you and never heard any complaints. I dare say, Edgar, she should make the ideal wife, so docile and demure. Not at all like her mother, by all accounts."

It took every scrap of strength and willpower Renée possessed to keep her skin from flooding an angry red. It

was not the first time she'd had to practice such restraint;
the long months she had spent in London had been one
test of endurance after another. As it was she could
scarcely believe her mother and uncle had emerged from
the same womb, or that they had grown into two such
opposite individuals. To compound matters, her aunt was
a jealous and resentful old crow who enjoyed picking at
open wounds. She referred to Antoine as "that stupid
little boy" and openly implied that he was not just mute,
but slow-witted.

He was standing behind Renée, hoping to use her as a
shield, but Lady Penelope could not let an opportunity
pass. "Come out from behind there, Nephew, and greet
our guests properly."

Antoine edged forward. He looked solemnly at Lady
Entwistle and offered a polite bow, then duplicated the
gesture for his aunt.

Pronouncing every word with exaggerated care as if it
were the language posing the barrier, she asked, "Can
you not say hello yet?"

Antoine's lips moved, delivering his reply silently in
French, and beside him, Renée was forced to lower her
lashes to keep her expression blank.

"What did he say?" her aunt demanded.

"He said"—*you hideous fat cow, I hope you choke on a
mouthful of your own dung*—"welcome to you Madam, it is
a pleasure to see you again."

"Well." Lady Penelope expanded her already prodi-
gious breasts with a lungful of air. "At least he is civil."

* ☽

# Chapter 21

The evening dragged on for three endless hours. Somewhere in the five carriages there had obviously been crates of food and wine, for they had a late feast of roasted plovers, fresh trout, and grilled lamb, all of it accompanied by great bowls full of buttered vegetables and savory sauces—delicacies neither the cook nor the housekeeper had thought to squander on Renée and her brother. Antoine ate so many fresh custards and twists of cream-filled pastries his eyes were glazed.

When the men were left to their cigars the two older ladies and Miss Beaker declared they were too weary to linger overlong in the drawing room. This suited Renée just fine, for her eyes burned with fatigue and her cheeks were numb from maintaining a frozen, polite smile all evening.

Finn was waiting to tend to Antoine. He reported that he had looked in on Tyrone Hart and there was, quite simply, nothing else that needed to be done for their patient. He would be gone by morning and frankly, it was not soon enough to suit James Finnerty.

Renée wearily agreed, but when she was in bed and her arms were hugged around a fat feather bolster, she found she could not keep her eyes closed. She kept seeing Tyrone Hart bending over in front of the fire, his body naked and gleaming, or Tyrone beside her in the bed, his eyes smoldering like flames as he rose up above her.

With a sigh, she rolled over onto her back and stared

up at the shadows overhead. The firelight threw moving patterns onto the ceiling and she remembered the last time she had watched them dance and writhe—her hands had been twisted around the sheets and Tyrone's tongue had been tracing wicked patterns across her belly and between her thighs. She closed her eyes and let the memories wash over her, arching into the flow as her nipples gathered and tightened, and her skin rippled with the remembered sensation of his hands roving from her breasts to her waist to her thighs. A soft groan recalled how his fingers had stroked deftly over places so sensitive she thought she would faint from the pleasure. An even softer sigh noted that the ache was still there, throbbing and insistent, and the heat caused her to throw off the blankets and quit the bed. She walked to the window and stood looking out over the darkness. And a moment later, she drew on her bathrobe, lit a stub of candle and, peering cautiously out into the hallway first, slipped through the door and along the corridor, refusing to even think of what she was doing until she was behind the tapestry and easing open the door to the old tower.

She ran up the steps, slowing only when she reached the top landing. A slit of light was fanning out across the stone floor and, with her heart throbbing in her throat, she turned the latch and eased the door open a few inches. The bed, the room was empty.

"M'sieur?"

A cool, metallic click brought her whirling around. Tyrone emerged out of the darkness of the landing behind her. He had one of the snaphaunces in his hand and even as her eyes were registering the shock of seeing him, he released the hammer and uncocked it, then lowered the gun to his side.

"What were you doing?" she asked on a gasp. "Where were you going?"

"I was just coming back, actually. I found it tiresome

listening to Paxton and Sir John Entwistle debate the vagaries of fighting a war on two fronts."

"You were in the main house?"

"I was careful." The cool, pale gray of his eyes followed the wild tumble of her hair down over her shoulders. Her belt had slipped its knot in her haste and her robe hung open, revealing the thin wisp of linen beneath. "And you, mam'selle? I might ask the same thing: why you are out roaming the halls in such a fetching state of dishabille."

"I . . . came to ask if there was anything else you needed before I . . . before I went to bed." She paused and swallowed hard.

"Finn was already here." The dark slash of his eyebrow crooked upward. "I was left with the distinct impression it was a farewell appearance, for he conveyed your fondest wishes for my speedy departure. In fact, he very clearly indicated that he did not see any reason why either of us should have to see each other again, and that it would be for the best if we did not."

"He said the same thing to me," she admitted with a faint smile. "He even threatened to sit outside my door all night."

"But you came anyway," he mused, "to see if I needed any more broth, or wanted my forehead bathed, or my blankets tucked in?"

They stared at one another through a small, suspended silence, each acutely aware of the other's closeness. His shirt was open at the throat and his hair was tied back with a strip of torn linen. Through the sheer white fabric she could see the wide band of bandaging that was wrapped tightly around his ribs. Above it the muscles across his shoulders and upper arms filled out the shape of the garment nicely, bulging farther as he bent over to set his guns on the table.

Finn had already expressed amazement at Hart's speed of recovery, but Renée had difficulty believing the man who stood before her now, as cool and confident as the first time she had seen him, was the same one who could barely sit upright without help two days ago. Here was the jungle-cat again, dark and sleek and dangerous, just a little bruised under the eyes but equally as wild and unpredictable. She took what she hoped was a casual step toward the door, and when he followed, she took another and another until her back came up hard against the rough stone wall.

"So why are you really here?" he asked quietly.

"I t—told you why."

Tyrone's gaze touched on the pale pink blush that warmed her cheeks, on the gaping edges of her robe that trembled with the same soft vibrations that shook her body. He had often taken pride in the fact that he could read a person's intent through the way they stood or held their bodies or conveyed what they were thinking, feeling, saying with their eyes. Renée d'Anton wanted something from him and it had brought her to him at the run without a thought for Finn's warnings or her own common sense.

Was it the rubies again? A woman's mind was a fickle thing at best, not easily understood by the bravest of men, but if she had come to ask for his help again . . .

"Look at me," he ordered softly.

When she did, when she lifted the protective shield of her lashes, each and every hair stood up across the nape of his neck. The blue of her eyes was darker, more intense than he had ever seen it, filled with such an utter depth of loss and loneliness it would be easy to mistake what he was seeing for fear. It was not fear, however. It was desire and longing and a thousand other emotions all tangled up with a helpless appeal for understanding.

"I h—have to go," she stammered.

She started to turn out the door but his arm came up, blocking her way.

"Please, m'sieur. I should not have come. Finn will be very angry if he looks in my room and I am not there."

"Actually . . . while I was standing outside your door a short while ago, I could hear him snoring to wake the dead."

She risked a sidelong glance. "You were outside my door?"

"I may be a thief and a scoundrel, but I am not ungrateful. I know the risks you have taken—that all of you have taken—and I thought I might have sounded a tad ungracious earlier this evening."

"You do not have to thank me, m'sieur."

"You save men's lives every day, do you?"

"It was just as much Finn and Antoine—"

"It was you, mam'selle," he murmured. "You saved my life, and I wish to express my gratitude." His hand slipped up from her shoulder to her chin, turning it so that when he bent his head, her mouth was there to meet his. The warm, heady taste of him caused her to part her lips around a faint breath, but he did not take advantage of the invitation, and when she would have taken the initiative herself, he pulled away. Not without great reluctance. And not without a hardness in his jaw that belied the casual gesture he made as he tucked a few strands of blond hair behind her ear.

"You had, indeed, better go," he said quietly. "You had better get the hell out of here while I am still feeling noble enough to let you leave."

Her hands, clenched up to now in fists by her side, crept up to his chest, spreading flat when she passed the strips of bandaging and encountered the heat and texture of his skin. Her fingers combed through the soft dark hairs and she ran them higher, making no effort to pretend she had any claims left to modesty or pride as she slipped them beneath the open edges of his shirt. His skin was warm and smooth. The dark hairs tickled her palms and teased her fingertips as she ran them up his breastbone to his collar, then around to the back of his neck where she broke contact long enough to unfasten the frayed strip of linen that bound his hair. With a look that was still half pleading, half frightened of being rejected, she threaded her fingers up into the thick black waves, combing them forward so that the silk was on his cheeks, touching hers as she rose up on tiptoes and pressed her lips to his.

Tyrone stiffened slightly in resistance, knowing that of the two of them, he should be the one strong enough to stop it before it went any further. The trouble, of course, was that he did not want to stop her. He very much wanted the staggering pleasure of holding her in his arms again, of hearing her cry out his name until there was no strength left to give it sound or substance. Before Renée d'Anton, he had taken his pleasure with casual, careless thanks, even wild recklessness when his blood was hot and singeing with tension. But he had never felt this excruciating level of urgency before, never this unrelenting restlessness that built all day and night and had him searching for scraps of toweling she had touched, snuffling into it like a bloodhound as if he could detect the scent of her lingering on it. Nor had he ever wasted a scrap of conscience standing outside a woman's bedroom door debating the consequences of going inside.

Her lips were soft and supple and he opened his mouth, responding to her entreaty with a ferocity that drew the breath from both their bodies. He returned her kiss with bruising force, damning the jolt of pain in his side that reminded him he was neither as mobile nor as flexible as he would have liked to be. Finn had bound the ribs tightly that afternoon and the only real difficulty came when he tried to bend over or lift anything above the level of his shoulder. But his legs had not given out yet and his breeches were growing tight enough to suggest he was fully recovered elsewhere. Fully, dangerously, incautiously recovered.

Renée welcomed his hunger, matching it with her own. The mindless drumming in her blood compelled her to run her hands down the heat of his body again and with each stroke she melted deeper into his embrace. She was not unaware of the growing bulge at his groin and leaned into it, using her hands to circle his waist and pull herself even closer.

"Wait," he grabbed her wrists. "Wait, for God's sake."

He saw the instant blush of shame rise in her cheeks and shook his head. "You don't understand," he explained with a groan. "Much as I want to oblige you—" He stopped again and gazed into her eyes, the centers wide and black and shining up at him with a volatile mixture of desire and desperation. He stared at her mouth and his thumb moved of its own accord to brush away the faint glistening of moisture.

"I am not the man you want, Renée," he said hoarsely. "I am not the man you deserve."

"I know that. Believe me, m'sieur, I know that."

His eyes narrowed and his blood roared through his temples and he could feel her hands skimming across his flesh again, smoothing over his chest, exploring the shapes and contours of muscle.

"Renée, dammit . . . I am trying to be noble here, but I swear to God if you touch me—"

"Here?" she asked in a whisper, putting her lips to his breast.

When her tongue swirled around his nipple he closed his eyes and groaned. He bowed his head, burying his lips in the silken mass of her hair, cursing softly as he did so for her hands were prowling lower, plucking the buttons free one by one until his breeches were gaping and his flesh was springing hard and urgent into her welcoming grasp.

"You *will* be the death of me, you know," he gasped.

Her fingers were cool, her breath warm, her voice

husky against his throat. "Does this mean it is all right to touch you now?"

He groaned again and tilted her mouth up to his for another hard, lashing kiss. She continued to cradle his flesh, to stroke it until he had to break away again and grab her wrists in order to avoid the ignominy of exploding against her belly. He kept her hands tight in his and led her to the bed. Once there, he let her take command again, the lust rising hotter and faster in his blood as she helped him out of his shirt and breeches and cast the crumpled garments away in the shadows. Her gaze went briefly to his bandages, but there was no sign of pink leaking through. She looked lower, at the thick spear of hard flesh rearing against his belly, and he had to steady her as she wavered and swayed weakly forward into his arms.

His hands went to her shoulders and peeled off the robe. Beneath it she wore a shapeless cloud of linen, primly fastened to the neck by a row of thin pink ribbons. He freed them one at a time until he was accorded the same privilege of being able to slip his hands beneath the fabric and cradle the lush ripeness of her breasts. Her nipples were already taut enough to draw a moan from the lovers' throats, and the night rail quickly joined the robe in a puddle around her ankles.

Gloriously naked she stood before him, her skin pale as cream in the candlelight, her hair spilling around her shoulders in a waterfall of tarnished gold. Her eyes were still dark with desire, innocently trusting, and Tyrone realized, suddenly and shockingly, that this lustrous wisp of a beauty was capable of destroying every iron clad rule he had made himself obey for the past twenty-eight years.

And Renée, who thought he was hesitating for other reasons, bowed her head and captured her lower lip between her teeth. "If this is not possible . . . I will understand. I do not want you to hurt yourself, m'sieur . . ."

He offered up a ragged laugh. "As you so eloquently pointed out, it would have been possible the first day if you had not been so quick with the laudanum. It only requires a minor adjustment—"

"—in technique," she finished for him.

With their mouths joined, he eased himself back onto the bed and guided her down over him, parting her thighs and positioning her legs on either side of his hips so that she straddled him. Obeying the firm command of his hands, she slid forward and settled slowly, blissfully, back over the rampant thrust of his erection. A fierce streak of pleasure shuddered through her belly at the first touch of hot, sliding flesh, and as the solid heat of him continued to furrow high and hard and deep within her, she felt herself tighten eagerly around him.

"Easy, *ma innocente*," he gasped, his teeth clenched against his own impatience. "We're almost there."

Renée shuddered again and shook her head in awed disbelief, for there were still inches to go and no possible place to fit them. But he only smiled and stroked her hips, and eased her gently forward and back until they were bound snugly together.

When she could, she drew a slow, steady breath and held it. Her eyes were closed and her head hung forward between her outstretched arms and, lying still as stone beneath her, Tyrone watched every flicker and shiver that passed across her face, waiting until she had become accustomed to his inflexible length and unyielding angle of penetration. Her body was taut, trembling with anticipation, thudding with excitement yet immutable and determined to prolong each sensation as long as possible. He was none too stable himself feeling each subtle adjustment she made, each warm throb of lubricant her body squeezed around him. But he dared not move, dared not allow her to move until he was well and sure he could weather the impending storm.

She wriggled against the restraint of his hands and shivered through a threatening volley of spasms. "*Je pense que je me meurs,*" she cried softly.

"You are not dying," he assured her. "You are just discovering how to come alive."

She looked helplessly at him through the silvered fall of her hair, and he smiled again then slid his hands up from where they were clamped around her waist. He cupped her breasts in his palms and rolled the calloused pads of his thumbs across the tightly peaked tips, and while the cry was still in her throat, he drew her forward, closing his mouth around a nipple, suckling it with hard, sharp motions of his lips and tongue that perfectly matched the harder, sharper streaks of pleasure that began to tear through her body. Of her own accord she began to move over his flesh, stretching forward and pushing back, forward and back, in increasingly longer, bolder strokes that soon drove him to abandon her nipples, abandon her breasts, and hold on fast to the frantic motion of her hips.

As shocking as it was for Renée to open her eyes and see how feverishly she moved over him, it was twice as astonishing to see Tyrone staring defenselessly back up at her as his body strained and arched into her rhythm. She could feel the powerful muscles beneath her, inside her contracting and expanding. She experienced the thrill of absolute ecstasy when his head pressed back into the ticking and his body surged upward, rigid and shaking in the throes of a release that she had only fractions of a second to appreciate before the brilliant flare of her own stunning climax swept through her. Through unrelenting, undiminished waves of rapture, she clung to him and shivered his name and her body moved in a desperate blur until one by one, all the myriad fluttering spasms were spent and she collapsed, utterly nerveless and replete, in his arms.

After several minutes, when the wildness of his own

pulsebeat calmed, Tyrone raked up the handfuls of hair that were smothering his face under a golden cloud and twisted them into a thick coil at the nape of her neck. He heard a hushed and resentful little moan and smiled.

"May I assume you are still among the living?"

A long, warm breath bathed his neck before Renée lifted her head off his shoulder. Careful to avoid acknowledging the gentle mockery in his eyes or his smile, and despite his earlier assurances, she inspected his bandages again.

"Did I hurt you?"

"If you did, I was too distracted to notice."

Her shoulders slumped a little in exasperation. "Must you make a joke of everything?"

"I was not joking. The bed could have caught fire and I would not have noticed. Roth and his dragoons could have burst into the room with bayonets drawn and I would not have noticed. And in case *you* did not notice, *ma petite*, you did most of the work. Like the true rogue I am, I only had to lay back and reap the benefits. I still am," he added in an appreciative murmur as he studied her body.

Renée followed his gaze. The muted yellow light from the single, flickering candle suddenly seemed as bright as a roomful of sunshine, and her cheeks warmed despite the glaring lack of any and all modesty over the past several minutes. She had never been naked in front of anyone other than a maid before, and because their previous encounter had been mostly in darkness and shadow, she had not felt particularly exposed. Certainly not to the degree she was now. There were mottled pink flush marks on her hips where his hands had gripped her and a similar blush on the insides of her thighs where the skin had been chafed by the coarser hairs on his legs.

She was, she realized with appalling chagrin, straddling him like a peasant would a plow horse: without a shred of shame or contrition. She glanced up quickly, but any fear she might have had concerning the impression she was leaving in Tyrone's mind was banished the moment she saw the pleasure in his eyes. Far from looking at her as if she had behaved like a hellion in heat, they were telling her how lovely she was, how exquisitely perfect the shape of her breasts, the line of her throat, the slope of her shoulders.

"You are," he murmured, "as beautiful as moonlight."

It was such an unexpected compliment, her body responded with another silky throb.

The pale eyes flicked up immediately.

"Do not try to tell me no one has ever said that to you before."

"I have been told," she admitted with a shrug. "Many times."

"But you don't believe it?"

Responding to the astonishment in his voice, she gave a little sigh. "I believe it. But I have lived with this face all of my life and wish, at times, that I looked more like Miss Beaker."

"Who?"

"Miss Entwistle," she said, blushing.

"Good God, whatever for?"

"Because then, perhaps, I would not just be a pretty decoration on someone's arm. People might actually seek intelligent conversation and not assume my knowledge or interests were limited to ribbons and furbelows, or how best to set a feather in the hair."

Tyrone ran his hands thoughtfully up her arms and brought them to rest on either side of her neck. "While it never occurred to me you might be an expert on feathers, it also never once entered my mind that you would ever be anyone's pretty decoration. Furthermore, if it would set your mind at ease any to know, you are not entirely without flaws. Your nose, for one thing, is crooked."

"My nose?"

"Indeed. It tilts the tiniest bit to the left side. You also have a habit of chewing on your lip if you are nervous or frightened or angry—I warrant you bit your nails when you were younger—and you have a scar on your temple, just at the hairline."

She raised a hand self-consciously, touching a fingertip to the place where she had tumbled into a rosebush and cut herself on a thorn. It had happened when she was barely three years old—she could not even recall the incident—and the scar was all but invisible; she needed bright daylight herself to find it.

"Too high," he said, guiding her hand lower, pressing her fingers over the faint tracing. The fact he had noticed it left her somewhat short of breath and speech, and when he laced his fingers through hers and brought them back down, pressing them against his mouth, she felt the effect of his tender, nibbling caress all the way to her toes.

"I . . . should go back now," she said haltingly.

"Whereas I was thinking . . . you should stay right where you are."

She looked down again in surprise, for she could feel him stirring inside her, a distinct and vigorous hardening where there had been only luxuriant softness a moment ago. To ward off any further thought of protest, he skimmed his hands lightly down her thighs then up again, bringing them to rest at the golden juncture. With his thumbs, he parted the dewy curls and spread the slick folds of flesh, probing and stroking until he found the tiny pink bud he sought.

Renée had nowhere to look but into his eyes. Even they could not hold her too long as his thumbs continued to tease, and she arched back, bracing herself on outstretched arms while he brought her to the gentlest of peaks. When it passed, he started again, using long, deft strokes of his fingers this time to supplement the pressure building inside and out. As she drifted with the pleasure, the haphazard twist of her hair uncoiled and dragged across the tops of his thighs.

"Oh! M'sieur . . . !"

Tyrone groaned and pulled his hands away. He caught her wrists, then her upper arms, bringing her forward until her face was an inch from his and there was nothing to see but the sparks blazing from his eyes.

"Not ten minutes ago you were all but screaming my name. If you do not want me to turn you out of the bed this instant, you will stop calling me 'm'sieur' or 'capitaine.' You will call me Tyrone. It is a fine Irish name and I rather like the sound of it said with a French accent."

She expelled a gust of air, her body still molten and rife with sensation. "So you *are* Irish? Finn guessed as much."

"My mother was. I was named after the county where she was born."

"And your father?" She wriggled her hips, seeking friction and pressure where she needed it most.

He scowled. "You are trying to distract me."

She considered the charge and the threat that preceded it for as long as it took to contemplate the fine dark lashes, the strong straight nose, the full sensuous lips that were more intoxicating than the purest French cognac.

"And if I am?"

"It will not work."

She refrained from calling him a liar, for he was thick and full and straining with impatience inside her, and he would no more toss her out of his bed at that moment than she would let him leave this place without taking some indelible memory of her with him.

She leaned forward, swamping him with her hair as she kissed him. "Tyrone," she murmured, kissing his chin, the underside of his throat. He gave a little grunt of satisfaction and she licked a path down to the hollow at the base of his neck, punctuating each caress with muffled whispers. "Tyrone, Tyrone, Tyrone."

Her body shifted lower and released its warm hold on

his flesh, but before he could protest, she closed her lips around the dark velvet of his nipples, using her teeth and tongue to elicit a startled hiss of breath from his throat.

"The same time I was calling out your name, 'Tyrone,' you were calling me innocent. Do you remember that?"

"You thought you were dying."

"I *am* French, you know."

"Yes?" His voice was wary. "And?"

"And"—she slid lower on his body and paused to admire the solid bands of muscle that sculpted his waist and belly—"the French call it *la petite morte*, the little death."

"An authority on the subject, are you?"

"I am not as innocent as you might think. I read books. I listened to court gossip. The French Court, you know, was very . . . mmm . . . liberal. The women spoke of many things, of men and pleasure, and ways of insuring a lover did not grow bored. Of course, I have always been curious to know if they truly worked." She curled her lip between her teeth as she continued to stroke her hands down his belly and over the tops of his thighs. "Jean-Louis was very sweet and attentive, but I think he would have been too easily shocked."

She sat back on her heels a moment, and while Tyrone was wondering what she was leading up to, she let her hands trail along his outer thighs and inner thighs, just as he had done, then curled her fingers around the various shapes of his flesh, lingering if she saw a response, smiling if she heard a soft oath or saw him tense himself against a particularly creative pattern of strokes.

"Tyrone?"

"Yes?" The word came out through the grate of his teeth and she smiled as she bent over him again.

"You will tell me, *s'il vous plaît*, if you are feeling bored?"

Tyrone sucked in a lungful of air and looked everywhere, at everything but the slow, deliberate movements of her mouth and hands. He gripped the wooden slats that formed the sides of the bed and curled his toes so hard they started to cramp. Beads of moisture broke out across his brow and his entire body flushed as if in the grips of another fever. If she wanted to know if he could be shocked she had succeeded, but not for the reasons she supposed. He was stunned because this, definitely, was never supposed to have happened. He was never supposed to have been the one reduced to whimpering volleys of sensations, never the one to writhe and arch and plead for a release that was promised, then withdrawn, promised and withheld.

Far past any limit he had achieved in his most robust moments, he growled and reached down, twining his fingers into her hair, dragging her back by gleaming fistfuls until it was his mouth she was suckling with such splendid enthusiasm and her body that was stroking his flesh with such explosive vigor. They strained into the oblivion of ecstasy together and this time, when the fever of their passion was spent, it was Tyrone who lay immobile and completely bereft of the strength it would have taken to open his eyes. He lay spread-eagled like a starfish, his feet and arms hanging over the edge of the bed, his head lolled to one side obscured by locks of damp black hair.

Renée fetched blankets and covered him, then tucked his limbs into the warmth without rousing so much as a sigh of thanks. She smoothed the hair back off his face and kissed his temple and his cheek, and after insuring the candle was fresh enough to last out the night, she drew on her night rail and robe and lit a taper to take her down the stairs.

She hesitated one last time at the door, but there was nothing else to be said or done. She had made her farewells and he had made his and this was the end of it.

He would be gone by morning and she would never see him again.

"*Au revoir, mon Capitaine Clair d'Etoile,*" she whispered. "And thank you for making me feel warm again, even if it was just for a little while."

$\mathcal{I}$t was six o'clock the following evening when the knock came on her bedroom door. Renée had been dressed for over an hour; her hair was curled and pinned, woven with thin strips of ribbon. She had chosen to wear a plain white round gown, made of watered silk, with a fitted upper bodice, a loosely flowing skirt and train. The neck was cut low, the sleeves were long with delicately puffed caps at the shoulders. Jenny had taken extra care with her hair, piling the curls at the crown and leaving just the right number of golden spirals trailing down her neck to emphasize the whiteness of her skin, the smoothness of her shoulders.

Tyrone Hart had told her she was as beautiful as moonlight, and last night, she had believed it with all her heart. The look in his eyes, the tremors in his body and hands had made her proud of her beauty for the first time in longer than she could remember. She had wanted him to lust after her, wanted him to touch her, kiss her, hold her. She had wanted to be the moonlight for him, and for a little while, she was.

Tonight there was no one she wanted to impress. The man she was dressing for was brutish and crude, and the company she was preparing for was ugly and hostile and cruel. She wanted no hungry eyes watching her, following her every move. She wanted no one's hands to touch her, no one's body to press next to her, no one's heated breath to scald her cheek. She did not want to have to smile and dance and talk about foolish, inconsequential things when her heart was breaking and her body was aching in places she never thought would preoccupy nearly every one of her senses. Her breasts were tender, her thighs seemed to chafe at every step, and no matter how many times she washed, how long she soaked in the bath, his scent was on her skin. His heat was inside her body, making her slippery with despair.

What had her mother said? That one day a complete stranger would look at her from across the room; they would dance one dance and her heart would be lost forever?

Tyrone Hart may not have danced with her, but she was lost all the same.

He was gone. Finn had reported the tower room was empty and dark when he had gone up just after dawn. The bedding was neatly folded, ready for the next captive, and there were already colonies of spiders busy at work attaching the table and chairs to the walls.

"Miss?"

Renée's eyes flicked to Jenny's reflection in the mirror.

"Shall I answer the door, miss?"

"Yes. Yes, answer it." She had not even heard the knock, and she busied herself now, quickly picking up a comb and fussing with an obstinate curl. She heard Edgar Vincent's voice scrape along her spine and her heart sank another few inches into her belly.

Not surprisingly, it was the first time he had visited her room and the look on his face suggested he was not overly impressed with the sparse accommodations. Renée was seated in front of the small vanity and did not get up when he entered. To do so would have accorded him a measure of respect and here, in the privacy of her bedroom, she did not have to accord the fishmonger anything at all. Instead, she nodded at Jenny to go and fetch Antoine while she put the finishing touches of rouge on her cheeks.

"Ready and waiting, I see," Vincent observed. "Promptness is a quality I admire in a woman."

Renée refrained from remarking that the same did not hold true with regard to his own habits. He was an hour later than the time originally designated.

Like a great ugly bull, he strode into the center of the room and gazed openly at the bed. Renée, following his progress in the mirror, would not have been overly shocked to see him lean his hands on the mattress and test the firmness. But he came up behind her instead, stopping close enough for her to feel his body heat against her back.

He just stood there, staring at her, watching her fingers manipulate a curl, seeming to be intrigued by the way the candlelight played over her skin.

"You are one hell of a beautiful woman," he murmured, giving into the temptation to take up another of the slippery gold spirals and run it through his fingers. "Even if you weren't nobility, I would marry you just to keep another man from having you. And while I might not be a count or a duke or an earl and I may not have the right pedigree or color of blood in my veins, you will not be disappointed, my dear. You will be dressed like a queen and draped head to toe in the most exquisite jewels money can buy. Jewels like these"—he popped the clasp on the velvet case he was carrying—"that barely do you justice anyway."

Renée had not seen the Dragon's Blood rubies since her hasty departure from London and despite everything that had happened between then and now, her breath still caught at the sight of them. They were darkly magnificent, as compelling and mesmerizing as the first time she had seen them worn by the Duchesse de Blois.

"Exquisite, are they not? They're just the thing to remove the . . . virginal temperament of your gown. May I?"

She set the comb on the vanity table and folded her

hands in her lap. Vincent took the necklace out of the case and draped it around her neck, bending down as he did so. It brought the heat of his breath brushing against her cheek and with it the smell of strong spirits and stale smoke. Judging by the amount of redness in his eyes, he had been drinking heavily for most of the afternoon, and while he appeared to be steady enough on his feet, his hands, when the clasp was fastened, remained on her throat, cradling either side as he inspected her reflection in the mirror.

The necklace was heavy and felt like a wide, cold yolk around her neck. Against the whiteness of her skin, the rubies looked like fresh blood, dark and glittering, spilling in a deep vee to the edge of her bodice. They were far too gaudy to wear on an evening when there was not even to be any dancing, but she had not offered any objection when Vincent suggested it. Perhaps, because they were all under the same roof now, he would not be so diligent about taking them back at the end of the night.

Vincent's fingers were digging so tightly into her shoulders, the gold filigree was cutting into her skin. His gaze was fixed on the large tear-shaped ruby that sat between the press of her breasts, and she could almost see the spittle filling his mouth.

"Beautiful," he murmured. "I never thought I would ever have the chance to own something as beautiful as you."

Renée moved slightly, hoping to ease the pressure from his hands. He took a breath and turned his attention to the bracelet, waiting until it was fastened around her wrist before he sought another opportunity for intimacy. He kept her slender fingers hostage in his larger, hairy fist, raising her hand to his lips, planting a long, wet kiss on her wrist. His breath was starting to rasp in his throat and his tongue was beginning to lick her like a salt lick when she pulled her hand away and—not knowing what

else to do to keep from wiping it frantically on her skirt—
reached for the earrings.

Her fingers were shaking so badly she had difficulty
threading the loops through her lobes, but she managed
to only stab herself twice before the pendants were hanging, red and white fire, against her neck. Before he found
another reason to touch her, she stood up and waited
expectantly for him to move out of her way.

He crowded closer instead. "In two days' time we will
be man and wife."

"I am well aware of that, m'sieur."

"Since you will have to thaw to me then, mademoiselle, might it not be . . . advantageous . . . to show a
little warmth, possibly even a little gratitude, sooner,
rather than later?"

Some small spark of defiance caused her to raise her
eyes above the level of his cravat. "Advantageous to
whom, m'sieur: you or me?"

He leered and blew another hot, stinking breath into
her face. "To both of us, of course. You won't have to
spend another cold night alone in this big bed, and I
won't have to wear myself raw thinking about you up
here all alone."

"But I am not alone, m'sieur. As you can see"—she
glanced pointedly at the door where Antoine and Jenny
stood rooted to the spot—"I have all the company I care
to have for the time being."

She started to brush past him but his fist closed around
her arm and twisted her back around to face him.

"You might think your blood is better than mine," he
said in a snarl, "but it's all the same color when it comes
out of the vein, and if you don't want to see proof of that,
you won't ever turn your back or push me away again."

His face was mottled and his eyes were blazing and
Renée had but a moment to realize it would be foolish—
stupid, in fact—to anger Vincent or Roth or anyone in the
house tonight. She bit down hard on her lip and lowered

her lashes before she turned her face shamefully to the side.

"You must forgive me, m'sieur," she whispered. "Everything has happened so quickly, and I have had no one to turn to for help. The highwayman almost raped me. I was very nearly shot by mistake. Colonel Roth acts as if it was my fault his trap failed, and my uncle still refuses to believe it was not Antoine who shot him." She looked up and her eyes swam with silvery tears. "Believe me, m'sieur, when I am your wife and you have taken me away from this terrible place, I will not push you away. I will not *want* to push you away. I will want your strong arms to hold me close and make me feel safe and protected again. You will . . . keep me safe, will you not?"

The anger in his eyes wavered a moment, then mellowed completely when he saw the single bright teardrop that trickled down her cheek. "Rennie . . . do you really mean that?"

"I swear it. As soon as we are wed—"

"We don't have to wait," he said huskily, leaning closer. "I will gladly hold you now, by God, and if Roth or anybody else so much as looks at you sideways, I'll rip his lungs out through his throat."

"No. No, we must wait, m'sieur," she countered with a piteous sob, as much for the lie as for the sudden, eager look on Vincent's face. "We must have the blessing of the church. I am . . . am Catholic, and a—a virgin, and . . . it would be a sin before God."

"You let me worry about God," Vincent stated flatly. He started to lean forward to mash his lips over hers, when Antoine nudged his foot against the door, causing it to bang on the wall behind him.

"We should not keep our guests waiting any longer," Renée gasped. "My aunt has gone to a great deal of effort to make this a special evening."

She dashed away the wetness on her cheeks and hurried to the door. Antoine's face was chalk white as he fell into step beside her.

"*Mon dieu*," she whispered, "the man is a *cochon*. A pig. I feel the need for another bath."

*We will be free of him soon. Then Finn and I will protect you.*

She attempted a smile. "I know you will, *mon coeur*."

They followed the main hallway to the central staircase and Renée was forced to wait at the top for Vincent. His eyes were still hard and cold as he extended his arm, and she tried tò look calm as she descended the stairs at his side, but her stomach was in her throat and her skin was crawling everywhere he touched her. The sounds of noise and laughter were coming from the main drawing room and a couple of the guests were standing out on the landing, enjoying a glass of punch and quiet conversation. One of those guests, who could barely contain his excess of emotion, stood frozen in place, his cheeks inflamed with ardor. Renée, in dire need of a friendly face, saw Corporal Chase Marlborough and smiled, hoping he would take it as an invitation to approach.

He did so with such pathetic eagerness, she suffered a small pang of guilt for the torment she had been putting him through the past few days. Since he and his dragoons had been ordered to Harwood to "guard" her, she had treated him to little more than cold stares and icy silence. Her mind, of course, had been too preoccupied with her own troubles to sympathize with those of a lovesick soldier. Now, however, she used the excuse of his approach to disengage her hand from Edgar Vincent's arm and extend it in a friendly greeting to the corporal.

"Miss d'Anton. May I say . . . may I be permitted to say how extremely lovely you look tonight."

"Of course you may," she said with a small, forced laugh. "I am happy you could be here in an unofficial capacity."

He blushed and while it appeared obvious he would

have liked to keep her fingers pressed against his lips the entire night, he was forced to give way as a small commotion in the lower landing, followed by quick and angry bootsteps ascending the stairs to the second floor, announced Colonel Roth's arrival. He was in full uniform, with ropes of gold braid at his shoulders and trimming the wide lapels of his jacket. He wore his own flame red hair dressed in precise curls above his ears, with short wings brushed forward in an effort to conceal or at least lessen the ugliness of the wound on his cheek. Much like the damage he inflicted on the torn and savaged flesh around his fingernails, he had obviously been picking at the scab and there were spots of fresh red-raw skin showing through gaps in the dried crust.

"There you are," Vincent scowled. "I was beginning to wonder if you were going to join us at all."

"Forgive my tardy arrival." Roth offered a polite bow to Renée, his tawny eyes glittering as he admired the rubies against the shimmering white silk. "We took a man into custody early this morning and have been attempting all day to question him."

"Attempting?"

Roth nodded at Vincent. "He was gravely wounded when my men brought him in and has had only brief periods of lucidity."

"And?"

"And"—Roth let out a small huff of air—"it was another false alarm. I am seriously contemplating declaring it a crime in itself to possess a greatcoat and tricorn. At least this one had the height and breadth for it, though, as it turned out, he was a Scotsman on his way home to Glasgow and so blind he could barely see a candle held in front of his nose."

"A blind Scotsman from Glasgow, y' say?" The high-pitched query came from another guest leaning casually against the banister behind them. "And y' thought he might be masquerading as the rogue Starbright?"

Renée could barely believe her ears or her eyes as she turned and saw Tyrone Hart strolling over to join their group. He was the image of startling elegance in buff and green striped satin. The collar of his jacket rose incredibly high around his neck, framing a cravat knotted in a bow as wide as the foolish grin he was wearing as he addressed the colonel.

"I say again, a blind Scotsman from Glasgow? What did they expect he was out to steal? Lamp oil?"

Roth forced a polite smile. "My men are still under strict orders to arrest anyone who has no good reason for being out alone on the roads late at night."

"Yaas, well, dash me if I can see why should it matter to a blind man what time of the day or night he travels." The cool gray eyes sought Renée. "A very great pleasure to see you again, Miss d'Anton. Might I say"—he executed a formal bow over her hand then raised her fingers and pressed them to his lips—"I find m'self agreeing with the corporal. I vow I have quite lost m' appetite in light of such a *glittering* feast for the eyes."

It should not have surprised her that he was there. Nothing about Tyrone Hart should have surprised her, least of all that he would come to her house bold as brass, taunt the man who had shot him, and openly admire the jewels he had been formerly hired to steal. The fact he *was* admiring them caused her to take an involuntary step back and pull her hand out of his with more force than was intended. A rough link of gold snagged on the extravagant fountain of lace on his cuff and the ruby bracelet became entangled, a situation which allowed him to catch her hand in his and hold it tighter than before.

"Allow me," he said, raising her hand and angling it into the light that he might locate the errant link.

Beside them, Vincent started to step angrily forward, but Roth halted the movement with a quick frown. He watched Tyrone closely, his eyes narrowing when the bewigged and powdered fop continued to turn the bracelet and examine the rubies after they were released.

"Positively exquisite, m' dear," he pronounced. "Yet their beauty does you no justice."

A slow, smug smile curled Roth's lip as he met Vincent's gaze again, but there was only confusion in Renée's as she reclaimed her hand and stared wordlessly up at Hart.

The fact she had spent all day worrying about him, wondering if he had made it safely to Coventry, if his wound had caused him pain on the ride home, or if the boat had overturned and he had drowned . . . none of that had probably occurred to him. Nor would it follow that he would be the slightest bit aware that each time she looked at him she would see the gloriously naked lover she had assumed she had bid her final farewells to in the tower room last night.

"If you gentlemen will excuse me," she murmured, "I—I should see if my aunt and uncle are looking for me."

She whirled away before any of them had a chance to object and made her way numbly along the hallway, barely able to see where she was going through the pressure squeezing on her temples. At the entrance to the drawing room she realized her aunt and uncle were the last people she wanted to see at that moment, and she veered away before she reached the door. She kept walking, her shoulders stiff, her hands held rigid by her sides. She did not know where she was going until she found herself inside the music conservatory with her back pressed against the wall and her eyes closed tight against the emotions swirling inside her. Thankfully the room was empty. Chairs were arranged in a semi-circle facing the piano, suggesting there would be entertainment later in the evening, but for the time being she was alone.

She stood in the shadows, gulping at deep lungfuls of

air to calm herself, and was not aware of anyone beside her until she heard the door click shut behind him.

"Are you mad," she gasped. "What are you doing here?"

"We have, I believe, already established the fragile nature of my sanity," Tyrone said. "And as it happens, I was invited. A card was waiting for me when I arrived home, requesting the pleasure of my company to help celebrate the marriage of Lord and Lady Paxton's niece to a London fishmonger. It did not say the fishmonger part, of course. A mild embellishment on my part, but—"

"Tyrone—"

"Ah, you remember my name!"

"Your wound—!"

"My wound only hurts when I laugh—which I have not had much occasion to do today. On the contrary, I have been scowling a great deal, shouting at Robbie and the servants, kicking occasional pieces of furniture—"

"What if someone comes in?"

"If they do, we will be standing here in rapt awe, admiring"—he looked above their heads and saw a particularly uninspired oil of a woman playing a lute—"this. It rather begs for comment, do you not agree? The artist must have painted it while taking poison and suffering cramps."

She raised her hand, resting it briefly over the cold breastplate of rubies, but finding no comfort there, let it slip down by her side again. "You could have refused the invitation."

"To be honest, mam'selle, I almost did. It is a cold and damp night and you are probably right: I should be at home in a warm bed with a hot snifter of buttered brandy."

"Then wh—why are you here?"

His jaw clenched grimly. "I am here to rescue you, of course. Is that not what all heroes are supposed to do?"

"Rescue me?" she whispered.

"*Noblesse oblige.* The obligation of the nobility, is that not what they call it?"

"You are not of the nobility," she reminded him through a tremor. "You have no obligations to me or anyone else."

"True enough," he admitted. "There isn't an ounce of noble blood in me, nor do I harbor any vast admiration for the principles of honor unto death or the battlecry of the doomed: *l'audace, toujours l'audace*! But alas, you seem determined to make of me more than what I am, so"—he spread his hands and shrugged—"I am come to offer my services, common though they may be."

His perceived mockery was cruel and she turned away. "I do not want or need your help, m'sieur."

"No? You were planning to steal the rubies all by yourself? Pack them up in a bag and heigh away with a thirteen-year-old boy who can't speak to defend himself and a sixty-year-old manservant who creaks when he walks? Just how far do you think you would get? And what do you think those two vultures out there would do to you when they got you back?"

Tears shivered brightly along her lashes as she stared up at him. "Is that why you are here, m'sieur? Because of the rubies?"

"If it were just the rubies, *mam'selle*," he said bluntly, "I could take them now and be long gone before Roth or your fiancé were able to revive you enough to tell them what happened. And if you still don't believe me, leave the damned things behind. It might be a good idea anyway, to make greedy bastards less inclined to chase after you. The choice is yours, however. I honestly do not care."

The truth of what he was saying was in his eyes, but her emotions were no better off for knowing it.

"What do you want from me?" she cried softly. "What more do you want from me?"

"Nothing. Or maybe everything. I don't know. We can work that out later."

"Later . . . ?"

It was a query with consequences Tyrone did not want to think about now and he waved it away. "Robbie is bringing a boat; he will be waiting in the base of the tower at midnight. The water in the river is still high and the current is moving fairly swiftly; we could be in Coventry in under a half hour. I know I am not much of an alternative for Finn's expertise, or even a preferred alternative, but I can get you out of Coventry, out of England, too, if that is what you want. It is the least I can do. I"—he hesitated, as if the words were teeth and he was extracting them one by one with rusted pincers—"owe you that much for saving my life. You have to understand, however, this is a new and somewhat singular position I find myself in—owing someone, that is. But despite what I may be and what you may think of me, I do pay my debts."

"Is that the only reason?" she asked quietly. "Because you feel you owe me a debt of gratitude?"

"No. But it is the only one I can make sense of at the moment."

She continued to stare up at him, her eyes soft enough, dark enough to make him sigh and brush the backs of his fingers down the curve of her cheek.

"Will it make you happier to know I am here with you because I cannot bear the thought of being somewhere else without you?" His fingers stopped at her chin and tipped her face up, holding it there while he kissed her. Neither one of them closed their eyes during the brief contact, and only Tyrone was able to manage a smile when he broke away.

"You might come to *my* rescue here and say something before I make a complete fool of myself."

"What if you are caught helping us?"

"I won't be caught. And neither will you so long as you

can endure the company of these pompous fools for another six hours without telling them all to go to hell. Do
you think you can do that?"

"If you will first do one small thing for me," she whispered.

"I am yours to command," he said, spreading his hands
wide.

The invitation was there and she took it, leaning forward with a small half sob to bury her face against his
chest. His arms remained spread in surprise for all of two
seconds before they wrapped around her, holding her
tight enough and close enough for her to feel the pounding of his heart against hers.

"Is this what you wanted?" he murmured.

She nodded and Tyrone felt a flush of icy prickles
shiver down his spine. She had not laughed at his arrogant
declaration that neither one of them would get caught,
and he wished he felt as confident as he sounded. It *was* a
new and uncomfortable position to find himself in, being
suddenly responsible for three other lives, and he wasn't
entirely certain he was suited to the task.

The urge he had, in fact, was just to fling her over his
shoulder and carry her to safety now, and in an effort to
dampen it, he eased her gently to arms' length.

"Come now. Not even very bad art inspires a red nose
and runny eyes. You don't want to make me regret my
noble impulses, do you?"

A faint sniffle had him fishing in the delicate lace of his
cuff a moment before producing a folded linen handkerchief. He opened it with a soft snap and carefully blotted
the wetness that spiked her lashes.

"What must I do?" she asked.

"Tell Finn and Antoine to be ready by midnight. If
you're late getting to the tower . . ." He paused and
waited until he saw the sudden flare of panic in her eyes.
"We will wait." He laughed and kissed her lightly on the
tip of her nose. "I came here determined not to leave

without you, mam'selle, and be damned, I will not, even if I have to cross swords with every man here."

"*Mon dieu*, do not even joke about such a thing."

"At best it would be a joke," he said wryly, "for I have not drawn a blade in several months."

He noted the returning threat of tears in her eyes and backed away, tugging on his waistcoat and jacket to smooth the wrinkles, plumping out the folds of his cravat, insuring his wig was seated firmly in place. By the time he was finished Renée looked composed again, although there was a radiant new flush in her cheeks that he wagered a blind Scotsman from Glasgow could not help but see.

He suggested she leave the conservatory first, and after giving her sufficient time to rejoin the other guests, he clasped his hands behind his back and sauntered out into the hallway as if he had just spent an utterly boring ten minutes studying an insipid rendition of a lute.

* ☽

# Chapter 23

$\mathcal{A}$t ten minutes past midnight, Renée excused herself, promising to return as soon as she had seen Antoine to bed. It was the first opportunity that had presented itself and as they hurried along the hallway, her heart was pounding and her feet felt weighted in lead. Finn had been pressed into helping the servants serve a late supper and see to the guests' needs. He had seen her leave and had exchanged a subtle nod to assure her he would not be too far behind.

Antoine walked nervously at her side. At first Renée had debated not alarming him ahead of time, for he was usually so quiet and withdrawn at these "family" affairs, any hint of excitement in his face or manner might draw a suspicious eye. But it was clear to her, as soon as she saw him following Tyrone's every move, that he would have to be told, if only to remove suspicion from Hart. It had proved to be the right choice in the end. He had all but ignored the Surveyor of turnpikes through dinner and no one observing him would have cause to think him anything but bored with the tedious, polite conversations that surrounded him.

Tyrone, on the other hand, sat with the Misses Ruth and Phoebe Entwistle and whatever they were discussing drew gales of laughter from the nearby guests, including Corporal Marlborough. For once, the officer seemed to be distracted from his usual intense study of Renée's profile, and by the conclusion of the meal, he seemed hardly

aware of her at all. Oddly enough, the glances began to go
the other way. Renée would catch herself leaning forward
to reach her wineglass or select a morsel of food from a
platter, and her eyes would travel along the table to
where Tyrone seemed to be enjoying his role as company
wag altogether too well and appeared to be listening
rather intently to anything Miss Ruth Entwistle had to
say. Once, when she was caught spying, she saw a corner
of Tyrone's mouth twitch as if to chide her for her fickle
thoughts. The impression did not diminish when the pale
gray eyes reminded her—she had no idea how—that she
had herself suggested there were more qualities to Miss
Entwistle than appeared on the surface. He then went on
to stare pointedly at the rubies, in particular the teardrop
pendant that hung between her breasts, and by the time
his gaze wandered lazily back to her face, she required
the use of her fan to cool her cheeks.

The same subtleness could not be applied to Edgar
Vincent's surly glares. He sat across the table from Renée,
draining his wineglass as soon as it was filled, glowering at
her in unbroken spans of two or three minutes' duration
before a comment would force him to break contact and
respond to the intrusion. And on the same occasion she
happened to need her fan, he stared deliberately down
the table at Tyrone then back again, making certain she
knew he had observed the exchange.

When the last course was cleared, Lady Penelope Paxton led the ladies away to refresh themselves while the
men enjoyed their porter and brandy. Afterward there
was entertainment in the music room, a number of guests
were called upon to play the piano forte and still others to
accompany them in song. There were card tables set up
in the drawing room—commerce and whist—as well as
tables for checkers and billiards in the game room. Renée
could rouse no interest in any of the planned activities.
She was conscious of the stares the other women sent her
way, most of them directed at the gaudy display of rubies.

Their opinions were being confirmed, no doubt, on why the penniless *Française* was willing to marry so far beneath her class.

What would they think, she had wondered, if they knew in whose bed, in whose arms she was willingly and happily prepared to go? A thief. A brigand slated as gallows-bait. A road hawk who had likely held his guns on the very people who sat laughing at his jokes, amused by his rolling eyes and wafting wrists.

Ten o'clock crawled by, then eleven, and by then Renée had worn a fair-sized hole in the corner of the handkerchief Tyrone had pressed into her hand. The worst abuse had come when her uncle had called for attention and proposed a toast to the future bride and groom; she had been forced to allow Vincent to kiss her on the cheek, and afterward, she had scrubbed the spot red.

With the supper cleared away, some of the guests departed. Those who had traveled longer distances had come prepared to spend the night and so were in no hurry to find their beds. They returned to their conversations and their games, while Renée listened to the chimes tolling midnight in the hall clock and excused herself to see to Antoine.

"You will have to be quick," she told him outside his bedroom door. "Finn should be up in a moment or two to help you change into warmer clothes."

She kissed him on the forehead and ruffled his hair, which earned her a wide grin and a soundless question.

*Do you like* le capitaine?

"Yes. Yes, I like him very much."

*I think he likes you too. He said you were* sous sa peau.

"Under his skin?"

*Here.* He scratched vigorously at the nape of his neck. *He says he always knows when you are close by.*

"Or he could simply have a rash." Renée turned him and gave him a little push into his chamber. "Hurry now.

Stay here until I come for you, and open the door to no one but me or Finn."

She hurried across the hall and ran straight for the dressing room. She retrieved her valise from the corner cupboard and pulled garments off the shelves, throwing them haphazardly in the case as she dragged it toward the door. She scooped her combs and brushes on top, along with the sandalwood box containing her powders and perfumes. Back in the main room, she felt beneath the bedclothes for the mended tear in the mattress. The few stitches she had used to refasten it came apart at the first yank and she withdrew the small canvas sack that contained, among her other treasures, the pearl brooch that completed the Dragon's Blood suite.

Seeing it, she reached around and worked the clasp of the necklace free. The bracelet and earrings were removed and all of the pieces returned to the velvet jewelry box. The box went into the valise and, after a last quick look around, she drew her cloak around her shoulders and headed for the door, reaching it just as a discreet knock sounded on the wood.

"Finn! Thank goodness."

She swung the door open and gasped.

Edgar Vincent was standing there, a bottle of wine in one hand, two glasses in the other. For all of the two seconds they stared at each other in surprise, a smile remained on his thick lips. But then he noticed the valise and the cloak, and his eyes, in contrast to her wide and horrified ones, narrowed down to two glittering slits.

"Going somewhere, my dear?"

Shocked, Renée stumbled back a step. A dozen lies went through her head, none of them remotely plausible enough to explain where she would be going this time of night.

"Here I was hoping we might finish the conversation we had started earlier in the evening." He held up the bottle and glasses. "I thought we could have a private toast to a long and fruitful marriage, but I see that perhaps the toast as well as the thought might be a little premature."

Renée's gaze flicked to the open hallway behind him, but Vincent's shoulders blocked the doorway. She took another stumbling step back, which he matched, and another that brought him far enough inside the room to hook the door with his foot and slam it shut behind him.

Renée retreated as far as the bed and could go no farther. She had not had time to fasten her cloak properly and when she came up sharp against the edge of the footboard, the cloak slipped off her shoulders, bringing attention to the naked whiteness of her throat.

"Well, well." Vincent came up in front of her and flexed the muscles in his jaw a time or two. "Shall I guess what you have in the bag?"

He threw the glasses to one side, causing Renée to flinch at the sound of them shattering against the wall. The bottle ended up on the floor, the glass too thick to break, and before it had rolled to a halt, Vincent had snatched up the valise and jerked it open. The velvet jewel case was on top and seeing it, he expelled a long, sour breath laden with oaths.

" . . . Cheap little whoring thief," he concluded with a disbelieving shake of his head. "No different from any other lying bitch."

Eyes blazing, he removed the velvet case and saw the canvas pouch beneath. He started to lift it out when Renée lunged forward, trying to dart past him, but he caught her by the arm and flung her back hard enough that her knees buckled against the footboard and she fell backward onto the bed. She twisted to one side and tried again, but this time when he swung out, he slapped her hard enough to knock her momentarily senseless with the shock and the pain. Keeping one eye on Renée's dazed efforts to struggle upright again, Vincent loosened the drawstring and emptied the contents of the sack into his hand. When he saw the pearl brooch, his jaw gaped, and when he saw that Renée had almost managed to regain her feet, he swung out again, this time with his fist closed and the full force of his anger behind the blow.

The agony exploded inside Renée's head, blinding her to the further pain of landing awkwardly on her shoulder as she was thrown back onto the bed again. Starbursts clouded her vision and sent her senses reeling; she did not know for long, wildly spinning seconds which way was up or down. Somewhere out of the pain and fog, she heard Vincent swear again, felt him grab a fistful of her hair, angling her face up and into the blurred glitter he shoved in front of her eyes.

"Where did you get this, bitch? *Where did you get this?*"

Even as the pain cleared enough for her to focus on the brooch, she was pushing herself to the side, trying to escape his clutches.

With a snarl he hauled her sharply back and before she could thrash her way free, he was looming over her, his fist tightened around her hair, his knee gouging into her belly to keep her body pinned to the mattress.

"I'll ask you one more time," he grunted. "Where did you get this? No, never mind. I *know* where you got it. The question I should be asking is how you got it and what you gave him in exchange."

Renée felt his spittle on her face and her temper flared. The rage of fifteen generations of noble blood coursed like fire through her veins and she reared up at him in defiance. "I could ask you the same thing. Where did you get it? Where did you get the rubies? No," she spat, "never mind. I *know* where you got them, m'sieur. I know whose blood is on them and whose blood was spilled that you might profit from their deaths!"

His grin was slow and evil. "So you know all about our little enterprise, do you? And what were you doing, trying to cut yourself in for a share of the profits? You stupid bitch, you could have had ten times as much if you'd waited another two days."

"But I also would have had to marry you, *marchand de poisson*, and I would not have been able to endure the stench for a thousand times as much!"

He stared and his face seemed to swell, purpling around the jowls as he responded with two vicious, open-handed slaps across her face. One of them caused her lip to split and her mouth filled with the rusty taste of blood.

"Whore," he snarled. "And me thinking you were a lady. A fine, noble lady of quality and virtue who had to be treated gently and patiently." He brought his face menacingly closer. "Won't Roth be surprised to hear exactly how well his little trap worked? You had Starlight eating out of your hand, all right. Eating out of something else, too, I wager. You must be good. Damned good for two hundred thousand pounds' worth of bauble."

He flung the brooch beside her on the bed and Renée braced herself for another blow, but he had caught the glitter of the diamond cravat pin amongst the coins he had discarded and he grabbed it up in his fist.

"And this? By God, who were you sweating under for this? Goddammit"—he bared his teeth and glared down at her—"am I the only one you haven't spread your legs for?"

"No," she countered furiously. "I have not yet had the gardener or the man who cleans out the gutters."

He struck her again and this time when her vision cleared, she saw the glitter of something else before her eyes. It was a knife, long and thin, sharpened to a needle-point at the end.

"We'll see how much of that clever little tongue you have left at the end of the night," Vincent hissed. "And we'll put this here"—he stabbed the knife into the corner post, leaving it vibrating easily within hand's reach—"for incentive, shall we? If I don't think you are worth every penny of the trouble you have caused us, you're going to find yourself cut ten ways to Sunday and wishing you were dead."

He straightened and started tugging at the buttons and fasteners on his jacket and waistcoat. Renée made another desperate lunge to the side, but he snatched her back with ease. His hands clawed at her breasts and he fell on her like a ravening beast, tearing at the delicate silk, plunging his mouth over the soft white flesh where it was exposed. Growling and grunting, he fumbled with his breeches and with the hem of her skirts, having to stop every few seconds to beat down her arms and legs as she fought to dislodge him.

He was big and he was drunk, and for every twist and blow of her fists, he struck her hard with the flat of his hand. She screamed—or at least she thought she did—as his teeth sank into her breast and dimly she was aware of another sound, another shadow looming up over the bed. His mouth was wide and the silent screams he made were coming from a nightmare—the same nightmare that forced him to relive the horror of seeing his mother being beaten and kicked to death on the wet cobblestones of a Paris street.

Antoine threw himself across Edgar Vincent's broad back, clinging like a dog with his teeth, his nails, his knees, anything and everything he could bring to bear. The fishmonger roared and heaved back, throwing the boy across the room, hard enough to crack his head on the wall. In a fresh rage, he turned back to Renée, his breeches gaping, the angry red spear of his flesh clutched in his hand.

Renée had scrambled to her knees and was holding the long, thin fileting knife between her clenched fists.

"Do not come any closer, m'sieur," she hissed.

"What are you going to do? Slit my throat? Stab me in the gut? Or maybe you'd like to try to geld me?" He approached the side of the bed, his hand working his flesh, his fist sliding back and forth along the thick protrusion, obviously aroused by the threat of the knife. His attention was all focused on Renée, on the blood that ran from her split lip, on the streaks of red that were smeared across the whiteness of her breasts where they glowed through the torn silk.

At the very last possible moment, Renée shook her head and ducked out of the way. The knife slashed sideways, cutting a ribbon across the back of Vincent's hand as he plunged forward, but he barely felt it and certainly did not notice it. The strike of the wine bottle against the back of his skull came with a sickening crunch of glass on solid bone and, after rearing back briefly to absorb the shock, Vincent shuddered once and collapsed forward, his weight landing in a limp heap across the bottom of Renée's legs. At the same time, the impact shattered the bottle and the contents exploded across the bed, spraying wine and shards of broken glass across the counterpane.

For five, ten full seconds no one moved. Antoine raised the jagged neck of the broken bottle and was prepared to swing again but Vincent lay still as death across the bed. The skin across the back of his neck was split like overripe fruit, and a thick, sluggish stream of blood started to ooze down through his hair and collar. Renée lay gasping beneath him, her legs pinned beneath his bulk.

"Antoine," she cried. "Antoine—help me! I cannot move!"

He dropped the bottle and dashed forward. Between them, pushing and pulling, they rolled Vincent over onto his side, then shoved him off the edge of the bed, where he landed with another dull thud. Renée choked back a sob and clung to her brother as he helped her up and off the bed. He managed to get her to her feet and together they stumbled across the room to the vanity table, where he eased her down into the chair then ran into the dressing room to fetch a towel.

Her dress was torn and gaped open to her waist. She went to clutch the edges together and realized she was still holding the fileting knife. For one final outraged moment, she stared at Vincent's body, then opened her fingers and let the knife fall to the floor.

Antoine returned with the towel and began to blot the splashes of wine and blood off her face.

"*C'est finis. La bête est morte. La bête est morte!*"

"The beast," she agreed with an angry shudder. "The bastard! I would have used the knife on him. I would!"

"I killed him for you, Renée. He cannot hurt you again!"

Renée shook her head, certain it was the ringing in her ears causing her to hear the proud assurances. But when he continued to say them and she continued to hear them, she stopped and looked up, squeezing her eyes to clear them of unshed tears. "Antoine . . . what did you say?"

"I said I—" he stopped too.

He closed his mouth, then opened it again and when he spoke, the words were rasped and broken with wonder, but they could both hear them.

"I killed him for you. He cannot hurt you anymore."

"Again, *mon coeur,*" she whispered, barely daring to breathe, to hope.

"I killed him for you." Stronger this time. "He cannot hurt you anymore! Renée—! Renée—!"

She brought him into her arms and hugged him. The tears she had not permitted herself to give in to until now came hot and fast, and a moment later, when Finn came running into the room, that was how he found them. Laughing, crying, hugging each other with the bleeding body of Edgar Vincent sprawled on the floor in front of the bed.

*

"Mary and Joseph! What happened here!"

Renée was still sobbing and it fell to Antoine to explain, which he did with a wide grin on his face.

"I believe I have killed him, M'sieur Finn. He was hurting Renée. He was hurting her like the soldiers hurt *maman*, so I killed him."

"Dear God in heaven, he is bleeding all over the—" the valet halted halfway to the bed, drew a deep breath, and stiffened. His eyes started to crinkle with surprise as he stared at Antoine, but then his gaze was drawn to Renée's torn clothing and the bloodied towel she was clutching over her breast and the smile turned into an expression of horror. "Good sweet God, mad'moiselle, are you all right?"

She nodded as he hastened over. "I am fine. Perfectly fine. Antoine came to my rescue just in time."

"I heard her scream."

"And he hit him with a bottle . . ."

"I smashed it over his head," Antoine repeated proudly. "And killed him."

"The blood?" Finn asked. "You are cut!"

Renée touched her cheek and her fingers came away red. "It must have been from the glass. Before that, he only hit me and—" she slid a finger along her bottom gum and a moment later produced a piece of broken tooth.

Finn peered anxiously into Renée's eyes. "You are not . . . hurt anywhere else?"

"No," she said, resting her hand over his. "No. He was . . . too drunk and too angry." She looked over at the body. "He was too clumsy, too stupid, too . . ." The words failed her and her temper flushed hotly into her cheeks again. *"Rien de tout!"*

"Yes, well, unfortunately, he is something. He is another body in your bedchamber that must be disposed of. Had I known this was going to become a habit," he added with dry sarcasm, "I might have insisted you take a bedchamber on a lower floor."

He returned to the body and knelt down beside it. "Is he dead?"

Before Finn could answer, Vincent groaned. One of his legs dragged forward a few inches then slumped flat again.

"Unfortunately not. It appears his skull is as thick as the rest of him. He is leaking quite profusely, however. Antoine—another towel, if you please? Or something we can use to wipe up the mess."

Antoine disappeared into the adjoining room and returned with two thick towels.

"What shall we do with him?" Renée asked.

"We shall have to tie him up and hide him away somewhere. But the first thing we must do is see you and His Grace safely to the tower. That rascal Hart said he would wait, but if someone should stumble upon us and the hounds of hell are released, he may not be able to wait too long. What is more, he was not looking too spry when last I saw him. No doubt his wound is playing him for the devil and while it is all very well for one to *think* one feels strong enough to caper about like a marionette, it is quite another to do it with a recently cauterized hole in one's side. I will just fetch the young master's bag—good God, I left it outside in the hallway!"

"I will get it," Antoine said, on his way before Finn could push himself to his feet. When he did, he had to grab at the bedpost to steady himself, suddenly looking every one of his sixty years.

"Can you manage on your own, mad'moiselle?" he asked Renée.

She frowned, then followed his uncomfortably indirect glance down to the torn edges of her gown. "Oh. Yes, yes I can manage."

"Good. Then dress quickly, if you please. We haven't many moments to spare."

While Renée changed in a shadowy corner of the dressing room, Finn gathered up the coins, the pin, the brooch, and the jewelry case, returning them to the valise. He removed the wine-splattered counterpane, bundling most of the broken glass inside, then turned down the corner of the sheets as if the bed had been prepared for the night. When he was reasonably satisfied with the appearance of the rest of the room, he took the braided cords off the curtains and began tying Vincent's wrists together.

Renée returned, pale as a ghost but freshly attired in a light woolen gown that closed all the way up to her neck. She had washed the blood off her chin and throat, but her lip was still leaking, as was the cut on her cheek. Her hands, though ice cold, were a good deal steadier however, as she placed them on Antoine's shoulders and gave him a fierce hug.

"You were very brave," she insisted. "Just like *papa*. He would have been so proud of you! When I saw you standing there, lifting that bottle, ready to smash it on his head, I could have laughed right in *le cochon*'s face!"

"Indeed, Your Grace," Finn said, "both your father and lady mother are likely smiling down upon you now, bragging to all their heavenly companions what a fine job they have done raising you. You have one more task to perform, however, before you puff out too much. You must take your sister quickly and discreetly to the tower."

Startled, Renée looked at Finn. "What about you?"

"I will be along directly, never fear." He retrieved her cloak from the floor and draped it around her shoulders. "I must insure this wretched swine cannot cry out an alarm or cause a disturbance until we are well on our way."

"We will help. Or we will wait."

"Not here, mad'moiselle. I would feel exceedingly more at ease if you waited in the tower. I will only be a moment behind you, I promise. And please," he crooked an eyebrow in anticipation of an argument, "Do exactly what Mr. Hart tells you to do. Even though I thought I should bite my tongue off before saying this, I believe you can trust the rogue. He will see you and the young master come to no harm. Quickly now. *Faites vite!*"

Antoine took her hand and started pulling her to the door. "We will not leave without you!"

Finn was already bending over Vincent again. "Yes. Yes . . . go."

After checking carefully down both ends of the hall, Antoine and Renée slipped out of the bedroom and hurried toward the tower stairs. Antoine bade her stop halfway and scampered to the bottom, peering cautiously down the long gallery. There was a couple strolling leisurely down the hall admiring the dusty old portraits, but they were still well along where the light was stronger. He retreated quickly and, holding a finger over his lips to caution her, lifted the edge of the heavy tapestry to one side while Renée ducked behind.

The door made the faintest squeak as it swung inward. The sound was no louder than what a mouse might make scurrying away from a tabby but to Renée it was like a scream. It was also pitch dark inside the musty old tower and for another heart-stopping moment, she feared they were too late. Tyrone had gone without them. He had waited as long as he could, and despite his promise . . .

The sudden scrape of flint on tinder quelled the bubble of panic rising in her chest. It was dispelled altogether when the spark was touched to an oil-soaked taper and she saw Robert Dudley standing against the far wall beneath the curve of the stairwell. His features were stark, distorted by the weak flame, and as he held the taper to a fat yellow candle, the brighter light revealed the worried look on his face.

"I thought I was going to have to go looking for you," he muttered, obviously not pleased at the delay.

"Where is M'sieur Hart?" Renée asked.

"Here." The voice came from the blackness beside them. Dudley limped forward with the candle, while the shadows retreated to show where Tyrone was seated on the stone steps. He looked, as Finn had forewarned, terrible. His face was drawn, his eyes dulled by exhaustion and pain. His jacket and waistcoat were unbuttoned, his cravat was loose and the ends were trailing down the sides of his lapels. His right hand was cradling his ribs, his left was holding a gun.

"Have you packed all your trunks?" he inquired with mild irritation. "Are you certain there is nothing you have forgotten? Where is poor Finn—dragging them down the stairs?"

Antoine pressed his lips together. "Finn is upstairs dragging the body of M'sieur Vincent into the anteroom to hide it."

Dudley had lit a second candle by then and the light reached into the shadows behind Antoine. From where Tyrone was sitting, he could only see Renée's shoulders and the sagging crown of golden curls, but from where Dudley was standing, he could see the bright, dark rivulet of blood seeping down her cheek.

"Tyrone . . . ?"

But Hart was staring at Antoine. "Say that again."

"Finn is upstairs—"

"You have your voice back."

"Then you should have heard me when I said Finn is upstairs dragging the body of M'sieur Vincent into the anteroom to hide it! I had to hit him on the head because he was beating Renée and making her cry!"

"Tyrone"—Dudley crooked his head—"you might want to have a look."

Tyrone pushed to his feet. Renée quickly raised the folded wad of linen, both to blot up the blood and to shield her face from the probing eyes, but Tyrone took hold of her wrist with one hand and her chin with the other. She could feel his gaze hardening as it inspected every reddened blotch, every faint scratch and cut, settling finally on the slash that cut across her cheek.

"Vincent did this to you?"

His voice was so cool, so calm, it caused her to stammer when she answered. "Th—the cut was caused by a piece of g—glass. It must have happened when Antoine broke the bottle over his head."

"Is he dead?"

She shook her head. "He is insensible. Finn is tying him up so he cannot call out an alarm."

"Robbie"—Tyrone half turned, though his eyes did not leave Renée's face—"take them out to the boat. I'll just go back and see if I can help Mr. Finn along. We shouldn't be too far behind you."

"No," Renée cried. "No, you must not go back in there. Please, Tyrone. You must not go back. I am sure Finn will be along any moment!"

"I am sure he will. I just want to hurry him along."

As if to confirm her fears, Renée saw him check the charge in both firing pans of the snaphaunce before he reached around and tucked the gun into the waist of his breeches.

"Tyrone, please . . . it means nothing. Vincent means nothing. It is over."

"Go with Robbie. Finn and I will be right behind you."

But she had seen something else when the flap of his waistcoat flared open with the movement of his arms.

"M'sieur Dudley"—she looked imploringly to him for help—"do you know his wound is bleeding again?"

"What?" Dudley stepped forward and before Tyrone could stop him, he lifted the panel of the striped satin waistcoat. There was blood on his shirt, just a few spots to be sure, but it meant his stitches had suffered too much strain—probably when he had been cajoled into performing a foolish charade for the Misses Entwistle—and the wound was oozing into the bandages.

"I am fine," Tyrone said. "It has been like that all night."

Dudley held the candle closer. Some of the spots were older and darker, some were new and bright red.

"I am going back," Tyrone said evenly. "Take them to the boat and wait for us."

"My vote is with the lady," Dudley argued. "It's too dangerous."

"I was not aware this was a democratic assembly."

"All right then, go back. Blow Vincent's head off. The house is full of dragoons and as soon as the alarm goes out, you can bet the woods, the canal, the roads, and fields will be full of them too. Look at yourself. You can hardly stand without holding on to the wall and you still have to run through the tunnel, row a boat into Coventry, and possibly fight off a patrol of Roth's mongrels with or without an alarm going out. But if you feel you have to risk everyone's safety to go and kill him, then by all means . . . go and kill him. I am sure Mademoiselle d'Anton and her brother both will appreciate the gesture from their gaol cells."

A finely sculpted muscle in Tyrone's jaw twitched. There was no visible lessening in the fury that had turned his eyes a cold slate gray, but there was a faint glimmer of reason. It took a moment for the glimmer to spread, but it eventually won a reluctant nod of agreement.

"All right. I won't kill the bastard. But you *will* take Renée and Antoine down to the boat and I *will* wait here for Mr. Finn. Someone has to stay and see that the door to the cistern room is locked behind us."

Renée touched his arm. "Tyrone—"

"You have my most solemn word of honor that I will not go back and shoot the bastard," he said to her. "Not tonight, at any rate. And if my word is not good enough for you, mam'selle, then here, take this." He removed the snaphaunce from his waistband and handed it to her. "The other one is on the step, take it as well. Would you like my cravat, too, so I am not tempted to strangle him?"

It was obvious he was not accustomed to having to

answer to anyone or justify either his past actions or future intent, and Renée took his hand in hers, fighting against the minor resistance she felt as she raised it and held the long, tapered fingers against her lips.

"I am sure you could strangle him with your hands alone, m'sieur, but I shall happily accept your word that you will not."

The resistance wilted out of his hand. His fingers shifted and cradled the side of her neck. "Does this mean you finally trust me?"

"Yes," she whispered. "With all my heart."

"Never that much, I hope," he murmured.

"That much and more," she whispered, rising up against him. She blew out a soft, helpless breath as her lips touched his, but before he could react or respond to the words she pressed against his mouth, she moved quickly away, following Antoine and Dudley through the secret exit to the chambers below.

* ☽

# Chapter 24

*T*yrone stood there for a full minute without moving, his body dark against the shadows, his hair silvered by the candlelight. He stared at the fake prayer nave long after it was pulled shut behind them and he could still hear the faint echo of her words in his ears, he could taste them on his lips.

*Je t'aime.*

How many times had he heard variations of the same declaration from women he had known in the past? How many times had he just laughed and plied his mouth, his hands across their bodies until they cried it out again in wild, passionate abandon? For that matter, had anyone ever said it to him sober or fully clothed? Or even in those precise terms? Usually they loved what he did to them or how he made them feel or the fact he made no demands on them and gave no promises in return.

He stared at the nave until his eyes felt dry and he was forced to look away. When he did, he turned his head too sharply and the savage pounding in his temples began in earnest again. His ribs were on fire and his skin was clammy. Maggie had given him two packets of powdered willow ash to take if the pain in his side got bad, but they were both gone and the effects had worn off hours ago.

Where the devil was Finn? He had promised he would not go back into the house—not with the intentions of killing Vincent, at any rate—but neither could he stand here in the darkness and shadows hearing the whispered rush of her words against his mouth without being able to say something in return . . . though he was not quite sure what it was he wanted or ought to say.

"Damnation."

He started buttoning his waistcoat. He tied a hasty knot in his cravat and retrieved his jacket from the steps. The muscles were stiffer than he had let on and it was agony fitting his arm into the sleeve, but he managed with a great deal of cursing. After shielding the glare from the candle, he slipped out through the low archway and stood in the darkened niche, listening for any sounds from the other side of the tapestry.

✳

Finn felt a bead of sweat slither down the bridge of his nose and drip off the end. It landed directly in Vincent's gaping mouth, but neither of them noticed. Finn was too busy struggling to haul the oblivious man's bulk through the door to the dressing room, and Vincent's mouth was stuffed too full of dirty linens for one more salty drop to matter. He was dazed and disoriented, his eyes rolled back into his head at every bump and jostle, but he was still weakly fighting to resist being dragged into the anteroom.

"Mary, Joseph, Jesus, and all the saints!" Finn grunted and heaved and shoved the lumbering hulk into the corner, then staggered back and stood bent at the waist, his hands on his knees, his breath coming in shallow, labored pants. "Might I recommend moderation in the future, sir," he gasped. "In food as well as drink."

"I doubt he would take your advice on either count, old man."

Finn whirled around. Colonel Bertrand Roth was standing in the doorway, one shoulder propped against the jamb, his arms folded in a leisurely fashion across his chest.

Under his amused and curiously flat stare, Finn

straightened and gave his jacket a prim tug to smooth it. "Forgive me, Colonel, I did not hear you knock."

"I confess to the boorish indiscretion," Roth said wanly. "Having noticed both the bride and groom absent from the company below, I thought I should come and insure they were behaving themselves. And here I find no bride, the room smells of a distillery, and the groom is trussed like a heifer about to go to the butcher block."

"He was interrupted in the act of attempting to rape my mistress," Finn said archly. "Rather violently so, I might add."

Roth followed a thin, pointing finger to the evidence of the torn, cast-off silk Renée had discarded on the floor. There was more evidence—towels with blood on them and a piece of jagged glass she had picked out of her hair.

"I have sent her to safety in another part of the house," Finn added. "I was trussing this—this vermin to keep him secure until I could fetch the proper authorities. The man is an animal. A drunken, fornicating creature of the devil and he should be hung as such, sir."

In the corner, Vincent groaned and contorted what he could of his face, demanding a release from his bonds.

"Rape, you say?" Roth regarded Finn through narrowed eyes. "A serious charge."

"Mad'moiselle d'Anton was quite seriously hurt. In her attempts to defend herself, she was struck several times—a heinous crime in itself to anyone who would consider himself even partially civilized. When I attempted to dissuade Mr. Vincent from his drunken course—to no avail—he left me no choice but to deter him with violence."

"You did this to him?"

Finn lifted his chin. "I did. And I would most heartily do it again if the circumstances warranted it."

"Smashing things over the backs of peoples' heads seems to be a particular habit with you, Mr. Finnerty," Roth said dryly. "Untie him."

"But Colonel—"

"I said . . . untie him."

"He could easily overpower us, sir, and if he does—"

Roth reached beneath his tunic and withdrew a steel cannon-barrelled pocket pistol. "Lucky for us, I brought this along, then. It carries a small charge, but at close quarters, will stop a man of any size and nature. If you please—" He waved the nose of the pistol in Vincent's direction and thumbed the hammer into half-cock for emphasis.

Left with little choice, Finn unfastened the bindings around Vincent's ankles first, then his wrists.

"Help him up. Bring him in here."

Again, Finn obeyed and despite Vincent's clumsy efforts to push him away, he was hoisted up onto his feet and helped back into the main bedroom. There he slumped down into the vanity chair and cradled his head in his hands, groaning.

"Now then, old boy, is what Mr. Finnerty says true? Were you trying to ravish your betrothed?"

Vincent gargled an answer for a moment, then reached with disgust for the linens still crammed into his mouth and flung them aside. "I only wanted what I paid for. The little bitch was trying to sneak out on us. She had the jewels packed and was heading out the door when I got here." He lifted his head out of his hands to squint up at Roth. "She had the brooch too. She had the damned pearl brooch; I saw it in her bag."

Roth's face hardened instantly. "The Pearl of Brittany? She had it? Are you absolutely certain?"

"I saw it," Vincent hissed. "I held it in my hand and asked her where she got it, but then I figured there was only one place she *could* have gotten it, only one man who could have given it to her."

Roth whirled around just in time to see Finn sidling toward the door. "Wherever the hell you think you are going, Mr. Finnerty"—he thumbed the hammer into the fully cocked position and aimed it squarely at Finn's head—"I would not advise it. I am a crack shot and your fine gray hair makes an excellent target."

Finn's hand curled back from the brass latch and dropped back down by his side.

"Over here," Roth snarled. "Away from the door."

Finn obeyed the jerking motion of Roth's gun and moved at a dignified pace to stand in front of the window.

"Is what he says true? Does Renée d'Anton have the Pearl of Brittany?"

"I am not kept apprised of mad'moiselle's personal possessions, sir."

"It was on the bed," Vincent said. "The last time I saw it, it was on the bed."

Roth glanced over, but there was nothing on the bed or beside it. He looked sharply back at Finn. "Where is she?"

Finn pursed his lips but said nothing.

"We can do this the easy way, or we can do it the hard way," Roth warned. *"Where is she?"*

Finn still said nothing and Vincent scowled up from his seat. "She was dressed and had a packed bag with her. My guess is she has gone to meet *him*. As usual," he added, "you seem to have underestimated the strength and resources of your opponent, not to mention the fact that she must have been using us all along to get the brooch."

"What do you mean?"

"Think about it, you arrogant bastard. If there is already a French agent in London sniffing around, asking questions about the Dragon's Blood suite, she must have known its value from the moment I put it around her neck. I warrant she would have stolen it before now if it wasn't for the fact that the brooch was missing. I'll also wager my front teeth she has been playing along, biding her time, hoping we would lead her to the Pearl of Brittany, and we did, didn't we. Or should I say *you* did. *You* led her right to it with your clever, fail-proof scheme to catch Starlight." Vincent paused to wipe a dribble of blood off his neck. "You stupid bloody bastard. I told you you should have let me handle this my way, but no. You had to prove you were smarter than Starlight, smarter than all of us. Well who is looking smarter now? Who had the foresight to exchange the real rubies for glass imitations? Who do you think is going to laugh the loudest when the little whore and her road thief find out they went to all this trouble for a few bits of colored glass, and who do you think is going to keep the real rubies now?"

"We had a deal," Roth said evenly.

"*Had* . . . a deal. You lost Starlight, you lost the girl, and if it wasn't for me, you'd have lost the rubies too. By my way of thinking, that makes them mine. And that makes you a fool . . . *again*."

Roth's eyelids closed until there was just a shiver of white showing along the bottom lashes. In a move so shockingly swift it caused Finn to stumble back in surprise, the colonel lashed out, swinging the pistol hard and sharp against the side of Vincent's face. Had the bigger man not been half-dazed by the previous blow to his skull, he might have seen it coming and been quicker to react, but he took the force of it fully on the temple and was thrown sideways, landing awkwardly against the delicate vanity table. Bottles, pots, jars went flying, crashing on the wall, on the floor, but Roth barely paid heed as he stalked toward the corner where Finn was standing.

"Is what he said true? Has she gone to meet Starlight?"

Finn merely glared in disdainful silence along the length of his nose and Roth's eyes narrowed to yellow slits.

"By God, you know who he is, don't you? You know who Starlight is and you know where he has taken her."

"I have no idea what you are talking about," Finn declared. "And even if I did—"

"Yes?"

He looked down at his thin, age-spotted hands and scraped a bit of lint out from under one manicured nail. "I would still have nothing to say."

"Your loyalty and bravado are commendable, old man," Roth said, baring his teeth in a sinister grin. "But utterly and completely futile."

With Finn staring calmly into Roth's eyes, the colonel swung the gun up, squeezed the trigger, and fired.

✳

Tyrone had been just about to edge the tapestry aside when he heard a tinkle of laughter on the other side. There was a flurry of whispers and breathless queries, followed by the patter of slippered feet and another laugh as the woman was caught and spun into her captor's arms. There could be no mistaking the nasally whimpers of Miss Ruth Entwistle as she was swept up in the passion of the moment, though who her companion might be was anyone's guess. It had been on the tip of his tongue last night to enlighten Renée to the fact that most men were not attentive to Miss Entwistle because of her intelligence. They were drawn to her because she would lift her skirts anywhere, anytime, and give them a rousing good ride in the process.

Under any other circumstances, Tyrone might have found the situation comical. Standing not two feet away, with only the width of the tapestry separating him from the lovers, he could hear the moist, suckling sound their mouths made and the whispered crush of linen petticoats as one body crowded another against the wall. Making matters worse, they could be no more than a few inches from the opening of the archway; one amorous roll and they would find out the wall was not as solid as they supposed.

A lusty groan brought renewed sounds of rustling garments and Tyrone leaned on the cold stones, cursing under his breath. If Finn was at the top of the stairs, he would be trapped there also until the lovers moved on.

"Can you not go and find a bed somewhere, for God's sake," he finally muttered after five minutes—each of them ticked off in long, agonizing seconds.

"Did you hear something?" the woman gasped.

Tyrone bit his tongue and mouthed another oath.

"No, no," the denial came on a strangled moan. "I heard nothing."

"I am certain I did," Miss Entwistle whispered. "Listen . . . there it is again."

Tyrone's head was throbbing too much for him to hear anything above the pounding of his own pulsebeat, but the frantic suckling noises on the other side of the tapestry stopped, and he could picture them: two startled faces, mouths open and chafed from kissing, staring into the gloom, waiting for a shrill reprimand from an outraged chaperon.

The sound of a gunshot brought Tyrone's head jerking forward off the stone.

"There!" Miss Entwistle shrieked. "You must have heard that!"

"Stay here," the gentleman ordered.

"Oh! You cannot possibly abandon me!"

"I will only be a moment. Wait here, I beg you."

The erstwhile lover's boots scraped briskly on the stairs as he mounted them. The echo of the shot must have carried down the main hallway as well, for there were now shouts from the upper landing and the sound of running footsteps converging on the east wing. Out of patience, Tyrone expelled a short gust of air and thrust the tapestry aside, drawing another startled shriek from Miss Ruth Entwistle who was still standing frozen against the wall, not three paces away.

"Clever where they hide water closets these days, is it not?" he remarked casually, hooking a thumb over his shoulder. "Am I mistaken, or did I hear a gunshot?"

Miss Entwistle shrieked again and whirled away in a cloud of pale blue holland. Tyrone barely gave a thought to her shattered modesty as he turned and took the stairs two at a time. There were half a dozen people already gathering outside the door to Renée's bedroom and more coming by twos and threes. He was able to slip unobtrusively into their midst and to look as concerned and surprised as the others when Colonel Roth strode out of the room.

Lord Paxton arrived at almost the same moment, huffing and out of breath. "Someone said there has been a shooting?"

Roth held up the steel pocket pistol. "It appears the French have an odd way of showing their gratitude for being taken in, fed, clothed, treated like royalty. Edgar Vincent is dead. He has been shot. I did what I could to revive him, but alas—"

"Dead!" Paxton's gasp was almost lost in the rumble of disbelief that went through the crowd of guests. "Vincent is dead?"

"Shot in cold blood by your niece's manservant, Finnerty. Luckily I was close enough to apprehend the culprit before he could make good his escape. I found him standing over the body, the gun still warm in his hand!"

"My niece?"

"Gone. Your nephew too. And the rubies Vincent gave her as a betrothal gift have mysteriously gone missing with them."

This last observation was obviously added for the benefit of the shocked audience, who reacted accordingly, raising their voices in outrage and disbelief.

Roth held up his hand to call for order. "According to Mr. Vincent's dying gasps, he arrived unexpectedly at his fiancée's chamber only to discover she was in the process of fleeing the premises. Moreover, he said the theft was accomplished with the help of the infamous Captain Starlight, with whom, it would appear, Mademoiselle d'Anton has had several clandestine meetings over the past weeks."

There were one or two women in the hallway and at the mention of the highwayman's name, they swooned and required immediate removal to couches or chaises.

"He was here?" Paxton demanded, looking suddenly faint himself. "Starlight was in this house?"

"That, we have yet to discover. And we will, by God, before the night is through." Roth stood aside and signaled to Marlborough and another gentleman, who dragged Finn out of the door between them. One side of his face was awash in blood from a crease in his forehead. He had been struck hard enough to lay the flesh open to the bone, and even though he was stunned and too unsteady to stand on his own, he made several feeble attempts to do so and to shake off the hands of the two men who held him. He also attempted to speak, but Roth's voice rose above the hoarse whispers, issuing orders to his men to search the grounds, pressing the male guests to make use of Lord Paxton's fowling pieces and hunting dogs to help search the stables and adjoining woods. He handed the cannon-barrelled pistol to Marlborough, declaring it to be evidence, then gave orders for the prisoner to be taken away, to be put into a coach immediately and driven under heavy escort to the barracks gaol in Coventry.

On his own, without a weapon of any kind, there was little Tyrone could do but watch as Finn was unceremoniously dragged past. The old valet seemed to catch his foot in the edge of a carpet as they drew abreast and for a brief moment, the eyes of the two men met. The contact was quickly broken when Roth saw Tyrone standing against the wall and strolled casually over to join him.

"You are looking a little damp about the temples, Hart. I could have sworn I saw you being carried off with the other fainthearted ladies."

Tyrone removed his handkerchief from his cuff and

dabbed his temple. "I readily confess neither the hunt nor the kill are m' forte, Colonel, though I must say, the thought alone is rather debilitating, that the fellow should have been right here in the house while we were playing at charades. You don't suppose he took offense and thus became homicidal?"

"What the devil are you on about?"

"Can you have forgotten already? Dash me if I was not assigned the task of playing Captain Starlight. No one guessed it. Not even you. Suppose he was hid behind a curtain watching?"

This drew a few more murmured speculations from the crowd but Roth did not allow for more than a contemptuous sneer. "If he was watching you portray him, sir, I rather think it would be you he shot."

"Well!" Tyrone sniffed and looked around for sympathy as Roth strode away. "No wonder he has had no luck catching the bounder. I warrant he could be standing right beside the rogue and never know how close he came to being run through."

\*

It was almost another full half hour before Tyrone was able to slip away unobserved. For the second time in less than twenty-four hours, he made his way into the belly of the ancient keep and exited through the old escape tunnel. He had to walk most of the distance doubled over to avoid scraping his head on the ceiling, and somewhere between the tower and the canal, he lost his wig and discarded his cravat. The smell of dampness and fresh, cold air assailed him about twenty feet from the last bend in the passage and for that he was grateful. The chill cleared his head and gave his strength a boost for what lay ahead.

Dudley, Renée, and Antoine were waiting at the mouth of the tunnel. It was raining again, falling in sheets that increased and decreased with the strength of the

wind. Tyrone had doused the candle he had brought with
him from the cellar and as he came quietly up on the
entrance Renée's was the first silhouette he saw. She was
pacing anxiously back and forth, her skirts and cloak dragging across the rough earth underfoot. Antoine was seated
on a rock, huddled in a blanket for warmth. Dudley stood
leaning against the side of the earthen wall, looking well
planted as a deterrent against what must have been repeated attempts to go back and find out what was keeping Finn and Hart.

"Tyrone!" Renée saw him first and ran to greet him.
The smile of relief on her face passed before the silk of
her cloak had stopped swirling around him. "Where is
Finn?"

There was no easy way to tell her. "He has been arrested."

"Arrested? How? By whom? On what charge?"

"Roth is charging him with the murder of Edgar Vincent."

*"Murder!"*

Dudley and Antoine both came to attention.

"What condition was Vincent in when you left him?"
Tyrone asked.

"He was alive," Renée insisted. "Antoine hit him
fairly hard, but he was alive."

"Well, he is very dead now. And Roth is claiming it
was Finn who shot him."

"Shot him?" Renée gasped. "But he had no gun!"

"Roth is also claiming Vincent interrupted you in the
midst of a robbery. He pointed out that you and the boy
were gone, along with the rubies, and he even managed
to suggest it was part of an elaborate scheme all along;
one you had conspired to commit with the help of Captain Starlight."

Renée shook her head and started to go back into the
tunnel. "I must go to him."

"And do what?" Tyrone asked, catching her gently by the arm. "What can you do for him?"

"I—I can tell the truth. I can tell them what really happened."

"What really happened? How do you know?"

"Finn did not kill M'sieur Vincent!"

"I'm sure he didn't. But that only leaves him and Roth in the room, and who do you suppose the people back in that house are going to believe?"

Dudley had only allowed a small, hooded light for a reference point, not enough to clearly read the expression on her face, but Tyrone could see the fear welling in her eyes.

"I cannot just abandon him! I cannot just leave him behind."

"You are not abandoning him and you are not leaving him behind. Roth has already had him removed to the barracks in Coventry, and if you do go back now, you will only end up in the cell beside him." He tilted his head to one side, catching the faint sound of dogs braying in the distance. "It could very well happen anyway if we don't get the hell out of here and back to town before the militia arrives."

"We can give the rubies back," Renée declared, resisting Tyrone's efforts to steer her toward the mouth of the passage. "We can trade them for Finn."

"I very much doubt a handful of pretty stones would be enough to soothe Roth's vanity at the moment," Tyrone said grimly.

"But sir," it was Antoine, stepping forward. "M'sieur Vincent said they were worth two hundred thousand of your English pounds. Surely he cannot think Finn is worth that much."

Tyrone stared at the boy a minute, thinking perhaps he was more exhausted than he realized. "Two hundred thousand? Where did you hear that amount?"

"I have learned to listen very well, m'sieur. And when

I heard shouting in Renée's room, I put my ear to the door and I heard him say you—you 'must be damned good for two hundred thousand pounds' worth of baubles.' "

Tyrone frowned and looked at Renée. "Do you know anything about this?"

She was staring into the blackness of the passageway and had to forcibly redirect her attention before shaking her head. "No. When he first gave them to me, arrogant goat that he was, he made a large point of bragging they were worth fifty thousand pounds, as if I had never seen a jewel in my life and should die of awe over his generosity. Had they been worth more than that, I am sure he would have told me."

"Did he tell you he had a duplicate set made?"

"Duplicate?"

"Glass. Very good imitations, but practically worthless."

"No," her voice fell to a shocked whisper. "No, he did not tell me this. How do *you* know he did?"

"Robbie overheard them talking in the coach the other day. Apparently Vincent wasn't prepared to risk the real rubies on another of Roth's schemes. Or maybe he realized he had made a mistake when he gave them to you."

"Then . . . the jewels I wore tonight are worthless," she said in horror, "and we have nothing to trade for Finn?"

The sound of the dogs was drawing closer, prompting Dudley into taking command of the situation. "We'll have nothing at all in a few minutes if we don't get moving. The boat is tied up to the scrub and loaded. How are the ribs holding up?"

"They will feel a hell of a lot better when we get out of here," Tyrone agreed.

With Dudley leading the way, they climbed carefully down the shallow embankment to where the boat was tied. The current in the canal was swift and strong from

the recent storms and the current downpour was adding
still more runoff, making it muddy and turbulent. The
banks of the river seemed to streak by, most of the landmarks blurred by the rain and darkness, but Dudley kept
a firm grip on the tiller, and drawing on his experience
from his smuggling days, moved them through the gloom
like wraiths.

Renée, huddled with Antoine under the blanket,
barely heard the two men whispering back and forth,
scarcely noticed the time or the bridges or the lights they
slipped past as they approached the city proper. Once,
Dudley signaled a halt and they pulled up under a
wooden bridge, waiting while a patrol of four dragoons
rode by, the hooves of the horses clattering like thunder
overhead. At the very next bridge, they moored the little
skiff and climbed up a steep flight of steps to a street
lined with tall, narrow houses, the upper storeys jutting
out over the road, the roofs steeply pitched and seeming
to lean into one another for support. It smelled of fish and
dampness and slime-filled gutters. Each building had a
wooden sign creaking above the door carved with a name
and picture; some had lights in the windows and noise
spilling out of the crowded taprooms, but Dudley hurried
past, guiding them down one alley and up another until
the sounds faded and the stench eased. A coach was waiting down one of these side streets and while Dudley
slipped a few coins to the faceless, shapeless shadow who
stood watch over it, Tyrone assisted Renée and Antoine
inside.

They were all soaked and chilled to the bone. The
shock of Vincent's attack, the race through the tunnel, the
news about Finn, and the rocking, lurching flight along
the canal was finally taking its toll on Renée and she felt
physically ill. She had been fighting a continuous battle
with the contents of her stomach since they left Harwood,
and it was only by the slimmest margin she managed to
hold on through the wild boat ride and equally breakneck

course the coach took through the twisted lanes leading to Priory Lane.

Dudley drove straight around to the back of the house and pulled up in the small cobbled courtyard. While he put the coach away and stabled the horses, Tyrone ushered Renée and Antoine inside. Maggie Smallwood was waiting there with hot tea, broth, and biscuits, but she took one look at Renée's pale, battered face and whisked her away up the stairs. Renée was stripped of her sodden clothes and chafed dry with a thick, warm towel. Maggie stoked a fire and left her bundled in several layers of quilting while she hurried back down the stairs to fetch hot water for a bath.

It was only then that Renée stopped fighting. She leaned over an enamel basin and wretched. She wretched and sobbed and convulsed until there was nothing left in her stomach to void, and when she was finished, she sagged gratefully back into the strong arms that were waiting to scoop her up and carry her to a warm seat in front of the fire.

✳ ☽

# Chapter 25

"*I* am hurting you," Renée exclaimed.

"You're fine."

"But your wound," she said, trying to struggle upright.

"My wound is fine," Tyrone reiterated, "as long as you refrain from wriggling about like a worm."

She stopped and looked at him, nose to nose, then melted slowly back into the warm crook of his shoulder. His arms settled around her again, blankets and all, and she felt his lips brush her forehead. She snuck one hand free of the woolen folds and rested it against the curve of his neck, feeling slightly ashamed that he should have found her helpless and nauseous but somehow comforted and content to be held so protectively in his lap.

She tried, surreptitiously, to inspect her surroundings. When Maggie had ushered her up the stairs, her head had been spinning far too wildly to notice much more than dark wood paneling and high, ornately plastered ceiling, but she realized now she was in an elegantly masculine bedroom, with heavy mahogany furniture and dark velvet draperies. The fireplace was wide enough to fit a five foot log, the floors underfoot were thickly carpeted with Persian rugs. For a public servant cum notorious highwayman he possessed very expensive tastes, not the least of which was reflected in the Italian marble mantelpiece and enormous tester bed. She was not exactly certain what she should have expected to see in the way of living quarters—something spare, utilitarian, impersonal as befitting someone who might have to flee the city, the parish, the country at a moment's notice. Or something completely foreign, gaudy, flamboyant, gilded in fakery like the caricature he presented to the world.

"I am sorry," she whispered.

"For what?"

"For . . . this. For not being very strong."

One of his hands shifted and smoothed down the wet tangle of her hair. "Little fool," he murmured. "You were stronger than anyone ought to be under the circumstances."

Her hand tightened on his throat and she buried her face a little deeper into his neck and above her, Tyrone's eyes closed briefly, savoring the sensation.

"What are we going to do? I cannot stop thinking of Finn."

"Finn will be fine. Roth would not dare do anything to him; Finn is his trump card and as long as he has him, he knows you will not go very far."

"He saved our lives. It was only because of Finn that Antoine and I were able to escape Paris."

"And I promise you, we will get him back. We may have to wait a day or two to see what develops, what Roth wants, but my guess is, if we sweeten the pot enough, he'll agree to an exchange."

"Sweeten the pot? *Qu'est-ce que tu dis?*"

"A gambler's term. Increase the stakes. Make the pot too rich to pass up."

"But how could you do this?"

"I will offer him something he cannot refuse."

"What could you possibly have that would satisfy a man like—" She stopped as the breath caught in her throat. She pushed herself upright again and Tyrone winced, as much from the palpable twinge in his side as from the very large, very blue eyes that were suddenly peering intently and fearfully into his.

"You would not be so foolish as to offer him yourself, would you?"

He was held by the look in her eye for several more long moments, wishing he could justify it, wishing that whatever she imagined she saw inside him was really there.

"There you go, overestimating me again," he murmured gently, "while sadly *under*estimating my talents."

Leaning forward, he eased her carefully to her feet. With a cryptic crooking of his finger he indicated she should follow, then led the way through his dressing room to the adjoining study.

Curious enough to obey, she gathered the folds of quilting around her shoulders and rustled after him, so close on his heels and so distracted by the sight of still more opulence in the upholstered chaises, enormous oak desk, and wall-length shelves full of leather-bound volumes, that she nearly ran into him when he stopped. As the flames took hold on the five-pronged candelabra he lit, more of the detailing emerged from the heavy shadows. Cornices and moldings were hand-carved, the squares of paneling had been fashioned to look like sheets of linen cloth. There was another fireplace, not quite so impressive as the one in his bedchamber, but supported nonetheless by marble caryatids, naked and full breasted. And commanding attention in the center of the room was one of the grandest pianos she had seen outside the walls of Versailles.

He seemed oblivious to her uplifted eyebrows as he lit more candles and placed them on the desk, the piano, the mantelpiece. He had taken off his satin jacket and looked much like he had on the steps of the tower, with his waistcoat unbuttoned and his shirt gaping open over his chest. His hair was wet, bound in a tail at the nape, but strands had broken free of the riband and straggled down his cheek and throat. The rain had washed away most of the cosmetics, and a brisk toweling had removed the rest, restoring his complexion to a deep and weathered bronze. The fop was gone and in his place was a man of such breathtaking beauty, an enigma comprised of so many contradictions and so many hidden facets, that Renée felt a trembling deep inside that had nothing to do with their flight tonight.

It worsened when he glanced over his shoulder and smiled, for now, it seemed, it was time for the boy in him to emerge.

"Come," he said. "Stand over here."

When she was positioned where he wanted her, he went to one of the long paneled sheets and released a hidden catch. The panel swung open and behind it were three multi-collared greatcoats, several black tricorns, gloves, and tall leather boots. The next panel revealed a gun case with shelves holding pairs of long-snouted pistols, pouches of shot and powder, as well as a rack holding at least a dozen swords of various styles and weights, from the lethal slimness of a dueling rapier to the solid deadliness of a Highland clai' mór.

At the third and last panel he stopped and held out his hand. When she put her smaller, cooler fingers into his, he pressed them to his lips first, then guided them to the latch concealed in the intricate wood carving. As the panel swung open, he held the candelabra higher, and Renée could not stop the gasp that escaped her lips. The cupboard was lined with shelves, all of them divided into compartments, most of them covered with felt or velvet. There were necklaces and bracelets and earrings of every gem imaginable; diamonds, rubies, emeralds, tourmalines, pearls glittered up at her in the candlelight, as did ropes of gold chain, watches and fobs, coins in gold and silver.

"*Mon dieu*," she whispered. "All this?"

"The spoils of a misguided sense of humor," he mused. "Was that not what you accused me of having?"

"But . . . so much!"

"Yes, well. There is more in London. Definitely more than I can spend in this or any other lifetime."

"Then why do you keep doing it? Why do you keep taking such risks?"

"Let's just say I have not found anything quite as exciting to take its place."

Incredulity widened the glorious blue of her eyes as she looked slowly up at him. "And you would simply give all this away?"

His gaze went from her eyes to her mouth to the jewels, then back again. "Half of it, anyway. We would not want to reward Roth too much for his greed. Then again, half of what is here is probably ten times more than he will ever steal on his own."

"You would do this for Finn?" she whispered.

He hesitated again and brushed aside the wisps of damp hair that had fallen over her cheek. "No. But I would do it to see you smile again."

He walked past her toward the open panels and this time it was Renée who was left staring at the bright flames of the candles, his words echoing softly in the shadows. She turned swiftly, intending to say something—though she was not certain what she would have said—and saw Maggie standing in the doorway of the dressing room.

"I've brought hot water for a bath, miss. And ointments for those bruises and cuts."

Renée pulled the quilts tighter around her shoulders. "M'sieur Hart needs tending more than I do. His wound has opened again."

The look in Maggie's eye was enough to confirm the fact that she had already seen the spots of blood on his shirt and was not pleased. "The boy is almost finished in the tub downstairs and there is more water boiling for a fresh turn. We will get you warm first, miss—though you aren't looking half so pale as you did when you first arrived—then you can be sure I'll be giving Mr. Tyrone a rare strip of my tongue while I'm after seeing what manner of mischief he has done to my handiwork."

"How is Antoine?" Renée asked, startled that she had all but forgotten him until now.

"Just fine," Maggie assured her. "He has already eaten half a loaf of bread and honey, and I've given him tea laced with brandy to keep the dampness out of his chest. I might add that once the chill was gone out of him he started talking and hasn't stopped for breath, not even with his cheeks full and his head under water."

"I do not understand what happened."

"Sometimes, when you're frightened badly enough to lose something, you have to be just as frightened to find it again. Come along then, Robbie has put the tub in front of the fire. I've a nice hot pot of special chocolate ready for you and the bricks are in the bed, getting it rare cozy and warm."

Renée felt a pang of uncertainty as she glanced over her shoulder and watched Tyrone close and latch each of the panel doors. "Will you come back later?"

He did not glance up. "If you want me to."

"I want you to," she whispered. "Very much."

＊

Renée soaked a sinfully long time. For the first time in more years than she could remember, she found herself sitting in a tub that was larger than she was. Maggie had sprinkled the hot water with herbs and while the steam did not exactly bring to mind a rose garden, each deep breath she took seemed to ease away another cramp, another ache, another knot of tightness in her muscles. She was almost drifting off to sleep when the Irish girl returned with clean buckets of warm water to rinse her hair and skin, and it was with a most regretful sigh that Renée stood and let herself be wrapped again in warmed towels.

"Did you try the chocolate, miss?"

"Two cups," Renée said dreamily. "It was *merveilleux*."

Maggie's smile was wide enough to bring out two dimples. "That would be the Irish in it. Warms the very marrow of your bones, it does." She finished blotting the excess moisture out of the long blond hair then peered closely at the cut high on Renée's cheek. "You were lucky with this one, miss. A bit to the left, you could have lost your eye. I'll put some salve on it, though I cannot promise you'll not be left with a mark. If I was a proper doctor, maybe I would know some way to stop a scar from forming, but . . ."

Renée reached out and laid her hand on the girl's arm. "It is all right, Maggie—I may call you Maggie, may I not?—I would be happy to have a scar, truly."

Maggie gave her an odd look, but continued applying ointments and salves to the various bruises on her arms and legs. When she was finished, she apologized again. "I had a quick peek in your bag, but everything you brought is soaked in rain and river water. I'm sorry, but I don't have any proper nightdresses to offer you. Robbie prefers me to sleep naked and Mr. Tyrone never brings any of his lady friends here, so—" She caught herself just after the words tripped off her tongue, but although Renée turned her head slightly, waiting for the rest of the sentence, she did not ask for clarification. "But I did find one of his shirts that should do in a pinch. Very soft it is. And likely large enough to feel like a nightdress."

"I am sure it will be fine."

Maggie helped her into it and it was, indeed, soft as another skin, long enough to reach her knees. After that she was belted into one of Tyrone's Chinese silk dressing robes, the sleeves of which had to be folded back almost to the elbows. She was ordered to sit again and enjoy a third cup of chocolate laced with the "Irish" while her hair was brushed dry in front of the fire.

"M'sieur Tyrone? His wound is all right?"

"Oh, aye. It was just a bit of weeping, naught to worry about. He's bound up tight as a drum again and had a healthy dose of the brandy himself. No doubt he will be carrying on in the morning like nothing is amiss. You've seen his back? Aye, well, a beating like that would have killed a normal man, but according to my Robbie, his only complaint at the time was that he had to carry Dudley half a mile before they could steal a pair of nags. Just when you think he should be dead, he"—the crackling strokes of the brush stopped and both women turned to gaze in the direction of the adjoining study, where the lightest, sweetest notes of music were coming from the other side of the closed door—"plays the piano," Maggie concluded with a wry chuckle. "Claims it relaxes him, heals him, helps him think. All hours of the day and night, I vow, and for days on end sometimes, he sits there and creates these heavenly sounds that—"

"*Forcer les anges de pleurer,*" Renée murmured.

"Aye, I suppose. Whatever that means."

"Why was he beaten so badly?"

"He doesn't like to talk about it." Maggie paused, cursing her loose tongue again. "But my Robbie told me. It was the first time the two of them came together."

"M'sieur Dudley and M'sieur Tyrone?"

"No. Mr. Tyrone . . . and Colonel Roth."

Renée turned so quickly, the action almost dragged the brush out of Maggie's hand.

"Colonel Roth? He did that to Tyrone?"

"He was only a sergeant at the time and stationed in Aberdeen. As full of himself as he is now, with a vicious temper and a cruel taste for inflicting pain. Mr. Tyrone had been caught running with the rustlers and Roth thought he could lash the location of their main camp out of him. The more stubborn Mr. Tyrone proved to be, the more brutal the beatings."

"And all this time . . . Roth does not recognize him?"

"It happened seven years ago, when they were both gangly and young. Mr. Tyrone, especially, was so skinny and filthy—a bag of bones and raw nerve, as my Robbie described him. Add to that this tomfoolery with the wigs and the powders and the rouges." She shrugged and set the brush aside. "I doubt his own mam would recognize him."

Renée stared into the fire a long moment and listened to the music, wondering why she had ever doubted, from the first instant of their meeting, that Captain Starlight would turn her world upside down. It was end over end now, and her emotions were paying the price, ebbing and flowing like tides on the shore, building, she was certain, toward the ultimate crash against the rocks.

"If that's all you need, m'lady, I'll be going to my bed now."

"What? Oh, of course. Antoine?"

"Is fast asleep downstairs. I can ask Robbie to carry him up if you would rather have him here with you."

"No. No, let him sleep."

"I'll say goodnight, then."

"Goodnight. And thank you so much for everything you have done."

Maggie's eyes twinkled in the direction of the study. "Thank *you*, miss. I was beginning to lose hope for him."

The door closed behind her and Renée was left alone with the fire, the shadows, and the music. Her eyes were heavy and her body tired, but she stood and walked through the dressing room to the study, hesitating with her hand on the latch for a moment before she quietly turned it and opened the door.

Tyrone was sitting with his back to her, his head bowed forward in concentration. He was playing Mozart, and she waited until the long, magical fingers finished displaying their artistry before she walked over and stood beside him. He glanced up once . . . then twice as his eyes registered surprise and pleasure seeing her wrapped in his robe. Her hair flowed smooth and sleek over her shoulders, tamed free of curls, shimmering with every slight move of her body.

"You play beautifully, m'sieur."

He smiled and touched his forefinger to his brow in a salute. "Since I believe that is the first compliment that has not contained the words 'madman' or 'buffoon,' I shall accept it with thanks."

"You *are* mad," she allowed with the faintest hint of a smile. "But you play beautifully nonetheless."

"Do you?"

She shook her head. "*Maman* tried in vain to teach me, but"—she held up her fingers and wiggled them—"they always wanted to go one way and the music the other."

"Here," he said and edged the bench back enough to make room for her on his lap. "Put your hands over mine; I'll take you in the right direction."

His fingers were much longer and the music he played was simple and slow, the tune familiar enough that she was able to anticipate which keys he would carry her fingers to next. His body was warm against her, beneath her, and by the time his hands came to a standstill, her body was a mass of hot and cool sensations, thick and sluggish in places, molten and fluid in others. The skin across her breasts was tight with anticipation, while elsewhere, it was throbbing with the shame of wanting him.

"I feel so guilty," she said on a shallow gasp. "Finn is in gaol and all I can think of is . . . how wonderfully warm I feel."

With her hands still splayed over his, he brought them up and circled them around her waist. "You can do nothing else for Finn tonight. And I shall take it as another compliment, mam'selle, that you feel so warm."

She closed her eyes and melted into the heat of his lips where they pressed into her neck. His breath scented with brandy, was soft on her skin, and she tipped her head back, needing to feel him, taste him in her mouth.

Wary of her damaged lip, he kissed her so gently, she could have wept. Aware of the freshly bandaged injury to his ribs, she turned in his arms, deepening the kiss herself, holding his face between her hands, guiding his mouth down onto the curve of her throat where there were only sighs of pleasure to welcome his explorations.

He loosened the belt at her waist and his hands slipped beneath the silk. They skimmed upward to cup her breasts in his palms, lifting them, raising them to his mouth as it descended to claim them through the soft layer of lawn. Renée arched back with the pleasure and her bottom brushed against the piano keys, producing a broken chord of mismatched notes. With slow, leisurely strokes of his lips and tongue, he teased her through the fabric, leaving two wet circles clinging transparently to her nipples. His hands meandered down her thighs and when they rose again they brought the hem of the shirt with them, exposing the milky whiteness of her bared limbs to the candlelight.

The chords were stronger this time, lingering on the air as she leaned against the row of ivory keys. When he eased her thighs apart, her hands struck other notes, startled notes that resonated softly throughout her body, for his mouth was on her belly, then buried in the silky triangle of golden curls. She gasped at the outrageous wickedness of his tongue as it flickered and swirled across the tender folds and peaks. She groaned at the first deep incursion, a slippery, sliding thrust of sensation that nearly lifted her off the keys entirely. Her hands spread wider to brace herself for each new onslaught as he explored the sleekly sensitive surfaces and probed the mysterious, lustrous depths. Shivers ran down her thighs while her hands, her fingers, skidded involuntarily over notes that were alternately sweet and sharp, jarring and gentle. He played her with the skill and expertise of a master musician building toward a shattering crescendo, each time holding back a single thrust, or a single stroke, holding her firm until her inner vibrations calmed, only to start again and again until she was in a trembling agony of wanting.

When he grew impatiently envious of his own skill, Tyrone stood and unfastened his robe. He was naked beneath, his erection standing strong and vigorous against his belly. With her body shivering and tightening around him, he drove himself deeply and urgently into her, groaning when he felt the eager grasp of her flesh, knowing by the sheer heat of her body that she was well beyond any desire for delicacy or finesse. He was hard and full inside her and she moved with him, against him. The combined effects of their rushing thrusts created an irrepressible cacophony of sound beneath them that was as rhythmic and frenetic as the motion of their bodies. It stretched into a single, prolonged chord as he stiffened into one last, explosive thrust—their climax mutual, wild and fiercely unrelenting, stunning in its absolute purity.

Then it was only their gasps they heard. Their shivered, disbelieving cries rent the air, and it was the fractured, ragged moans of their own unstructured ecstasy that eventually caused them to dissolve, panting and blissfully spent, into each other's arms.

* ☽

# Chapter 26

"*W*here did you learn to play the piano so well?"

They were lying in bed, arms and legs twined together. The curtains had been deliberately left open so the daylight would waken him, but Tyrone had barely closed his eyes all night. He lay staring up at the ceiling most of the time, replaying the events of the past two weeks, wondering at exactly what point he should have listened to his instincts—which had noticeably been in turmoil since the first time he had clapped eyes on Renée d'Anton—and walked away.

"Are you referring to the fine symphony we played last night? To that I can only say . . . inspiration. Lovely ivory skin to stimulate the passion of the composition, stirring crescendos to inspire my baton . . . ouch!"

She released the pinch of flesh she had between her teeth and angled her face to look up at him. "If you would rather not tell me—?"

"There are some things that are awkward for a rogue and scoundrel to admit to. Like an excellent education and a life of relative privilege few who possessed my inferior bloodlines would have thrown away so cavalierly."

"There is nothing inferior about you," she assured him, snuggling back into the curve of his body. "And I pity those who would underestimate you because of your blood."

"The truth is difficult to underestimate. I was born the son of a game warden and, had fate not intervened at an early age, I would likely be doing the same now with a wife and seven mewling children about my ankles looking to me to improve their predetermined lot in life."

"I rather doubt that," she said, smiling. "I think you were born a rogue and shall die a rogue and"—her breath caught a moment in her throat—"and whoever is lucky enough to share a part of your life along the way will be forever changed."

While he thought about that, his hand continued to stroke her hair and when he responded, finally, he was frowning. "It was never my intention to change anyone, nor did I anticipate anyone changing me. I have always been content to take each day as it came. I have made no plans, plotted no courses in life. All in all, a poor prospect for domestication."

"And yet you have all of this," she said, indicating the richness of their surroundings.

"I do not deny I like my creature comforts. But if I had to walk away from it all, I could. And I would, in an instant. It is hardly the kind of life," he added in a murmur, "that I could ask—or expect—anyone to share."

Renée propped her chin on her hand and looked up at him, at the smoky gray of his eyes, the seductively inviting fullness of his lips. *You could ask me*, she mouthed silently in French. *You could ask me and I would walk . . . no, I would run to the ends of the earth with you.*

But he did not ask. His eyebrows quirked a little with curiosity as he watched her lips move, but in the end, he only kissed her briefly on the top of her head and gently untangled himself in order to sit up.

"I have been giving it some thought," he said, stretching out his arms, testing the pull on the bandages, the mobility in the wounded ribs. "The first order of business should be to find out exactly where Roth is keeping Finn. If he is in the town gaol, the cell has a lock that could be picked with a dull knife. If he is in the converted wine cellar at the Black Bull, we will have to rely more heavily on Roth's greed."

Renée reached out and gently ran her fingers over the old lacerations that crisscrossed the slabs of muscle on his back. "Why did you not tell me he did this to you?"

His head turned slightly. "It happened a long time ago. And it was personal, between Roth and myself."

She slipped up onto her knees behind him, "Do you still think of me as business?"

Tyrone looked down at where her hands circled his waist. His flesh stirred, betraying the very unbusinesslike pleasure he felt at such a simple gesture, and he sighed, "That was not what I meant. I just didn't think you should feel obliged to worry about something that has nothing to do with your present predicament. Or with getting Finn back, for that matter."

"I do not mind worrying about you," she said softly.

"Yes, well," he pushed himself off the side of the bed, "I mind."

After casting a cursory glance around the room and not locating his robe, he walked naked into the dressing room, but he had barely opened the door to the commode when Renée appeared in the entryway behind him, her shoulders swathed in the bedsheet.

"You will let me help you, will you not?"

He looked at her, looked at the commode, then shut the cupboard door again. "I gather you mean with Finn?"

"Roth will not hurt him, will he?"

"No." The word alone did not seem to be enough to appease her, so he walked back to where she was standing and took her face in his hands. "This is not France," he said gently. "And Roth is not Robespierre, regardless of how much power he thinks he has over everyone's destiny. In this country, an accused man has to stand trial, regardless of the charge or the evidence against him—a process that could take weeks, or months, depending on the crime. Even I would have my day in court, to be judged innocent or guilty by a jury of my peers, before they led me up the steps of the gallows."

"How can you joke about such a thing?" she asked in a whisper.

"I do not joke about it, mam'selle. I simply choose not to dwell on the reality of it twenty-four hours a day. If I did, I would not be able to breathe. Just like now," he said, tenderly kissing her bruised mouth. "I am having great difficulty breathing because I cannot stop thinking of what I was about to do when you interrupted me."

She blushed and withdrew with an impatient sigh. "I want to help," she insisted. "Finn is my responsibility. He is only in gaol because of me, because of trying to help me. Nor do I want you to put yourself at any more risk because of us."

"A kind thought, but unfortunately we haven't time to fit you for a tricorn and greatcoat."

As soon as she heard the door to the commode shut, she was back at the doorway. "You are going to meet with Roth as Captain Starlight?"

"Would he negotiate with anyone else seriously?"

He poured fresh water into the washbasin and reached for his shaving gear although the reflection in the mirror suggested there would not be much improvement in his overall appearance. There were dark circles under his eyes and an underlying pallor to his skin. His ribs ached like hell and he longed for another forty hours in bed without having to think or move or find a way to save the world.

"This hero business can be quite taxing," he muttered as he scrutinized his reflection.

"Will you let me shave you?" she asked, brightening, anxious to help in even so small a way.

"Have you ever done it before?"

"No. But I watched Finn shave my father a thousand times. It does not look the least bit difficult."

"Ahh. Well, we will give you a lesson another time."

"May I at least watch?"

"If you promise not to make me laugh when I have the blade over my throat."

She came into the dressing room and sat on a straight-back chair. Tyrone took up a fine-bristled brush and a bar of soap and worked up a lather, spreading it thickly on the shadow of dark stubble that had sprouted overnight on his chin and neck.

"Does M'sieur Dudley usually do this for you?"

"Robbie is not my servant. Maggie sometimes obliges when I am too hung-over to see clearly, but otherwise, I have it done by a barber or"—he tilted his jaw to foam the underside of his chin—"I do it myself."

"None of your other lady friends obliged?"

The pale eyes narrowed as he looked at her. "Is there anything else you and Maggie discussed that I should know about?"

"She only mentioned that you do not bring your mistresses here, therefore, it must be assumed that you visit them elsewhere."

"Them? I have more than one?"

"I cannot see you with just one, m'sieur. I should think you would get bored very easily."

He glanced warily at her out of the corner of his eye for she had stretched her neck at the same time and the same angle as he stretched his. "You think that, do you?"

"*Oui. Absolutement.* As *maman* would say, you would make someone a magnificent lover, but a poor husband."

He reached for his razor and stropped it several times on a length of hard leather. "It sounds like your mother was a wise lady."

"She was. And she would have liked you, I think, and been happy for me even though we did not have a chance to dance."

Tyrone looked at her again and frowned. "Did I miss something? Were we supposed to dance?"

Her laugh was soft and a little sad. "No, m'sieur. As it turned out, it was not necessary."

Still frowning, he turned back to the mirror. He did not like cryptic little smiles, especially when they came at his expense. On the other hand, it was the first time he had heard her laugh, not that there had been many opportunities over their brief acquaintance to inspire jocularity. Nevertheless, like the various degrees and shades of blushes he had discovered she was capable of producing, the sound of her shy, husky laugh intrigued him—enough so that he thought he ought to change the subject.

"How long has Finn been with you?"

"He left England with my mother, thirty years ago. He loved her very much."

"Loved . . . as in *loved*?"

"I think he loved her all his life, but he would never dare tell her so or even admit it out loud to himself. When he saw her beaten to death outside the prison gates," her voice and eyes lowered with the memory, "I thought he, too, would die of a broken heart. Do you know his hair was brown the night before it happened and white the night after?"

Tyrone scraped the edge of the razor down his cheek, clearing the first stripe of lather and stubble. "I have heard of it happening, but never seen it."

"There was nothing he could do to help my mother, but he saved Antoine and me. He had made a promise to *maman*, you see—she made him swear it every morning, for she did not know how long any of us would be safe from Robespierre's tribunals. He promised to guard us and protect us and he swore this to her on his life." Her expression was solemn and haunted again as she looked up at Tyrone. "I do not think we can wait a day or two. If Finn believes Antoine and I are safe, and if he believes that by sacrificing himself he will protect us . . . then he will do it."

Half of his chin was clean and Tyrone allowed a wry

chuckle before he started on his neck. "What makes you think he would believe you are safe in my clutches? I should think I would be the last person he would want to see taking care of you."

"In truth, he told me to trust you. He said he believed you were a good man and I should do everything you say to do."

The razor took a nick out of his skin, leaving a curse and a small bead of blood behind.

"Does that not sound like goodbye to you?" she persisted. "Do you not think he might do something foolish to avoid being used as a—a trumpet?"

The second bite of the razor was deeper, the curse louder, but when he glared at Renée, all she did was blush and point out the obvious. "You have cut yourself, m'sieur."

"I am well aware of what I have done to myself. Could you possibly"—he clenched his jaw and forced a smile— "go and put some clothes on. Maggie left them on the chair while you were sleeping. In your present condition, you are enough of a distraction to have me slicing ribbons all over my face."

She stood, hauling the profusion of sheets with her. "I am sorry if my appearance disturbs you," she said primly, "but I have not exactly been looking at a blank wall."

She exited in a swirl of linen and Tyrone glanced down. He was, he realized, still naked save for the strip of bandaging, and, as was becoming a noticeable tendency when Renée was wearing little but roses in her cheeks, he was half aroused.

He finished shaving without any further bloodletting and when he emerged from the dressing room—safely confined in buff breeches and a white shirt—Renée was standing by the window. Her hair was catching enough of the morning light to make it glow silver, and he decided she was as beautiful in the sunlight as she was in the moonlight. Not even the cut on her cheeks, the scabbing on her lip, or the bruises that marred the whiteness of her skin could detract from the gentle radiance that seemed to glow from within. At the same time there was nothing fragile or fainthearted about her. She had survived the Terror in France, endured Roth's manipulations, withstood Vincent's assault, even bared her neck to a murderous highwayman and defied him to throttle her if he thought she was lying. Now here she was, refusing to even consider Finn's willingness to sacrifice himself for her safety, something not one in a thousand aristocrats of so-called noble blood would think twice of accepting—even expecting—from a mere servant.

Coming so close on the heels of admitting she intrigued him, of acknowledging that he became as randy as a billygoat if she just looked at him, and of knowing he would give more than just half of what he had in his cabinets to see her smile at him the way she smiled at Antoine . . . well, he did not trust himself to speak or to move, nor did he do either until she sensed his presence and turned toward him.

She might just as well have taken up a hammer and hit him in the chest, for the expression on her face was so full of despair, he was concerned enough to join her by the window and take her gently into his arms.

"I may have my faults, Renée, but I do not count making false promises to frightened young women among them. I have said we will get Finn back, and get him back we shall."

"It was not Finn I was thinking about," she said with a guilty, tremulous smile. "I was . . . only wondering what it would be like to have seven mewling children about my ankles."

He tightened his arms around her and buried his lips in her hair, but before he dared put any of his thoughts into words, they were interrupted by an urgent knock on the door.

"Come," Tyrone said, straightening.

It was Antoine, and for the moment, running up to throw himself into Renée's arms, he forgot he could speak. *M'sieur Dudley told me to come up here and be very quiet. There is a big enormous fat lady in the kitchen and twenty people at the rear door!*

"That would be Mary, the cook," Tyrone explained with a laugh. "Every urchin in Coventry knows when she is baking bread, for they gather like geese and wait to fill their pockets." In response to the startled look on Renée's face, he offered up a small shrug. "I remember many a hungry morning myself."

But that was not what had amazed her. "You read his lips! Yet in the tower room you professed ignorance."

"Did I? Perhaps because he spoke French and my skills are a little less proficient in that language. As for knowing how to communicate without making any sound, the knack has come in handy on more than one occasion." He glanced at the boy. "But Dudley was right. It would be best if you stay up here and be very quiet. Mary only sees what she chooses to see, but urchins have been known to have prying eyes and loose tongues. I will have Maggie bring a tray."

He went back into the dressing room and emerged a few minutes later with his hair scraped severely back into a tail at his nape and a heavy dusting of powder to dull the rich ebony shine. It was a small adjustment, trifling really, but it aged him ten years and tamed a surprising amount of wildness from his appearance. He had donned a chocolate-colored jacket and striped silk waistcoat as well, and while he headed for the door, he was tying a cravat about his neck.

"Tyrone?"

He stopped and looked back.

"You will not do anything . . . go anywhere . . . without telling me?"

"I will be just downstairs. When Robbie and I decide what must be done, I will come and fetch you. Oh, and

you might want to stand back from the window. You glow
like an angel with a halo around her head; I would not
want to shock any poor sinners passing by."

\*

Dudley was waiting in the library. There was fresh
mud on his boots and his nose was red and dripping.

"You look like jolly hell," Tyrone remarked.

"Aye, well, while some of us have been lounging in a
warm bed, me and my ballocks have been all over this
blessed town. And I would not be surprised to discover I
have caught the lung rot after last night." He took out an
enormous square of linen and honked into it with great
gusto before cramming it back in his pocket.

"Any news about Finn?"

"He's at the Black Bull with double the sentries outside, double the guards inside."

"Any way of getting a message to him?"

"Not unless it's from the cell beside him."

"Renée is worried he might do harm to himself in
order to free her and the boy."

"You believe her?"

"I am not discounting the damned old rogue's sense of
loyalty."

Dudley twitched an eyebrow. "Like him, do you?"

"He grows on you." He swore and shuffled through a
sheaf of papers on his desk. "Where the devil are my
sketches of the streets around the Black Bull?"

"On the left," Dudley said calmly, pointing. "And unless you have some secret army of your own that I don't
know about, there is no way you can get near him as long
as he is being held there."

"Then the trick will be to get him out in the open."

"We're agreed on that, but how?"

"We get Roth to bring him to us. We propose an exchange and offer the greedy bastard something he can't
refuse."

Dudley patted his breast pocket and withdrew two folded sheets of parchment. "I don't know if this measures up, but it seems the boy was right about the value of the Dragon's Blood suite; the value increases dramatically when the rubies and the pearl brooch are put together. After I overheard Roth and Vincent talking about it in the coach, I asked Jeffrey Bartholomew to make some discreet inquiries. The jewels belonged to some old baron way back when men wore armor and kings killed their own blood kin to gain a throne. The Pearl of Brittany is unique, one of a kind, named after the princess who, it is rumored, gave birth to a son who not only could have challenged King John's right to the throne, but could have changed the course of history by uniting France and England under one crown. The revolutionary government is understandably anxious to get the suite back, while the French court in London will pay almost anything to keep it in monarchist hands."

"You *have* been busy this morning."

"Aye, well that's not the best of it." He paused and handed the second sheet of paper to Tyrone. "This is a list of the contents of a certain bank vault in London. The approximate value and the name of the claimant is on the bottom."

Tyrone unfolded the sheet and skimmed down the list, but just as his lips were pursing to whistle their astonishment, he came to the bottom line. He shot a quick glance up at Dudley for verification and got a wry smile in response.

"Kind of gives you a warm feeling all over, does it not, to know her uncle was taking such good care of her, finding her a fine, *fertile* husband, keeping the boy in close check with a false arrest warrant."

"Son of a bitch," Tyrone muttered.

"Aye. It also makes you wonder if the pearl alone will be enough to draw Roth out. What is a mere two hundred thousand when there are millions being held in trust for the Duc d'Orlôns."

"Millions?"

Both men turned at the sound of the soft query. Renée was standing in the doorway, looking battered and fragile and frightened anew.

"I thought I told you to stay upstairs."

"You said you were going to discuss what to do about Finn. I . . . thought I might be able to help." Her gaze went to the list in Tyrone's hand. "I heard what you said about the pearl. I knew it was of some *indigène* value to the government of France, but . . . to be worth so much. It is difficult to believe."

"Well, brace yourself for another surprise." Tyrone came out from behind the desk and extended the sheet of paper. "It seems we have also discovered the tree where your grandfather buried his treasure."

She took the list and read the inventory of jewels, bullion, and coin, and when she finished, her hand was trembling.

"This is not possible," she whispered.

"Your grandfather must have believed your uncle had a change of heart. *Noblesse oblige* again. The unspoken bond of the nobility to take care of one another."

"It must have taken months to remove so much . . ."

"And I wager every box, crate, or pouch must have passed through Roth's hands, then Vincent's, then your uncle's."

She swallowed hard and looked up. "This belongs to Antoine. How did they expect to get it?"

Tyrone pursued his lips. "I can offer a guess, but it is a rather unpleasant one."

She stood a little straighter. "There has been very little about this past week that *has* been pleasant, *capitaine*. Please go on."

"To put it bluntly, then, I do not think your uncle expected you or your brother to escape France alive. I think he was counting on the fact Robespierre would be very thorough in removing any legal claimant to the fortune they had smuggled out of Paris for your grandfather. If that happened, the vaults would be discreetly emptied and because no one could be sure what measures the *duc* had taken to safeguard his wealth, no one would ever know it had gone missing. I would further speculate the three of them—Roth, Vincent, and your uncle—were on the verge of toasting their very good fortune when you and your brother arrived on Paxton's doorstep seeking his protection. Rather like rabbits fleeing into the fox's den to take shelter from a storm."

Renée looked from one somber face to the other. "My uncle never mentioned anything about any inheritance to either me or my brother. If anything, he—he treated us as if we were a great burden."

"I don't doubt that you were. But like all good thieves they came up with a viable alternative, or at least your uncle did."

It was too much to absorb at once and Renée shook her head. "I do not understand."

"Going back to what you said the other day, as the last surviving male heir, any titles and assets accorded to the Duc d'Orlôns now belong to your brother. Finn does not, I imagine, refer to him as Your Grace without reason."

"Yes," she whispered. "Antoine is the twelfth Duc d'Orlôns, Marquis de Mar, Comte de Laborde, Baron de Dreux-Brézé, Maréchal Beauvau, and Chevalier de Valenciennes; possibly there are more, I cannot think."

Dudley and Tyrone exchanged a glance, with brows raised. "Yes, well, for the sake of brevity, let us just say your uncle saw the perfect way to make a legitimate claim on at least a portion of the fortune locked away in his bank vaults. By having himself declared your brother's legal guardian, any assets your brother had would be held in trust until he came of age, and Paxton, naturally, would control the trust. The fact that a written inventory exists would tend to support the idea that your uncle was planning to use it as collateral, perhaps, or proof to his creditors that he would one day make them regret their efforts to bankrupt him. Fortunately—or unfortunately for Paxton—Roth and Vincent discovered his little scheme and assumed, probably correctly, that he planned to cut them out of the deal. Roth retaliated by showing your uncle how easily *he* could be cut out of the deal, and—"

"Are you saying Colonel Roth shot my uncle?"

"In the same conversation Robbie heard about the duplicate gems, he heard Roth admit that he shot your uncle because he was getting greedy and had been making plans to double-cross them."

Renée stared at Tyrone for a full minute before she turned and paced from one end of the library to the other. "It is almost too *fantastique* to believe they would go to such lengths."

"I'm still guessing, but I would say they were prepared to go even further," Tyrone said quietly.

"What do you mean?"

"Your marriage. Apart from the prestige of marrying into an old and noble family, Edgar Vincent would not have benefited from the union financially or otherwise. But suppose he and you had wed and you had produced a male heir? A legitimate heir to inherit should an unfortunate accident befall your brother, or . . . should he be hung for committing a crime he did not commit."

She paced another length of the room. "For any of this to be possible, they would also have to have known Antoine was the last heir. How could they know this for sure?"

"Between the three of them, with their various connections in the army, the black market, and the banking industry, they obviously had a good scheme going to smuggle gold and jewels, even émigrés out of France. They were by no means the only ones engaged in saving lives for profit. Many enterprising English businessmen have made a tidy profit charging a percentage of what they have smuggled out of France in both human and monetary cargo. But I am guessing somewhere along the way, our greedy triumvirate must have decided their shares could be much larger if those fleeing aristocrats never made it out of Paris. Oh, they brought a few out safely so they could offer proof of how successful and reliable their routes were, but the rest were left to fate and likely never made it past the first guardpost. Roth, for instance, would only have to pass an anonymous tip to the Committee of National Security telling them where and when the *aristos* would be trying to sneak out of Paris."

"You are saying they deliberately betrayed men and women to the *gendarmerie*?"

Alarm and disbelief had turned her eyes the color of midnight sapphires and Tyrone required a deep breath. "Renée—"

"The Duc de Blois and his family were arrested at the gates of Paris," she gasped. "Jean-Luis, his father, his mother, his brothers . . . their children! And . . . oh!" She froze for a moment before her pale, shaking fingers flew upward to cover her mouth. "*Grandpère*—he was taken away to prison the night before he was to leave for the country."

"I imagine Roth and Vincent were both pleasantly surprised to discover Paxton had a sister married into one of the noblest families in Paris, whose father-in-law was one of the wealthiest *ducs* in the old régime."

Renée let out an anguished cry and the hot splash of tears ran down her cheeks. She stumbled back and her leg hit the corner of a chair. It threw her off balance, not enough to cause a fall, but enough to send her staggering against the wall.

Tyrone was beside her in an instant. She flinched from his touch at first, but he was adamant and drew her into his arms. Across the room, Dudley looked down at the floor, out the window, up at the ceiling, anywhere but at the young woman weeping bitter tears into Tyrone's shoulder. As for the dauntless highwayman, rogue, and steely nerved thief, he felt the sobs wracking her slender body and he did not know what to say or do to make the hurt go away. He buried his lips in her hair and tightened his arms around her even more, though he doubted he could hold her much closer than he was already. He met Dudley's gaze over the top of her head and signaled quietly that he should leave, a request Robbie did not hesitate to oblige.

Renée curled her hands around the precise folds of Tyrone's lapels and choked the sobs to the back of her throat. When she was steady enough, she lifted her face from his shoulder and saw the truth in his eyes.

A huge silvered tear slipped over her lashes and she bowed her head again.

"How can a man," she cried, "betray his own family?"

"Greed does funny things to people. It makes them do things they would never have dreamed of doing in a normal, rational state of mind. The same thing can happen with love, I'm told," he added under his breath.

She shook her head with incomprehension and though she tried valiantly to dash the spent tears off her cheeks she only succeeded in smearing the wetness further. With a grim twist on his lips, Tyrone undertook the task himself, then held his finely monogrammed handkerchief over her nose.

"Blow," he ordered.

She obeyed with such childlike compliance it only heightened the fury blazing through his veins. There was a decanter of wine on the sideboard and two empty glasses and he steered Renée gently into a chair before he filled both glasses to the brim.

"Drink this," he ordered.

She started to refuse but he pressed a glass into her hand and insisted. "Drink. You have been nursing me for almost a week now, I should think I have learned a little about ministering to the wounded."

Huge, dark eyes filled with incomprehension and pain rose to his, causing another hot flush of emotions to tighten his expression.

"What are we going to do?" she cried softly.

"We are going to give the bastard whatever he wants," Tyrone said calmly. "And then I am going to kill him."

*✶ ☽

# Chapter 27

*B*ertrand Roth leaned back in the hot, steaming bathwater and drew deeply on his cigar. He felt much, much better. The pressure of the past few weeks had been building up inside him with the strength to test the willpower of a normal man ten times over and tonight, he had finally succumbed. The whore had served him well; he had come so many times, he had lost count, in every unwilling orifice she had tried to deny him. Unfortunately, because of his exuberance, it had been necessary to pay extra to the proprietor of the brothel for the discreet removal of the broken and bleeding body. It was not the first time, nor likely to be the last, though he did try to control his rages during these episodes.

He glanced down in disgust at his chest, at the four glaring stripes clawed across his flesh. Frowning, he tested the marks with the tip of a gnawed finger to see if they had stopped bleeding yet, then muttered a small oath as he dribbled some brandy over the open wounds. The liquor stung and burned and gave rise to a deliciously sadistic throb in his flesh, but the surge was brief and the pleasure faded as quickly as the pain, and he took a deep swallow of the brandy before leaning his head back again.

The door opened behind him, the draft causing the steam to swirl away in tiny circles.

"I gave specific instructions I was not to be disturbed.

If you have brought more water, take it away and keep it hot until I ring."

He heard the door close again and the distinct *snick-t* of the key turning in the lock. A second later, something else equally distinct and ominously cold was pressed against the back of his neck, just behind his ear.

"Colonel Roth. Sorry to interrupt your bath. I would have arranged a more convenient time to meet, but I wanted to be certain there would be no unexpected interruptions."

Roth started to turn his head but the muzzle of the gun gave a quick jab to discourage him. His hand jerked at the same time and the inch of ash at the end of his cigar dropped into the water, sinking beneath the surface in a scattering of gray and black flakes.

"Who are you? What do you want?"

"I think you know who I am, and I think you know what I want. The only thing we have to discuss is the terms of the exchange."

Roth's eyes widened. Starlight! How the hell had he found him here, in a ratty little brothel in Spon End?

"I know most of your habits," Tyrone said, correctly interpreting the cause of Roth's scowl. "The bad as well as the abhorrent. And for what it is worth, I am exquisitely close to just pulling the trigger now and blowing your brains across the room."

"If you do, you will never see the old man alive again."

"Ah, but neither will you." A shifting of wool brought the ominous baritone closer to Roth's ear. "And I would at least have the immense pleasure of seeing you dead."

Roth's fine, pinched nostrils flared. He was aware of half a dozen things at once, beginning with the fact he was at a glaring disadvantage. He was naked in a tub of water. His gun and sword were on the opposite side of the room. He had not told anyone he was coming here tonight, nor did he particularly want anyone to find him, dead or otherwise, in an establishment known to cater to the less palatable tastes of its clientele.

"You surprise me, Captain. A beautiful woman, I might understand, but I did not know you harbored an affinity for old men as well."

"Let's just say I cannot fully enjoy the company of one without easing her concerns about the other."

"Indeed. I should think Mademoiselle d'Anton would be quite enthusiastic in expressing her gratitude in getting her manservant back. May I inquire what you are offering in exchange for all this bliss?"

"What do you want?"

Roth felt a measure of composure returning. Despite his threat, the bastard had not come to kill him; if he had, he would have done so by now. He had come to negotiate for the old man's release and he could not do that if he killed the man who held the key to the gaol cell.

"What do I want? What is an old man's life worth?" Roth drew consideringly on his cigar and exhaled a slow, thin streamer of blue-white smoke. "The property that was stolen from us, of course. In particular the pearl brooch and the rest of the goods you took from Edgar Vincent several months ago. I presume you still have them?"

"I might."

"As well, Lord Paxton is terribly worried about his niece and nephew; I would be remiss if I did not convey his fondest desire that they be returned to the bosom of his family with all due assurances, naturally, that there would be no repercussions for their unseemly behavior."

Tyrone snorted. "Tell Lord Paxton he has about as much chance of seeing his niece and nephew again as he does getting his hands on the fortune belonging to the Duc d'Orlôns."

"I am afraid I do not follow—"

The muzzle of the gun gouged deep again and Roth bared his teeth in a grimace.

"Shall we agree not to play stupid here, Colonel? I have seen the inventory, I know all about the jewels and the bullion being held in Paxton's bank. I also think I have it pretty well figured out how your little scheme worked. So has Mam'selle d'Anton and her brother. What they choose to do about it is their business, of course, but I doubt either of them are feeling particularly generous toward anyone who was a party to having their family murdered."

"Nor are they likely to see a pence of it themselves should they be charged with the brutal murder of Edgar Vincent."

"Which we both know is as valid a charge as the one against Antoine d'Anton for the attempted murder of his uncle."

"As it happens, the burden of proving or disproving the charges has been removed. The old man wrote out a full confession this morning wherein he admits that he not only assaulted Lord Charles Paxton some weeks ago in London, but he killed Edgar Vincent last night. Shot him point blank in the head, right between the eyes."

"Which you, naturally, are prepared to accept, even though it is a lie and an innocent man will go to the gallows?"

"Has your opinion of the state of my conscience improved over the past five minutes?" Roth inquired wryly. "Do you honestly think I give one whit if the man lives or dies, if he is innocent or guilty or merely convenient in providing me with an opportunity to rid myself of a noisome, arrogant, blundering fool."

"Such high praise for your own partner."

"Vincent was getting careless. It was only a matter of time before he outlived his usefulness. The same with Paxton. I should have done away with that yellow-livered coward when I had the opportunity. It might amuse you to know he departed Harwood for London before dawn this morning. I imagine by this time tomorrow he will have emptied the vaults of any and all evidence of anything held in trust for the Duc d'Orlôns."

"Including your share? How unfortunate."

"He will not get far with it," Roth said, clamping his teeth around the end of the cigar. "Edgar Vincent had men in every seaport. A word in the right ear and the fat oaf will find himself wearing chains around his ankles and going for a swim. And if Vincent's men do not get him, the French will. They have agents watching his bank day and night. If he thinks he can walk in empty-handed and walk out again carrying chests of gold and jewels, well, more fool he."

"You are taking the loss rather casually."

"It has been a profitable venture for three years now. I have an appreciable amount put aside already and once we conclude our negotiations for Mr. Finn's release, I shall have considerably more."

"What guarantees do I have that you will let the three of them walk away?"

"My word, for one thing."

"Don't make me laugh. These triggers are extremely sensitive, I would not want to blow your head off by accident. I will want full pardons in writing, duly signed by a magistrate of my choosing."

"Mmm." Roth pondered it a moment, then waved his cigar in a circular motion. "And what guarantee will I have that you will not simply steal the jewels back once you have the old man?"

"You will have my word on it."

Roth chuckled. "You're right: it is rather amusing. But even so, I still have a problem. I still need to hang someone for the crime of murder. And if it isn't the old man, or the girl, or the mute . . . who else is there to step forward and take the blame? Who else might have been in the room at the time of the killing? Who else might have collaborated with the girl to rob her fiancé of a fortune in jewels? Who else might write out a confession and use it—along with the aforementioned return of stolen goods—not only to buy but to *guarantee* the freedom and future welfare of three innocent people?"

"No doubt you have someone in mind?"

"The capture and conviction of the infamous Captain Starlight would certainly add a singular feather to my cap, so to speak. Moreover, you *have* become somewhat of a personal challenge," Roth conceded.

"If it is a personal challenge you want, I would be more than happy to oblige."

"A duel? A fight to the death? You and me, with the victor taking all the spoils?" Roth tipped his head back and laughed. "How refreshing! A common thief with pretensions of being a gentleman! The insult alone makes the offer tempting, and I promise I shall give it some thought with regards to the method of your death. In the matter of saving Mr. Finn's life, however, the time for playing games is over. You have my terms. Return of my property, a full confession, and yourself, presented without arms or deception of any kind. Once you have met those conditions, the old man will be released, set free and unharmed to whoever chooses to claim him."

After several moments of throbbing silence, Roth risked turning his head a fraction of an inch. There were only two candles alight in the room, neither of which were strong enough to reveal more than a figure in a black greatcoat, raised collar, and tricorn.

"You must agree," he mused, "it would make for a splendidly noble sacrifice, all things considered."

"Even for a common thief?"

"Especially for a common thief. Think of the lore the name of Captain Starlight will garner down through the ages. Why, you might even come to rival that other fox . . . what was his name? Turpin?"

There was movement in the shadows and a heartbeat later Roth found himself staring into the double barrels of the gleaming over-and-under snaphaunces. The colonel held his breath. He was confronting his enemy up close for the first time and he did not miss an inch of the awesome sight, from the fully extended arms and broad shoulders, to the raised collar and black-edged tricorn. He was a magnificent creature, even to the glittering stare that had been said to freeze a man's bones to the marrow.

"I am not in the habit of making sacrifices, Roth. Noble or otherwise."

"How unfortunate for Mr. Finnerty," the colonel rasped. "For those are my terms. My only terms. And they are nonnegotiable."

One by one, a black gloved thumb cocked the four hammers, revealing four primed firing pans and four full loads ready to be shot simultaneously, capable of delivering enough power to obliterate most of Roth's upper body.

"If they are so nonnegotiable, perhaps you can tell me why I don't kill you right now."

"Because if you kill me now, the old man will hang at noon tomorrow."

*"Tomorrow?"*

"We have a full written confession, remember. The magistrate need only sign it. What is more, if you kill me now, the warrants for theft and accomplice to murder will remain outstanding against Mademoiselle d'Anton and her brother. Every port, harbor, and ship will be searched, every road patroled, *every one of Vincent's waterfront mongrels given the scent and told to find her.* Moreover, every agent of the French government will be informed of the theft of the Dragon's Blood suite; that alone would put the hunters on her trail like flies on shit. She would be running and hiding for the rest of her life."

Tyrone's fingers squeezed a shade tighter around the front triggers. "I am sure you have been told this many times before," he hissed, "but you are quite the rare bastard."

Roth savored the piquant rush of power, growing almost lightheaded with the strength of his erection. "Oddly enough, though, I never tire of hearing it. I expect you will want some time to contemplate your answer? I should not wait much past eleven o'clock tomorrow morning to deliver it, if I were you. After that, it might prove awkward to delay the proceedings. Now, if you don't mind"—he gave way to the weight of his eyelids as he sank deeper into the water—"I would like to finish my bath."

"I don't mind at all. And if you don't hear from me by ten o'clock tomorrow morning, you can take this as my answer."

Roth glanced up in time to see the blur of one of the flintlocks swing hard and sharp across his face. The barrel caught him high on the same cheek marked with the barely healed slash from their last encounter. The force of the blow split the flesh open to the bone and sprayed a fan of blood across the wall behind him. His head whipped to the side, knocking solidly on the rim of the tub, dazing him long enough for Tyrone to unlock the door and stride out into the darkened hallway.

Roth had dropped both the cigar and the glass of brandy into the tub. He tried to lever himself up, but he had been soaking for over half an hour and the callouses on his feet were spongy. He slipped on the metal and went under, spluttering and choking out a scream as the soapy water swirled into the open wound on his face. When he lunged upright, the plastered red streaks of his hair were bleeding into the dark red streaks of blood that ran down his neck and he screamed again, in rage this time—rage for the man he vowed to kill with his own bare hands.

*

"You did what?"

"I pissed Roth off," Tyrone said, shedding his great-coat in a swirl of black wool. It landed in a heap by the door of the library, followed a few angry paces later by the tricorn, the gloves and lastly the two guns, slammed down on the top of the desk. "Then I robbed a coach on the way home. Here"—he tossed a small canvas pouch beside the guns—"fourteen shillings and a gold ring. A rippingly satisfying night all around, wouldn't you say?"

Dudley was not all that surprised to hear that Tyrone's meeting with Roth had gone more or less as anticipated. He was, however, mildly alarmed to hear about the unscheduled robbery. "May I ask what inspired you to take such a risk?"

"That's what I do, remember? I take risks. I put on my hat and my coat and my gloves"—he pointed contemptuously to each garment in turn—"and I wait in the shadows until some unsuspecting fool rides by. I sleep with loaded guns by my bed and I spend nights crouched in ditches while patrols of dragoons search the woods for me. I spit in the eye of danger and laugh at the hand of fate, and by God . . . I love it! I really do!"

"I can see that." Dudley pursed his lips and clasped his hands behind his back. "You want to tell me what happened?"

"What happened?" Tyrone halted in the middle of pouring himself a hefty glass of brandy. "You want to know what happened? I'll tell you what happened. I came out of that stinking brothel and rode north. I rode north for ten, maybe fifteen miles until I damned near blew Ares' lungs out his throat. He isn't talking to me by the way. Damn near bit off my hand when I tried to unsaddle him."

"No doubt he'll forgive you in the morning," Dudley murmured, watching the first glassful of brandy flow down Tyrone's throat without a pause for a breath. "So you were sitting by the side of the road, and . . ."

"And I'm asking myself why. Why do I care? Why do I care what happens to a hundred-year-old valet who wants to make a grand gesture to save his mistress? Why should

I spoil his moment of glory?" He paused and waved a hand airily by way of explaining. "He has made a full confession to the fact that he shot Edgar Vincent in cold blood. He is to be hung tomorrow at noon if Roth does not hear from me."

Robbie only said, "Ah."

"By noon tomorrow we could be in Manchester. Roth has threatened to unleash the hounds, but we have a few contacts of our own. Getting her out of England would not be an unsurmountable problem. And once we do, well, she is a young, beautiful woman, an exile from the French court and sister to a *duc*, goddammit—she would have no trouble finding a rich husband to protect her in New Orleans or wherever the hell it was she said she wanted to go."

"New Orleans," Dudley agreed calmly. "And I believe it was Antoine who mentioned it."

"Yes, well, she will survive. They will both survive without any gestures, noble or otherwise, from me."

"I am still not sure what this has to do with robbing a coach."

Tyrone refilled his glass and carried it to the window, watching the scene play out in his mind as he retold it.

The coach had appeared, literally, out of nowhere. He had given Ares his head, urging the stallion to run like the wind in whichever direction the moonlight took them. When at last he had reined the lathered beast to a halt, the two of them had stood by the road, panting and heaving for breath, with Tyrone calling on every oath and expletive he could remember. He had heard a distant, yet familiar sound coming along the road toward them, and without thinking, he had raised his collar and taken both pistols out from beneath his coat.

It had been a small traveling chariot drawn by a pair of matched grays. It boasted one postillion, a driver, and a liveried coachman, none of them too alert.

He had waited until they were abreast then spurred

Ares out of the shadows. He had cocked and fired one of the flintlocks into the air as a warning, and at his shout to stand and deliver, he heard a scream inside the coach and a cry from the outrider who nearly toppled out of his saddle in his haste to rein in.

"This is a robbery, gentlemen," Tyrone had snarled. "If you know what is best, you will lay down your arms and do nothing to tempt me to shoot off the tops of your heads."

There was another shriek from inside the coach, but he had ignored it, waiting until the driver had thrown his musket and handgun over the side of the box. The outrider seemed frozen in place, but thawed quickly when the pistols were trained in his direction.

"It's Captain Starlight," he had cried, owl-eyed with fear. "It's Captain Starlight! Don't shoot! Don't shoot!" Then he had thrown his weapons onto the road as if they were red hot and searing holes in his flesh.

Tyrone had turned his attention to the narrow door. "Inside! I am not a patient man tonight. Do not make me ask twice."

The door was flung open and a young man of about twenty years disembarked, his face looking ruddy with indignation even in the dim glow of the lamp. His companion was an equally young, fresh-faced girl in evening dress, sobbing and terrified.

"I demand you let us pass," the young man had declared. "My wife and I have done you no ill will."

"You are on my road," was Tyrone's answer. "That is ill will enough. But I will overlook the offense if the weight of your purse is convincing."

"Y—you are a bounder, sir!"

"I'll not sleep tonight, knowing that."

"M—my purse is in the coach. I—I have to fetch it."

Tyrone had jerked the nose of the snaphaunce to indicate consent, shaking his head as the earnest young fool reached inside and bravely produced a pistol instead. By

the time the valiant groom had balanced the weight of it
in his hand and swung the weapon around, Tyrone had
fired again, the flash of powder preceding the cannon-like
explosion in the darkness.

"You didn't kill him, did you?" Dudley asked, drawing
Tyrone's stare away from the window.

"No, I didn't kill him; I just gave him a sting in his
fingers. But I made him hand over his pathetic little purse
with his fourteen shillings. His wife was weeping all the
time, begging him to do whatever I asked if I would only
let them pass unharmed. They were hardly more than
children and there I was waving my guns around and
scaring them half to death for fourteen shillings."

He took a deep swallow of the brandy and faced the
window again. What he did not tell Dudley was that he
had very nearly gone back and returned the miserable
pouch. He had ridden away with the image of the child-
woman's face twisted with fear and he had had a sudden
glimpse into the future, seeing himself as the one who
was a hundred years old with nothing to show for it but a
reputation for terrifying helpless young lovers.

He should have gotten out of this business a long time
ago. He should have just taken his profits, boarded a
ship—bought a damned ship for that matter—and pursued his quest for adventure elsewhere, if that was what
he needed.

*If that was what he needed?*

Now where had that damned thought come from? He
was a thief, for Christ's sake. A highwayman, a rogue, a
heretic who lived from one breath to the next and thrived
on danger and deception! What was the alternative? A
cozy home, a warm hearth, a wife and—and seven mewling children clinging to his ankles at every turn?

"Jesus Christ," he muttered, shaking his head as he
stared out at the darkness. The thought of respectability,
of hearth and home, had never even occurred to him as
the faintest, most distant possibility. Not until he had

stood in the shadows and watched a half-naked French beauty walk through a path of moonlight to press her hand against a windowpane. The look on her face had been one of such utter sadness and loneliness, he had almost forgotten why he was there. And when he had kissed her, he had forgotten why he had to leave.

His instincts had warned him then and he had ignored them. They were warning him now, and, as he turned and hurled the half-empty glass into the fireplace, he knew he was going to ignore them again.

Dudley stared calmly at the spray of shattered glass and the sudden burst of flames where the liquor splashed the burning logs. "What did Roth demand?"

"The jewels, the pearl. Me."

Dudley almost missed it. "You?"

"And a full confession in writing or he sets Vincent's hounds loose on Renée and her brother."

"And in exchange?"

"The three of them go free, with full pardons."

"Do you believe him?"

"No farther than I can smell him. But if I go through with it, he will have to agree to some of my nonnegotiable terms, such as the time and place for the exchange, the proceedings witnessed by an officer of my choosing who will respect the terms of the agreement even if the colonel does not."

"Roth will never agree to all that."

"If he wants me badly enough, he will. And I made sure he will want me badly enough."

Dudley started to rake a hand through his hair, but stopped halfway, leaving one tarnished lock flopped over his eye. "What do you mean . . . if you go through with it?"

"I don't really see that we have another choice, do you?"

"We can hire some men of our own and when Roth shows up, we grab the old man and show them our dust."

"How far would we get? An old man, a young boy, two women—one of them pregnant—me not in peak form and you . . ."

"A cripple?"

Tyrone frowned. "I was not going to say that. But you have to admit we would make for an easily identifiable group of travelers."

"Well, there must be something we can do!"

"I gave my word."

"*What?*"

"I gave Roth my word. If he met all my conditions, I would meet his."

Dudley glared and pointed his finger. "You're not thinking clearly, that's your problem. Two weeks ago, this would never have happened. You would have laughed, spit in Roth's face, and blown a hole in his scrawny chest."

"Two weeks ago, you were the one laughing. Your fondest wish, if I recall correctly, was to be able to say 'I told you so,' that one day someone would get far enough under my skin I wouldn't be able to get her out. Well, I am admitting it. It has happened. And the only thing I am thinking about now is how to get her out of harm's way and guarantee her safety."

"At the cost of your freedom? Your life?"

"I gave him my word," Tyrone repeated tautly. "Something I have bandied about all too freely these past few years. Something that has not meant too much either until recently."

Dudley stared, too shocked to answer for a full minute. "This is a hell of a time to turn noble on us. And what about Miss d'Anton? How impressed do you think she will be when she finds out what you plan to do?"

"She isn't going to find out," Tyrone insisted quietly. "Not now. Not ever. I'll want your word on that, Robbie. I do not want her to have any reason to doubt we will all be together tomorrow, toasting yet another triumph at Roth's expense."

"But—"

"She is young, she is beautiful. She will survive. These past two weeks have been an infatuation, like playing with fire, and she will get over it. I doubt it would have worked out anyway. I could hardly have expected her to—to . . ."

"Love you just for the surly, mean-spirited bastard you are?" Dudley supplied dryly.

Tyrone's eyes narrowed. "Among other things."

"One of those being, of course, the lack of blue in your blood?"

"It does pose a certain barrier."

"When she was standing over you in the tower room, aiming a gun at the door, prepared to fire on anyone who entered, I did not get the impression she cared too much about her rank in society, or anyone else's."

"It is a moot point," Tyrone countered evenly. "I have made up my mind."

"Aye, well, it's not like you to just give up so easily. Dammit, you can't just walk up to Roth with your tail between your legs and offer up your neck to the noose!"

"I have no intentions of dying at the end of a rope. Not if I can help it."

"Well thank God for that!"

"Actually, I have always found the thought of hanging quite offensive. I would much prefer to end it with a bullet through the head or a blade through the heart."

"Marvelous." Dudley threw up his hands in exasperation. "You're going to meet him with your chest bared and large bullseye painted over your heart?"

Expecting some sort of wry retort, Robbie lowered his hands and stared at the somber expression on Tyrone's face. "You can't be serious."

"If I anger him enough, he might just offer me the opportunity to take him with me."

"He is a crack shot and a master swordsman. He has fought a dozen duels that we know about and never lost one yet."

"I did not say I would beat him, just that I would relish the chance to damage him a little."

"You do realize we are standing here calmly discussing the method of your suicide?"

"Would you prefer ranting and foaming at the mouth? Would it change anything?"

Dudley's shoulders drooped. "No, probably not. But it might make me feel better."

Tyrone came around from behind the desk and clapped his hand on Robbie's shoulder. "Don't feel bad, old friend, and don't get maudlin on me either. We *have* had a good run at it. And we both knew it was bound to end one way or another. Just promise me you will take care of Renée and the boy. And for God's sake, make an honest woman out of Maggie before she poisons you in one of her fey fits."

Dudley could not even muster the imitation of a smile. "What are you going to tell Miss d'Anton?"

"Nothing. Only that I am taking Roth a sackful of ill-gotten gains and exchanging them for Finn."

Robbie looked intently into the pale gray eyes and cursed. "Of all the bloody, useless wastes . . ."

Tyrone clapped his shoulder again and returned to the desk. "I'd best start writing before the entire discussion becomes irrelevant. Maybe you could ask Maggie to mix me up some of her special Irish? I've never penned a confession before; am I expected to list all my past indiscretions or only the highlights of a blazingly successful career?"

Robbie shook his head, not trusting himself to speak. He quickly exited the library, his limp more pronounced than usual, and when he was gone, Tyrone felt his shoulders sag. Alone, he turned to the window, his fists clenched so tightly by his sides the knuckles threatened to pop through the skin.

*

He was still seated at the desk writing when Renée found him two hours later. She had obviously been sleeping; her face bore pink creases and her hair hung in a loose, fat plait over one shoulder. She was wearing his Chinese silk robe, and because the hem was so long and dragged behind her, he could see glimpses of pale white legs peeping through the edges as she walked across the room. It was equally apparent that she was wearing nothing underneath and watching her approach, Tyrone suffered a painful tightness in his chest, a sensation he was coming to realize had nothing to do with his wound or the rigid layers of bandaging.

"I fell asleep in the chair," she confessed. "When I woke and you were not there—"

Tyrone gathered up the sheets of paper that were in front of him and stacked them neatly before placing them in a leather folder. "I would have been up in a minute or two. I was . . . just writing out some letters for business associates. I am still the Surveyor of turnpikes, until tomorrow, anyway, and there were some things—"

"Did you find Roth? Did you meet with him?"

She was close enough for him to reach out and invite her gently forward onto his lap. "I did, and I did. Everything is arranged."

"He is going to set Finn free?"

"He wanted a bit more than I went prepared to give him, but," he shrugged, "in the end, we agreed on a price. All that is left to do is arrange where to make the exchange and you shall have your Mr. Finn back."

"And Roth?"

"Roth . . . will be a very rich man."

"That was all he wanted? Money?"

"Were you under the mistaken impression he was

dedicated to his profession?" She was looking so intently into his eyes, he was afraid she was detecting something he could not control, and with a sigh he added, "I do have a bit of bad news for you, however. It seems your uncle has gone back to London already, hell-bent on clearing out his vaults before the firm hand of the law steps in and starts asking too many questions."

"Can he do this?"

He pursed his lips. "I suppose you could pursue the matter through the courts, but that would take time. I gathered from what Roth said that by next week the pair of them will have vanished to a place where no creditor or court can find them. It is unfortunate and unfair, but how many fortunes do you expect you can spend in one lifetime? Even after I pay off Roth, we will have more than enough to live in the extravagance befitting a *duc* and his kin."

Renée followed the motion of his hands as they slipped down to the belt that held her robe closed. So intent was she on watching him loosen the knot, she almost missed the most important thing he had said.

"We?" she asked in a whisper, looking up again. "Did you say . . . we?"

"You don't really think I have gone to all this trouble just to stand on a dock and watch you sail away, do you? Robbie and I have discussed it and we figure Portsmouth is our best bet. It is usually full of ships waiting to sail to all manner of exotic places. I served on a privateer for a while, did I tell you that? At any rate, I have been meaning to take another look at the West Indies. The sun is always hot and the water cool, the breeze is clean and sweet and"—he leaned forward, pressing his lips over the heart-shaped mole he had uncovered with his roving fingers—"you can swim naked with the dolphins. I know you mentioned New Orleans, and certainly we can go there if you are anxious to drink lemon tea and wear tight corsets again—"

"No," she gasped. "No, I—I never want to wear a corset again. But what about you? What about—?"

"My life of larcenous indulgence?" He looked deep into the blue pools of her eyes. "I somehow doubt I will be bored. Seven children, you say?"

His mouth, his tongue, the gentle nipping pressure of his teeth claimed her flesh again as he opened the vee of her robe wider, exposing the white and pink velvet of her breast. A single warm roll of his tongue and the nipple was as hard as a berry. Her hands were in his hair, combing the glossy waves off his face, angling it upward that she might distract him long enough to keep hold of her wits a few minutes more.

"I thought you said any manner of commitment was certain death to a man of your nature."

"Yes, well, I have no doubt you will be the death of me, mam'selle," he murmured. "But I do not imagine I shall have any regrets, all things considered."

While she was absorbing the shock of his admission, he tipped his head and touched his mouth to hers. The cut on her cheek and the split on her lip made her look like a marred Grecian statue, but there was a soft shine in her eyes that made his own sting uncomfortably. She was radiant in the moonlight, spectacular by candlelight, dazzling in sunlight, lush and silky in no light at all and because he thought this might very well be the moment he would hold closest to him when the end came, he pushed aside the guilt he felt at deceiving her and concentrated instead on loving her.

He trailed a path of warm caresses down the curve of her neck and from there to her breast, her belly, her thighs. She complied without protest as he pulled her gently down onto the floor, and, on a bed of their cast-off clothing, with the fire gleaming red and bronze on their bodies, he expressed his love the only way he dared. He loved her there, on the floor, with her body naked and golden beneath him, and he carried her up the stairs and loved her in the bed. He loved her until the air shivered with her cries and he had no more strength left to give her, no more of her courageous heart to steal.

And when dawn came through the window, he extricated himself gently from the tumble of sheets, kissed her softly on the bare curve of her shoulder, then went down the stairs to find Dudley.

* ☽

# Chapter 28

*R*enée wakened to the sound of voices in the next room. She looked quickly around, blinking the dullness out of her eyes, and when she realized she was alone in the bed, she scrambled into the silk robe and was still belting it tightly around her waist when she walked through the dressing room to the study.

Maggie and Antoine were there, carefully emptying the drawers and shelves behind one of the hidden panels.

Antoine was kneeling on the floor beside an open leather chest, packing between layers of clothing the jewels and coins Maggie handed down to him.

"M'sieur Tyrone said we were to pack up everything of value," he explained. "He said that when we left here today, we would not be coming back."

"Where is M'sieur Tyrone?"

Maggie glanced over briefly. "He and Robbie left about an hour ago. They . . . had some errands to run. Mr. Tyrone had to stop at the bank, and the solicitor's office; Robbie had to go to the livery to make arrangements for a coach and purchase vouchers for a change of horses. I'm sorry if we disturbed you."

"No." Renée's gaze strayed to the clock on the mantelpiece and she was surprised to see it was past two. "*Mon dieu*, you should not have let me sleep so long!"

"There was no reason to wake you," Antoine declared. "And besides, M'sieur Tyrone gave orders we were to leave you be."

"He gave orders, did he?" Renée did not know whether to frown or smile, but in the end she just felt relieved to have someone else making the decisions. "Is there something I can do to help?"

"No." Maggie turned back to her work. "You have done quite enough already."

The dismissal was disconcertingly abrupt and at first, Renée credited it to the fact that Maggie was probably not entirely pleased at the turn of events. Even though Tyrone had said last night that both Robbie and Maggie had accepted their impending departure from England, she could understand how a pregnant woman might be upset, resentful having to leave behind everything familiar and flee her home in the middle of the night.

Renée walked over to the piano and ran her fingers lightly over the polished wood. She still blushed to think of herself propped on the keys, a dark, silky head moving flagrantly between her thighs.

*Forcer les anges de pleurer* . . .

To cover her embarrassment, she crossed over to the window and lifted the edge of the heavy curtain aside. The stronger light caught Maggie full on the face and she turned to avoid the glare, but not before Renée saw the redness around her eyes, the puffy, swollen look to her face.

She let the curtain fall back into place. "Maggie, I am so sorry to be the cause of this. Do you have family here?"

"Robbie and Mr. Tyrone are my family." She looked over, then turned away again. "Since you are up now, miss, perhaps it would be best if you get yourself dressed. I've left you something in the wardrobe, nothing fancy, you understand; we do not want to be calling any more attention to ourselves than is necessary. We also have to leave here no later than five, if we're to be at the rendezvous on time."

"The men are not coming back here first?"

Maggie moistened her lips. "They didn't think they would have time."

"When is the meeting with Colonel Roth?"

"Six o'clock. Mr. Tyrone sent him a note first thing this morning and it came back just after noon, with Roth agreeing to all his terms."

"That is good, is it not?"

"Aye. I suppose, if there is anything good about it . . ."

"What do you mean?"

Maggie shook her head. "Nothing. I meant nothing, miss. I'm . . . just tired, is all. The babe has been putting the boot to me all morning and I am just tired."

"Then let me help you. Let me finish for you."

" 'Tis all done." She shut the last drawer and closed the oak panel. "Will you be wanting a bath?"

Something in the girl's emerald eyes sent a sudden chill along Renée's spine and she hugged her arms. "If there is no time, I will manage with just a wash."

Maggie's shoulders bowed forward slightly and she shook her head again. "It may be the last chance you have for a while. And there are kettles waiting on the stove, already hot."

"I will carry this down the stairs," Antoine announced, closing the lid of the chest and buckling the two straps. "Then I will bring the water upstairs for your bath. A pot of tea also, perhaps, and something to eat?"

Renée reached out and ruffled his short blond curls. "You sound just like Finn."

"*Vraiment*, and he would scold me terribly if I did not take care of you. Both of you," he amended quickly, glancing at Maggie. "Especially since I am the only man here at the moment."

He lifted the chest and started out of the room, but before Maggie could follow, Renée reached out and placed a hand on her arm.

"Is something wrong? Have I said or done something to upset you in some way?"

"No, of course not, miss."

"And M'sieur Tyrone? He *was* telling me the truth last night, was he not? Roth *has* agreed to make the exchange for Finn . . . ?"

"Yes," she whispered. "Yes, he has."

The green eyes flooded with fresh tears and although Maggie tried to twist her arm away and hurry past, Renée stepped in front of her to block her way.

"Maggie . . . *s'il vous plaît*. Please. Is something wrong? If something has happened, you must tell me."

Maggie pressed her lips together over a stifled sob. "I wasn't supposed to say anything. Robbie made me swear I wouldn't, but . . . I know if it were me, I would kill him with my own bare hands if he tried to keep such a thing to himself."

Renée was starting to become truly frightened now. "Has something happened to Mr. Tyrone?"

"Not yet, it hasn't. But oh, miss . . . ! Miss, it is so dreadful, I cannot even think how to put it into words."

\*

Tyrone had thought it fitting they should make the exchange where it had all begun. From Dudley's vantage point in the trees, he had a clear view of the road and the flat countryside beyond. It was the only patch of forest for a mile in any direction, and from Tyrone's own position on top of the adjacent hill, he would know if Roth intended to keep to his end of the deal. Dusk had recently settled, smothering the surrounding countryside in shades of blue and purpling shadows, and for a change, the sky was perfectly clear. As the purple faded out to black, stars appeared by ones and twos, then in clusters. A thin layer of mist rose off the puddles and patches of mud that lingered from the recent rains, but it was a clear, cold evening with the twinkling lights of Coventry visible well off in the distance.

Dudley had not said more than two incomplete sentences to him throughout the day. He wore a wide-brimmed felt hat jammed low over his forehead and did not glance in Tyrone's direction any more than he had to and seemed almost relieved when dusk came and the gloom settled heavy around them.

It was just as well. There was nothing more to say. Just as there had been no reason to linger at the house any longer than was necessary. It had been bad enough leaving Renée all curled up like a kitten, asleep on the bed. If he had to see her or speak to her again or hear that soft little catch she made in her throat when he kissed her, he was not sure he would have been able to go through with it. It was better this way, less painful for both of them, and even as the thought was forming in his head that it would all be over in under an hour, he saw riders off in the distance, moving at a brisk, official pace along the road.

*

Roth rode in the lead, his saber slapping his thigh on every cantering stride. He was in full uniform, as were the six blue-clad Coventry Volunteers who rode in box formation around Mr. Finn. The latter had his wrists bound and tied to the saddle. He was not the most accomplished horseman at the best of times, and with his body jostling erratically up and down, side to side, his bony shoulders hunched forward, and his long legs slipping periodically out of the stirrups, he looked like he might almost prefer the comparatively predictable swaying motion of a ship's deck.

In contrast to Finn's loose-limbed discomfort, Corporal Chase Marlborough rode a wary half length behind Roth. He had no idea where they were going, no inclination as to why they had removed the old manservant from his cell and brought him out to the middle of nowhere in the dark of night. He had an uncomfortable feeling, nothing he could identify, but the six men who rode escort had been handpicked by Roth, brutes and undisciplined troublemakers who had only joined the militia to avoid being tossed in a gaol cell themselves. They were also unusually heavily armed, with each man carrying a brace of pistols as well as a heavy musket. Corporal Marlborough had his sword and a growing sense of unease.

"Just around this next bend, I warrant," Roth said, glancing into the small patch of woods they passed. "We should find ourselves in a gulley between two hills, or so the map indicates."

"Might I ask, sir—"

"No. You might not. You are here to observe and to do what I tell you to do and nothing more. Is that understood?"

"Yes, sir." He adjusted his seat in the saddle and muttered under his breath.

"Did you say something, Corporal?"

"No sir. I was just . . . thinking out loud, sir."

"Well, think to yourself. And keep your eyes open. I have no intentions of dying from a bullet in the back."

They snaked around the final bend in the road and rode into a shallow gulley. They had not gone twenty strides along this new stretch when Roth held up his hand, halting the men behind him. The trees were on the left now, a steep slope rose on the right. At the bottom of the gulley, a ring of lanterns had been lit and parked a few feet beyond, a covered coach with its bright lamp blazing like a beacon in the darkness.

"Hold your position," Roth growled and urged his horse forward at a slow walk. The only sound was the soft clopping of his horse's hooves, the only movement came from the flickering shadows outside the ring of lanterns. When he had covered half the distance to the coach, he heard the latch twist and saw the door swing open. The man who stepped down wore a tall silk hat and a swirling black cape slung at a capricious angle over an impeccably tailored jacket, stark white cravat, and skintight buff breeches.

"Good evening, Colonel. Dash me if I was not beginning to wonder if someone was playing a bad prank on me."

"*Hart?*" Roth's eyes narrowed with disbelief. "What the bloody hell are you doing out here?"

"Well, as you can see," Tyrone swirled aside his cape to display the fine cut of the garments he wore beneath, "I was on m' way to a soirée. Thunder strike me if I am not assailed at gunpoint instead and ordered out of m' rig. I vow it was Captain Starlight, no less, who instructed me to wait here until I was informed otherwise. Took m' driver, so he did. Led him off into the woods at gunpoint, and . . . good gracious, sir! What happened to your face?"

Roth's stitched and swollen cheek gave a vicious throb as he dismounted. "I cut myself shaving. What else did he say to you?"

"Only that I was to give you something and you were to give me something, and when he was satisfied you were not up to any tricks, he would show himself and . . . er . . . fulfill his part of the bargain. Yes, that was it. That was what he said: fulfill his part of the bargain."

Roth tried to peer into the nearby trees, but the glare from the ring of lamps had ruined his night sight.

"You're a clever bastard, Starlight," he shouted. "But how do I know you will keep your word and not just take the old man and vanish into the night?"

"How do I know you will keep your word to grant free pardon to Mademoiselle d'Anton and her brother?" came a rejoinder from somewhere deep in the blackest of shadows.

"Because I gave it as an officer and a gentleman, and I give it to you again, now, in front of witnesses."

"Then I give you my word again, as a thief and libertine, in front of these same witnesses, that as soon as Finn is on board the coach and the coach has driven away, I will surrender myself as per our agreement."

The voice was distorted by the trees and sent a hollow echo through the dampness. It was also moving between each exchange, making it difficult to pinpoint an exact location.

Roth considered his options a moment, then beckoned to Marlborough to bring the prisoner forward.

"If you renege, Starlight," he added, withdrawing a packet of folded documents from beneath his uniform lapels, "these pardons will not be worth the paper they are written on. Moreover, there will be no one to call off Edgar Vincent's men and when they find your little French whore, they will carve her up in pieces so small the fish won't have to chew."

Beside him, Tyrone dabbed a folded handkerchief under his nose. "Dear me. That *would* be most unpleasant."

Roth glared at him. "You said he gave you something to give to me?"

"Eh? Oh yes. Yes, the threat of violence does make the mind wander, does it not?" Tyrone reached inside the coach and drew out a similarly folded, beribboned sheaf of papers which he handed to Roth in exchange for the pardons.

By this time, the horses carrying Marlborough and Finn had reached the circle of lanterns. In the glare of the lamplight, the cut on Finn's temple was an ugly blotch, thick with scab. His hair stuck out in spikes and his skin resembled crushed parchment.

"Untie him," came the voice from the woods, "and help him into the coach. Corporal Marlborough, were you informed of the terms of this exchange?"

The corporal's eyes scanned the woods as he cleared his throat. "Actually . . . no sir. I was not."

"In exchange for Mr. Finn's release, and the expunging of all charges against Mademoiselle Renée d'Anton and her brother, Antoine d'Anton, I have agreed to surrender myself along with a full written confession."

Corporal Marlborough was clearly shocked.

"Do you happen to know of any treachery lurking around the next bend in the road, or any reason why I should not trust Colonel Roth's assurances that Mr. Finn is now a free man?"

"No, s—sir," the corporal stammered, then repeated in a clearer voice, "No, sir, I do not."

"Or any reason why Mademoiselle d'Anton and her brother should fear any legal repercussions?"

The young officer flushed with adamancy. "No, sir! I do not!"

"Will you give me your word as an officer in His Majesty's Royal Dragoons to uphold the terms of the arrangements?"

"Absolutely, sir. My word as a gentleman as well."

Roth had opened the papers and had tilted the pages into the light, scanning the neatly written script. He looked up briefly to jerk his head in Finn's direction. "Untie him. Put him in the coach."

Marlborough swung down out of the saddle and did as he was ordered. Finn had been considerably weakened by the cold and the jouncing ride and had to be supported when his wobbly knees failed to hold him up, but his eyes were clear and hard; they had not wavered from Tyrone's face since hearing the terms of the exchange. When he drew abreast, Tyrone offered a slight bow and handed him the pardons.

"These would, perhaps, be best kept in your care. You will have to give the lovely mam'selle my sincerest felicitations when next you see her," he said. "Tell her . . . tell her I am so sorry we were never able to have that dance."

Finn swallowed hard enough to set his adam's apple

bobbing, but although he tried to speak, the words were just a mumble of sounds.

A moment later there was a rustling of brush and saplings and Robert Dudley came limping out of the woods. He was glaring over his shoulder, straightening his jacket with small indignant jerks. "'Ee said as 'ow I was to drive away now, sar. Up in the box, 'ee says. Ply the whip an' don't look back. Soon as we're on the wheel, 'ee'll come out."

"Well then," Tyrone said. "I should think that means I have done m' part. If you have no objections, Colonel?"

"Get the hell out of here, Hart. And if you know what is good for you, you will forget everything you saw and heard here tonight."

"Indeed. I have quite forgotten it already."

With a swirl of his cape, he boarded the coach and closed the door. There was a lengthy delay while Dudley maneuvered his stiff leg up into the driver's box, and, after glancing down once and muttering something under his breath, he took up the reins and spurred the horses forward.

Roth was still skimming the contents of the confession when the coach passed by. He watched the eye of the riding lamp until it vanished around the sharp bend at the top of the gulley, then half turned to smirk at Marlborough.

"I guess we will see now if Starlight is a man of his word."

The young corporal was frowning, staring at the edge of the woods. "Sir . . . ?"

Roth twisted fully around. Where the coach had been, a figure was now standing by the side of the road. He wore a long greatcoat with a standing collar and his tricorn was pulled low over his brow, leaving only an inch of shadowy space for the glitter of his eyes to shine through. He had a saddle pouch slung over one shoulder and the twin barrelled snaphaunces in his hands.

"Odd that you should have doubted my word, Roth. Thieves are supposed to trust one another. Our own peculiar brand of *noblesse oblige*, if you will. Murderers, on the other hand, are an entirely different breed. You just never know when a shot will come at you out of the dark."

Roth's amber eyes flickered in the lantern light as he stared at the guns. "And is this your idea of complying with the agreed terms?"

There was but a moment's hesitation before Tyrone reversed the direction of the guns and held them out, stock end first, toward Corporal Marlborough. "I agreed to surrender, unarmed, to an honorable representative of His Majesty's government."

Roth's lips thinned to a flat line. "Collect the guns, Mister Marlborough."

The corporal hurried forward to obey, then backed slowly away, holding the heavy weapons down by his sides.

"I am surprised to see you only brought six men with you," Tyrone said, crooking his head slightly in the direction of the Volunteers who were edging their mounts closer to the ring of lights. "Then again . . . suppose it is a sufficient number for a firing squad. I am presuming, of course, that you have no intentions of letting me walk away from here alive."

"Did you really think I would?"

"I would have been shocked if you had, Colonel. After all, you did murder Edgar Vincent in cold blood; why should I anticipate any better treatment?"

"The old man confessed to the crime," Roth countered evenly.

"Indeed, and while he was in your custody writing out his confession, did he happen to mention how he came to be in possession of such a distinctive weapon? A cannon-barrelled pocket gun with a diamond-patterned steel grip. Ever seen one like it before, Corporal Marlborough?"

The corporal glanced uncomfortably at the colonel, but Roth's attention was fixed on the saddle pouch slung over Tyrone's shoulder. "I assume you have complied with *all* of my terms?"

A black gloved hand reached up and unslung the leather sack, giving it a careless swing before tossing it into the closest pool of lantern light. The neck was not fastened tightly and the contents spilled out onto the ground in a glittering array of jewels, coins in gold and silver. In the silence, each of the half dozen Volunteers could be heard gasping, muttering under their breath.

"The return of your personal property, Colonel, as requested, and as near to what I can recall Edgar Vincent having in his possession that night. I'm sure Lord Paxton can tell you if anything is missing; he does seem to keep rather detailed inventories of what he steals from his own bank vaults."

Roth unsheathed his sword. "If you are trying to bait me, Starlight, you are succeeding. But before this little farce progresses any further, perhaps you will oblige us all by stepping into the light and showing your face."

Tyrone reached up slowly and removed the tricorn. Dark, gleaming waves of hair fell forward over a wide brow and cheeks that wore no camouflaging paints or powders. He unfastened the two buttons at the top of the greatcoat and shrugged the heavy garment off his shoulders, standing in waistcoat, shirt, and breeches while the point of Roth's sword wavered and sank in astonishment until it rested on the ground.

"What the devil—? What are you playing at now, Hart?"

"Absolutely nothing, I assure you," Tyrone promised in his own rich baritone. "As you said last night, the time for games is over."

Marlborough's jaw dropped open. "*You? You* . . . are Captain Starlight?"

"In the living flesh, Corporal, although to hear some of

the wild tales of wraiths and phantoms, I can only hope I am not too great a disappointment."

"Good God," Roth rasped. "How have you managed to get away with it all these years?"

"In truth, it was ridiculously easy. Skulk about like a thief and men see a thief. Caper about like a fool and you fit in so well with the rest of the fools, no one thinks you capable of buttoning your own breeches without assistance. The theory does not always work, of course. Take yourself, by way of example. You look like an officer in your scarlet and buff. When you are strutting about issuing orders on a parade ground, I imagine you even act like an officer. But last night, when you were in that brothel in Spon End beating a whore half to death because she couldn't stop laughing at you, I shouldn't think anyone would have thought you anything but a pitiful deviant."

Marlborough sent yet another startled glance in Roth's direction, but the colonel only shrugged it off. "He has a vivid imagination. I was nowhere near Spon End last night, nor do I frequent brothels of such low repute."

"No, you generally prefer raping and beating victims of a higher quality," Tyrone mused. "Like the daughter of the magistrate in Aberdeen seven years ago. As I recall, you beat her so badly she never walked again, and the magistrate was so distraught he hung himself."

"Aberdeen?" Roth's eyes narrowed. "What do you know about Aberdeen?"

"I was there. I was a guest in one of your prison cells. You used to fetch me into your office every other day and lay stripes across my back for the sheer pleasure of it. You tried to do something else to me as well, as I recall, having been so thoroughly aroused by all the blood, but there was still enough life in me to reach around and grab you by that puny little finger of flesh you call your manhood, and to give it such a twist you were squealing and flopping on the floor like a beached fish."

Two of the Volunteers who were not mesmerized by

the spilled jewels guffawed as Roth's face flushed a deep red. He took several jerky strides forward, and raised his blade, bringing the tip to rest at the base of Tyrone's throat. Over the bright slash of steel he peered intently into Hart's face trying to see something familiar in the nose, the mouth, the pale, almost colorless eyes. The lanterns on the ground were throwing the shadows upward, distorting the present, confusing the past, but it was the eyes, at last, he settled upon, staring into them, seeing the same cold hatred he had seen seven years ago.

Roth grinned, slowly and maliciously. "Well, well, well. We do seem to have traveled a full circle, have we not? You had a different name then and you were . . . stealing cattle, were you not? Cattle and cabbages and crusts of bread. Now it is diamonds and rubies and pearls, by God. Still a thief but one with pretensions of being a gentleman."

He swished the blade away from Tyrone's neck, leaving a bleeding nick behind.

"At least I manage to fool the general population into believing it," Hart said, "which is more than you have been able to do."

Roth had already turned away, but in response to Tyrone's taunt, he spun around, slicing out and up with the sword, carving a mark in Hart's cheek to equal the wound on his own. Tyrone flinched back, cupping his hand over the wound. Blood oozed instantly through his fingers and ran down his wrist in shiny red rivulets, soaking the cuff of his shirt.

"They used to brand thieves with red hot irons," Roth hissed. "A pity the custom went out of fashion. They used to geld bastards, too, to prevent the corrupted bloodlines from procreating."

He lunged, thrusting the blade forward, but Tyrone anticipated the strike and was able to deflect the blade onto his thigh. It cut through his breeches and slashed the muscle, drawing an involuntary grunt of pain from between his clenched teeth.

"From what I heard, Roth, you might as well be gelded. It's really only the soft-faced boys who make you feel like a man, isn't it? Soft-faced boys and whores who take the blame when you aren't able to perform."

Roth's next move came with the swiftness of a viper's tongue, a thrust and slash that caught Tyrone's right hand and forearm, laying both open to the bone and sending him to his knees with the pain and shock.

"Sir—" Marlborough started forward to object. "Mr. Hart is unarmed! He has surrendered himself into our care!"

"Stay out of this, Corporal, and stay out of my way!"

"But sir, he has surrendered himself into *my* care, and I have given my bond—"

*"I said, stay out of it Corporal!"*

With fury mottling the whiteness of his complexion, Roth waited until Tyrone had staggered to his feet again, then brought his blade arcing across the lantern light, intending to leave yet another red stripe in the gore that was already spreading across the front of his shirt. Once again Tyrone anticipated the strike and turned so swiftly, the colonel stumbled over a rut in the road as he tried to recover from the follow-through.

The faux pas only infuriated him more and he slashed out with a decided lack of finesse, catching Tyrone high on the shoulder, hacking through cloth and flesh with enough force to send the wounded man to his knees again.

White-faced, Marlborough leaped forward, placing himself between Roth and Hart. The colonel's outraged eyes focused on the young officer's face, then on the fully cocked snaphaunce he held outstretched in his hand.

"I will not stand by and let you attack an unarmed

man, sir. You will set down your sword or suffer the consequences!"

Roth tilted his head in disbelief. "You are defending
this man? You are protecting a thief and a murderer? A
man you are pledged to see brought to justice?"

"This is not justice, sir. This is murder."

Roth's grin did not waver by the smallest degree.
"Mister Hugo, if you please!"

One of the Coventry Volunteers raised his musket and
pulled the trigger. But Marlborough swung his pistol
around in time, firing through the glare of two lanterns
and catching the militiaman high and square on the chest.
Being unaccustomed to the sensitivity of the double
serpentine triggers, he caused both barrels to discharge
almost simultaneously, the double blast tearing a gaping
hole in the man's torso. The nose of the musket flew
upward, the shot exploding harmlessly into the air, while
the Volunteer toppled back off his saddle, dead before the
echo of his scream faded.

Marlborough scarcely batted an eye as he cocked both
hammers on the second snaphaunce and raised it threat-
eningly in the direction of Roth and his phalanx of five
remaining Volunteers.

"I am sorry, sir." His voice, if not his body, was trembling with integrity. "I cannot and will not allow you to
murder an unarmed man."

"You only have two shots left, *Mister* Marlborough,"
Roth snarled, "and I have five armed men, each of whom
will earn a handful of whatever they choose from the
saddle pouch when they bring you down. On my command! Fire!"

There was no sound, no movement and Roth spun
around, glaring at the Volunteers. "I said fire, you stupid
bastards! Fire!"

But none of them was looking at Roth. None of them

was even looking at the jewels or Marlborough or the bleeding highwayman. They were all staring at the side of the road where a string of shadowy figures had emerged from the mist and the trees, pistols and muskets in hand, the muzzles trained on the remaining militiamen.

✴ ☽

# Chapter 29

To Renée, it seemed as though her heart had stopped several times while Maggie Smallwood told her of the agreement Tyrone had made with Bertrand Roth. It was nearly stopped again now as she held the heavy gun in both hands, her finger curled around the trigger, her eyes daring the flat-nosed militiaman to move his musket so much as an inch. She knew where she was, she knew why she was there, but the blue and white uniforms of the Coventry Volunteers were so much like the blue, red, and white uniforms of the Paris gendarmes, it seemed as if all the injustices of the world had come together on this damp and dark stretch of road. The five burly men were no different from the guards who had attacked her mother—they were no different from the zealots who roamed the streets of Paris looting and burning in the name of *liberté, égalité, et fraternité*, or the cheering beasts who marched innocent men, women, and children up the steps to the guillotine and forced them to lie on a blood-soaked plank of wood.

She would gladly have pulled the trigger. She was no longer afraid to fight, and, as she had told Maggie, she was tired of the people she loved making sacrifices so that she might live to have her heart broken another day.

The wagon that was supposed to carry them to the rendezvous with Finn and Dudley on the road to Manchester had brought them here instead. They had intercepted the coach not five minutes after it had abandoned

Tyrone to his meeting with Roth, and even though Robbie had given Hart his solemn word to drive on and not look back, there was no argument strong enough to turn the women around. The Brown Bess that Maggie thrust into his hands prompted him to switch loyalties instead and he led them through the woods, all of them armed and determined to save Tyrone Hart from his own reckless bravado.

Renée was closest to one of the lanterns and Roth recognized her at once by the strands of blond hair that escaped her hood.

"Well, if it isn't the little French whore herself. I was hoping to have the opportunity to see you again, mademoiselle, but this is too rich. Too rich by far."

Renée heard his ugly laugh but she had eyes only for Tyrone. Half of his face was wet with the blood that ran down his cheek and throat, his right arm was cradled against his chest, the ruined hand limp and dripping. His expression, when he whirled around and saw her standing there with Antoine, Maggie, Dudley, and the stalwart Mr. Finn, was a mixture of horror and disbelief.

"Renée! For God's sakes, what are you doing here? You were supposed to be at the rendezvous!"

She kept the pistol trained on the militiamen as she edged carefully closer to where he stood. "Waiting for whom, m'sieur? For you? If so, we would have been waiting a very long time, *n'est-ce pas?*"

"Renée—"

"*Non*! When Maggie told me of this foolishness, I could not believe my ears! I could not believe this was the same man who boasted he had no conscience, no sense of obligation, no desire to revenge himself upon the world."

"Renée, you don't understand—"

"*Non*! I understand perfectly what Roth has threatened to do. I know he has threatened to send Edgar Vincent's *salopards* after Antoine and me, but I do not care."

She cast a scathingly contemptuous glance in Roth's direction as she crossed in front of a lantern. "You have managed to thumb your nose at men like this for seven years, and I would rather spend the next seven weeks or days or hours running and hiding with you, *mon capitaine*, than seventy years living without you."

She was close enough now for him to see the defiant jut to her chin, the fierce determination burning in the depths of her eyes. He saw the same ferocity in the eyes of the other motley rescuers and knew he did not have the strength—or in truth, the desire—to fight them all.

His shoulders sagged as he reached out with his one good arm and drew her against his chest. "You intend to deny me my one noble gesture, do you, mam'selle?"

"Be assured I do, m'sieur, for noble gestures do not keep me warm at night. Only your heart and your body are able to do that."

He closed his eyes briefly and pressed his lips to her temple, but in the next instant, the sound of loud, mocking applause caused her to lift her head from his chest and nervously raise the cocked pistol in Roth's direction again.

He had tucked his sword beneath his arm and was clapping his hands together slowly and deliberately in response to the tender exchange.

"How very, very touching," he declared dryly. "I vow it makes my heart swell to hear such sweet, sentimental pap. Unfortunately, it will probably not affect a magistrate or a court of law the same way, for you are still a wanted man, Hart, and you, Miss d'Anton, have now voided any prior arrangements for leniency by attempting to interfere at gunpoint with a formal arrest. Seven hours? I should think you will be lucky to enjoy seven minutes together on the gibbet before they hang you both for your crimes."

"Then it should not matter if we add one more," Tyrone said, taking the gun out of Renée's hand.

Roth was quick to laugh again, quicker to cast his

sword to the ground. "By all means, add the murder of an unarmed officer of His Majesty's government to the already impressive list of charges. You will undoubtedly have to deal with Corporal Marlborough's rigid code of honor, but then what is honor to a man whose word is not worth the spit expended to pledge it?"

Renée felt Tyrone's body stiffen beside her. She also saw the look on Marlborough's face as he turned, clearly torn between his sense of revulsion for Roth and his obligations as an officer and gentleman.

Tyrone's eyes narrowed. "We needn't put the Corporal through such angst, Roth. We needn't trouble a court or a magistrate or waste the cost of a hangman's noose either if we agree to settle our differences here and now, once and for all."

"A duel?" Roth arched an eyebrow. "To the death?"

"But you are hurt," Renée gasped. "You cannot fight him!"

In this, Marlborough concurred. His gaze went from Renée's horrified expression to Tyrone's right hand, which was bleeding and held tightly against his chest. "Miss d'Anton is right, sir. It would not be a fair fight. Your hand is useless and you can barely balance any weight on your leg. You would not survive the first party." He glared across the lantern light to where Roth was standing. "You crippled him deliberately, sir, a blatant act of cowardice and cruelty that *will* be reported, you may depend upon it."

"He still has one good hand he can shoot with," Roth said through the gleam of his teeth. "And you may be sure, Corporal, that when I finish dealing with him, I will deal with your insubordination in a manner which will forever define the word 'cruelty' for you."

Marlborough paled further, but stood his ground. "Might I suggest you leave now, Mr. Hart? I cannot guarantee how much time I can give you, but I would be in your debt if you could remove Miss d'Anton to safety."

Roth's grin widened. "Indeed, Hart, take the corporal's advice and run. You won't run very far, and you surely will not be able to hide behind your lady love's skirts for very long, but by all means, take your chances and run."

"Do not listen to him," Renée begged, pulling on his sleeve. "He is only trying to bait you the way you baited him."

"And he's doing a damn fine job," Tyrone murmured.

Roth laughed and held up his hands. "I would not want to be accused of taking unfair advantage. Listen to your little French whore, Hart. Run while you have the chance. Run while your belly is yellow enough to light the way."

Tyrone blinked the sweat out of his eyes and pressed the gun back into Renée's hands. "Here, take this. If the corporal has no objections, I prefer the weight and familiarity of my own gun."

Renée shook her head. "Tyrone, no . . . please . . ."

"A new deal, Roth? We count out the ten paces and the others go free?"

Roth drew a triumphant breath, swelling his chest. "Agreed. I have no real interest in them anyway. It was always your head I wanted the pleasure of spiking in the town square."

"Tyrone!"

"It will be all right." He cradled her chin in his hand and gazed deeply into her eyes. "You did say you trusted me, did you not?"

"Yes, but—"

"Then trust me now." He kissed her hard and fast then pressed his mouth to her ear. "Go and stand with Robbie and for God's sake, don't make the mistake of trying to shoot anyone with this gun. It isn't loaded."

She stared at the pistol then looked up into his face, seeing a completely incongruous twinkle of humor in the cold steel of his eyes. His mind was made up. There was nothing she could say or do to stop him. It was partially her own fault, she realized, for she had accused him of being a man without purpose or conscience, yet she had not seen that beneath the casual indifference he hid a strong sense of honor and pride, coupled with more courage than she thought she could bear.

"With all my heart, m'sieur, I wish you had remained a rogue and a scoundrel."

Tyrone smiled and brushed the backs of his fingers across her cheek. "Be careful what you wish for, mam'selle. It has been a long time since I turned my hand to honest trade."

"Just turn it to me. That is all I ask."

He kissed her, softly, briefly, then steered her gently toward the edge of the wood. When she was safely back in the shadows he took out his handkerchief and started wrapping it around his injured hand.

"Corporal Marlborough," he glanced pointedly at the heavy snaphaunce trembling in the young officer's grip. "If you would be so kind as to empty one of the chambers. God forbid the tables should turn and I am later brought to account for having two shots to the colonel's one."

Roth smirked and began to unfasten the buttons down the front of his tunic. "You could have ten, Hart, you would still be dead before you pulled the first trigger."

Marlborough bowed his head and proceeded to remove the shot and charge from the lower chamber of the flintlock. He appeared to be clearly uncomfortable with all aspects of the situation, not the least of which being the fact that he should have been arresting Tyrone Hart, not aiding him in a duel against his commanding officer.

"The colonel is an expert marksman, sir," he murmured. "I have seen him shoot the eye out of a fox at thirty paces."

"Then I am well advised to keep mine firmly shut and cheat him of a target."

Marlborough looked up, startled.

"You are a good man, Corporal," Tyrone said quietly. "I am grateful for what you did earlier. And I am still holding you to your bond. Whatever happens over the course of the next few minutes, I expect you to insure Mademoiselle d'Anton's safety."

The dark, earnest eyes searched the blood-smeared face and nodded slowly. "You may count on it, sir."

Roth was waiting. Having removed his scarlet tunic, he wore a collarless white shirt beneath, with braces over the shoulders to keep his breeches snug about his waist. He ran his thumbs down both suspenders to adjust the tension, then retrieved his pistol from his saddle and checked that it was loaded and primed.

Tyrone did likewise, insuring the corporal removed the right priming charge from the right barrel, then, with the pain in his slashed leg causing him to limp slightly, walked forward to where Roth waited in the middle of the road. He stood half a head taller than the colonel and with his loose-fitting sleeves and shiny satin breeches, knew he would present a wide, clear target against the background of night shadows.

Marlborough insisted on positioning the lanterns to provide equal advantage to both duelists, while the five militiamen were ordered to dismount and leave their weapons in a pile beside the road. When the corporal was satisfied there would be no ambush out of the dark, he fetched one of the pistols and stood with the two challengers.

"You will each count off ten paces. I will call one, two, three, and on three, you will turn, aim, and fire. Should both shots miss—"

"Both shots will not miss, Marlborough," Roth said. "Back away."

"Should anyone anticipate the count of three—"

"Mister Marlborough, you are going to have a difficult

enough time as it is explaining your actions when this is over. I suggest you *back away. Now!*"

The young man flushed, taking three long strides back toward the side of the road, and Roth grinned up at Tyrone.

"Well, Hart, I cannot say it has been a pleasure to make your acquaintance . . . in either of your incarnations. But to prove my sincerity in wishing you a fond farewell, I shall aim low, for the belly, so that we can all enjoy hearing you scream your way into the devil's hands."

Tyrone smiled tightly and balanced the snout of the gun over his wounded hand while he wiped his left palm down his breeches and took a firmer grip on the stock.

Roth pursed his lips. "Do you need an extra moment or two to accustom yourself to the aim or balance? I should not want you to shoot a horse by mistake."

"You're too kind, Roth."

The colonel laughed and turned, presenting his back. Tyrone was slower to take the set position and his strides were less even than Roth's as they counted off the required ten paces apiece. He glanced up once into the brilliant canvas of stars, suffering the smallest regret that the moon was not riding high and pale in the sky. He glanced a second time to where Renée was standing, her hands clasped over her breast, her eyes wide and dark and shining with tears. He was not sure if she could see his face clearly, but he moved his lips anyway, saying the words he had been too stubborn to say before. He said them in English, then in French. He might even have shouted them had he not heard Marlborough begin to count off one . . . two . . .

On the count of three both men turned. They straightened their elbows and extended their arms and there were two flashes of powder, two explosive blasts that shattered the absolute stillness of the air.

For half an eternity, no one moved. Renée had covered

her mouth on the count of three and her hand remained
frozen in place. Antoine was beside her, his chest expanded with the pressure of a pent-up breath, his eyes
round as saucers. Maggie clutched Dudley's arm with one
hand, Finn's with the other, but the two men forgave the
gouging pain of her fingers; indeed, they were barely
aware of it. The militiamen looked from one combatant to
the other, waiting for the haze of the smoke to clear.
There was so much blood on Tyrone's clothing already, it
was difficult to see if there were any new stains appearing
on his body, whereas they all saw the gleam of the smile
that began to spread across Roth's face.

Tyrone wavered. His shoulders sagged and he went
down hard on one knee.

Twenty paces away, Bertrand Roth started to walk
back toward his horse. He managed to go only a couple of
steps, however, before his legs buckled like snapped kindling and he crashed facedown on the ground, landing
close enough to one of the lanterns that the fresh new
hole in the center of his forehead glistened red in the
light.

Renée broke free and ran to where Tyrone was teeter-
ing, trying to maintain his balance. He had dropped his
gun and both hands were folded over his belly now. With
Dudley and Antoine a close step behind her, she skidded
painfully onto her knees beside him, almost dreading to
ask, dreading to see what horrible new injury had been
inflicted. His head was bowed and the shaggy black
waves of his hair fell forward over his cheeks. It took him
a moment, but he responded to the soft plea in Renée's
hands as they cradled his face and begged him to look up
at her.

"Is Roth dead?"

"Yes. Yes, you shot him. He is dead."

He offered up a lopsided grin. "Then you may rest
easy, mam'selle, for if I was truly reformed and truly a

gentleman, I would have told him from the outset that I was left-handed . . ."

"Tyrone!"

But he could not hear her. He had already toppled sideways, senseless in her arms.

* ☾

# Épilogue

Renée leaned back in the chair and tried to keep her eyes from closing. She heard the door open behind her and sat a little straighter, offering up a tired smile as Antoine came into the cabin.

"Where is Finn?"

"Puking over the rails again," he offered up cheerfully. "I came to fetch him a clean handkerchief."

"And M'sieur Dudley?"

"Puking right alongside him," Maggie said, coming through the doorway behind Antoine. "You would think, for two such fierce brigands, they could hold their biscuits and ale through a few little swells. You should go and take a turn around the deck, miss. It really is a lovely evening, clear and cool, full of stars, and the moon so bright it paints a silver river on the surface of the sea."

"I can see the moon from the window," Renée pointed out. "And if I had to *watch* the ship going up and down I am afraid I might end up standing with Finn and M'sieur Dudley."

Maggie peered at the wooden supper tray she had brought down earlier. "Well, I am glad to see *someone* has not lost his appetite. He ate all the meat, I see, and the cheese. Did he drink all the tea I brewed for him or has he been spilling it out the porthole again?"

"I drank every last wretched mouthful," Tyrone grumbled from the bed. "I had no choice; the minx would have poured it down my throat otherwise."

"So you're awake, are you?"

"Awake and pondering the cruel circumstances that have brought me to this fate. Three weeks ago, I was happily unfettered, in full possession of my health, my faculties, my creature comforts, free to come and go where I chose, to do it with whom I chose, when and where I chose to do it. Now look at me," he sighed, lifting the curved sweep of his black lashes to stare up at the lantern where it swayed gently from its hook on the ceiling. "Freshly quit of one set of bandages and bound in another, forced to flee hearth and home in the dead of night and take up residence in a berth no wider than a coffin, on board a vessel run by pirates—"

"Enterprising merchants, or so Robbie told me," Maggie corrected him, "who prefer not to pay the exorbitant export prices for West Indies rum."

"Pirates," Tyrone reiterated, "and a pair of women who treat me like a recalcitrant child."

Both Maggie and Renée frowned a moment over the meaning of the word recalcitrant, but in the end, decided he had said it with enough of a scowl to make it a compliment.

Maggie went to the bed and inspected the bandages on his hand. They were clean and dry, as were the strips around his arm and thigh. The cut on his face was healing to a thin red line, dotted with scabmarks where the stitches had been taken out the previous day. When they had first carried him on board ship, he had looked like a mummy, with bandages around his ribs, his leg, his arm, his hand, even slung diagonally across his chest. Roth's bullet had caught him high on the right shoulder but Maggie had found it on the first pass of the knife. It was the deep cut across his palm that had worried her the most, although they had found a doctor in Portsmouth before they sailed who had inspected her stitchery and said he could not have done a better job. With care and vigorous strengthening exercises he would likely regain the use of the hand, though it was doubtful the grip would be as powerful as before. Tyrone was just thankful he could move his fingers and that the numbness of the first few days was gradually giving way to sensation, even though that sensation was pain.

Ignoring the frowns from all three observers, he swung his legs over the side of the bed and struggled to sit up. In the end, it took the combined efforts of Antoine and Maggie to haul him fully upright, but he wore such an inanely happy grin when they were finished, they forgave him his bullheadedness.

"Well, that's me then, off to my berth," Maggie said. "You too, Your Grace. Especially if you are to be up early to stand the morning watch. Badgered the captain, he did," she added by way of explanation, "until the poor man agreed to let him drill with the crew."

When Maggie and Antoine were gone, Renée found the pale gray eyes waiting for her, narrowed in anticipation of a protest.

"He asked me first, and I couldn't see any harm in it. Would you rather have him comfortable and knowledgeable about the workings of a ship, or terrified and propped at the rail alongside Finn and Dudley?"

Renée, who'd had no intention of arguing with anything that served to bring her brother farther out of his shell, smiled and murmured, "Why did I know you would be a corrupting influence on him?"

"Turnabout is fair play, mam'selle. Why should others not suffer upheavals when I am but a mere shadow of my former self?"

Her smile faded slightly and she averted her gaze, turning to her portmanteau instead to begin searching for a clean night rail. They had been on board the ship two nights and she had spent both curled in a nest of blankets on the floor, refusing to leave the cabin for more than a few minutes at a time in case Tyrone called out or needed her. In that time, her relief over his surviving Roth's bullet had gradually turned to dismay, then a creeping sense of guilt, for she knew precisely what it had cost him to spirit her and Antoine away from Coventry. He had declared a willingness to walk away from all he possessed at a drop of a hat, but she suspected that was not entirely true. He had settled himself into a comfortable home, a comfortable life, and managed to acquire a degree of respectability in the community that might have continued indefinitely had he given up his nighttime activities. And all for what? A hasty departure for a foreign country, burdened with a woman, an old man, and a boy who were now dependent upon him at least until they could find some way of supporting themselves in the new world.

Biting her lip, Renée pushed aside the silk underpinnings in her valise and withdrew the velvet jewel case. She had all but forgotten it, and, as she opened the lid and stared at the glittering array of stones, she suffered another pang of guilt. Guilt and anger that so much had happened, so many lives had been changed because of a few strands of red glass.

"I suppose I could save these as a memento," she said softly. "Though I should prefer to simply toss them into the sea."

Tyrone, who had been adjusting his seat on the edge of the bed, glanced over just as she was about to fling them through the open porthole.

"Good God, don't do that! You will be throwing away a healthy portion of our future if you do."

Renée's fingers curled around the stones, grasping them back just in time. "But . . . in the passage . . . I thought you said they were worthless imitations, just glass."

"I said they had a duplicate set made. *You* were the one who assumed you were wearing the worthless imitations."

With a great deal of effort, he maneuvered himself off the bed and, with the sheets draped around his waist, limped over to where she stood in front of the bank of gallery windows.

"The night your uncle arrived at Harwood," he said, plucking the necklace out of her hand, "when I said I grew tired of listening to them debate politics? I paid a little visit to Edgar Vincent's room. Not very imaginative for a clever man to hide his valuables under his mattress. I switched the pieces from one case to the other, just for the hell of it, not really thinking he wouldn't notice the exchange." He paused and clumsily unhooked the tiny gold clasp with his bandaged fingers before draping the sparkling camail of rubies around Renée's slender white throat. "Imagine my surprise when I caught my cuff on the bracelet and realized they were the real stones, and that he hadn't noticed the switch." He let his hands linger on the curve of her neck, let them stroke gently up beneath the fall of her hair. "I did notice him and Roth watching me closely however, waiting for my reaction, testing me perhaps to see if I would question their authenticity."

"So . . . they both thought I was wearing the fake suite?"

Tyrone shrugged. "The lighting was poor, and they both had other things on their minds."

"And your declaration in the music room, that I could bring them with me or leave them behind . . . ?"

"Was delivered with genuine sincerity, I assure you. I was as sincere then as I was when I told Corporal Marlborough to divide the jewels in the saddle pouch among Roth's men; that it was a fair price to pay for them to ride away and forget what they saw on the road that night."

His hands went around her waist the same time hers crept up and curled around his shoulders. "My only regret, of course, is that we do not have the Pearl of Brittany to complete the Dragon's Blood suite, but"—he shrugged again and brushed his lips over hers—"with what Maggie managed to remove from my cabinets, we should have enough to live on for the next, oh, thirty or forty years anyway. After that, I should expect at least one of our seven children will be able to support our dotage in some style."

His lips were warm, their rovings invitingly mischievous, but Renée's remained unmoving and unresponsive. When he straightened and looked down at her inquiringly, her eyes were wide and dark, a deeper, unfathomable blue than the midnight waters that creamed back off the hull of the ship.

"Thirty or forty years?" she whispered.

"You did say if I asked you, you would run away to the ends of the earth with me, did you not?"

"You read my lips? But you said—"

"Yes, well, perhaps my French is a little better than I let on." He bowed his head, silencing her embarrassed protest with a kiss. This time she relented willingly, but he was the one who hesitated to accept the invitation, and it was the probing gray of his eyes that were searching hers with absolute seriousness. "I cannot promise you I will become a changed man, Renée. I cannot promise you there will not be nights when I want to ride with the wind and howl at the moon. But what I can swear to you here and now is that I love you with my whole heart and soul, and so long as my nights and days are filled with you, I will do my damnedest to be the kind of husband, lover, man that you deserve."

"You are already more than I deserve," she said, tears of happiness shining in her eyes as he kissed her closer into his arms.

It was with no small surprise she felt the further evidence of his amazing powers of recuperation, and with no objection at all, she let him abandon her a second time while he threw the bolt across the cabin door. He had forsaken the bedsheet as well and was gloriously naked, splendidly aroused when he took slow, stalking steps back to where she stood.

"We may have to make a few more minor adjustments in technique," he murmured, "but where there is a will—"

"There is a way," she finished, holding up something else she had retrieved from the valise.

It was the Pearl of Brittany, the huge and lustrous center gem encircled by the fiery red body of the ruby serpent.

He looked at the brooch, then looked at the smile in her eyes and swore softly. "And you wonder that *I* have been a corrupting influence on your brother?"

The smile spread to her lips, turned into a joyous laugh, as she opened her bodice to the moonlight. "Come then, *m'sieur le capitaine.* Do your best."